My

My Hands Are Tied
First published in Great Britain by De Minimis 2018 as Double Blind.
This edition published by Partners in Crime Publishing 2020 as
My Hands Are Tied
Cover design by www.nickcastledesign.com[1]

10 9 8 7 6 5 4 3 2 1
By Sean Campbell:
Dead on Demand
Cleaver Square
Ten Guilty Men
The Patient Killer
Missing Persons
The Evolution of a Serial Killer
Christmas Can Be Murder (a novella)
My Hands Are Tied

---

1. http://www.nickcastledesign.com/

Chapter 1: Behind the Hedge

H e didn't even want to go to the damned wedding anyway. It was just Morton's luck. Today was the day of his eldest son's nuptials and, as Morton knew it would be, it was a disaster before it had begun.

Stephen had always been a contrary git. Whatever Morton expected, Stephen did the polar opposite. When Stephen got into Cambridge, he turned down his place to go travelling around Southeast Asia. When he finally did manage to get his degree, it wasn't from the University of Cambridge. It wasn't even from Durham or St Andrews. Instead, it was from one of those former polytechnics turned diploma mills, and the less said about that the better. Despite all that, he'd still snagged a place in a prestigious grad scheme at one of the big accountancy firms. He turned that down too as he 'wanted to write the next great British novel'. That sold all of a hundred copies and Sarah had bought at least half of those.

The latest hare-brained plan was getting married to a woman that they hadn't even met, not even in passing, and, to top it all off, the ceremony was being held on a *farm* of all places. Until today, Morton didn't realise they had farms out in the suburbs of Putney.

Now, he was lost. Soon, they'd be late too, and the Sat-Nav wasn't helping a jot. Nor was the navigator sitting beside him.

'It's *got* to be around here somewhere,' Sarah said in a flustered voice. She put down the hand-written instructions of how to find Terra Farm to lean out of the passenger-side window. Beyond her, all Morton could see were rows of hedges with no wedding venue in sight.

Morton glanced at his watch. It read ten minutes to ten. Why on earth had Stephen and Abigail chosen to have the ceremony so early in the morning?

'I told you we should have left earlier.'

Morton ignored her. 'I can't see it,' he said flatly as he idled in the road. There wasn't a soul in sight. He killed the engine and unlocked his mobile with his thumb. He squinted against the sun and struggled to find the maps application. The little dot denoting their location confirmed they were in the right place, and yet they appeared to be in the middle of nowhere.

'This *is* the right road,' Sarah said. 'I told you it was.'

Morton bit his tongue. Three decades together had taught him not to start an argument on such a big occasion. Especially since this was the first time they'd get to meet the legendary Abigail. Sarah had been fretting about meeting her future daughter-in-law ever since Stephen had shocked them with the wedding announcement a fortnight ago.

'We'll find it,' he said. 'Let me pull over and we'll call him again.'

While he was calling the groom for the tenth time, only to reach Stephen's answerphone once more, a man walking an enormous Great Dane strolled into view. Morton leant out of the window.

'Excuse me. Could you point me towards Terra Farm?' Morton asked, hoping that the man had heard of the place. From what Stephen had said, Terra Farm was a huge estate, and dog walkers usually knew the local area better than most. 'Couldn't miss it,' Stephen had said. So much for that.

The man ambled over, stroked his beard, and then leant in towards the car. His dog jumped around excitedly, its paws pressing up against the rear window. 'Terra Farm? What do you want with those nutters?'

Nutters? Morton wondered what the man meant. It was one thing for him to think that his son was a bit weird, but he didn't want the world to agree with him. 'Do you know where it is or not? We're late for a wedding there.'

'They're desperate enough for cash to rent the old barn out now, then? Interesting. I'd still keep well clear of that lot. But if you're sure you want to know, it's right down there, you can't miss it. But don't say I didn't warn you.' The man pointed at the very same hedge that Morton had been staring at for the last five minutes.

Morton couldn't stop irritation from creeping into his voice. 'That, sir, is a hedge.'

'Aye,' the man said with a crooked grin. 'It is. Look about fifty feet further along.' He pointed with a gnarled finger, chuckled, and straightened up. 'Be seeing you!'

The strange man had to be joking. Morton looked both ways for traffic, opened the car door, and got out. As he jogged along the grass verge, he grudgingly told himself to be thankful for small mercies. At least he wasn't wearing a formal suit, as both he and Sarah had complied with the bride's ludicrous request that they wear a 'plain white shirt/blouse' rather than proper wedding attire.

The dog walker was right. Less than fifty feet from Morton's parked car, there was a gap in the hedge about five feet wide, beyond which was a second hedge. He could have driven past it a hundred times without noticing it.

Morton stepped into the small gap. The path immediately turned a sharp left, running parallel to the road. A gravel path ran between the two hedges for at least a couple of hundred feet or so in Morton's estimation. He called out to Sarah to say he'd found the place. He waited just inside the entrance where he spotted a lopsided sign atop a wooden stake. The sign read '*Terra Farm*'.

'Woah,' Sarah said as she appeared behind him. 'D'ya think the path goes all the way along the southern edge of the farm? Seems a bit... creepy? Like a tree tunnel made of hedges. I wouldn't want to walk along here late at night.'

Creepy was the right word for it. The shadows and quiet of the narrow path gave a sense of moving away from the modern world towards a place of solitude, nature, and, thanks to the looming shadows, a sense of foreboding.

In some ways, the abrupt change in mood reminded Morton of holidaying on the Isle of Wight. There he always felt like he'd travelled back in time several decades the moment he stepped off the ferry.

This felt similarly otherworldly and altogether more isolated. The road noise faded until all they could hear was the crunch of gravel underfoot. At the end of the path, they came to a wrought iron gate, rusted and weather-worn. The bars were twisted like roots, snaking and organic, into an intricate letter C. The gate was attached to iron railings which seemed to disappear inside the hedges, evidence of a fence hidden in the foliage. Presumably, the fences had come first and the hedges were added later to conceal them. The greenery did make it look a little prettier. The effect was unsettling and excessively draconian. A simple group of hippies living off of the fat of the land didn't need such a convoluted entranceway.

'What now?' Sarah asked.

'Unless you can see a doorbell, I think we just wait.' Morton pointed up at a small red light hidden among the bushes. Someone was watching via a security camera.

'Quick, how do I look?'

Morton suppressed a smile. 'Just as lovely as you did when you asked me an hour ago. Chill your beans, woman. This is going to be fine.'

Before Sarah could hit back with a retort of her own, they heard footsteps and a woman appeared on the other side of the gate. Like them, she was wearing all white. Unlike them, her look was somehow catwalk-chic rather than farmgirl-clumsy. Her simple white gown began just off her shoulders and flowed all the way down to her ankles, accentuating the curve of her hips. It was made of a material so light that it fluttered in the gentle breeze, giving her the appearance of floating along the gravel path. Taken with the woman's porcelain skin, long golden hair, and a complete absence of make-up and jewellery, she looked angelic and ethereal.

'Mr and Mrs David Morton?' she asked, her voice melodic and lilting.

After Morton nodded, she waved a hand, and, as if by magic, the gate clicked unlocked. Morton eyed the camera warily. The red light continued to blink as if they were still under surveillance. With a mighty heave, Morton pushed the gate open, leaving a deep gouge in the gravel. Sarah trailed close behind him with her hand on the small of his back.

'Before we head down the hill to the barn, could I have your phones, please? Today's ceremony is, as you no doubt know, technology-free. Lorenzo would hate for an errant phone call to ruin the celebration. After that, would you be so kind as to close the gate behind you, please?' the woman said.

They exchanged glances. Why couldn't they just put their phones into Airplane Mode? And who on earth was Lorenzo? Sarah shrugged and handed hers over. Despite his misgivings, Morton put his phone into Airplane Mode to conserve battery, locked it, and then handed it over. Thankfully, he'd only brought his personal phone with him and not his Met-issue iPhone. The woman put the mobiles into a small safe hidden behind the gatepost and then walked on ahead of them like the Pied Piper. She looked back over her shoulder. 'Don't forget the gate, Mr Morton.'

He rolled his eyes. Nevertheless, he pulled against the gate once more, his arms aching with the effort. He hoped he wouldn't end up covered in sweat as a result. He probably would. The damned thing weighed a ton. Finally, it clicked shut. Morton fished in his pocket for a tissue and then dabbed at his brow to mop up the beads of sweat which threatened to ruin his look.

He couldn't resist giving the gate a quick rattle, his hands searching for a release lever that wasn't there. The lock was as solid and unmoving as the gate itself. There was no way to unlock it from either side without a key, and it was thick enough that there'd be no way to break through it short of ramming it with a car. Not that a car would be able to squeeze between the hedges. He felt a shiver run down his spine. He could understand using a gate to keep the world at large out, but this gate also served to keep all of the Collective's residents *in*. If he hadn't already been regretting his decision to attend the wedding, he would be now.

His wife called out to chivvy him along. 'Hurry up, David!'

When Morton turned to follow them, Sarah and the woman were ten paces ahead of him, walking down another hedge-lined path identical to the first one. From here Morton couldn't see anything but hedge, path, and the two women. He felt the hackles on the back of his neck rise again. This didn't feel quite right. He wanted to call out to Sarah, but she was deep in conversation with the woman. He lengthened his stride to close the gap. As he caught up, he noticed that Sarah was lifting her feet high with every step so her heels didn't get caught among the stones. He gave a wan smile. Perhaps he was overreacting.

The path had snaked back on itself, turning them through one hundred and eighty degrees so that they were now walking perpendicular to the first path. The whole thing was like a giant privacy guard, ending fifty feet further in where they came to an opening barely wide enough to pass through single file.

When Morton walked through the gap, he emerged into the main compound and felt his jaw drop.

'Blimey.' The place was *huge*. It was practically a hamlet, an isolated little community tucked away in the folds of a steep valley, one Morton wouldn't have believed existed if it weren't right in front of his eyes.

The field sloped downwards and away from the road towards a huge barn that dominated his view. It was right in the bottom of the valley at the very lowest point. On either side of the barn, the land sloped steeply back up, and it was on these slopes that Morton could make out the glint of red roof tiles tucked away, barely visible among leafy beech, sycamore, and hawthorn trees. By his estimation, there were three buildings on the slope nearest him, and at least three more on the far slope on the other side of the barn, with identical arrangements on the slopes rising east and west from the barn. That made for a grid-like layout three buildings wide and three deep with the barn at its heart, each dwelling so far from the next that everyone enjoyed privacy.

'Like a little chocolate box village in South-west London, isn't it?' Sarah said. 'I never imagined Stephen living somewhere like this. Abigail must be very well-to-do.'

'Suppose so,' Morton agreed. Except, on closer inspection, he realised that instead of quaint little cottages, Terra Farm was made up of squat, ramshackle bungalows in dire need of some TLC and a fresh coat of paint. They reminded Morton of the bungalows that had dominated the tiny Hampshire village where he'd grown up.

The woman turned to see that they'd stopped to admire the view. Rather than explain the lie of the land, she simply beckoned them with a long index finger. 'Come on. Everyone's waiting for you.'

Feeling very much the recalcitrant schoolboy, Morton followed her. The ground was soft underfoot from the previous night's rain, and Sarah kept sinking into the mud. By the time they reached the barn, her new shoes looked ruined. The leggy blonde lady waved them inside, curtsied, and left them by the barn door. She still hadn't introduced herself.

'*He* could have told us we'd be in a field,' Sarah muttered. 'I'd have worn flats.'

Their son hadn't told them much at all about today's proceedings. All he'd told them was where to turn up, when, and that her ladyship had decreed they dress solely in white. But that was Stephen: enigmatic, quirky, and uncommunicative to the last.

Inside, Sarah perched her handbag upon the nearest bale of hay, and then, leaning against Morton, removed each of her shoes in turn so that she could wipe them clean. It didn't work very well and before long, all her tissues were gone, but, on close inspection, muddy streaks remained.

'I suppose that'll have to do.' She motioned for Morton to help her back to her feet, and together they proceeded further into the ramshackle barn. It wasn't decorated at all except for some candles scattered about which were, as yet, unlit. The shape and size of the barn meant that the hay bales cast long, ominous shadows across the room, giving it a gloomy vibe at odds with the bright sunshine outside.

They found the groom, alone, in the centre of the room. The guests were not, as the woman had announced, waiting for them after all. Nor was the legendary Abigail anywhere to be seen. Presumably, the bride was off somewhere preparing for the wedding ceremony. Morton still couldn't fathom why they hadn't met her before now. Was Stephen hiding something until it was too late? Even as a boy, he'd been a fan of the adage that it was easier to ask for forgiveness than permission. Morton scrutinised his son as Stephen knelt on a fluffy white woollen mat, his back to them as if deep in meditation. Like everyone else they'd seen on this tinpot farm, he was wearing the ridiculous long white robes.

'He looks like Gandalf,' Morton muttered. 'Should have bought him a staff as a wedding present.'

Sarah elbowed him, her eyes flashing darkly. 'Play nice.'

Thankfully, Stephen didn't hear them. Or if he did, he was too diplomatic to call his father out on his comment.

'Stephen?' Sarah called out as they approached.

Morton watched his son rise gracefully to his feet, spin around one hundred and eighty degrees and then hold out his arms to offer his mother a hug. They embraced tightly, and only when Stephen had released her did he turn his attention to Morton. As Morton watched and waited, he saw Stephen's body language shift from one moment to the next. Where before he had been languid and relaxed, his muscles tightened as he turned to gingerly offer his father a limp handshake.

'Not today, son,' Morton said, pulling Stephen into a bear hug. Neither of them was touchy-feely, but if ever there were a day for such an event then surely it was today.

No sooner had Stephen broken free of Morton's embrace than he resumed his position kneeling on the floor.

'What're you doing, son?'

'Meditating. It's part of the binding.' He straightened his back as if he were in agony.

'Just how long have you been down there?'

'Twenty-three and a bit hours if you must know, Father. That's the rule. One day of meditation, a lifetime of bliss. First the ablution, then we can kiss. I'd appreciate it if you didn't mention that I've given you both a hug.'

Morton resisted the urge to snigger at the terrible rhyme. Surely this had to be a wind-up. He looked at his son. Stephen had his eyes closed and there was no sign of mirth on his handsome features. Had his son really been kneeling for a whole day? If Stephen wasn't pulling his leg, the dogwalker's warning was justified: Terra Farm *was* full of nutters.

And now Stephen was one of them.

Chapter 2: The Ceremony

The ceremony took place a little less than half an hour after they'd arrived. It promised to be a dreadfully dull affair. Gone were the pomp and ceremony of a big church wedding like the one that he and Sarah had had nearly three decades ago. Instead of a beautiful, ornate building like Chelsea Town Hall, Stephen and Abigail's wedding was to take place in a mouldy barn that reeked of pigs though there was no livestock in sight. It just wasn't the same as a proper church. So far, the occasion could have been any low-rent London garden party though that was one opinion Morton was wise enough to keep to himself. There weren't even any flowers.

The residents of Terra Farm entered one at a time. As each guest entered, they grabbed a bale of hay and placed it in front of Stephen to form an enormous semi-circle around him and then their gazes focussed upon him as if they were about to watch some sort of rustic play.

Except it lacked any of the solemnity that Morton associated with a real wedding. All of a sudden, the guests surrounding them stood as if music had begun to play except the barn was still totally silent.

He elbowed Sarah as Abigail entered the barn. It was their first-ever glimpse of her. Short, mousy-faced and with long, tasselled hair tucked back over her ears, Abigail wore the same robes as all of the others. She kept her eyes down as she was paraded in, flanked by two men.

The men escorting her looked less like a father giving away a bride and more like security guards manhandling a shoplifter towards the back office, each man clinging onto one arm.

'So that's our new daughter-in-law,' Morton whispered. 'Why on earth are there *two* men dragging her in like that? Who're those two, anyway? They can't be old enough to be her father. And they don't look like they could be her brothers either.'

Sarah shushed him. 'At least she looks nice.'

That much was true. Abigail had one of those round, friendly faces that immediately invited trust. Morton could see why Stephen would have chatted her up. The man on her left carried a bouquet that consisted of drop-like flowers that Morton didn't recognise. Finally, something a bit more normal.

'I've never seen those flowers at a wedding before either.'

'May bells. Royal brides always carry them. Very fashionable. And I haven't a clue why there are two men there. Or why one of them has taken the bridal bouquet hostage. Now would you please keep quiet for five minutes, it's starting,' she whispered and, as emphasis, raised a finger to her lips.

Morton looked on as Abigail was paraded once around the barn, stopping for a few seconds in front of each guest. When it was time for her to stop in front of him and Sarah, Abigail didn't even meet their gaze. Instead, she stared at her feet. Up close, Morton could see a clumsy, almost childlike letter "C" sewn into her gown in a repeating pattern, the metallic red thread occasionally glinting as sunlight filtered into the barn through the open doors. The creepy factor increased when Morton's eyes traced her arms, which he could now see were tucked behind her back. As she was paraded past, he heard a sharp intake of breath from Sarah, followed by her bony elbow in his ribs. Her eyes met his then darted back to the bride. The unease Morton had felt since their arrival deepened. Abigail's wrists were bound together by a red ribbon tied in a bow. That had to be why the grumpy gentleman was carrying the bouquet for her.

There was little fanfare to celebrate the couple themselves, and nearly all the guests – none of whom Morton recognised – had adhered to the white clothing only rule. The only man wearing anything remotely colourful was the elderly gentleman leading the ceremony, and he wore a silver-grey robe that would not have been out of place at a comic book convention. The old man's robe was more ornate than any of the others. Silver threads traced a tree of life on each arm, its roots entwined around a larger and more ornate letter "C" than the one on Abigail's robes. It looked much more like the wrought-iron emblem that Morton had seen at the front gate. When Morton looked at Stephen and Abigail's guests more closely, he realised they were all wearing nearly identical robes, all of which featured the letter C pattern running down their sleeves. It was so subtle that he'd missed it before: the C was embroidered in white thread on white cotton robes.

Before them all, Stephen knelt in silence, his eyes cast down at the floor in reverence. He hadn't moved for twenty minutes now. Perhaps he wasn't exaggerating about the day of meditation. Surely that was hyperbole? Even with practice, that had to be knee-numbingly painful. And he looked like he was waiting to be invested by the Queen herself. Morton half-expected someone to produce a giant sword and anoint him Sir Stephen of the Barn.

Despite the rearrangement of the bales of hay, the barn still felt spartan rather than ceremonial. There were no wedding tie backs or bows, which was just as well as there weren't any chairs to put them on. All that Sarah and Morton could do was stand up or perch their backsides upon one of the filthy-looking bales of hay which one of the guests had kindly set down next to them before taking their own seat. It was a no-brainer. They had chosen to remain standing. The way the bales were arranged reminded Morton of an illegal cockfighting ring more than it did a wedding.

Eventually, Abigail was brought around next to Stephen. The men each pushed down on one shoulder, forcing her to her knees next to her betrothed. The groom glanced sideways, giving his bride a tiny smile. As Morton watched, the elderly man in the silver robes, who was clearly their idea of a priest, took centre stage, standing over them like a lord about to exercise his *jus primae noctis.*

The priest's countenance was unsteady as he waved his hands over them and murmured. He looked so disoriented that Morton wondered if he even knew where he was, let alone what was going on. After a few moments of incoherent mumbling, Morton found himself losing patience. The rest of the guests paid him rapt attention anyway as if his nonsense were the word of God. It wasn't that he was talking in tongues; it was a complete inability to form a proper sentence.

Morton elbowed Sarah. 'The lights are on but nobody's home,' he whispered.

'Shh.'

After a few more minutes, the adoring gaze of the crowd gave way to furrowed brows: Morton wasn't the only one having trouble understanding what was being said. Furtive glances were exchanged among the crowd, until eventually, a handsome young man stood up.

'That'll do, Pa,' he said, laying one hand gently on the officiant's arm. 'I'll take it from here.'

The elderly man allowed himself to be led over to a bale of hay at the far side of the barn where he sat down and stared forlornly at the bride and groom, his eyes glazed over and defocussed. Then his head lolled forward as if sleep or death had taken him.

'Ladies, gentlemen, I apologise for my father's confusion. It seems that the energy of a special moment like this can be too much for even the great Giacomo himself. Stephen, Abigail, would you consent to let me officiate for you in his place?'

All eyes turned back to the bride and groom. They were still kneeling on the soft white mat in the centre of the barn. They looked at each other lovingly, smiled and then nodded.

The son proved markedly more eloquent than his father though his words bore little relation to what Morton thought of as a wedding ceremony.

The replacement officiant waved his hands over them, gesticulating as he spoke to the crowd. 'We are here today to celebrate the Collective movement and the parts which Stephen and Abigail have to play within it. They have both meditated upon their relationship, found peace within themselves, and attuned themselves to the will of Mother Earth, gaining priority in her eyes and with it the hope of ascendance to a higher plane. It is with great pleasure today that I, Lorenzo di Stregoni, son of Giacomo di Stregoni, invite Stephen and Abigail to pledge themselves anew to our cause. Abigail, would you rise and give your vows?'

So, Morton thought, this was the great Lorenzo, he who had declared that none shall enter Terra Farm with a mobile. There was no doubt in his mind that this was the man who was really in charge.

· · · ·

LITTLE KINGS IN LITTLE fiefdoms drove the world of the Collective. Not a bad opening line. It was Lucy Reed's attention to detail and turn of phrase that made her so good at her job. While everyone else was entranced by the proceedings, Lucy tore her gaze away from the bride and groom to scrutinise the room.

She'd been on the compound for just over six months now, and today was the first time that outsiders had been allowed in. Apparently, even a binding ceremony only merited two outside guests: the groom's parents. No siblings, no friends, nada. The bride's family was conspicuous by their total absence.

The binding of Stephen and Abigail had been fêted for weeks, not for the celebration of them and their love, but as a celebration of the growth of the declining community. Having Stephen in the fold meant one more able-bodied man to tend the land and the promise of the first children on Terra Farm in years. Perhaps that was why everyone was so enthusiastic about bringing Stephen Morton into the fold. It had been many moons since there had been the pitter-patter of tiny feet on Terra Farm, and a new generation would bring fresh impetus to the group.

Lucy's mind drifted as she tried to filter out Lorenzo's nonsense. He was banging on about Stephen and Abigail renewing themselves so that they could dedicate their lives to the Collective's cause.

That was its original name. His father, Giacomo, had dreamt it up.

It had started out innocuously enough as far as Lucy could tell. Giacomo, or Dr Giacomo di Stregoni as he ought to be called, had once been a renowned psychiatrist in private practice. He had risen to prominence as a radio psychiatrist and television personality specialising in rehabilitating former cultists, and part of that treatment had been a transitional phase living with other former cultists.

Back then it had been a sort of counter-culture movement, roving from squat to squat, occupying the empty period homes of the rich and famous, never settling in any one place long enough to get in trouble with the law. It was only when the movement was left a generous bequest that Giacomo had been able to scale up the Collective's operations. The result was that Terra Farm had evolved to become an enormous complex, tucked away behind leylandii hedges in Putney. Over time, Giacomo had built eight bungalows around the existing barn to create a tiny village for the cultists who lived within its limits. It was just about big enough to be self-sufficient, producing its own electricity, rearing its own meat, and growing its own fruit and veg. Lucy could see the obvious appeal in a "back to the earth" movement that could largely ignore the world outside the gates. It was something she herself wouldn't mind having once she got home to Raleigh, living off the fat of the land like she was in a Steinbeck novel.

What struck Lucy as odd was that nobody had questioned the logic of former cultists being recruited into what was tantamount to another cult. Perhaps it was Giacomo's immaculate academic pedigree, his charming kindness, his results, or merely the fact that the Collective operated in a secluded farm in west London, out of sight and out of mind. Whatever the reason, the benign cult, or benign-ism as Lucy knew it ought to be properly called, had grown unchecked and unfettered throughout the years until Giacomo was too old to carry the mantle alone. Nowadays there were only thirteen other full-time residents on the Collective and the average age was creeping upwards every year.

As Lucy's eyes drifted back to the ceremony, she saw Lorenzo, Giacomo's only son, smirk as he led the blessing. Unlike his father, he was neither well-educated nor kind. He had a cruelty to him, an edge that he could barely conceal. Where his father had tried to liberate and raise up those under his care, Lorenzo sought to degrade and control them. Even now, in the midst of a happy day, Lorenzo seemed to delight in playing puppeteer. The bride didn't even have her bouquet by her side. It had been thrown upon a nearby bale of hay where it lay looking as sad and forlorn as the bride.

Lorenzo locked eyes on the groom, his hazel stare intense and unblinking. Every time Lucy watched him stare, she felt the urge to stare too, but her eyes always watered long before he finally blinked.

'Stephen, you have completed the ritual of contemplation, a period of twenty-four hours to cleanse the mind and ensure that the supplicant is ready to be bound. If you are indeed ready, rise up now to take your place among your new family.'

Stephen rose, his eyes still downcast. He didn't appear happy as he looked around the room. Instead, he had the demeanour of a dog which had been kicked and still crawled back to its master.

The ceremony was now ready to draw to a close. The bride rose from her kneeling position. Each turned inwards until they were face to face.

Lorenzo walked around Abigail, running his hands over her in a gentle, plainly unwelcome caress. He ignored her repulsed shiver, instead chanting more nonsense before he untied the ribbon that had been used to bind her hands.

'Stephen Morton, are you ready to be bound, in this life and the next?'

The groom gave a terse nod. When he did so, Lorenzo handed him the ribbon. Stephen began to wrap one end around his wrist, looping it around and around until he had used half of the ribbon. By now it was pulled so tight that it was practically a tourniquet. Only when his hand turned white was Lorenzo satisfied. He nodded, permitting Stephen to repeat the words which would bind him to his new bride.

'I, Stephen Morton, do freely and of my own accord confirm my wish to be bound to this woman and this movement. In this life and the next, I pledge to obey without question or delay, to act for the greater good of us. I pledge everything I have, everything I am, and everything I ever will be to you, Abigail.'

He smiled at Abigail, revealing a row of crooked yellow teeth.

Lucy tried not to barf. The words were an empty platitude laden with multiple meanings. Lucy wouldn't have put it past Lorenzo to have added them for the benefit of their guests. Stephen wasn't pledging himself to Abigail. He was pledging himself to the Collective, a movement which demanded everything from its members: every penny they earned, every minute of their time, every ounce of their fealty. While Stephen and Abigail might be bound together today, it would be as a cog within a larger machine.

The whole shebang was, Lucy thought, a very literal interpretation of being bound together as if Lorenzo had made it up on the spot, which he pretty much had. His father's vision of the Collective had emerged out of a period of hippie free-love. It was only under him that it had become a nascent religion, adopting bits and pieces of other religious movements until it resembled a Frankenstein's Monster, the cobbled-together parts somehow more gruesome in combination than any single element would suggest.

Abigail echoed Stephen's vows. Lorenzo slowly wrapped the other half of the ribbon around her left wrist until there was no ribbon left, and Stephen and Abigail were pressed up against each other, their noses touching in an Eskimo kiss.

'I, Lorenzo di Stregoni, pronounce you bound in the eyes of the Collective.' Then he added, almost as an afterthought, 'You may kiss the bride.'

Lucy rolled her eyes. Surely this wouldn't hold water in a court of law. The rest of the members seemed not to notice this, however, and had begun cheering with wild abandon. With great effort, Lucy hauled herself to her feet and began cheering loudly with the rest of the lunatics. It wouldn't do for one of them to notice the journalist in their midst.

Chapter 3: The Reception

'Lighten up, David.' Sarah glared at him from the other end of the hay bale.

Morton worked his jaw, the muscles tightening as he did so. He couldn't pretend any longer. The post-ceremony celebrations had been going on for a couple of hours and he was itching to make good on his exit plan.

'I'm trying.'

'Try harder.' Her glare softened into a smile. 'Please. Try to enjoy the day. For Stephen's sake. Have a beer. We paid for them, after all.'

A long fold-out table had appeared from nowhere after the end of the ceremony and now groaned under an assortment of Tupperware, each member of the Collective having contributed at least one home-cooked dish. One lady with an American accent had referred to it as a potluck.

On top of that, Stephen and Abigail had arranged a BBQ. It had only taken two hours to get going, but now the smell of hot charcoal filled the air. Morosely, Morton eyed the packs of frozen burgers and fuchsia pink sausages stacked neatly next to the BBQ.

'With the money we gave them, you'd think they could have got in ribs or steak,' Morton grumbled.

Sarah shot him a withering look. 'It's catering for fifteen people. What did you expect for a thousand pounds? Most of the money probably went on the booze.'

There was plenty of booze, and the guests were guzzling it with gusto. One young man in particular was trying to demolish his way through half the bar. Morton wasn't the only one watching him do it, either. Several of the Collective members were eyeing him disapprovingly.

'Don't mind him,' said a raspy, croaky voice which suggested a lifetime of smoking. Morton turned to see a woman pushing Giacomo's wheelchair around. 'Poor Guy... he was doing so well.'

'Was?'

She tutted disapprovingly. 'Six months sober. We've worked so hard to keep that boy out of trouble. The first chance he gets, and this is what happens. I do apologise, Mr Morton. We're not usually this out of control. I'll have a word with him. I'm Dori, by the way, and you already know Giacomo of course. Don't mind his lack of words. He's one of the ascended.'

Ascended? Morton wondered. Was that another word for dementia? He shook his head in despair as she ambled off, Giacomo's wheelchair squeaking as if in protest. He watched as she fetched a pitcher of water and offered it to the drunk, trying desperately to pry his bottle of beer from his fingers. When he got bored of watching the man try to drink himself into an early grave, he decided to examine the tables groaning with homemade food and bottles of cheap booze. Cheap pizza, sausage rolls, a curried concoction of some kind, and cold, soggy chips. The dessert table, a diabetic's worse nightmare, wasn't much better. It was piled high with cheap biscuits, gelatine sweets, and just one baked dessert, a fruitcake that Stephen had no doubt baked himself. He recognised it as being one of Sarah's recipes, but they hadn't brought anything edible with them.

No matter how he totted it up, there wasn't a grand's worth of food and booze there. They were feeding fifteen, not fifty. And with no wedding photographer, no honeymoon, and no venue costs, there wasn't much else for the money to have been spent on. There weren't even any ushers. No rented suits to pay for. No rings. No something old, or something borrowed, or something blue. It didn't feel like a wedding at all.

After nibbling the end of a stale biscuit, he headed outside to where the barbeque was set up. As soon as the charcoals were hot enough, he started piling on chicken wings and sausages.

'Hey, you can't do that, you're a guest.' The speaker was an older man, greying and ruddy-faced.

'It's no trouble,' Morton said. 'I like cooking.' And it got him out of awkward conversations like this.

'Suit yourself,' the man said.

As he cooked, he watched Sarah as she circled the room, mingling and chatting easily even though it wasn't their sort of crowd. It was a trait Morton admired in her. He couldn't make small talk to save his life. Before long, an older woman approached holding a beer. Coors. Not exactly his drink of choice.

'I can't drink and drive,' he protested.

'Don't be a sourpuss, young man,' the woman said.

He hadn't been called young man in forever. He smiled at her in gratitude. 'I'm not that young.'

'Compared to me, you are,' she said. 'Go on, have a beer. One won't hurt. You've got to have a drink in this heat.'

She was right. Next to the barbeque, it was particularly sweltering. She was right about the booze too. One beer didn't hurt at all. Nor did beers two and three. Each of the half-pint bottles seemed to evaporate in the sweltering heat. Whenever he finished a bottle, the elderly woman played the perfect host, a fresh, cold bottle appearing in Morton's hand as if by magic.

'Thank you...'

He paused expectantly, hoping she'd take the hint that she hadn't introduced herself. After a moment's hesitation, she smiled a broad, gummy grin that revealed she had, at some point, lost most of her teeth.

'Marta,' she said. 'And you're welcome. We don't usually drink alcohol on Terra Farm. I feel like a schoolgirl again, swigging pilfered lager in the park.'

That explained the loss of control among the group. Despite the social lubricant, Morton struggled to make headway socialising with the other members of the Collective. It wasn't that he couldn't. It was that he didn't want to. He couldn't even grab some face time with his son and Abigail. They were too busy mingling with their brethren.

The residents of Terra Farm were a bizarre bunch. It was as if they were in their own little universe where the normal rules didn't apply. Nobody was dancing, and the smiles were few and far between. The bar was slowly emptying but even that hadn't lifted the mood much. If someone had told him he'd accidentally stumbled into a funeral, he'd have believed them.

'We're very happy to have Abigail and Stephen,' another older woman said. This one looked even more wizened than the first two. Morton supposed she had to be in her late sixties or early seventies. He was losing track of who was who. Was it the booze?

No. It was them. Just like the woman at the gate, the third old lady didn't introduce herself either. What was it with these people not revealing their names? Instead, she bumbled on about nothing as Morton nodded along and sipped at his beer. 'Ever since Giacomo started this place, it's been a haven for souls looking for a simpler life. I've been here since the beginning, and I've never seen a couple so ready to be bound.'

He bit his tongue. Apparently, a simpler life meant living in a run-down bungalow in a muddy field, totally cut off from civilisation with all of London lurking just outside the boundaries. He was about to suggest leaving when Abigail bounded over, her grin stretching from ear to ear. Morton's gaze trailed down, taking in the silk work on her tunic. Up close he could see how the repeating C pattern ended in a series of roots around the hem. Abigail must have mistaken his contempt for admiration.

'The roots of the tree of life,' she said proudly. 'They support us and bind us together as Stephen and I were bound. It is my honour to join your family today.'

Before Morton could scoff, Sarah's eyes flashed darkly as if to tell him to play nice.

When he didn't reply immediately, she leapt in for him. 'We're delighted to see you and Stephen so happy.'

He nodded along. 'I've not seen Stephen smile so much in forever.'

It was worse than that: he just hadn't seen Stephen at all. Except for high days and holidays, they kept themselves to themselves, which was how Stephen had always wanted it.

By the time that Abigail had shuffled off to talk to the elderly lady, Morton was desperate to get away from it all.

'We can't go,' Sarah said flatly.

'Why on earth not?' Morton said, his words coming out ever so slightly slurred. 'It's getting on a bit. We've been here for hours.'

'It'd be rude to go this early,' Sarah said. 'He hasn't got any other guests. Besides, you've been drinking. When will you be safe to drive?'

'I... I don't know.'

'Well, I've had most of a bottle of wine, so I'm not sober enough either. If you don't know, we'll have to stay the night. Abigail's already offered us their spare room. If we crash there, we can head out first thing to the Registrar's Office. They've got an appointment for ten o'clock and we're their witnesses, remember?'

Morton had wondered why he and Sarah were allowed to stay in their bungalow with them on their wedding night. He said as much. 'Isn't it a bit... well, cringeworthy? Having your parents stay over on your wedding night?'

Sarah gave a small shake of her head. 'I wondered about that too. The old woman – Martha, I think her name was? – was eavesdropping. She came over to tell me that "consummation is not a part of the binding ceremony". Maybe you were onto something when you said this lot are a bit weird. Or maybe we're just old fashioned.'

That boggled his mind too. In most marriages, a lack of sex usually happened *after* the wedding day. Perhaps it was the opposite: they'd already been shagging for aeons, so they didn't need to make a big deal of the wedding night. Or maybe they were saving it for after the formalities at the registry office tomorrow.

'But can't we just take a taxi home and then come back tomorr–'

She cut him off. 'David Morton, your son never asks you for anything. It won't hurt us to kip in a spare room for one night so you can drive him to the registry office. It's not exactly going to cost you anything, is it?'

But it did.

Chapter 4: 72 Hours and Counting

Her charge had been locked up for three days so far.

These things were not pleasant, but they were necessary. Besides, *he* had ordered it.

While the rest of Terra Farm ate, drank, and celebrated the binding, the groundskeeper snuck away to check on the girl. The cell was well hidden, tucked away at the back of her tumbledown bungalow, miles from the festivities and hidden behind several locked doors.

There were three locks on the final barrier, a thick oak door that required tremendous strength to open. Two of those locks were simple bolts fitted to the outside. They came undone easily.

The third was a padlock the size of her fist. Only the rusty key hanging around her neck granted her access. She slipped it off, placed it into the keyhole, and listened for movement from the creature within.

When she heard nothing, she turned the key, bracing her hand against the door. Sometimes, they were stupid enough to try to run.

Not this one. She cowered in the corner, backing away in fear, her eyes as big as saucers.

The groundskeeper ignored her as she set a metal bowl full of gruel on the floor beside an identical bowl of water. A whimper escaped the girl.

'Hush,' she said. 'It won't be long now.'

Chapter 5: The Wake-Up Call

wo shots. That was all it took for Morton's world to fall apart.

It was barely six o'clock on Friday morning when Morton was awoken by the sound of gunfire. Without even thinking, he rolled over on top of Sarah, duvet and all, the momentum pulling them both off of the bed and onto the floor with a thud. He suppressed a yelp as the impact ripped through his back. Then there was another sensation, a dull ache at the back of his head that made him wonder if he'd caught that on the way down too.

Then he remembered how much he'd had to drink the previous night.

'What's going on?' Sarah demanded groggily. Either she hadn't heard the gunshot or hadn't recognised the sound.

He held up a finger to his lips and whispered, 'Shh. Something's up. Hold your breath for a second, would you? You're breathing like a chain smoker.'

His own breathing was fast, adrenaline pumping through his veins, his heart thumping in his chest as he strained to listen for further gunshots. Nothing. Pure silence. How far away had the gunshot been? It didn't sound close. He sat up, his ears pricked. The only sound he could hear was coming from the other bedroom. Stephen and Abigail. He jerked his head towards the other side of the bungalow to indicate he was going to check on them.

'Stay here, push the bed against the door behind me. Call Ayala, tell him to get a rapid response team from SCO19 here. Don't open the door until I get back. Just don't move, okay?' He snatched up his shirt and trousers as he spoke, leaning against the bed to pull his trousers on. He didn't have time to put his dress shoes on. They were tight at the best of times and, as he hadn't planned to stay here, he hadn't brought a shoehorn with him. He looked at Sarah's scared expression, desperate to wrap her up in his arms and reassure her, but instead just nodded as if this was something he dealt with every day. In his head, he added: *And if I don't come back, wait longer.*

'I can't.'

'Yes, you can,' Morton reassured her. He touched her arm lightly. 'You've got this.'

'No, David, I literally can't. They took our phones at the gate, remember?'

Morton cursed. In his hungover state, he had forgotten that their phones had been placed in a lockbox by the gate 'so as not to disrupt the wedding'. They were on their own.

Still wrestling with his shirt, Morton opened the door and eased through it. He half-crouched to offer a low profile for any gunman, his eyes peeled for any sign of movement. He wasn't armed, but the bungalow they were in, which was in the north-west corner of the compound, had a small kitchen. Stephen and Abigail were in the bungalow too, albeit at the opposite end on the other side of the kitchen.

Morton considered risking calling out to them, and then, once his eyes were adjusted and he was reasonably sure there wasn't anyone else in the bungalow, he decided to shuffle closer first.

'Stephen! It's me,' he said. The door to the master bedroom opened a crack.

'Was... was that an explosion?' Through the crack in the door, Morton could see his son's eyes had gone wide with fear. He was trembling. Now wasn't the time to deal with Stephen's fear.

'Gunshot,' Morton said bluntly. 'Have you got a mobile? Mine's locked up at the gate.'

'Ours are too,' Stephen said. 'What do we do?'

'Stay here, blockade yourself in. Grab whatever you can to arm yourselves. Your mother's doing the same,' Morton ordered. 'Which direction did the sound come from?'

'A long way off, I think. If it was a gun, maybe it was the shotgun that Pauline uses to kill rabbits. She lives over in the western bungalow... but the sound wasn't that close, was it? It sounded like it came from the other side of the barn. Sounds can bounce around the valley.'

Valley or no valley, the sound was much too far away to have come from one of the neighbouring properties. If Stephen was right, the gunshot had occurred at the bungalow on the other side of the barn, right on the south-eastern edge of the property where the entrance was. To get there, Morton would have to go down the hill, around the barn, and back up the other side. He clenched his jaw, nodded at Stephen, and then, taking his own advice to grab a weapon, he swung by the kitchen and helped himself to the largest knife before heading for the front door.

He buttoned up his shirt as he ran. Why on earth had he chosen to wear such a horrendous billowy shirt? He hadn't even had time to grab a pair of cufflinks.

Alas, the members of the Collective were not of sound mind. Many of them had emerged from their homes and they were heading in the same direction as Morton: towards the south-easternmost bungalow.

He chose to take the shortest route, running down the valley, winding through the barn, and out the other side. As he passed through the barn, the detritus of the previous night's celebrations cut into his bare feet, eliciting a yelp. Out the other side, Morton began to climb the hillside towards the far bungalow.

As he ascended, he could see the outlines of several people clustered around the bungalow. Hearing gunfire had galvanised rather than terrified the Collective. He had not expected to see a soul on the grounds of Terra Farm. Anyone in their right mind ought to be cowering under their bed, waiting to be told it was safe. Instead, they were wandering like lemmings in the same direction as Morton.

'Get inside, for God's sake!' Morton yelled as he sprinted past a woman emerging out onto her porch. He must have looked like a madman brandishing the chef's knife while legging it across the compound. Adrenaline alone carried him through, and he arrived at the south-easternmost bungalow to find a crowd had amassed outside.

'Out of my way! Police coming through.'

It seemed to be common knowledge who lived in the bungalow, and the crowd were presuming the homeowner was the one who had been shot. They were probably right, especially as the rest of the group was milling around out the front, jockeying to see what was going on. Morton elbowed his way to the front of the group. Virtually the entire collective was there. He could hear them murmuring quietly, snippets of conversation floating on the breeze.

'Did you hear? Guy's *dead*.' Morton turned to see that the speaker was the girl from the gate. This morning, she looked far less angelic and far more hungover. Although she was speaking to the fat groundskeeper, her gaze was fixed firmly on the porch where Lorenzo di Stregoni, the man who'd led yesterday's ceremony, stood in the doorway, his arms folded across his chest. Each arm was tattooed with the intricate roots that traced his arms like deformed veins. 'Nobody goes inside,' he shouted to the crowd. 'Nobody.'

Before confronting him, Morton paused to scan the crowd once more, cursing his lack of mobile phone once again. If he'd had his with him, he'd have snapped a few surreptitious photos of the group so he'd know who had got there before him. It was odds-on that one of the looky-loos outside was the killer. He couldn't have got there any quicker as Stephen and Abigail's home was in the north-west, as far away from here as was possible within the confines of the Collective. Perhaps that explained why he wasn't the first on the scene, but what it didn't explain was why the entire group had run towards the source of the noise. It took a great deal of courage – or insanity – to run towards the sound of gunfire.

'Let me through,' Morton demanded. The others were in various stages of undress, with most of the cultists wearing only the Collective's trademark white gown. Oddly, though, Morton was the only one who was bare-footed.

'Didn't you hear me? I said nobody,' Lorenzo said. From his vantage point on Guy's porch, he looked down his nose at Morton with a sneer. 'I'm not letting anyone in, least of all a geriatric who couldn't even find his shoes.'

'I heard gunshots. Let me through or I'll have to arrest you for obstruction.'

He cursed himself for leaving his warrant card back in the bungalow. In his rush, he hadn't thought to grab it on the way out.

'No need,' Lorenzo said. 'I've got the gun here, safe and sound.' He held up an object the shape of a shotgun, wrapped in two large bin bags. 'I found it inside. And no, I didn't shoot it. I just checked the chamber – for my own safety. No doubt you'll want to test my hands for gunshot residue to prove that,' Lorenzo said loudly. 'It's not as if I've had time to go and clean my hands and bleach my clothes.'

Found it? That was convenient. And while he hadn't had time to get clean, he had had the time to stick the gun inside a bin bag. 'And the gunman?' Morton demanded. 'Where have they gone while you're standing on the porch?'

Lorenzo gave a languid shrug and said: 'Long gone, by the looks of it. But the body's inside. I haven't touched that either. I'm assuming you'll want to call your colleagues.' He turned towards one of the crowd, an elderly woman shivering as she wrapped her arms around her tatty gown. 'Marta, would you be a dear and get my mobile phone from my bungalow? It should be locked in my safe – you know the combination.'

'I want mine too,' Morton demanded.

He wasn't sure whether Marta heard him or chose to ignore him. As she hurried off towards the nearest bungalow, Lorenzo turned to the rest of the crowd. 'There's nothing to see here, folks. Go back to bed, and I'll summon you all to the barn when there's news. And could one of you fetch Mr Morton's shoes for him?'

Morton's mind clunked along at half-speed, the effects of last night's indulgence dulling his thinking. A horrible choice had to be made. He could force his way past Lorenzo to enter the crime scene and look at the body. That would leave Lorenzo on the doorstep with the gun. If instead he took the gun, Lorenzo could go and wash his hands and then the chance to prove whether he'd recently fired it would be gone. Neither of those options would work.

That left him with the safest choice: waiting with Lorenzo until he could get his team on-site. That too posed plenty of problems. Someone could interfere with the crime scene by entering the bungalow through a window or back door. Then there was the obvious flight risk. The killer could flee the compound at any moment.

The most immediate threat was the shotgun. He had to keep it in sight at all times. That meant staying with Lorenzo. For now.

'Can you confirm who the victim is? Is it the man who lived here?'

Lorenzo nodded. 'Yep, Guy Rosenberg. He's been with us forever.'

'And he lives alone?'

Another nod.

Now that he knew who the deceased was, Morton's priority shifted. He had a finite suspect pool and there was only one way out of the compound as far as he knew. 'How many of your members have a key to the front gate?'

Lorenzo lifted a necklace from under his gown. The key, which was cut so that it resembled the "C", hung from it. 'Just me. If you're worried about someone leaving, don't. There's no way in or out of here without my say-so.'

'And what about this bungalow?'

'One door at the back. I locked it before you got here. Want to walk around and verify that?'

Morton nodded. 'But first, you're going to have to let me have that gun. Set it down for me nice and slow, then take a step back.'

Lorenzo smirked as he did so. 'Paranoid much, Chief Inspector?'

Chapter 6: Digging for Dirt

Three-quarters of an hour later, Morton was still standing on the front porch outside Guy's bungalow. Rain had begun to pelt down and little droplets were rolling off the tin roof of Guy's porch, pinging loudly as they struck before slinking down into a rapidly filling storm drain. Ten feet away, Lorenzo was splayed out on a chair, apparently unfazed by either the weather or the morning's events. Morton kept a watchful eye on him. Until Purcell's gunshot residue test came back negative, Lorenzo was still a suspect.

Conversation between the two men had been stilted and not just because of the thundering rain. What little Morton had managed to cajole from him concerned the history of the Collective. Lorenzo was far more willing to talk about the past than to answer questions about the present. Morton learned that Guy had been a part of the group ever since he was a child, that he flitted around doing various jobs on the compound from minor repairs to lifting and shifting, and that, as far as Lorenzo knew, 'everybody loved him'.

Morton now had his shoes and cufflinks thanks to Marta fetching them from Sarah and bringing them down. In theory, everyone was now at home, staying well away from each other. News that Guy had been murdered had no doubt travelled throughout the group at lightning speed. A killer was in their midst.

When Morton's team arrived, Lorenzo deigned to let Pauline borrow his gate key to let them in. Unlike yesterday, they kept their mobiles with them. Rafferty and Ayala arrived simultaneously. The former had evidence bags and swabs to hand from the get-go and leapt into action straight away. She put the gun into an evidence bag, swabbed Lorenzo's hands for gunshot residue, and then headed straight for the lab.

'Get a rush on it,' Morton said. They needed to rule out their prime suspect – or arrest him – as soon as humanly possible. The Met's Forensic Science Laboratory was in Lambeth, twenty or so minutes' drive away. With a bit of luck, they'd have the results of Lorenzo's gunshot residue test within the hour.

Once Rafferty was gone, he turned to Ayala, who was bouncing on the soles of his feet, his eyes scanning the horizon as if trying to take everything in at once.

'Earth to Ayala?'

'Yes, boss?'

'I need you to help secure the crime scene. And our witness.' Morton nodded at where Lorenzo was pretending to twiddle his thumbs but was no doubt listening to every word Morton said.

'Gotcha,' Ayala said. 'How'd you end up being here first? Don't you live miles away?'

'Stephen and Abigail got married yesterday.'

'Oh yeah. How was the ceremony? Did they have a lovely church?'

'Here, Ayala. They got married here. In that barn over there.' Morton pointed towards it.

A look of confusion appeared on Ayala's face as he took in the decrepit barn in the distance. His brow furrowed as he wrestled with this new information.

'Oh... but this is...'

'A cult?' Morton said. 'I thought much the same. Stephen is convinced it's not, and you know what our relationship is like. He thinks I just don't like Abigail.'

'Do you?' Ayala asked sharply.

'Do I what?'

'Like Abigail?'

Morton squirmed. 'Honestly, I don't know her from Adam. She barely said a word to me yesterday. But Stephen clearly adores her and she him. Isn't that all any parent can ask?'

The look Ayala gave him said he wasn't buying it. 'So you're not a fan, then. But you're keeping quiet to try to repair your relationship with Stephen? I'm impressed. It takes a lot for a stodgy old git to be so modern.'

Morton scowled. 'And then look what happens when I do try: someone gets shot.'

Chapter 7: Not Quite Murder

Doctor Larry Chiswick would have had the same problem that Morton did in finding the place if it were not for the line of familiar cars parked in what appeared to be a dead end. Despite all the activity, it still took some faffing to get past the security gate. In the end, Detective Inspector Bertram Ayala came down to the gate to escort him to the body.

'I think the boss has gone to put his shoes on,' Ayala said. 'Or something like that. Don't ask.'

Chiswick flicked an eyebrow northwards. 'Wasn't going to,' he said. Not that he'd need to. Ayala would no doubt tell him anyway. He had the pained look on his face of a man who was desperate to spill the beans.

'If you're going to tell me, get it over with. Some of us have work to do,' Chiswick said as he dragged his kitbag behind him, leaving a trail in the gravel pathway that led between the hedges.

Ayala grabbed the rear end of the bag. 'Blimey, Doc. What've you got in here? Feels like you're taking the body to the crime scene, not removing it.'

Another oft-repeated joke. Chiswick forced himself to smile. If he didn't keep Ayala sweet, he'd be lugging the bag on his own again in no time. 'Go on then, what's the gen?'

'Morton's son got married last night.'

'Congratulations?'

'Here, Doc. His son got married here. On this farm.'

The pathologist dropped his end of the bag and spun around to face Ayala. They had just reached the end of the gravel path and were about to step foot onto Terra Farm proper. 'Were they here when the victim was shot?'

'Well, yeah—'

'Then he's a suspect,' Chiswick cut him off. 'And Morton needs to recuse himself.'

'No, no, no,' Ayala said. He'd just had the same conversation not two minutes earlier. 'Morton already explained all this. He and his family were in the north-west bungalow. They were all there when Morton heard the gunshot. Stephen couldn't be involved.'

Chiswick regarded him thoughtfully and stroked his chin. 'Look, that may well be the case, but I'm still not happy about this. He should really be passing this off to another—'

'And he will, I promise, as soon as he can,' Ayala interrupted. 'But for now, can we just get you inside so you can take the body away, and then Morton can hand it all over when he knows the perimeter is secure, the evidence is collected, and none of our suspects have fled. That gate you just came through is the only entrance, and the fencing runs right through the middle of those hedges all the way around the compound.'

He gestured to where the kit bag lay on the ground. 'Shall we carry on? It's not much further.'

'So now you're telling me that not only am I walking into a conflict of interest, but I'm walking onto premises where we know there's a killer nonchalantly wandering around?'

'Suppose so. All the more reason to get a shift on then, eh, Doc?'

The ageing pathologist huffed as he picked up his end of the kitbag. 'Then you'd best stay close.'

• • • •

THE DECEASED AWAITED Chiswick in the bedroom at the back of bungalow number seven. Guy Rosenberg's corpse lay in a four-poster bed around which the curtains were tightly drawn. When Chiswick peeled them back, he found his victim wearing only boxers. He wasn't even wearing a t-shirt, a wise choice given how hot and muggy the previous night had been. This morning's drizzle had abated, and now sunlight was streaming in from a locked window, making the scene both eerily sinister and remarkably calm. From the foot of the bed, Chiswick could see everything and hear nothing. It was rapidly approaching midday, and his new assistant hadn't yet arrived to help remove the body.

The victim had been shot twice in the chest at point-blank range, leaving burns on his exposed chest. The bullets were still in there, which would make it dead easy to match up the shotgun they'd recovered by comparing striae, markings which resulted from the bullet rubbing up against the linear grooves on the inside of the gun barrel. Except... Something was off.

There wasn't much blood. What little there was had pooled underneath the body. Chiswick turned his attention to the curtains around the bed, inspecting them carefully for any sign of splatter. He found none.

'Ayala!' the doc shouted.

He called back from his place on the porch. 'What?'

'Get in here. Close the door behind you.'

He heard the door slam, and then footsteps as Ayala shuffled along the long corridor to the master bedroom.

'We've got a problem. Your victim was *not* murdered with a gun.'

'What?' Ayala exclaimed. 'Doc, are you sure you're not having a senior moment? There are two gaping bullet holes in his chest.'

Chiswick glared. 'Young man, if you ever suggest I have dementia again, I will see to it that you have to complete every form in triplicate just to get an appointment to come into my morgue. Do I make myself clear?'

'Yes, Doc,' Ayala said sheepishly. He tried to steer the conversation back to the topic at hand. 'So how do you know the gunshots weren't what killed him?'

'The gunshot wounds are post-mortem. We know that because there's an insufficiency of blood. There's pooling underneath, but it's all gravitational. If his heart had been beating when he was shot, his blood would be all over the bedding.'

'How did he die?'

'I need to do a full autopsy to confirm my suspicions, but it looks like he was smothered. There's petechial haemorrhaging in the eyes, which is usually a giveaway. I just need a tox screen to rule out poisoning and the like.'

'Then two people tried to kill Mr Rosenberg last night.'

'Not only that,' Chiswick said. 'It means Stephen is still a suspect. And Morton too. He needs to recuse himself. Now.'

Chapter 8: The Square Kilometre

An odd tension ran through the Morton bungalow over breakfast. The suspects had been corralled and then ordered to wait in the barn under the watchful eye of DS Mayberry and a couple of uniformed officers. The immediate need to secure the Collective's grounds had been met, and now the scene of crime officer had arrived with his team, ready to undertake a grid search and secure all the available forensic evidence. For now, Morton's job was to stay out of the way until another detective could assume control of the investigation.

'Can we go home now, then?' Sarah asked.

'Soon, I hope. We'll have to rearrange the registrar's office.' Morton glanced at his watch. 'There's no way we're making our appointment on time now. We've got to make formal statements before we can leave.'

'Why?'

'We're each other's alibi. At the time the gunshot went off, I was with you. You can alibi me and vice versa.'

Sarah gestured towards the bedroom where Abigail and Stephen were still hiding. 'What about them?'

'I spoke to Stephen straight after the gunshot when I checked on them. There's no way he could have made it back from the other side of the compound in the time it took me to run the length of the bungalow.'

'There's a "but" in your voice.'

He fidgeted on his stool uncomfortably. 'I didn't see Abigail, though. All I could see was Stephen through the crack in the door.'

45

'So? Were they supposed to both jam their faces against the door to establish an alibi? We got woken up by gunshots. Nobody was thinking about that.'

'She didn't speak, either. I don't have first-hand knowledge she was there. I can't be her alibi.'

A voice boomed from behind him. 'But I can.' Stephen emerged from his bedroom, already dressed in one of the cookie-cutter gowns the Collective's members wore. His eyes were bloodshot, great dark circles hanging underneath them as if he hadn't slept a wink.

Morton's hackles rose. 'Spying on us, son?'

'Don't you dare start. You're in my kitchen, Father, in my home. As it happens, I wasn't eavesdropping. I was coming out to make myself a cup of coffee. Do you want one?' When Morton nodded, Stephen set about making a V60 straight away, washing the filter before blooming his grounds. Morton recognised the coffee set as the one he'd given his son only yesterday, complete with a kilogram bag of medium-roasted Peruvian coffee and a pack of disposable filters.

The wedding had come out the blue, so it was a regifted present that Morton had fished out of the back of the cupboard and handed over at the BBQ after he finally remembered that it was in the boot of his car. He'd never tell Stephen where it really came from, not when Stephen was so happy with it. Originally, it was a not-so-secret-Santa present from the pathologist, himself a coffee nerd. It was a gimmick in Morton's opinion. Coffee was coffee, wasn't it?

The awkward silence was punctuated by the slow drip of coffee.

Stephen was the first to break. 'Why is it a problem that you didn't see Abigail this morning, Dad? I'm her alibi. We were together the whole night.'

'Because you're her other half,' Morton said. 'An alibi from a partner isn't exactly bulletproof.'

Four mugs were set on the counter. Stephen began filling them with boiling water then emptying them. 'Warming the mugs,' he explained. 'But seriously, you can alibi Mum, but I can't alibi Abigail? Where's the logic in that?'

'First, I'm a detective. Second, we don't have any connection with the victim or the Collective. It's simply not a credible argument that one of us decided to find a gun – which we didn't know existed – and then murder a man neither of us had spoken to in our life.'

Sarah bit her lip. 'Actually, I did speak to him. His name is Guy something or other.'

'What did you talk about?' Morton asked as his son handed him a mug of coffee.

'Not much. The poor boy was drinking a lot last night. I get the impression he was drinking to escape something.'

This wasn't going well for Morton. He took a sip of his coffee. Not bad. 'Okay, but I know you didn't do it. Stephen knows we didn't do it. I know he didn't do it. He knows Abigail didn't do it.'

'But you don't believe him.'

Morton wanted to protest that yes, he did trust his son. But before he could muster the courage to lie, his phone buzzed. Ayala. And the message wasn't coming in on the official channels. Instead, it came in via an encrypted and self-deleting messaging app that he'd only had installed to keep up with the kids. It was the team's way of communicating off the record. His heart thundered in his chest as he read the message. Seconds later, it deleted itself, all trace gone forever. No wonder criminals loved smartphones.

'Sarah, you're going to have to come with me to talk to the coroner. Right now. Ayala just texted. He says Chiswick's on the warpath.' He set his coffee down on the kitchen counter with a thud, spilling it all over the show. 'Sorry,' he said as Stephen dashed to wipe it up.

'But what's that got to do with me?'

'Outside,' Morton said, jerking a thumb towards the front door. 'I'll explain everything on the way.'

Sarah pulled on her shoes, hauled herself to her feet, and followed him. He felt her hand shake in his as they left a quizzical-looking Stephen in the kitchen.

As soon as they were out of earshot, Sarah stopped dead in her tracks as if her feet would carry her no further. 'David, you're scaring me now. What on earth's going on?'

'Guy Rosenberg wasn't shot to death. Someone smothered him first. The gunshot occurred post-mortem.'

Her eyes went wide. '*Two* people tried to kill him last night?'

'Looks like it.'

'And this affects me because...?'

'Because it changes the timeline. We can alibi each other all night. But we can only alibi Stephen and Abigail this morning when the gun went off.'

'You think one of them did it?'

'No, I don't. But another detective certainly might. When I turn this case over to whoever ends up being senior investigating officer, they'll look at everyone. That includes Stephen and Abigail.'

'You can't. It's supposed to be their wedding day. The happiest day of their lives. And you're going to let one of your colleagues–'

'Probably DCI Brissenden. You met him at the Christmas party the year before last. Tall, lanky bloke with the chubby wife.'

'Right. And he'll be fair, will he, this DCI Brissenden?'

'Doubt it. He hates me. If he's got a chance to nail my son for murder...'

'Why would they think Stephen did it?'

This was the time to share the titbit he'd learned from Lorenzo while waiting outside for the pathologist, and he knew Sarah wouldn't like it one bit. 'Because, darling, the dead man, Guy Rosenberg, was once betrothed to Abigail.'

Chapter 9: Pleading for Time

The pathologist was apoplectic.

By the time Morton cornered him, Dr Larry Chiswick had turned ruddy-faced, the vein in his temple throbbing.

'It's time to recuse yourself, David,' he demanded. The "or else" was left unsaid, but his tone conveyed the threat. He stared at Morton unblinking.

'And I will,' Morton said bluntly. 'I know Stephen and I have had our differences, but he's not a killer. If I turn this over to one of the other murder investigation teams now, then he'll be suspect numero uno. Give me a chance to clear his name. You've got kids. Imagine it was one of them in trouble.'

The doc's expression softened a fraction. 'I can't, David. Rules are rules. You're asking too much of me.'

Morton looked away for a moment and then turned back to meet Chiswick's fury with his own. 'I'd do it for you and you know it. How about this? You give me the weekend, no more, no less. It's Friday morning. Don't file your autopsy report until Monday. If I can't solve the case by then, I'll recuse myself the moment your report is on record. Until that time, I can proceed on the assumption that Guy Rosenberg was murdered by gunshot, and neither Stephen nor Abigail is a plausible suspect because they were with me on the other side of the compound. Nobody would ever blame you for letting an autopsy report slip one working day. Find us something to buy a little time if you have to. Can't you send off Guy's blood for lab analysis to rule out poisoning?'

'It doesn't matter if he was poisoned or not. Neither asphyxiation nor poisoning would fix Stephen's lack of a proper alibi. And what if it turns out he did actually do it?'

The thought had crossed Morton's mind. If he kept this investigation and Stephen or Abigail turned out to be the culprit, he'd be staring down the barrel of an accessory to murder charge, and while he was pretty confident his wouldn't-say-boo-to-a-goose son hadn't killed anyone, he didn't know Abigail at all. 'Then I'll turn in my warrant card. Sarah's wanted me to retire forever, and if I'm going to go down without a pension to show for it, I'd rather go out fighting for my son.'

The doc's lower lip trembled. 'One weekend?'

Two days. Not nearly enough time to catch a murderer. But it might be enough to prove Stephen's innocence. If he could solve the murder into the bargain, great. So long as Morton succeeded, Silverman wouldn't even know that Chiswick had done him a favour.

The risk was self-evident. If Silverman caught wind of the delay, she'd be onto them in no time. Anyone who knew Chiswick would guess something was amiss. The man was renowned for his efficiency, and a three-day delay, even over the weekend, was unheard of. But it was the best Morton could do in the circumstances.

'One weekend,' Morton echoed. 'There are only a few working hours before it's the weekend, so nobody ever needs to know. Come nine o'clock Monday, you do what you have to do. Just take your time today and let the paperwork slip until after the weekend. Please, Larry. If this goes tits up, I'll make sure it's only me that gets in trouble.'

'I don't like this, David, not one bit,' Chiswick said. 'But on your head be it.'

Chapter 10: Huddled in the Barn

Morton couldn't hold them there forever. For now, the suspects were playing ball, probably because Lorenzo had given them the same order that Morton had: go to the barn and stay there. There wasn't much to go on until the scene of crime officers could do their job. Mayberry had been dispatched to find out how and where the CCTV footage was recorded and to check the perimeter fence for any gaps a suspect could fit through. Morton didn't expect to find much on either front.

Until Purcell's team had worked their magic, Morton's best bet was to interview all the cultists to get their accounts of the wedding night and the morning after down on record. Then he could pore through those accounts for any inconsistencies, pursue any leads, and start to rule out the least likely suspects. In short, all the normal investigative techniques but without the usual time and manpower.

Except this wasn't normal. His family was involved. Not that Stephen would ever appreciate it, but Morton cared far more for Stephen, and, by proxy, Abigail, than he did for solving Guy Rosenberg's murder. The challenges were obvious. Firstly, he only had until Monday morning before the pathologist's report would be filed, which gave no slack time at all for forensics to be processed. Collecting, processing, documenting and transporting trace evidence would take Purcell's team the better part of Friday. The chief scene of crime officer was already hard at work, but diligent forensics took time, and lab analysis took even longer. And it was a weekend. Morton couldn't bank on getting back anything useful before Monday morning.

That meant he had to rely on his team more than ever. And that was problem number two. While he might be willing to risk his own professional reputation to save his family, he couldn't demand that his team do likewise.

He assembled his team inside Stephen's bungalow, except for Rafferty, who had yet to return from the forensics lab. Stephen's living room was now the de facto incident room for the investigation and had begun to fill up with the paperwork and other detritus of a major investigation. Morton had debated bringing in Stuart Purcell and then decided against it. Purcell was competent but he was not yet Morton's man in the way that DS Mayberry was, and he was too busy to pull away from his work without good reason. If Morton needed to read him in later, he'd do so when that became necessary.

The most dangerous team member was Ayala. Morton wouldn't have called him in if he'd had any choice but not calling him in would be a huge red flag. The problem was that Ayala had been gunning for Morton's job for years. He could only hope that even if the team chose not to help investigate, then they would at least keep quiet until Monday. It was a big ask.

The pair of them sat on the sofa in the tiny living room while Morton strode back and forth like an expectant father. Ayala and Mayberry were chalk and cheese. While Mayberry sat forward, notepad in hand and pen at the ready, Ayala sat back, casually crossing one leg over the other. Their clothes were so different too. Mayberry's suit was cheap and cheerful, probably off-the-peg from Marks and Spencer's, while Ayala wouldn't be caught dead in anything less than Saville Row. What it must be like to have an inspector's salary, complete with London weighting, and no kids to syphon most of the cash away as surely as rain fell from the sky on a British bank holiday.

While he was waiting for them, he'd made a quick filter coffee for the caffeine hit and could delay no further. Even in his rush, he had to admit that the fancy-pants brewing method did add something to the coffee's flavour.

'This is going to be quick, and it's going to be dirty,' Morton said. He paused, watching Mayberry and Ayala closely. While the former was as loyal as a Labrador, Ayala was a pragmatist at heart. For a while, he'd entertained the thought of lying to them, letting them investigate Guy Rosenberg's murder as just a gunshot death. That would have been the coward's choice, and it would have made Morton's life far more complicated in both the short and the long term. In the short term, the investigation would be hamstrung by the falsehood. In the long term, he'd have betrayed his team and undermined years of earning their trust. It wasn't worth the gamble. He had to trust them as they had trusted him over the years. 'My family is intricately tied up in this mess, and I have no choice but to fight Stephen's corner. The evidence as we know it so far is this: Guy Rosenberg attended Stephen's binding ceremony last night. That's what this lot call a wedding. Accounts so far suggest that he drank heavily and retired late. Sometime between then and this morning, he died, probably as the result of asphyxiation. Then, a little after six o'clock this morning, someone shot his corpse twice at point-blank range.'

Ayala swore. 'That's a bloody mess, boss, if you'll pardon my French. Why the hell are we even here? Shouldn't we be handing this investigation off to another team?'

Not an unexpected question. Nor an unreasonable one. From the look in Ayala's eyes, he knew it too. He just enjoyed making Morton squirm. Like Morton, Ayala was usually a strictly by-the-book detective. Except he lacked Morton's imagination. That was the real reason he wasn't ready to be promoted.

'It's a fair question,' Morton said finally. 'If either of you wants to call in sick, recuse yourself, and stay well away from this mess, I don't blame you. I would in your shoes. This isn't your mess; it's mine. If you want to walk away, then now is the time to do so.'

Neither moved.

'Then if you're both staying, you'll need plausible deniability. We have two aims here. One is to solve the murder. That's the gold standard here. Two is to exculpate Stephen and Abigail. With a bit of luck, we do both. And we've got to do it by Monday morning.'

Disdain and doubt met his words. Ayala was disdainful, Mayberry doubtful.

'H-h-h-how, sir?' Mayberry said.

Another good question. The fuzziness of last night still lingered in Morton's mind. 'As far as the cult is concerned – and our colleagues at New Scotland Yard too for that matter – we're investigating a simple gunshot murder. We know the gunshot didn't kill him. But whoever shot him might not. If we're canny, we can interrogate the cult under the guise that Guy was shot without them realising that we know better.'

'H-how did he d-d-die?'

Ayala turned to him. 'He told you already. He was smothered.'

'I said he was asphyxiated, not smothered,' Morton corrected him. 'And that won't be on-record until Monday morning.'

'Same diff, no?' Ayala said. 'I don't see how he could have drowned in his bed.'

Morton couldn't help but agree with that. 'We have to be seen to investigate the gunshot. I don't want anything but the gunshot appearing on the paperwork. Investigate everything, but don't write any of it down unless it chimes with the official cause of death. Until Dr Chiswick's report is officially on the record, Guy Rosenberg died from two point-blank gunshots to the chest. Are you two willing to play along? You need to be seen to be whiter-than-white here. That way, if this all blows up, it blows up in my face and not yours.'

The hint of a smile crossed Ayala's face. He won either way. If they solved the case, Morton owed him one. No doubt he'd try to cash that favour in sooner rather than later. If he lost, Morton was disgraced, and Ayala could finally poach his job. The promotion he craved awaited him either way. Morton just had to keep Ayala thinking that the easiest way to get that promotion was to keep him on side.

'You on board?'

Both junior detectives nodded.

'Does that mean we're really looking for two would-be killers?' Ayala asked.

'Bit strange that two people choose the same night to try to kill one man,' Morton said. 'It would be natural for us to assume we're only looking for one killer. Who's so unpopular that he gets murdered twice in one night? But then again, why would someone asphyxiate him and then come back with a shotgun later on?'

'S-s-same p-person c-covering their t-tracks?' Mayberry suggested. 'It's g-g-got us c-confused.'

It was a defence lawyer's wet dream. To get a conviction, the Crown Prosecution Service had to prove guilt beyond reasonable doubt. Two murder methods would be catnip for defence solicitors who would quickly argue that their client, whoever that was, was the innocent party. Usually, killers weren't that smart. Morton had seen a few killers try to point a finger at someone else, sometimes even an accomplice. The so-called cut-throat defence was inherently risky, as juries had little patience with such shenanigans, but this might just confuse enough jurors to deadlock the jury.

Morton shrugged. 'Could be. It'd be a weird one. If the killer wanted to throw off the time of death to help establish a fake alibi, there are easier ways to do it.'

'Especially here,' Ayala said. 'It's a cult. They've got a secretive little community. If one of them died and you weren't here to witness it, would they have even called us? Or would they have just buried the body in the vegetable patch and carried on with the world none the wiser?'

'Good point, Ayala. Someone here chose to commit murder on the one day they had external visitors. They knew they had a police officer coming. So why kill Guy Rosenberg now? Why not next week when the wedding celebrations are but a memory?'

'M-m-maybe they want to get caught.'

Morton stopped pacing. 'Whoever shot Guy did so at nearly point-blank range. We're left with either a killer who was so desperate to change the timeline that they shot a dead body and thus risked being caught by the policeman sleeping a few hundred yards away, or two different people wanted Guy Rosenberg dead, and both saw last night as their best opportunity to see that through despite my presence.'

The room fell silent as they contemplated why two people might try to kill one man on the same night. It seemed far-fetched unless the trigger was a single event.

'Are you sure they knew that you're a police officer?' Ayala said to bring them back to task.

Morton nodded. 'Stephen said as much.'

'So, what's the plan then, boss?'

'We talk to the lunatics. How many people are there in the barn, Mayberry?'

'A d-d-dozen?' Mayberry said hesitantly. 'Ish.'

It sounded about right. Add in Stephen and Abigail who were with Sarah in the other room and that made for fourteen.

Morton tried to pair the people with the property. How did everyone fit in? Who lived where? What did they do all day? How did they afford to eat and keep the lights on? Nothing about the setup made any sense.

'Twelve-ish?' Morton echoed. 'Go check. And while you're at it, talk to Stuart Purcell. Tell him to run the gun for prints if he hasn't already. We'll need exclusionary prints from every member of the Collective. DNA too if we can get them to agree to be swabbed. If anyone refuses, bump them to the top of my list of interviews.'

'What about Lorenzo?' Ayala said. 'His prints are bound to be on the gun. He's admitted to handling it.'

It was all a bit academic; the gun wasn't the murder weapon anyway. 'He's a suspect either way. If Rafferty returns and says his gunshot residue test was negative, we rule him out of the second attempted murder. But the fact he made such a big deal of not being a suspect makes him a bigger suspect in my mind.'

Ayala leant forward, doubling up as if in pain. 'This is such a headache. We can't investigate one murder properly while pretending to investigate another.'

'We c-can do the b-b-basics though. W-what's common to b-b-both?'

This met with Ayala's approval. He sat back up, his back straight as if the idea was ground-breaking. 'We can't keep them all in that barn forever. Why don't we let Purcell take his team and sweep the premises one bungalow at a time? Mayberry can go run background checks on the names we do have so far, and then you and I could try to work out who's who in the Collective.'

Morton had already planned as much. But he'd let Ayala think it was his idea if it meant an easy life.

'And remember,' Morton said, 'nothing gets put in writing until I say so, got it?' He couldn't afford for any of the paperwork to contradict the idea they were investigating a simple gunshot murder. 'And remember, the killer is in that barn. Tread carefully.'

They had one weekend to solve a murder... and find a killer... or two.

Chapter 11: Dead Man Talking

The body landed on the pathologist's slab a little after midday on Friday. In life, Guy Rosenberg had been a heavyset man, and in death, he seemed even more so. It was with great effort that Dr Chiswick's assistant helped him remove the corpse from the body bag.

Once he'd double-checked that the toe tag was still where it was supposed to be (Chiswick had once had a toe tag slip off before autopsy and had nearly lost his job for "losing" the corpse), Chiswick began his work.

Today's assistant was a newbie. His old diener had retired to the south of France – Beziers or somewhere of that ilk – so Chiswick was forced to babysit as she stood anxiously peering over his shoulder. He had the feeling she hadn't seen inside too many dead bodies yet.

'Maria, you're standing in my way,' Chiswick said. 'Make yourself useful and put the SLR onto the camera mount and document the body for me. Here in England, documentation is everything. We'll do photos while he's in the body bag, photos before we wash him, and then another set of photos once the cadaver is clean. Only then will I start cutting. While we're looking at the internal organs, I want you to photograph each and, when I read out weights, enter them into the laptop over there on the sideboard for the record. Can you do that for me?'

'Yes,' Maria said. She was Spanish with the merest trace of an accent.

'Yes, Doctor,' Chiswick said.

She cracked a broad smile. 'But I am no doctor.'

'Ha, ha, ha,' Chiswick said sarcastically. 'As if I haven't heard that one before. You're so witty and original. Just so you know, I've got a video camera up in that corner' – Chiswick pointed up – 'which is to protect us both. Now, assuming you're done with the stand-up routine, let's take a first look at the body and you tell me what you observe.'

She leant in close, scrunched up her nose, and looked at Chiswick with disgust. 'He smells bad, as if he has... defected himself?'

Welcome to pathology, he thought with a silent chuckle.

'Defecated,' Chiswick corrected cheerfully. 'And corpses do that, I'm afraid. This one appears to have had diarrhoea. I'm going to have to get you to clean him up. Before that, let's start with the in-situ so you can get used to the camera.'

While she figured out how to use the camera to take shots of the body in-situ, Chiswick watched her carefully, intervening when necessary to make sure everything was done according to procedure. Each time she took a photo, it automatically synced to his laptop via Bluetooth and was then displayed on the big screen on the wall. Chiswick examined each photo, asking her to repeat angles where the lighting or focus wasn't spot on.

'What else you want me to do?' Maria asked.

'I expect my assistants to do all the little things around the lab. I've only got one pair of hands, after all. Today, I'll have you take blood samples so we can confirm his blood alcohol level. I'll also ask you to swab around his mouth and face. If he's been smothered – and I suspect he has, from the lack of damage to his throat that would have occurred with strangulation – then we might get lucky and find trace evidence telling us what he was smothered with. But don't get ahead of yourself, young lady. What do you think your next task is?'

'More photos?'

He shook his head. 'We have two more batches to do. But you can't do the next one until you've stripped the body. Chop chop.'

Maria slowly removed Guy's gown. She did so by cutting from the bottom to the top, removing the fabric carefully and methodically. Chiswick nodded approvingly. Perhaps she did know what she was doing after all. The last newbie he'd trained had wanted to yank a t-shirt over the deceased's head, which would have disturbed crucial evidence.

'Now we do more photos?'

'Indeed. Take one set before you clean him up, and then, when he's been washed, we'll do another set.'

Again, he supervised her from a distance. This time, the photos came out perfect without any do-overs, and soon Maria was taking the hose to wash the dirt and grime off Guy's body.

'Yuck,' Maria said, grimacing.

Then again, Chiswick thought, once a newbie, always a newbie. He peered past her, expecting to see just two gunshot wounds. The gunshot wounds were there, all right, though the bullets had gone right through and out the other side.

Then he saw it. Mottled, burnt skin interspersed with tiny, darker splotches.

'What it is?' Maria asked.

He stroked his chin thoughtfully. 'The tiny spots are hyperpigmentation, which can be caused by many things. Hives, sunburn, poison ivy, allergies... this isn't any of those, though.'

The pattern was much too regular. Guy Rosenberg's skin looked like it had been traced over with tiny tendrils. 'Got a photograph? Can you get another one? Use the lens marked macro this time, and then we can flip him over.'

A quick lens swap later, the camera flashed as Maria depressed the button on the SLR. Once the close-up photos were done, Maria turned him over.

'Blimey,' Chiswick said. The tendrils continued on Guy's back, this time tracing a blotchy yet unmistakeable letter C. Guy didn't have a skin condition. This was *deliberate*.

'What caused it?' Maria asked.

Shudders ran through the pathologist as he considered how someone could deliberately inflict such a horrible burn. He knew that the cult called itself the Collective. This had to be their handiwork. It wasn't a simple branding with heat. That would have been more humane. 'This,' he said, keeping his tone neutral, 'is a chemical burn. It's called phytophotodermatitis. In technical terms, Guy came into contact with a light-sensitizing agent and was then exposed to ultraviolet light, causing a cutaneous phototoxic inflammatory response.'

She looked at him blankly.

'Someone painted his back with something, probably plant-based, something from the *Apiaceae* or *Rutaceae* genera, and then made him lie out in bright sunlight to burn the letter C into him. Disgusting stuff. You might have heard it called a Margarita Burn.'

'Should we tell someone?'

'I'll call Morton. But first we need to complete the autopsy. Pass me that Stryker saw.'

For a while, they worked in silence. Maria watched half-fascinated and half-disgusted as Chiswick performed the typical Y incision to begin taking out Guy Rosenberg's organs one by one.

'Here,' Chiswick said as he thrust the liver he had been cutting from the body into her gloved hands. 'Weigh that, would you?'

As she wrote down the measurement, Chiswick watched her closely.

'Notice anything unusual about his liver?'

Maria looked at him, confusion evident in her eyes. Was he testing her? 'Should I?'

'He has cirrhosis, so, yes, you should have spotted that. His liver ought to be smooth; instead it's bumpy with the texture of baked beans. That's a classic sign of alcoholism. If you saw white lumps as well as bumps, you'd think hepatocellular carcinoma.'

'Should I take the notes?'

'I don't care if you write it down or not. Just remember it for next time either way. Now, look at the body. What else tells us he liked a drink?'

She shrugged.

'Look at his face. He's got a ruddy complexion because there are broken capillaries. See here.' Chiswick pointed. He was beginning to enjoy playing teacher, though his student seemed reluctant to pay much attention. He had a feeling this one wouldn't last long.

'And?' She sounded bored.

'He's an alcoholic. But more than that, look at the eyes.'

She peered in close. 'They are red?'

Chiswick sighed. 'That's petechial haemorrhaging. It means he suffocated to death.'

'He was shot. See?'

Dieners. They weren't the brightest bunch, and Chiswick always seemed to get lumbered with the worst of them. She'd come highly recommended too. The pathologist was beginning to get the feeling he'd been short-changed.

'You've spotted the obvious and missed the subtle. Yes, he was shot. Whoever shot him did so at close range after he was dead.'

Her confusion became more apparent. For a moment it looked as if she was puzzling out what the pathologist had said, perhaps thinking she had misunderstood. He watched her patiently.

'Why would someone do such a thing?' she finally asked.

Chiswick waved one hand as if it were none of their concern. 'It is not for us to reason why. All we can do is follow the evidence. This man was dead when he was shot, and before that, someone suffocated him to death.'

'Someone else?'

'That's the million-dollar question, isn't it?'

Chapter 12: The Longlist

'So?' Morton demanded as soon as he met Rafferty at the gate.

'He didn't fire the gun. Lab ruled out gunshot residue.'

'Thought as much. Wouldn't it be nice if it were that easy?'

She laughed. 'Yeah, but then we'd be out of a job. What's the plan?'

'Divide and conquer. Ayala is with them at the moment. The whole group is holed up in the barn. We're going to split them up and interview them separately before anyone has time to coordinate their stories. While we're doing that, Purcell can check them all for gunshot residue.'

'And nab any clothes they might have ditched before we rounded them up,' Rafferty said.

'Good thought. I'll brief Purcell. You divvy up the suspects as you see fit. I want all of them interviewed by someone. Standard questions. We need background on the cult, how and why each of them ended up here, and what their relationship was like with Guy.'

Rafferty rolled her eyes. 'I'm sure they all *loved* him. Nicest fella ever. Not a bad word to be said. The usual.'

Morton and Rafferty entered the barn a little before midday. The grumblings of the cultists were obvious: Ayala had been left to corral them together on his own, and they were asking for all sorts of things. They wanted more food, drinks, bathroom breaks, and time to meditate in the Collective's meditation garden. No doubt those irritations were getting on Ayala's wick, each request taking up a little more of his time and sanity as well as those of the uniformed officers assisting him.

The final task of the morning, which Morton had delegated to Mayberry, had been to clear out Abigail and Stephen's living room. Mayberry had done it in record time, and it now felt like a proper incident room rather than an old lady's home. The dining room had been stripped of all decorations and knick-knacks, furniture had been stored in the small box room at the back, and a makeshift interview suite had been set up using a divider to create an enclosed space where before there had been a small armchair piled high with yarn and knitting needles. Mayberry assumed the craft materials were Abigail's rather than Stephen's, though he wasn't entirely convinced. He squeezed a small desk in there together with four chairs and the usual array of audio recording equipment to interrogate each of their suspects.

In the barn, the first thing that struck Morton was how the group had divided itself around the room. The old man, Giacomo, had been rolled into the sunniest corner in a wheelchair. Next to him was an elderly woman whose name Morton didn't yet know. She had perched her bum on the very edge of a bale of hay next to him while leaning towards him as if to cater to his every whim.

At the other end of the barn was his son and replacement officiant, Lorenzo. Unlike the other cultists, who wore expressions of mixed annoyance and boredom, Lorenzo seemed to be enjoying the drama. The tall ethereal blonde girl who had met Morton and Sarah at the gate was now draped across him, her hands running up and down his biceps. Morton fished in his pocket for his phone. He'd had Ayala take down the names and dates of birth of each of the members of the Collective and text him the whole list. He scanned down the last column. Judging by her date of birth, she had to be Lana. She looked much too young to be Lucy, and the only other woman in her early twenties was Abigail.

Morton cleared his throat loudly until silence fell and all eyes were on him. 'Ladies and gentlemen, thank you for assembling in the barn to talk to us. As you all know, Mr Guy Rosenberg was murdered last night. My colleagues, Inspector Rafferty' – Morton pointed towards Ashley and then Bertram – 'and Inspector Ayala will be helping me talk to each of you in turn this afternoon. Before that, our chief scene of crime officer will be swabbing each of you for gunshot residue as well as taking a DNA sample. We will let you know when it's your turn to talk to us. In the interim, please can I ask that you do not talk to each other about Guy's death. Thank you.'

As the chatter resumed, Morton turned to his team. 'Ayala, stay with the group for now and I'll swap with you in a bit. Double-check that Purcell has swabbed everyone, hands and clothes, and then expedite those samples for me. Keep an eye on anyone who looks unhappy about it. Feel free to make it damned obvious you're watching them. I want them to sweat knowing that you're listening to their every word. Rafferty, can you start interviewing the women in the group? They may be more open with you.'

Both nodded and moved off to carry out Morton's orders.

'Lorenzo?' Morton called out. He watched as the cult leader's son shoved Lana off his lap and stood up languorously. He waltzed over slowly as if to convey that he was complying at his own whim and that Morton wasn't in charge. The big man was surprisingly lithe for a man of his frame and build. Lorenzo effortlessly commanded the attention of all within earshot.

'Me first, huh?'

Morton forced himself to smile politely. 'Purcell here is going to swab your hands for GSR and then, if you don't object, he'll swab your cheeks for a DNA sample too.'

The cogs turned as Morton watched Lorenzo grind his jaw. For a second, Morton thought he might object. Then he said: 'Fine. Get it over with.'

* * * *

AS USUAL, MAYBERRY had drawn the short straw. After spending much of the morning checking every inch of the perimeter for gaps – there were none, as the iron fencing continued right through the hedges for its entirety – he was dispatched to do preliminary background checks on all the residents of Terra Farm.

It wasn't going well. As could be expected for a group that lived largely 'off the grid', there was little in the way of records. Only Giacomo's name appeared on the paperwork. He owned the land, he paid the council tax, and he was responsible for the utilities.

Only two of the Collective's members were registered to vote. None of them had a real job outside the confines of Terra Farm and so there wasn't any tax documentation either. They were, as far as the government was concerned, ghosts.

The Morton family, Abigail included, had been excluded. It didn't sit quite right with Mayberry that Morton remained in charge of the investigation, but after all the chief had done for him, Mayberry was willing to ignore that unsettling knot in his stomach for one weekend.

His notepad had the names of all the residents written down in the neat, curly handwriting for which he was well known. He'd added a few notes next to each name. This was the first draft of his "longlist", every person who could feasibly have murdered Guy.

Giacomo di Stregoni. He was the original cult founder, landowner, bill payer, and, unfortunately, not of sound mind. In another life, he had been a psychiatrist, though he had long been considered inactive. At seventy years of age, he was too physically frail to easily commit murder. Moreover, his nursemaid, Doreen Brown, was with him twenty-four-seven. She was likewise an unlikely suspect. Oddly, Giacomo wasn't on the electoral roll. Perhaps that was down to dementia.

Lorenzo di Stregoni. Lorenzo was the son of Giacomo. He was the obvious suspect for the shooting: he'd been caught red-handed holding the offending gun. The evidence cleared him of that particular attempt as his hands and clothes bore no trace of gunshot residue. He couldn't have fired the gun. That didn't necessarily make him innocent, however, as he still could have smothered the victim. Mayberry had managed to find a birth certificate for Lorenzo, but little more than that. The man had grown up inside the Collective, and as far as anyone could tell he had never even been to school.

Lucy Reed. She was a ghost, a quiet woman with an American accent who didn't officially exist. There was no record that Mayberry could find of her ever having entered the country. It was such a common name that Mayberry was drowning in Lucy Reeds with no way to work out which she might be other than age. There was something about her that rubbed Mayberry the wrong way, so he put a great big star next to her name, which flagged her as someone Morton would want to interrogate personally.

Pauline Allchin. The butch groundskeeper had been a member of the Collective for decades. She was one of the two registered voters among the group and had been on the electoral roll for as long as the Collective had been in Putney. Just as she'd told Ayala when protesting about being sequestered in the barn, she had a legitimate firearms licence for the shotgun.

Marta Timpson. Mayberry had barely seen the older woman. She had been sitting serenely on a bale of hay since the group had been corralled into the barn. While Mayberry didn't think she was physically capable of shooting a shotgun without keeling over from the kickback, he did find one peculiarity: her name was on the electoral roll, unlike almost everyone else. Had she lived at Terra Farm before the Collective? Or was Mayberry's information wrong?

The other residents of the Collective – Lana Hayworth, Tracey Cox, and Darren Heggerty – were harder to investigate. Like Lucy, they had managed to go off the grid. No official record of them appeared anywhere in connection with Terra Farm or the Collective. They weren't on the electoral roll, held no jobs, appeared to have no bank accounts registered in the UK, and were not responsible for any of the Collective's bills.

For all official purposes, they might as well not exist. Mayberry scribbled question marks in the margins of his list, unable to come up with any leads to pursue.

How on earth were they going to sort through so many names in just one weekend without a single concrete lead?

• • • •

MORTON'S FIRST SUSPECT wasn't taking it seriously. Lorenzo smiled nonchalantly, walking with the cocky swagger of a man who owned all that he surveyed as Morton led him to the makeshift interrogation suite in the bungalow. When they sat down, Lorenzo gestured towards the kitchen.

'Any chance of a cup of tea?'

Once drinks had been made, the men sat either side of the dining table, Lorenzo's larger-than-life frame making the chair look comically small. Lorenzo leant forward, his elbows resting on the well-worn edge of the table. He seemed to delight in leaving as little personal space between him and Morton as possible. It was a tactic Morton had seen many times: closing the gap between them would force a novice detective to subconsciously pull away, thereby ceding control of the interview process to the interviewee.

'Tell me in your own words what happened this morning,' Morton said once he had read out the standard caution and set the tape to record.

The big man jerked his head towards the tape recorder. 'That really necessary? I feel like I should be asking for a lawyer if this is a formal thing...?'

'That's your right. I'm afraid the tape stays on.'

Lorenzo said nothing for a moment, apparently contemplating whether to call a lawyer. Another power play. 'Fine,' he said finally. 'You were there too. You know as much as I do. I heard the gun go off. Two shots. It sounded nearby.'

'And you weren't expecting to hear a gunshot?'

'Obviously not,' Lorenzo said. 'Not at six in the morning. Pauline rarely rises before nine, and she's the only one who ever fires that gun.'

'What happened next?'

'It sounded like the gunshots came from the direction of Guy's bungalow, so I headed over. He was dead and I found the gun just lying there in his hands.'

Morton leant back as if to consider this apparently new information. He already knew it wasn't suicide as the victim had been long dead before he was shot. Even if they hadn't known that, it was difficult, though not totally impossible, to shoot oneself in the chest with a shotgun. Even if by some miracle Guy *had* contorted himself just so, there was no way a dead man could have scrubbed himself clean of gunshot residue from the afterlife. 'You think he killed himself?'

'Looked like it to me. He was dead. He was holding the gun. Put two and two together, Chief Inspector.'

'Then why take the gun?'

'Can't leave a shotgun lying around where just anyone could pick it up, can I?' Lorenzo said, his tone that of someone talking to a small child. 'That reminds me. I must have a word with Pauline. She's *always* forgetting to lock her gun safe.'

'Is it her gun? Registered?' Morton asked for the benefit of the tape. He knew the answer but he didn't know if Lorenzo knew.

'Yep,' Lorenzo said. 'She uses it to keep pests away. We get a lot of rats coming through the hedges. I'm sure it's one hundred per cent legit. Our Pauline's on the up and up.'

Morton paused. Was he trying to imply that someone else in the Collective *wasn't* on the up and up? If so, that much was self-evident given that Guy Rosenberg had just been murdered.

If the gun was lawfully owned as Lorenzo had just said, it ought to have been securely locked away. For a single gun inside a bungalow within a secure compound, the licensing requirements were relatively lax. A gun safe or even a clamp would be enough to tick the right box. Neglecting to lock the gun safe was criminal, but it wasn't murder. There was no point chasing the lesser crime while a murderer was on the loose, especially when Morton had a ticking clock racing away in the background. He had to solve the murder, and he had to do it by Monday morning. Anything else had to wait.

'How long has she had the gun?'

'Dunno. Ages. You'll have to ask her.'

'Who else knows about it?' Morton felt like he had to ask the obvious question, though he suspected the answer would be equally obvious. It was.

'Everyone. It's pretty loud, and we've all seen her taking pot-shots at rats and woodpigeons.'

Morton was fast exhausting the gun-based line of questioning. It wasn't the murder weapon. Lorenzo hadn't fired it. Everyone knew about it. The very tape he'd set up to prove that he was investigating the gunshot was proving his undoing. It stopped him asking about the asphyxiation because he didn't officially know about it.

Could Lorenzo know that they were doing a pointless dance? If Lorenzo had strangled Guy Rosenberg, then he would know the gun was a red herring. It would explain his nonchalance.

'Tell me about your relationship with Guy Rosenberg,' Morton said, switching topics quickly.

Lorenzo's brow creased up as if the breadth of the question was too much. 'What exactly do you want to know?'

'How long have you known him?'

'All my life,' Lorenzo said. 'We grew up together.'

'Where?'

Lorenzo leant back, spread his hands, and looked around. 'Here. This very bungalow was where his mum lived. There weren't many children back then, and we were the only boys. His mum taught us to read at this dining table.'

'So, you were friends?'

Lorenzo nodded. 'We were.'

Were. Past tense. Had Lorenzo merely echoed Morton's phrase, or had he deliberately used the past tense because Guy was dead? That adjustment would be far quicker than most in Morton's experience. Perhaps then he simply meant that they used to be friends? The nuances of the English language fascinated Morton.

To clarify, he probed deeper. 'Until?'

'Until we weren't.'

'You fell out,' Morton accused him.

'We grew apart,' Lorenzo said. 'We grew up together, but as we got older, Guy and I took different paths. After his mum died, he went travelling for a year or so. When he came back

– booze-addled and emaciated – the man I had once called my friend was gone, and in his place was a shallow husk of a human being.'

'Are you saying he suffered from depression?'

Again, Lorenzo held his hands up. 'I'm not a doctor, but it always seemed that way. I've heard that the best way to tell if someone is clinically depressed is to ask if they bring you down by being around them. Guy did that. He was the drain to everyone else's radiator.'

Lorenzo was trying awfully hard to push the suicide narrative. It would have been easy to dismiss him as brash and arrogant. So far, his tone was far too matter-of-fact for Morton's liking. But Morton's gut said there was more to Lorenzo. His shallow arrogance hid something deeper, more complex, and more cunning. While he had been found proudly toting the gun, he couldn't have fired it without leaving gunshot residue all over his hands. He simply didn't have enough time to fire the gun then clean up before Morton ran from the north-west bungalow down to Guy Rosenberg's home in the south-east. Was his arrogance because he thought he was off the hook?

Worse still, he wasn't grieving his former friend at all.

'Was Guy suicidal? Had he ever threatened to kill himself?'

'Who knows?' Lorenzo said. 'Guy seemed to be trying to drink himself to death. He'd been doing so, so well giving up the booze, but that all came crashing back to reality at the wedding when he tried to drink the bar dry. You must have seen it yourself, Chief Inspector.' Lorenzo looked at him accusingly, and Morton had a fleeting suspicion that Lorenzo knew Morton ought to recuse himself.

Morton let the silence continue for a few moments, each man watching the other with a mix of curiosity and wariness. Then he asked: 'What was it like growing up in the Collective?'

'How am I supposed to know? I haven't got anything to compare it to, have I? This life, these people, this place' – he looked around almost wistfully – 'is all I've ever known.'

There was a pang of loneliness in Lorenzo's voice. For just a moment the mask had dropped. Morton didn't like the brash younger man, but he could relate to the challenge of an isolated childhood; his own had been spent in a village where the local pub had served as a sub-post office twice a week and the nearest proper shop was two villages over.

The message the pathologist had sent right before the interview lingered in Morton's mind. He couldn't get the image of a scarred C on Guy's back out of his mind. As Lorenzo stood up to leave, Morton stopped him. 'One more thing, Mr di Stregoni. The pathologist found some sort of scar on Guy's back. Do you know anything about that?'

'Scar? You make it sound so tawdry. It's his mark. Look.'

Before Morton could say another word, Lorenzo lifted his tunic straight up and over his head to reveal that almost his entire body was covered in an enormously intricate tattoo. Roots criss-crossed his abs and chest.

He flexed his muscles. 'Not bad, huh?'

'Not my cup of tea. Guy's "mark" as you called it was on his back.'

Lorenzo spun around. Just like Guy, he had a large letter C covering his back from his rhomboid muscle right down to the base of his spine. Unlike Guy, Lorenzo's "mark" as he called it was in bog-standard tattooist's ink rather than the telltale white of a faded scar. Morton said as much.

'Yeah, well, Guy wanted to go all-natural, didn't he? That's why he planted all those lime trees in the greenhouse.'

'Is it something everyone does?' Morton asked. Could Stephen have been stupid enough to get such a ridiculous tattoo?

'Yeah. It's a mark of belonging around here. Nobody's forced into doing anything, of course.'

Morton arched a sceptical eyebrow. As if anyone had much choice around here. Whatever the di Stregoni men said was gospel.

'Is there anything else, Mr Morton?'

'Not for now,' Morton said. 'Thank you for your time.'

As far as the *official* investigation was concerned, Lorenzo was an innocent man. But in Morton's mind, Lorenzo di Stregoni was incredibly dangerous. He was far too laid back about a murder being committed on his farm. The lack of gunshot residue didn't rule him out as the real murderer. If anything, his callous and casual inference that Guy had committed suicide only made him more dangerous.

Morton watched him swagger out the door. One down, eleven to go.

Chapter 13: Something to Hide

Lucy leant back in her armchair and surveyed the man before her. The detective was tall, handsome, and impeccably attired. Despite the heat, Detective Inspector Ayala wore a full suit and his only concession to the scorching weather was foregoing a tie. He spoke with a soft, quiet voice that naturally made her want to lean forward to hear him better. His manner was practised, calculated, and designed to immediately put the interviewee at ease. It was almost impressive. But it wouldn't work on her.

He smiled at her like an old friend, and Lucy had to remind herself that, while the police were not her enemy, she needed to maintain her cover if she wanted to win the Pulitzer.

'How long have you lived here?' he asked as he folded one slender leg over the other.

Lucy smiled back. If he wanted banter, he'd get it. 'This bungalow?'

'Terra Farm,' Ayala clarified.

'Six months. And the same for the bungalow.'

Ayala leant forward in his chair as if he wanted to hear the latest gossip. He really was good. 'What are the living arrangements like around here?'

Lucy spoke with a dry, disinterested tone as if the Collective's housing arrangements were unremarkable. 'Some of us share. Some don't. The unmarried women share a bungalow, the widows have another of their own, the groundskeeper has her own place so she doesn't disturb anyone when coming and going early or late, and all the men have a house each.'

'That's rather sexist.'

'It is what it is,' Lucy said. 'It's a man's world. You yourself must have faced discrimination, no?'

The detective looked abashed. 'Because I'm black?'

'And gay. Where's the name from, anyway? Ayala's Spanish, isn't it?'

For a moment he looked surprised that Lucy had figured it out so quickly, but he recovered in an instant. 'My father's Spanish. He's from La Linea. My mother was from Mali.'

'Then the English accent... school in Gibraltar?'

Ayala's patience waned. 'This isn't about me,' he said tersely, and then, resuming the quiet, affected manner, he continued: 'So, Lucy, tell me what your role in the Collective is. A place this big must be organised somehow.'

Lucy shrugged. Her diversion hadn't been enough to get him riled. 'I do whatever is needed. Some days that's watering the plants or tending the chickens – we're largely self-sufficient for food – and on others, I hoover the bungalows, paint the barn, or cook dinner. The one thing I don't do, thank god, is the laundry. Poor Tracey gets all of that, and with just two old Bosch washer-dryers too. They're always breaking down. Our handyman Darren is in and out of that washroom like a yo-yo.'

'Do you eat communally?'

She shook her head. 'Not usually. For special occasions, we sometimes lay out a buffet in the barn. Otherwise, we take our meals in our own homes. The evening meal gets prepared here – we've got the largest kitchen – and then one of the girls takes a plate around to each house.'

Lucy stretched out. She had been standing in the barn for far too long waiting for her turn to be interviewed. The police were clearly on a fishing expedition. They had no clue that virtually everyone hated Guy.

'What was your relationship like with Guy Rosenberg?'

'I barely knew him,' Lucy said. 'We spoke maybe once or twice a week in passing. He did a lot of manual labour, drove the jeep to pick up supplies, and kept to himself as far as I could see. The poor man seemed miserable most of the time. I don't think I saw him crack a smile once in six months.'

'Do you think he was depressed?' Ayala asked.

'He wasn't suicidal, if that's what you're asking. He wanted out of the Collective. That much was obvious. He'd grown up with Giacomo as his surrogate father, and he felt there was more to explore out in the world.'

Ayala flashed her a smile revealing perfectly even teeth that couldn't possibly be natural. 'You got that from an occasional conversation here and there?'

Damn. At this rate, she'd give herself away. Lucy almost hung her head in shame. 'It was common knowledge,' she said matter-of-factly. 'Guy has been quite vocal about his... disagreement with how things are run. He obviously wanted to go but didn't quite dare to step out into the world on his own. Terra Farm has been home almost all his life, so leaving permanently must have been a daunting prospect.'

She saw Ayala shudder as if he were contemplating the same thing she was: the idea of a child brainwashed inside a cult run by a charismatic but egotistic leader. Guy had grown up alongside Lorenzo, and he'd never have had a chance to become his own man. He was destined to become the right-hand man to the future leader. In rejecting Lorenzo's leadership, he'd doomed himself to a lonely existence as the only young man in the cult without any semblance of power.

'That it must be,' Ayala said soothingly. 'Is there anything you think I need to know about anyone in the Collective?'

She paused. Six months of undercover journalism meant she knew a great deal, but she was not yet ready to show her hand. She shook her head slowly. 'I can't think of anything right now, Inspector Ayala.'

He rose from the opposite armchair, took a business card from inside his jacket and proffered it. He began to launch into a spiel beginning with 'If you think of anything, call me' but Lucy cut him off mid-sentence.

'I can't call you, can I? Nobody here is allowed a phone except for Lorenzo. All of the phones on the farm are in that lockbox by the gate. For emergencies only, of course.'

As if the phones left in the lock box would retain any charge, *Ayala thought.* 'Then come find me or Detective Chief Inspector Morton. As a last resort, talk to one of the uniformed officers at the gate and they'll be able to put you in touch with me. I expect we'll have an around-the-clock presence on Terra Farm until the murder is solved.'

• • • •

MORTON SHUT THE BATHROOM door behind him and slumped to the floor. The past few hours had been utter chaos as they'd worked their way through a merry-go-round of interviewees being frogmarched in and out of the bungalow. He was drowning in plausible suspects, three of whom were family, and the rest were so similar that they began to blur together, which was never a good sign.

He rested his head in his hands and exhaled deeply, the last of his energy finally depleted. He really shouldn't be on this case at all. The pathologist knew it too, and he'd probably lose his pension if Silverman cottoned on. Or worse. Morton had to pretend to investigate just the gunshots when he knew that wasn't the cause of death. And even if he could hide his own dishonesty from everyone outside the team, he still only had one weekend to solve the murder.

A wave of hopelessness crashed over him. In a normal investigation, he felt powerful, strong, capable. He was the predator and the criminals were his prey. Here the roles were reversed, the great detective becoming a sheep among wolves. It was enough that he almost felt sorry for the criminals he had to pursue. Almost.

Footsteps echoed in the hallway.

'David?' Sarah called out.

So little respite. His wife meant well, but she never quite understood that a good detective ran on a combination of adrenaline, caffeine, and cortisol. And she was another problem he needed to deal with: she couldn't wait around here indefinitely. He'd have to send her home.

With a grunt, Morton hauled himself to his feet. He flushed the unused toilet, ran the tap, and then unlocked the door.

'You okay?' she asked lightly, but her expression of concern said that she already knew the answer.

'Fine,' he muttered.

'David Gareth Morton, we've been married for over thirty years. You are not fine. Talk to me.'

Morton rolled his eyes. He never could get anything past her, and he did wish she would refrain from using his full name whenever things got serious. It reminded him far too much of his mother.

'I can't do this.'

'You can't do what?' Sarah prodded. When he didn't reply, she grabbed him by the arm and steered him towards the kitchen. As Morton watched in silence, Sarah fell back on that peculiarly British standby in times of stress: she put the kettle on.

A good few minutes later, the whistling of the old hob-style kettle heralded the end of Morton's contemplative silence. No sooner had she thrust a mug of steaming breakfast tea (milk, no sugar) into his hand than the interrogation began anew.

'What's bothering you?'

Morton took a slurp of his tea to avoid answering, then fetched a packet of digestive biscuits from one of the cupboards. When he could stand the silence no longer, he muttered into his cup: 'Everything.'

'Such as?'

'Such as the fact that you're still here. We're staying on the premises of a cult where a murder just occurred and I don't know for sure that you're safe. I should have taken you home by now. I'm sending you home with an escort. I can't force Stephen to leave, but I'll ask him to.'

'Okay, that's fair. But I'm not going 'til I know you're okay. What else is bothering you?'

'The obvious. I'm running an investigation that's procedurally negligent at best and a hair's breadth from perverting the course of justice at worst. If Silverman finds out, she'll sack me in a heartbeat. I wouldn't blame her for it, either.'

'If she finds out.'

'Big if. Then there's the fact that our son is involved with these lunatics, and now that I know Guy Rosenberg didn't die by gunshot, both he and Abigail ought to be on my suspect list, but they're not because I can only officially investigate the gunshots that didn't kill Rosenberg. I've got twelve suspects, three of whom are you and the kids. Even if I assume Abigail didn't do it, and that's a big if when we don't know her at all, that leaves me with nine plausible suspects.'

'But not all *equally* plausible,' Sarah said. 'You told me Guy was smothered to death. Doesn't that take some physicality? He was a big guy. He towered over Abigail when he dragged her into the barn for the ceremony yesterday. Wouldn't he have fought off any attacker smaller than, say, Lorenzo?'

'Well, yes,' Morton conceded. 'Normally a victim will fight and struggle and it takes far longer to suffocate someone than most people imagine. But by all accounts, Guy was drunk off his tits, and he'd passed out in bed. He wouldn't have been hard to smother. All it really takes is an unflinching determination to get the job done.'

'Could Giacomo have done it?' Sarah asked. 'If he's the big cheese around here, then surely nobody would kill without him being in the loop.'

He resisted the urge to tell his wife to stop trying to play cop. That would never end well. Instead, he said patiently: 'Lorenzo's more likely in my book, but as far as the official investigation is concerned, he's an innocent man. Unfortunately, the father has stage six Alzheimer's. Giacomo doesn't know what day of the week it is, and he can't physically do anything without his nursemaid, Doreen. She's with him twenty-four-seven.'

'Then they're each other's alibis?' Sarah asked. 'Doesn't that cut your suspect list to just seven?'

'Unless she nipped out when he was asleep. Or they did it together. If he was involved, there's no way a jury would convict him. I just can't definitely rule anyone out yet.'

Sarah drained the last dregs of her cup of tea and reached for another biscuit. 'Two attempts on Guy's life is already unlikely. What are the odds that one of those attempts involved two people as well? Unless you think all of them are in on it and this whole investigation is a charade for their amusement.'

'Nah,' Morton said. 'They're not that smart. The Collective is a weird bunch of hippies, idealists, and nutters, but I don't see them all being capable of murder. Stephen certainly isn't, and he's as shocked as anyone.'

Sarah put down the packet of biscuits and looked at Morton. 'Then you'd best give me the car keys so I can get out of here and out of your way. If you've got to solve this by nine o'clock on Monday morning when Silverman gets into her office, then you've got' – she glanced at her watch, which now read two o'clock – 'about sixty-seven hours to solve a murder.'

Chapter 14: Moral Flexibility

By mid-afternoon, several members of the Collective were making noises about being 'unlawfully detained' in the barn. No doubt that was Lorenzo's doing. As soon as his own interview was complete, he'd flipped a switch and stopped the pretence of being helpful. There was only one interview left, so the group was told they were free to go and they quickly scarpered back to the four corners of Terra Farm. The last interviewee was Marta, and she was on Rafferty's list. It wasn't a plum assignment interrogating an ageing hippie, but it beat standing guard by the front gate to watch who was coming and going. Rafferty didn't envy the uniformed officers who had that task: the afternoon temperature was edging towards thirty, and as she trekked towards the yoga lawn in search of Marta, Rafferty could feel beads of sweat on the back of her neck.

The lawn was on the eastern perimeter of the property, tucked away behind a row of leylandii. From what Purcell had told her, there were nooks and crannies hidden all around the perimeter with greenhouses here and a polytunnel there. Purcell and his team were working their way through a vegetable garden and pigsty on the western perimeter. No doubt that would take them all day. Rafferty hated pigs even though she knew that they were clean, intelligent animals. Ever since she'd seen the film *Babe*, she'd sworn off eating bacon. This was a much better place to be, a secret garden dedicated to meditation and yoga, a suntrap lined with beautiful flowers. Upon her arrival, Rafferty found two of the older women practising yoga. She knew from her notes that they were Tracey Cox and Marta Timpson.

Despite their age, they were more flexible than Rafferty had ever been. Unsure which was which, Rafferty coughed to announce her arrival, and without looking at either of the women in particular, said: 'May I have a few moments of your time please, Marta?'

The less-wrinkled of the two women looked up for a moment, and then resumed a pose that Rafferty didn't recognise. 'Pull up a mat then, young 'un. Trace, would you mind giving us a bit of peace and quiet, love?'

The other woman gave her a quizzical glance.

When she didn't move, Marta's tone grew harsher. 'Sod off, woman. Honestly, can't you see the nice police lady wants a chat without an audience?'

This time Tracey stooped, picked up her mat, slung it over her shoulder without saying a word, and disappeared off down the path towards the main compound.

Marta gestured at a stack of mats underneath a nearby tree. With a shrug, Rafferty headed over to collect one. It was better than sitting on the grass.

'On my right if you don't mind, lovely,' Marta said as she effortlessly changed pose. 'I'm mostly deaf in my left ear.'

Rafferty set her mat down a few feet to Marta's right as requested, sat down, and then simply watched the older woman as she held her downward dog pose. For her age, Marta was in great shape. She made it looked effortless. Rafferty knew that if she tried to mimic it, her thigh muscles would tire almost immediately.

'Have you been here since the beginning, Marta?' Rafferty asked as she assumed a much less taxing pose that she called sitting policewoman.

'Aye, I have,' Marta said. 'Longer than most of our lot.'

'What was it like in the beginning?'

'Fucked if I know. We were all high as shit back then.'

Rafferty was so taken aback by Marta's sudden profanity that she must have looked slack-jawed because Marta immediately burst out laughing.

'Sorry, young 'un. You must be one of them precious young things who don't swear.'

'Not when I'm on duty,' Rafferty said as she wrangled to put the interview back on a more serious footing.

'Back then, the movement was all about being free. Doing whatever the shit we wanted and damn the consequences. We moved squat to squat to avoid paying rent. None of us worked a proper job back then except Giacomo, so it was easy. We drank, we smoked some weed, and we partied. Then we came here fifteen years ago.'

'Why was that?'

'One of the original gang owned this place,' Marta said airily.

'Your sister,' Rafferty said smartly. Mayberry had already found that little titbit when he'd searched through the Land Registry records.

'Ho, ho, ho, you are a smart one,' Marta said. 'Yep, my late sister inherited this place off her deadbeat partner. It was the only good thing he ever did for her. After he was gone, we got turfed out of a long-term squat, and she rescued us.'

'Why?'

'Family loyalty, I suppose,' Marta said. 'Blood is thicker than water, after all. I'd tell you to ask her yourself, but that's a bit difficult, seeing as how she's dead and all.' As if blood explained everything. It was too casual, too rehearsed, to be the truth.

'There wasn't any other reason?' Rafferty shot back. 'She wasn't in love with Giacomo?'

Bingo. Rafferty's shot in the dark had hit home. Marta stopped her yoga, mirrored Rafferty's sitting policewoman pose, and grinned. This time, the smile didn't reach her eyes.

'We all loved Giacomo,' Marta said. 'He was tall, dark, handsome, and much too charming for his own good. It's impossible not to love him.'

Love. Present tense. 'You still love him?'

Marta's tone turned gruff. 'So what if I do? Can't a gal carry a candle for her Italian stallion in peace? It's not as if he loves me back, anyway. The husk that's left doesn't even recognise me anymore. Looking into his eyes is like looking into the abyss. Ascended, my backside.'

'He's got dementia, hasn't he? Late-stage?'

'Yep,' Marta said. 'He's been bad for a while, and *she's* got him on all sorts of treatments, herbal remedies, all-natural bullshit. I'm sure you've met the type. If she were forty years younger, she'd be one of those twats pyramid selling online.'

'Who is she?'

'Dori.'

'Doreen Brown?' Rafferty named Giacomo's live-in nursemaid.

'That's the harlot,' Marta said. 'She stole him from me, you know. Younger model and all that.'

Rafferty choked down her laughter. It was hard to imagine a fifty-nine-year-old woman as the younger anything.

'Giacomo was a bit of a ladies' man, then?'

'A bit?' Marta echoed. 'Look around, dearie. You see many other eligible men of his generation on the farm? His whole life has been a series of younger and younger women. The only men he tolerates being around him are those who don't challenge his authority.'

'But there are men here.'

'Two are too young to be a threat to Giacomo, and besides, his son has always been his pride and joy. Never have I seen him look prouder than when he was with Lorenzo. As for Darren, he's far too obsequious to be threatening. You've met him, haven't you? He rarely says a word. Bloody poofter if you ask me. I can't image why else he'd have stuck around this long.'

'What would happen if someone did cross Giacomo? He seems pretty harmless to me.'

Marta met Rafferty's question with a stare, her eyes flashing darkly. 'Giacomo might come over as a nice, doddery old man now, but make no mistake, Giacomo di Stregoni has held the reins of the Collective in an iron grip ever since he started it. It's his way or the highway.'

'And you chose his way.'

'I did. And I regret it every day.'

Chapter 15: The Pigs

Most of the original Terra Farm was long gone. Today, just one tiny sliver of it remained tucked away on the western edge of the property, a hundred yards from Darren Heggerty's ramshackle home. This was his domain. He set the heavy feed bucket down and wiped his brow. Feeding the pigs was his favourite part of the day. Everyone else saw them as dirty, smelly creatures that would eat anything. In Darren's experience, they were the smartest things on Terra Farm. Some of the others were all right, especially the less fervent believers. The farm was split down the middle. Some of the older lot had joined, as Darren had, hoping for a simple life. Others followed Lorenzo and his lunacy, even when he instituted arbitrary rules just to see who'd go along with them.

The west was so much better. Hidden away here, Darren could water and tend the vegetable patch in peace. He'd even grown pineapples and chillies in the two decrepit polytunnels that had been here almost as long as he had.

It was a quiet life. Most of the time.

But this weekend, the past threatened to haunt him. All because someone had been stupid enough to knock off Guy Rosenberg.

Not only that, they'd gone and done it when there was a bloody rozzer on the farm. Who waits for the one day a policeman's about before they commit murder? Bloody morons.

It wasn't the first death on the farm. Not by a long shot. The others... they'd just disappeared. And Darren knew exactly where to. He hadn't wanted to go along with it, but he'd had no choice. Lorenzo had given him his orders and, like the coward that he was, he'd complied without a whimper.

Hadn't always been that way. Once upon a time, he'd been his own man. A man with a future. A wife. A home.

That was all long gone.

All because of one mistake, a mistake that – somehow – Lorenzo had learned of.

Now he had to keep his head down, stick to the party line, and tell the police the truth. Not the whole truth, though. Just enough to keep them away from him, away from Lorenzo, and away from the secret he wished he had never learned.

Before they could learn what he'd done.

Chapter 16: The Unexpected

Stuart Purcell grumbled to himself as he worked. It was just too much. With less than his full complement of scene of crime officers on-site, he was forced to do all of the donkey work himself. The grounds were enormous. As well as eight bungalows and a barn, there were also hundreds of metres of perimeter fencing encased in hedges, the kitchen garden and its greenhouses and polytunnels, the pigsties, a smattering of sheds and other dilapidated outbuildings, and even a small pavilion complete with a statue of Giacomo in the tiny garden behind his and Doreen's bungalow. No doubt Lorenzo would replace that with a statue of himself if he had the chance.

He'd begun with a grid-search style, going from the north-east corner of the property across to the north-west. Next, he'd head south and then head east before, finally, heading down to the third and last row at the southernmost edge of Terra Farm, finishing up at Darren's bungalow in the southwest. It was a slow, deliberate method that meant a lot of climbing up and down the hillside, a hard slog for a man of his bulk made worse by the cloying plastic overalls and shoe covers that proper procedure dictated he wear.

So far today, he'd come up empty-handed. The only bit of evidence that indicated any sort of criminality was something that he'd spotted just outside the compound boundaries as if it had been flung over the northern fence in a hurry. It had to have been thrown by someone with a good arm, as the fence was high and the hedges were higher still, and this wasn't a small bag of cannabis. Weed would explain how they were financing the

Collective, because running a few yoga classes for outsiders down at Putney Village Community Centre a few times a week wasn't going to pay their way.

He'd just given Stephen and Abigail's bungalow, which Morton and the team had converted into a makeshift incident room, the most cursory of examinations. It had been so *weird* having to search his boss's son's home, and he'd finished his search in less than ten minutes. Not that there was much to rifle through anyway, as Stephen and Abigail had fewer possessions than a Trappist monk. The bedroom had only had a bare mattress on the floor, the bathroom only a lone, presumably shared, toothbrush in dire need of replacement and a single towel. It hadn't been much better in the kitchen, which had basic utensils available but precious little food. The tins in the cupboard were so out of date that they must have been there since the place was built.

Before he headed south, something caught his eye. There was a number five painted on the front door. Odd. He was sure he'd seen another door marked number five. How strange. Could he have made a mistake? Whoever did the house numbering was a bit of a lunatic. There wasn't any rhyme or reason to the order that Purcell could discern. Anyone with half a brain would have started at one and then worked around the farm either clockwise or row by row. That hadn't happened.

Even Giacomo's bungalow was oddly numbered. The door was emblazoned with the number zero as if it used to read ten but half the signage had fallen off except that the number was actually painted on the door so a digit couldn't have fallen off.

Purcell put that thought from his mind as he headed towards the western bungalow where the groundskeeper, a woman called Pauline Allchin, lived alone.

By the time he got there, he was drenched in sweat. The sweltering heat was working against him and his team, and it raised the real possibility that he might contaminate great swathes of the crime scene with his own DNA if he took off the protective suit for even a moment.

She was waiting outside, a constable keeping her company. Despite her name, Allchin was a big beefy woman with so little neck that her face melted into her body with no chin in sight. No wonder she lived alone. Even by Purcell's lax standards, the woman was a troll.

Purcell nodded at the constable standing guard and then headed in.

Inside, he was confronted by piles of junk. There were newspapers, old boxes, and knickknacks of all kinds littering every available surface. Muddy boots lay just inside the door, a trip hazard that elicited a yelp from Purcell as he stumbled over them.

'Everything all right in there, sir?' called the voice of the constable outside. Purcell thought he could hear a trace of amusement in the man's voice. No doubt he'd also spotted the boots and failed to warn Purcell.

'Fine, fine,' Purcell shot back. It didn't get any better as he progressed further inside. The bungalow was one of the messiest properties Purcell had ever been in, and he'd had to investigate the homes of hoarders, junkies, and the mentally disturbed.

It was a broad search looking for anything incriminating. The purported murder weapon, the gun, had already been found, and he knew that gun was registered to Ms Allchin. From what Morton had told him, he also knew the gun wasn't actually the murder weapon, which meant his entire grid search was tantamount to a fishing expedition. The only specific item he had to keep an eye out for was clothing. Every single robe on Terra Farm needed to be tested for gunshot residue. So far, no GSR had been found on any clothing, person or object. It didn't help that the robes were all *very* similar. Under close inspection, Purcell could tell which were men's robes and which were women's, but beyond that only Giacomo's slightly more flamboyant robes stood out.

'So messy,' he muttered to himself. Usually, the evidence drove the investigation, which was how it ought to be. Purcell was forever telling his staff to follow the evidence, but in this case, he was actively ignoring the real cause of death. Smothering someone took no special equipment and left little evidence. The odds were that the only valuable evidence to collect was back in Guy Rosenberg's home, and everything that Purcell had found there had long since been bagged, tagged, and sent off for analysis.

This bungalow was bigger than he had expected, and, unlike the other homes, there was no lack of technology. It appeared the 'back to the earth' motivations of the cult were of little importance when it came to security. High-end cameras at the gate fed through to a computer in the living room which recorded it all. When Purcell attempted to gain access to the system, he found himself confronted with a password screen. He quickly backtracked to the front door where Pauline Allchin was waiting impatiently, tapping her foot.

'Ms Allchin, I'd like you to come and enter your password for me, please.'

She looked at him with her muscle-bound arms tightly crossed, peering down menacingly at the man who stood at least four inches shorter than she did.

'No,' she said flatly.

Typical. They all tried it, and all it did was waste police time and resources, and this weekend they were short on both. 'You know we'll just have to break in.'

'Break in, then,' she said with the yellow, crooked sneer of a woman who hadn't seen a dentist in decades. 'If you can get a warrant.'

It was a rare flash of normality. These cultists oscillated between ethereal, aloof, and awkward one moment, and then surprisingly street-wise the next. Demanding a warrant was a sign of one of two things. Either the suspect was hiding something, which was no surprise given what Purcell had seen on many a laptop, or the suspect had watched too many episodes of *Law & Order*. Purcell left Allchin on the doorstep, spun on his heel, and marched back into the bungalow. A gentle breeze caused him to slam the front door behind him slightly harder than he needed to. It reverberated angrily in its frame, eliciting choice words from Allchin on the other side of it.

He hated dealing with the public. Where were Ayala and Mayberry when he needed them? This investigation was turning out to be shoddily run as well as unethical. Morton was trying to cajole his team into getting everything done in the one weekend he had, and it was spreading them all far too thin. Even with the forensics being marked top priority so the lab would process the samples collected straight away, there was a good chance that, come Monday morning, Morton would be out of a job, and questions would be asked of all of the extended team.

After failing to secure the password he needed, Purcell moved on to searching the master bedroom. He still hadn't found anything probative. Allchin's room was sparingly decorated with only a stack of old paperbacks, mostly genre fiction, not giving away anything except her love of bodice rippers. Life as a single woman in a cult must be very lonely indeed.

He swabbed all of the robes for GSR. Anything that had been worn by the shooter ought to flash up bright orange when subject to the Griess test. That would prove there were nitrite residues, usually indicative of a gunshot. Anything that tested positive for nitrites would then be tested again, this time for lead by using sodium rhodizonate. So far, nothing had tested positive for either. Nor had Purcell seen any physical damage that would indicate that clothing had been burned or otherwise damaged by a close gunshot.

By the time he reached the last door, a spare bedroom tucked at the rear of the bungalow, he was practically sleep-walking. The knob didn't turn straight away. For a moment he thought he had somehow lost the ability to open a door, but then he noticed the padlock, a big heavy affair like the kind most people had on their front door except that this was *into* a spare room. To top it all off, there was one deadbolt at the top of the door and a second at the bottom. He slid them both across and pulled at the door. No dice. He'd have to get the key or fetch bolt cutters to snap the lock.

Once again, he trekked outside. Pauline Allchin was still there, still smirking.

'Key to the back room, now,' he demanded, holding his hand out expectantly.

'Nope,' Allchin said again. This time she leant in so close to him that he could smell her stale breath. Allchin's oral hygiene left a lot to be desired.

'Fine,' Purcell said. He spotted Mayberry fifty feet away walking briskly north. He called out and the young detective turned. With a gnarled finger, Purcell beckoned him over.

'Y-yes?' Mayberry stuttered.

'I need a lock pick, or failing that, a door ram,' Purcell said. 'Do you have one?'

'In the c-c-car.'

'Then go get it, would you?' Purcell said, his frustration creeping into his voice. No sooner had he spoken than Mayberry scarpered towards the gravel path leading towards the gate. Purcell stood in awkward silence watching Allchin as he waited. For the first time, he thought he could see apprehension hiding behind the vacant expression. If there hadn't been a uniformed officer guarding her, Purcell was certain she'd have legged it, or worse, hit him.

After a few minutes of silent staring, Mayberry reappeared carrying a manual battering ram.

'Fine,' Allchin grunted. She fished inside her dungarees and then held out a key grudgingly. 'No point you smashing up my home now, is there?'

'Thank you,' Purcell said curtly as he took the key. Mayberry followed in his wake as he headed for the locked bedroom. 'Want to do the honours, Detective?'

'N-no, you g-go ahead.'

The key turned with an audible click, and then shuffling sounds came from within. Purcell barely had time for his muscles to tense up before he wondered if he'd made a mistake unlocking the door. What if there was a rabid dog inside? Or worse?

Mayberry shoved him to one side and yanked the door open, letting the sunlight stream in. Before Purcell could say a thing, the air was rent with the scream of someone howling in agony.

He risked peeking past Mayberry to see a young woman, no older than eighteen or nineteen, sprawled on the floor. Her hands were clamped over her eyes as if the merest sliver of light would burn them. Her skin was sallow, pale, devoid of Lorenzo's golden tan. Beyond her, Purcell could see a dog's water bowl, almost empty, which lay by her side, the final drops of moisture glistening in the sunlight. It was only when Mayberry had the presence of mind to partially close the door that she stopped screaming. Her eyes watered as they adjusted to the trickle of sunlight coming through the door.

As the woman squinted, Purcell let his eyes dart around the room. It was empty but for what appeared to be hundreds of old rags glued to the walls, a bucket that, by the smell of it, was being used as a toilet, and a filthy single mattress that was so thin that the girl may as well have been lying directly on the floor.

Now certain that the girl posed no threat, Purcell felt his courage return. 'Mayberry, go fetch help.'

As Mayberry's footsteps echoed on the wood floor, Purcell removed his Tyvek Coveralls. Forensics was important, but people always came first, and the poor girl was traumatised enough without seeing a strange man in a white plastic suit staring down at her.

He pulled a bottle of water from his kitbag and held it out to her. 'What's your name?'

She took the bottle and greedily downed the lot.

'Claudia,' she whispered hoarsely.

'I'm Stuart. Help is on the way, okay?'

Purcell looked around towards the door. Allchin had disappeared from her spot on the porch. No matter; she was Morton's problem, not his, and she couldn't get far.

As he waited for medical help to arrive, Purcell once again cursed the lack of manpower behind the investigation. The girl ought to have been found hours ago.

Chapter 17: Charing Cross

It took an age for Claudia to be cleared by her doctors at Charing Cross Hospital. By the time Morton was finally allowed into the ward to talk to her, he had been waiting for hours. He'd spent his time reading up about the Collective on his phone. He'd managed to verify that the land the Collective was on had indeed belonged to Marta's late sister and that Giacomo di Stregoni was now the lawful owner of the property. Council tax and utilities were all up to date, which suggested the Collective wasn't as hard-up as Morton might have imagined. That was about as far as he had managed to get. The same walls that had stopped Mayberry in his tracks stopped Morton too. Most of the residents of Terra Farm were digital ghosts with no records of them to be found anywhere in the databases that the Met had access to.

Claudia was his best bet yet at finding out just what was going on inside Terra Farm. She hadn't been at the wedding, so she wouldn't have a clue who he was. He'd have to tread lightly.

'Keep it quick,' her doctor warned. 'She's stable, but we don't know yet what caused this.'

Her symptoms were myriad, varied, and, taken one or two at a time, wholly generic: headache, vomiting and diarrhoea, blurry vision, elevated heart rate, hives, confusion, and disorientation.

'Do you have any idea what could cause these sorts of symptoms to occur at the same time?' Morton asked.

'It could just be dehydration and exhaustion. Or she could have been exposed to something toxic,' the doctor said. 'I've sent off a blood sample, but it'll be a few days before we get any results. I'm in a rush. I've got another patient to see, but if you have any questions, please speak to the ward sister.'

Morton was led by a nurse to the back of a single-sex ward. There were six beds, and Claudia's was the furthest in, tucked away behind a plastic curtain so flimsy that it afforded virtually no privacy. Morton's request for a private room for her had fallen on deaf ears. At least she had a window. She was staring out of it as Morton approached, her expression hollow and vacant. She took no notice of Morton's arrival.

At the foot of her bed, the name on her chart read Claudia Sozler, and her date of birth confirmed she was twenty-two, a little older than Morton would have guessed from her youthful demeanour.

'Hi, Claudia,' Morton said gently as he sat down in the little plastic chair intended for visitors. He waited patiently until her head turned in his direction. He could see that her eyes were red from crying. 'I'm Detective Chief Inspector Morton, and I came by to see how you're doing. Can you tell me what happened?'

Even though there was an IV hooked up to her arm to maintain her fluid levels, she spoke with the hoarse tone of someone who was severely dehydrated. 'I was... in seclusion.'

The words came slowly, laboriously, as if uttering them took the greatest of efforts.

'Seclusion?' Morton echoed, unsure if he had heard her correctly. 'What's that?'

She averted her gaze as if she were ashamed. As Morton watched, a tear rolled down her cheek before falling onto the bedsheets.

'You don't have to talk me if you don't want to, and if you'd like a female officer then you only have to nod.'

A shake of the head. Morton took that as permission to proceed. 'Is seclusion some kind of punishment?' he asked.

She nodded timidly.

'What did you do?'

'I... I bled.'

Did he hear her right? Before he could follow up to clarify, she pointed between her legs.

'You mean you were on your period?'

Another nod.

Morton felt bile rise up in his throat. Someone had locked her up for *menstruating* as if she had done something wrong. The hairs on Morton's arms stood on end. How dare they? If he had a daughter, and somebody had done this to her... It couldn't have been Guy Rosenberg, could it? This sort of abuse would be ample motivation for his murder, and he had been one of the men to parade poor Abigail around the barn just yesterday, so he was clearly capable of such misogyny. Or perhaps it was that monster Lorenzo. He clearly ruled the roost.

'Who?' Morton roared far louder than he had intended. Then, in a quieter voice, he asked gently, 'Who did this to you?'

Her face paled. She froze as if she couldn't speak.

Morton forced himself to calm down. The poor girl was terrified of him. He breathed deeply.

'I'm sorry, Claudia. I shouldn't have raised my voice like that. It must be hard for you. Perhaps you could just write down the name of the person who locked you in that room?'

A third, tentative, nod.

Morton passed her his notepad and the pen that Sarah had given him for his last birthday. He waited with bated breath as Claudia Sozler wrote down the name of her assailant. He fully expected to see Lorenzo's name. She handed him the note, still not meeting his gaze.

There, in shaky, barely legible writing was the name of the psychopath who had locked a young woman up just for being on her period. When Morton read it, he felt his jaw drop.

Pauline Allchin.

Chapter 18: Seclusion

It was nearly seven o'clock in the evening by the time Morton returned to Putney. He was still fuming at the idea that a young woman could ever be punished for something as normal as simply menstruating. The Collective had taken period shaming to a whole new level. He'd read about such things in the newspapers, but that was always in far-flung places that had yet to learn that it was now the twenty-first century and women were equal to men in every way. He'd never imagined something like this happening here.

Not even the beautiful sunshine could lift his mood. He barely noticed how verdant Terra Farm looked in the summer sunlight. Nor could his hunger pangs distract him. He didn't have time to eat. He forced himself to breathe in deeply as he marched towards Pauline Allchin's bungalow. He needed to keep his wits about him. These cultists were insane, not stupid. They had to know that what they were doing was wrong. That they didn't care made them dangerous.

Again, the contrast struck him over the head. The beautiful surroundings, the hippie beginnings, the unfalteringly polite older women. It was all at odds with the crazy, violent, controlling regime that was beginning to emerge from the cover of secrecy. Though he was mere miles from his corner office at New Scotland Yard, he felt as if he were in a foreign land. The hustle and bustle of the concrete jungle, replete with hunched-over commuters and jam-packed tube trains, was far removed from this oasis of birdsong and greenery.

His anger subsided, giving way to a cool and determined calm. If Pauline Allchin was so unfeeling as to throw a young woman – a girl, really – into a room and lock her away for days just because she was on her period, then what else was she capable of?

Morton could see the groundskeeper through the window as he approached her bungalow. She had clearly seen him coming on the CCTV because she rose to open the door before he had a chance to knock.

'Detective Chief Inspector Morton,' she greeted him. 'Come in. I'll explain everything.'

• • • •

MORTON FOLLOWED ALLCHIN inside in silence. The gruff woman that Purcell had described to him was nowhere in sight, and Morton felt wrong-footed by the sudden change. She made a beeline for the kitchen, put the kettle on, then perched her ample behind on a kitchen bar stool that looked much too small to be comfortable. Morton remained standing. He pulled out a Dictaphone.

'Put that away or we don't talk. You want to know why Claudia was locked in my spare bedroom,' she said bluntly.

'Naturally,' Morton said. He forced himself to remain dispassionate. He was far too curious as to why Pauline seemed so nonchalant about having a prisoner in her bungalow to allow his anger to show through.

'She asked for it.'

'*Excuse me?*' Morton's temper frayed immediately. '*She asked for it?*'

'Yep. Claudia asked for it. She knows the rules: women on their period go into seclusion until they're no longer bleeding. No ifs, no buts, no exceptions.'

Morton stared at her dumbfounded. She had explained the rules as one might explain how to play snap to a child. A million questions arose in his mind at once: Who had made these rules? Was it the now-doddery Giacomo? Or was this a recent invention? Why would anyone agree to abide by them? Why did someone think this was a good idea?

He took them one at a time. 'Who made the rules?'

'Lorenzo did,' Pauline said with just a hint of regret. 'When he took over as "leader", he introduced a host of new rules. This was one of them.' As she spoke, she made air quotes to make it clear that Lorenzo might be the leader but he clearly wasn't *her* leader. Morton filed away that information for later use.

'If it hasn't always been this way, why did everyone go along with the new rules?'

'We've had stranger rules, and this one didn't affect me.'

Morton looked at her closely. Of course, it didn't affect her. Most of the women in the cult were old enough to be post-menopausal.

Realisation dawned on him. 'That means it just affected Claudia, Lana, and...'

'And Abigail.' Pauline was no longer meeting his gaze.

His hands began to shake as Morton forced his rage down. When he spoke, it was in an icy-cold tone that was so calm that Pauline recoiled with surprise.

'You enforced the rule,' Morton accused her.

She hung her head in shame. 'I did.'

'Why?'

'Because it's my job to keep the rules,' she said plainly. 'Mine and Darren's, anyway. We don't make 'em, we just keep 'em.'

So the two middle-aged duffers were the enforcers in the Collective. It made sense. As groundskeeper and farmer, Pauline Allchin and Darren Heggerty were set apart from the rest by their responsibilities as much as their age.

'But why, Pauline? Why would you enforce the rules at all? Surely you can see how cruel and demeaning they are?'

'I just want a quiet life. I like my solitude, and I like my garden. I don't want to follow the rules, let alone enforce 'em, but if I don't, then Lorenzo would turf me out or worse.'

There was quiver to her voice denoting genuine fear. 'Worse? What's worse than being thrown out?'

'Losing *it*.'

The only thing Morton was losing was his patience with this wreck of a woman. 'Losing *what* exactly?'

'Priority.'

'And what, perchance, is that?'

Her eyes flashed darkly, her face tightening into an emotionless mask. Obviously, she hadn't meant to let that slip.

'Pauline, what on earth is priority?'

She set down her tea mug. For a moment, Morton thought she was going to throw him out and then he'd have to drag her down the nick where she would undoubtedly lawyer up. Instead, she said: 'My place in the Collective. All of us have Priority. Lower is higher. Giacomo's the only one of us to have a priority level of zero.'

'Right...'

'Then Lorenzo's priority one. I'm a three.'

It all began to click. The Collective was run like a pyramid with the lower numbered members sitting at its top.

'And it goes down to ten.'

A simple scale. Zero to ten, lower is better. It was simplicity personified and it worked. Pauline was genuinely terrified she might lose her status as a middle-ranking member of the Collective. 'Then the number on your door...?'

'Denotes my priority. It's not a door number.'

Crap. How had they missed that? Morton cast his mind back to the numbers that he could remember. Abigail and Stephen had a number five on their door. Guy Rosenberg had been a seven. Had he seen anyone with a worse ranking? He didn't think so. But they were getting off-topic. Pauline's slip had distracted him from the real reason he was here.

'And your damned priority is worth that much to you? Enough that you locked Claudia up like a mongrel in the tiniest room going? That it had to be filthy and sound-proofed? That she could only drink from a dog bowl? With no food and only the barest scraps of cotton for clothing?' Morton's voice grew louder with every question, his temper bubbling up once more. 'Look at me, Pauline. You know this isn't right.'

'I have no choice. This is Lorenzo's will, which makes it the Collective's will. I must carry out the instructions I am given, as must those who must follow my own decrees. I do not expect you to understand our ways.' She finally met his gaze. 'Am I under arrest, Chief Inspector? If not, I think it's time that you left my home.'

Morton reached into his pocket to fumble for his mobile phone. He was glad to have its reassuring weight back in his pocket once more. If he hadn't so blindly followed the rules himself, this all might have gone much more smoothly. Perhaps Pauline was a victim too. It was easy to imagine how following one rule could lead to a loss of control, each little restriction building upon earlier rules, a slippery slope which was too muddy to climb back up without help. He wished he could get this all down in a formal witness statement from Pauline, but no doubt she'd deny it all or, worse still, invoke her right to remain silent if he tried going down that route. He could just imagine losing a whole night stuck in with her and a solicitor, every question being met with 'no comment' until the clock ran out and he was forced to let her go. It was probably fruitless anyway. If Claudia had genuinely consented – and it was a big if – then the Crown Prosecution Service would be reluctant to bring a case without a complaining victim. Then there was the bigger, more immediate problem: if he arrested Pauline, he'd immediately set the entire Collective on edge. They'd shut down completely, all taking the same 'hide behind the lawyers' approach that Pauline was threatening, and then, in no time at all, it would be Monday morning and Silverman would be having his guts for garters.

'No, you're not under arrest,' he said, and then added under his breath: 'Not yet.'

Chapter 19: Without Question or Delay

A long walk around Putney looping back to Terra Farm didn't calm Morton down as much as he'd hoped it would. At a little after eight o'clock, his stomach now rumbling louder than ever, he walked into the bungalow to find Stephen and Abigail sitting at the tiny dining table waiting for him to show up. There was a big pot of casserole in the centre of the table together with a ladle and three wooden bowls.

'It smells wonderful,' Morton said to Abigail as he took his seat.

'Not me,' she said with an audible tut of disapproval at his assumption that she was responsible for dinner. 'Stephen cooked for us this evening. Everything was grown here, by us.'

'Oh. Thanks, son.'

'You're welcome, Dad.' Stephen began to ladle out the casserole. 'Usually, meals are prepared communally and then we just collect our portions, but, given the circumstances...'

They ate in awkward silence. No one wanted to tackle the obvious elephant in the room, and yet no one made the effort to engage in futile small talk either. Abigail, in particular, stared into her bowl until the dishes were ready to be cleared away. She and Stephen stood simultaneously, looking at their guest as if prompting him that it was time to make himself scarce. Morton had booked himself a night at an inn around the corner, though a uniformed officer would remain in the bungalow all night to secure the incident room.

Morton gestured for Abigail to sit back down. 'Abigail, could I speak to you for a moment? Alone.'

She exchanged glances with Stephen, who nodded encouragingly. She sat back down slowly as if reluctant to engage with the man who was, at least in the cult's eyes, her father-in-law. At the back of the room, Stephen set down the bowls and cutlery in the sink before making a hasty retreat himself. The sound of footsteps grew quieter until a door slammed shut.

When he was certain that Stephen was out of earshot, Morton cut to the chase. 'I know that you were in a relationship with Guy Rosenberg before you dated Stephen. Does he know?'

Abigail placed a finger to her mouth to shush him. 'No. Why would he need to?'

'Maybe he doesn't. But I have to ask you this – and please don't be offended – do you know anything at all about who killed him?'

She looked away for a moment, closed her eyes, gulped, and said: 'Lawyer.'

'Pardon me?!'

'Lawyer. I said I want a lawyer.'

Seriously? Morton thought. One innocuous question and she already wanted to lawyer up? First it was Pauline Allchin, and now Abigail was at it as well. Too many secrets among so few people. Pauline's words echoed in his mind. The lower priority members had to obey all those with higher priority without question or delay. Clearly, someone had told Abigail and Pauline that they had to lawyer up if they felt that they needed to. It had to be Lorenzo's doing; he was at the apex of the Collective hierarchy, after all.

'Is it you who wants a lawyer? Or has Lorenzo told you that you have to ask?'

'No lawyer, no talking,' Abigail said flatly.

'Then a lawyer you shall have... down at the station.'

• • • •

WITH NO MONEY TO HER name, Abigail got shafted with the duty solicitor. He was an elderly man by the name of Perkins, and he specialised in representing petty criminals charged with drug dealing, shoplifting and traffic offences. Despite working for the well-known Southwark-based law firm Perkins, Perkins and Perkins, he was neither the first nor the second Perkins, and he could, at best, be described as barely competent, just good enough not to get struck off the roll of solicitors, but not someone Morton would want representing him. In any other circumstance, Morton would never have allowed a family member to be represented by such a buffoon.

Abigail took her time consulting him, which gave Morton and Ayala plenty of time to get ready. They set up the interview suite, put out four chairs, filled in the first bits of paperwork, and got the audio recording equipment ready. As they worked, Morton outlined how he wanted the interview to be run.

'Ayala, you're going to take the lead on this,' Morton said.

Immediately suspicious, Ayala turned to Morton with a surprised look. 'Thank you?'

'Just the interview, Bertram. Don't get carried away.' *Only because I shouldn't touch this interview with a barge pole*, Morton thought.

Ayala saluted mockingly. 'Then what do you need me to get out of her, sir?'

Resisting the urge to call Ayala up on his insolence, Morton pondered the question. It was a fair point. They knew Abigail had been involved with the victim, but they also knew she had an alibi – his own son – for the time of the gunshot, and that was all they could *officially* investigate. As this interview was on the record, they'd have to be incredibly subtle to investigate the real murder without the transcript giving them away. Given that Guy Rosenberg had died during the night, Abigail *could* have slipped out while Stephen was sleeping soundly in his bed. But she'd have had to get past Stephen and then sneak out without disturbing either Sarah or Morton himself. All three of them were notoriously light sleepers, which made it highly unlikely.

And yet she had lawyered up quicker than a Bakowski caught with a kilogram of cocaine. Clearly, Abigail had a guilty conscience about something.

'Get a timeline going. Start with the wedding, or binding, whatever you want to call it, and log everything that's happened up until now. Keep it inconspicuous, but gather as much detail as you can. We want to give her enough rope to hang herself.'

'You got it, boss,' Ayala said.

Morton left Ayala alone and retired to the adjoining suite, from which he could watch the whole interview through a one-way mirror.

It didn't take long for them to get started. Ayala handled the preliminaries with aplomb, apologising for the late hour and expressing what appeared to be a sincere wish that they could all head home this side of midnight.

'Before we get to the matter at hand, congratulations on your nuptials,' Ayala said. Morton rolled his eyes. He'd started so well too. Alas, Ayala's attempt at the rapport-building stage of the interview was as subtle as a horse's head in a bed.

'Thank you,' Abigail replied cautiously.

'What time was the wedding? An early one, wasn't it? Not many people get married first thing in the morning.'

Abigail glanced at her lawyer as if to ask permission to reply. He gave the tiniest of nods and then lost focus as his mind wandered.

'The actual ceremony was supposed to be at ten, but we didn't get started until half-past,' Abigail said. 'We're usually punctual in the Collective, but our only guests were late.'

She shot a nasty glare at the one-way mirror. She had guessed Morton was watching.

Either Ayala didn't notice, or he chose to ignore Abigail's shift in body language and pressed on. As Morton had ordered, Ayala was going in with kid gloves to try to get as much information on the record as possible before she clammed up when he asked the big questions about Guy and whether she had ever been in seclusion.

'Right, right. You guys do things your own way. What was the ceremony like?'

'The binding went exactly as we had expected. We pledged ourselves anew to the Collective,' she said, and then hastily added, 'and to each other.'

This time Ayala reacted subconsciously. His right eyebrow arched so high that Morton almost laughed. Bertram 'Captain Obvious' Ayala had struck again.

'The... binding?'

'That's what we call it,' Abigail replied much too quickly. 'There's nothing wrong with having our own name for the ceremony!'

He's got her on the defensive, Morton thought. Not bad, but it might make her clam up.

'Okay, that's fair,' Ayala said soothingly. 'Everyone has the right to use whatever names they wish. How long did the binding take?'

'Not long. It's a simple ceremony in which we affirm before our friends that we are bound to the will of the Collective.'

Morton scoffed. She meant Lorenzo's will.

On the other side of the glass, Ayala leant forward as if he were sharing some juicy titbit of gossip. 'And then what happened?'

'We celebrated. There was lots of food, as everyone had brought something with them. Stephen's father cooked on the BBQ. And binding ceremonies are one of the few times that we're allowed to have an alcoholic drink, so the whole Collective got to enjoy a few glasses.' She shuddered theatrically as if this were an alien concept. 'And, as is our tradition, we spent the whole day together so we could talk to every member of the Collective and thank them for witnessing the binding. Of course, there was live music too. I love to swing dance, and we all had a wonderful time.'

By the end of her speech, she was practically breathless. She had spoken so fast that it took Ayala a moment to take it all in.

'*All* of you were there?' Ayala said. 'Even Guy Rosenberg?'

Abigail's nostrils flared. Morton immediately headed out into the corridor. He rapped smartly on the door.

Without skipping a beat, Ayala paused the interview, excused himself, and made his way out to the corridor where an irate Morton was waiting.

He shut the door behind himself and then glared at Morton. 'What now, boss?'

'You can't cut to the chase that quickly,' Morton said. 'She'll get her hackles up. Look at the body language. We need to nail down details. Ask her when she went to bed, when people left, that sort of thing. Don't focus on irrelevant and subjective nonsense like whether people were enjoying themselves or not, just get the facts. Don't start asking about Guy until you've nailed down as many concrete details as possible. If she wants to ramble, let her. If she's lying, she'll trip herself up on the details sooner or later.'

'Whatever you say, boss.' Ayala's tone was monotonous. He never took criticism well, even when it was constructive. Morton had once met Ayala's mother, an overbearing woman who encircled every aspect of his life. Her attitude toward life explained a lot about the man and his need to control everything and everyone around him. He resumed his position behind the safety of the one-way mirror and turned the volume on the speaker up a smidge.

'Interview resumed at... goodness me, is it ten to eleven already?' Ayala said. 'Present are John Perkins, Abigail... Morton?'

She nodded.

'...and Inspector Bertram Ayala,' he finished. 'Where were we? Oh yes, your wedding celebrations. What time did they end?'

She held up her hands. 'I don't know. Midnight? We were all a bit squiffy.'

'Squiffy?'

'We'd had too much to drink. Like I said, we don't normally drink, so it didn't take very much before we were all three sheets to the wind.'

'Ah. How much alcohol was there?'

'We had ordered three cases of wine, so thirty-six bottles. There was some beer too, and a few bottles of spirits.'

'For barely a dozen people?' Ayala asked.

'It *was* a wedding.'

Not a binding, then? Morton thought with a smirk.

'Okay. Was everyone drinking?'

Another good question. Ayala was beginning to find his feet.

Abigail hesitated before she answered. 'I think so. Nobody was totally abstemious, but I wasn't keeping track of who had what. You could ask Marta who drank the most, as she was the one refilling the drinks.'

'Marta Timpson?' Ayala knew the answer but wanted it on the record.

'Yeah, Guy's aunt.'

Morton watched as Ayala's eyes widened in surprise. The background checks hadn't caught that there was any sort of familial relationship between the Collective's residents other than the obvious father-son relationship between Lorenzo and Giacomo.

'She's his *aunt*?'

'Great-aunt, I think? She must be. But don't quote me on that,' Abigail corrected him. 'She's been with the Collective since the start. The poor woman must be suffering so much. Guy was her sole living relative after her poor sister passed away.'

'I'll be sure to check in on her when I'm next passing her bungalow,' Ayala said kindly. 'Did anything strike you as out of the ordinary that night?'

'No... wait. Yes, there was something. I noticed that Lorenzo and Lana were arguing. I don't know what about, so don't ask me.'

'When was this?'

'Late evening. It's probably nothing,' Abigail said, immediately trying to backtrack as if she hadn't just dropped a bombshell.

'Was it usual for them to argue?'

'I hadn't seen them argue in public before.' She looked to her lawyer, who was still staring off into space. With a disdainful flick of her head, she continued: 'Maybe that was just because of the booze, Inspector. The binding was different for us. We rarely have outsiders in our little corner of Putney. Emotions were running high...'

'Fair enough.' Ayala looked towards the mirror as if to ask if Morton wanted to ask anything else. 'Well, thank you for your time, Abigail. You're—'

A loud knock interrupted him. 'Excuse me,' Ayala said for the second time, irritation creeping into his voice.

Morton waited patiently for Ayala to pause the tape and extricate himself.

'Again? I was about to send everyone home. It's late.'

'You can't send her home,' Morton said. 'She could be our killer.'

'What? Are you serious?'

'Deadly,' Morton said. 'Keep her here tonight. We can easily justify a twenty-four-hour hold, and Perkins isn't going to put up much of a fight even if we try for longer.' Morton jerked his head towards the mirror, where they could see the elderly solicitor looking half-asleep, with a dribble of drool dripping from the corner of his mouth.

'Stephen will kill you,' Ayala warned.

'Let him get mad, then. I need to rattle a few cages and the Collective might blink if they think I'm willing to put my own son in the cross hairs. Right now, we've got nothing else to go on. If we hold Abigail, it might shake the cult up a little. If they think she's the killer, tongues could loosen, and we might find who the real killer is.'

'Why not just ask her to stay away for a day?'

It took Morton an enormous effort not to roll his eyes. Hadn't Ayala realised that they didn't know where Abigail's loyalties lay?

He ticked off the reasons on his fingers. 'One, she might not agree. Two, she might be loyal to Lorenzo. Three, I'm not convinced she's innocent.'

Could his new daughter-in-law be the killer?

He hoped not.

Chapter 20: Like Father, Like Son

After a restless night's sleep at the Red Lion Inn, Morton returned bright and early to Terra Farm, where two uniformed officers met him at the gate. Once he had confirmed that all was secure and that nobody had entered or exited the premises since yesterday, Morton headed north to the incident room in his son's bungalow.

He made it as far as the front porch, where he found Stephen waiting for him. Stephen was as angry as Morton had ever seen him. No doubt he'd had a terrible night's sleep too, especially with uniformed officers guarding his living room as if it were Fort Knox.

'Where the hell is my wife?' he demanded.

'Fiancée,' Morton corrected him. 'At least in the eyes of the law.'

Stephen took a step closer until his nose was inches from Morton's. 'I don't give a damn about the law, Father. Where is she?'

'Can we go inside and talk?' Morton looked around in case any other members of the Collective were eavesdropping, but he saw no one.

Before he acquiesced, Stephen made Morton wait. 'Fine,' he said. 'After you.'

As soon as the door had shut behind them, Stephen stopped. 'So?'

Morton let the silence linger for a moment. Something in his gut said that his son was hiding something. It was an instinct he'd learned to trust over the years, although the gut feelings had to be tempered by evidence. It came back to the ABC method that he taught his student detectives: assume nothing, believe nobody, check everything. That second one was especially hard when his own son was his prime suspect.

'She's at New Scotland Yard.'

For a moment, Stephen looked hopeful, earnest, and trusting. Morton felt a pang of guilt. He was going to have to crush that hope, no doubt destroying whatever trust they enjoyed in the process, to make the whole Collective believe that Morton was willing to throw Stephen under a bus.

'Helping you?' he asked.

Morton braced himself for a torrent of anger. 'No,' he said firmly. 'She's under arrest.'

He wasn't disappointed. Within seconds, his son's temper erupted. A fist was swung towards his face. Morton dodged out of the way, and Stephen's fist collided with the door behind him, eliciting a yelp. Stephen clutched at his hand, swearing so much in the next few seconds that, by Morton's reckoning, it was the longest conversation they'd had in years.

The uniformed officer posted outside the front door came racing into the living room.

Morton waved him off. 'My son tripped, didn't you, Stephen? I'll take it from here. Could you stand guard outside, please?' The constable looked as if he might protest. Morton cut him off with a stern look, grabbed his son's arm and steered him into the incident room where he shoved him onto the sofa.

'First hit's free,' he said, his nostrils flaring. 'But if you ever swing at me again, you'll be joining Abigail in a cell. You and I are going to do something we've never done before. We're going to sit here and talk man to man. I'm going to put my cards on the table and give you a chance to grow up. I suggest you take it. You understand me?'

Still cursing, Stephen met his father's stare and then gave an almost imperceptible nod.

'Abigail was engaged to Guy Rosenberg. Did you know?'

Morton didn't know what to expect. If his son knew, then there was no way any legitimate investigation could exclude him as a suspect. If he didn't know, would he be hurt? Angry? Morton half-wished Sarah were still on the farm. She'd know what to say.

'So what? That's all ancient history,' Stephen said.

'If it's ancient history, who did he have sex with on the day he died? The coroner found vaginal secretions on his genitals.'

Stephen's temper flared up again. He leapt to his feet, his hand balling into a fist once again. 'How dare you!' he yelled. 'Out! Get out!'

Morton held his ground. 'Nope. I told you we're having a nice, calm chat. I'm not going anywhere until Guy Rosenberg's killer has been caught. You're going to have to stay somewhere else tonight.'

'You're throwing me out of my own bungalow?'

'Temporarily.'

'But I was nowhere near Guy Rosenberg's place when he got shot, and neither was Abigail.'

'The gun didn't kill him.'

'What?'

'Someone else killed him first.'

The penny dropped. 'Then I... I'm a suspect. And so's Abigail?'

'If you weren't my son, I'd assume that Abigail was sleeping with the dead man and that you killed off the competition. I have to ask: is there anything you want to tell me? Anything at all?'

Stephen worked his jaw, secrets desperate to escape his lips. He avoided his father's gaze. Then, without saying a word, Stephen walked out.

The door slammed shut behind him.

'Well, that went as well as could be expected,' Morton muttered to himself.

Chapter 21: Point of No Return

Lucy spent Friday evening in the widows' bungalow just south of her own. The unmarried women's bungalow had seen so many changes in the recent past, the latest of which was Abigail moving out so that she could live with Stephen. Tonight, it was abandoned. Lana was no doubt in Lorenzo's arms and Claudia was still at the hospital. It was also a great opportunity to add some extra colour to her article on the cult by talking to the bickering widows, Marta and Tracey.

Despite the rules, Marta and Tracey were drinking. At some point during the wedding, one of them – probably Marta, given her light-fingered tendencies – had snuck several dozen bottles of wine away from the wedding and surreptitiously stashed them in their kitchen. The great Lorenzo was willing to turn a blind eye so long as the widows kept their drinking to the confines of their own bungalow and didn't cause any problems. They'd been drinking longer than he'd been in charge, and this wasn't a hill that he was willing to die on.

'They can't think dim little Abigail had it in her to kill Guy, can they?' Tracey said.

Tracey was such a gossip. Apparently, it hadn't always been that way. Tracey and her husband Rupert had been early members of the Collective, but he'd left when she refused to stop spending the night with Giacomo. It was, Lucy reflected, probably the sane decision.

'Why would Abigail kill my Guy?' Marta lamented. 'I know he was a bit of a wastrel, but they'd long since stopped being a thing.'

Tracey swung towards Marta, her wine glass swirling dangerously as she did so. 'A *bit* of a wastrel? Guy was a...'

'Careful, now. You're talking about my nephew.'

'Since when are you so easily offended? We've sat in this very lounge many a time talking about how much of a disappointment Guy was. He never worked. He drank far too much...'

Lucy coughed gently. 'Sorry, just clearing my throat.'

Tracey took another glug of wine and then resumed where she'd left off. 'He drank nearly every night, and he couldn't even keep the one available girl who was close to his own age. The man brought down everyone else around him, he was constantly miserable, and we're much better off without him.'

Marta leapt to her feet. 'How dare you! You know he'd been clean for six months.'

'And the binding ceremony was his undoing. Weakness. That's all it was. He couldn't fulfil the will of the Collective. No wonder he never made it beyond priority seven.'

By now, the old women were glaring at each other. In her time on Terra Farm, Lucy had seen several such flare-ups. Apart from her penchant for rosé, Tracey was a true believer. Whenever anything threatened her beloved rules, her hackles rose. Marta, on the other hand, was still very much the free-spirited "live and let live" hippie she'd always been.

'Ladies,' Lucy intervened, 'let's not speak ill of the dead. Whatever flaws Guy had, they've gone to the grave with him.'

The older women stared at each other, both indignant that anyone would dare hold an opposing opinion. They grudgingly backed down, sinking into their seats in an amicable silence punctuated only by the slurp of wine being drunk.

'Who do you think could be the killer?' Lucy asked.

'Isn't it obvious?' Marta said. 'It has to be Lorenzo. He could never stand the idea of another man competing with his authority in the cult.'

'No,' Tracey said. 'He wouldn't *need* to kill Guy. That wreck was incapable of standing unaided. Even on the night he died, Doreen had to bring him food and water so he didn't get too drunk. As if she didn't have enough handholding to do looking after Giacomo. But to answer your question, yes, Lorenzo is man enough to shoot someone, sure, but he didn't need to do that with Guy. There was no competition there. Whatever Lorenzo said, Guy did–'

'...without question or delay,' Marta finished mockingly.

As the insults began anew, Marta shot daggers at Tracey.

Lucy sighed. It was going to be a long night.

Chapter 22: Life Goes On

The Collective rose early that Saturday morning. As dawn broke, the men were sent to work the fields overseen by Darren Heggerty's watchful eye. Tracey was preparing to go off-site for her morning teaching yoga down at the community centre, leaving Marta to sit in a chair outside her bungalow and watch the world go by.

Old Marta always had been a people watcher. Body language, the way people dressed, even the way people moved; these all fascinated her. A swish of long blonde curls caught her attention.

'Morning, Lana!'

The ethereal young blonde reluctantly approached. 'Morning,' she said guardedly, as if she were expecting a dressing down.

'Staying over at Lorenzo's again, eh?' Marta chided. It appeared that she had caught Lana midway through her walk of shame home.

'It's none of your business, Marta. Stay out of it.'

Marta giggled 'Calm down, girl. We've all been there. Well, for most of us it was his father.'

'Eww.' Repulsion spread across Lana's face. Evidently, she was thinking of the older di Stregoni's now weatherworn features.

'But that was before his mind went. Such a shame. He used to be a real charmer. Have you spoken to him lately?'

'Nah, no point,' Lana said. 'The lights are on, but nobody's home. He doesn't have a clue who I am. Some days he barely recognises Lorenzo. He thinks he's looking in a mirror!'

'They do look mighty similar,' Marta said. 'Hang on a moment and I'll go grab some old photos so you can see the good Doctor di Stregoni in his heyday.'

Marta shuffled off into her bungalow to look in the little lockbox she kept under her bed. Inside were a lock of hair, a bundle of photographs, and a small ring. She found the photo she was thinking of and shuffled towards the front door.

By the time she got back outside, Lana was gone.

• • • •

LORENZO'S PHONE KEPT vibrating in his pocket. He was running late and he couldn't do a damned thing about it. The police were still all over his farm, which he was sure wasn't legal without a warrant, but that meant he had to sit on his hands. For now.

Thank God that Lana had had the presence of mind to toss the supply over the fence. The last thing he needed right now was an arrest for possession with intent to supply. Was it still there? If it was, had the police left it there just to see who retrieved it? That was what he'd have done.

Whatever, the weed was lost. He had more with a non-dweller down by the river, not that he could touch that either. The coppers might be following his movements, and the last thing he wanted to do was give them a heads up about his import-export business.

Bloody Morton. The curmudgeonly old detective had a hard-on for him during the first interview. Now, Lorenzo couldn't visit the khazi without the police knowing.

He swiped his phone until the WhatsApp screen appeared. Should he ditch the phone too? His WhatsApp was encrypted and password protected so only he could get into it. Could the police compel him to unlock it for them? Or just pin him down and put his thumb against the fingerprint reader? He made a mental note to find out.

Two more swipes opened up the group with all his customers. He typed deftly at maximum speed in case anyone was watching him:

Service is suspended. Do not contact or approach until I contact you.

He hit send, deleted the WhatsApp message, then sent the same message to his lieutenants, the dealers who hoped to gain his favour. That was a stroke of genius. Take a bunch of aimless wanderers, suggest they might get to "ascend" to a higher plane of existence, and then create a whole system to stop them getting there. He gave a chuckle as he recalled inventing the concept of "non-dwellers", those muppets who were so unimportant, their priority so low, that they didn't even have the right to set foot on Terra Farm. Some people would believe anything. Another swipe and he found himself on the menu which would allow him to reset the mobile to factory new.

No point throwing it in the bin if he could stick it on eBay or Gumtree instead.

Chapter 23: Comings and Goings

Rafferty arrived back at the compound at eight o'clock on Saturday morning. She nodded to the uniformed officer on the way in.

'You'll have to sign in, Inspector Rafferty, I'm afraid.'

Paperwork. There always had to be paperwork. There were records of what went on, records of where it happened, and records of who made the records. She swore ninety per cent of being a detective was dealing with more paperwork than even the lawyers and accountants had to get to grips with.

She scrawled her name, confirmed the time as being four minutes past eight, and then proceeded up the gravel path. She passed by Lucy Reed on the way in.

A sudden thought struck her.

'Miss Reed!'

Lucy spun on her heel. 'Yes?'

'I was wondering where you were going,' Rafferty said. 'If you don't mind indulging my curiosity.'

'I'm off out to pay some bills. One of my jobs here is administration. I take the money we make from selling vegetables and our popular yoga classes, put it in the bank, and then we can pay our electricity and council tax.'

Rafferty gave her a warm smile. 'Is there much money in that?'

'I'm afraid not, but we manage to get by. I really must dash. Lots to do, and the queues at the bank can be horrendous on a Saturday morning. Is there anything else I can help you with before I run?'

'No, that was it. Thanks very much for stopping to chat with me.' With a wave of a perfectly manicured hand, Rafferty dismissed her.

Terra Farm opened out before Rafferty at the end of the path. Once more she was struck by how much it felt like a hidden hamlet nestled between the hedgerows. Coming onto the Collective's property was like taking a step back in time to the mid-eighties or perhaps even earlier. It had to be the last place in London with such a strong gender bias in the division of labour, with men doing the heavy labour in the fields and women doing the domestic chores.

She didn't envy the men their role today. It was much too hot to be out digging up the fields. As Rafferty made a beeline for the Morton bungalow, she had a change of heart. There wasn't much point asking the boss what he needed her to do; he was all over the place with this investigation, and understandably so. It was time to take the initiative and crack on. He'd said many times that he trusted her judgement.

Just across from Morton's was the largest and most luxurious bungalow. While the other seven were in various states of disrepair ranging from needing minor paint touch-ups (such as those occupied by the widows and by Lorenzo) right through to needing gutting and rewiring (the groundskeeper's bungalow), Giacomo di Stregoni's home was fit for a king. The front façade had a fresh coat of paint, the gutters were empty, and somebody had taken the time to pressure-wash the nineteen-seventies roof tiles back to their original salmon colour.

The door was open as Rafferty approached. She stepped inside and then spotted the neat array of shoes by the welcome mat.

'Hello?' she called out.

'Coming!' a woman's voice called back. Doreen Brown hobbled into view, her right leg dragging behind her left as if it were struggling to keep up. Though Rafferty knew her to be Giacomo's nursemaid, Dori looked like she was mere months away from needing nursing care herself. She shuffled along at the speed of a tortoise, taking what felt like forever to cover the twenty feet from the end of the entrance hall to the front door.

'Hello, Dori, I'm Inspector Rafferty. May I speak with Giacomo?'

'I know who you are, dear. I might look senile, but I haven't ascended just yet.' Dori tapped the side of her head. She glanced at Rafferty's feet as a prompt that Rafferty ought to remove her shoes, and once Rafferty had done, Dori led on. They moved at a comically slow pace. Every time Dori took one step forward, Rafferty was hot on her heels, silently urging the elderly nursemaid to get a move on.

'Lovely home you have here,' Rafferty remarked. There were pictures on the wall of members of the Collective past and present, and the same few faces, Dori's included, cropped up over and over.

'Thank you, dear. It's been my home now for, oh, thirty years?' Dori said. She paused to turn around and smile at Rafferty.

Fighting her urge to chivvy Dori along, Rafferty smiled politely back. It seemed to take hours to reach Giacomo's bedroom, where he was sitting upright eating breakfast from an ornate wooden tray with fold-down legs, which allowed the tray to double up as a table.

Dori put a hand across the doorway to stop her and then whispered in her ear. 'Inspector, please try to keep your tone even and upbeat. Think slow and soothing. Giacomo began his ascension a few years ago, and his spirit doesn't like being dragged back to this astral plane.'

The poor woman genuinely thought he'd gone to a higher plane. Or maybe she just needed to believe it. Desperate people will believe big lies if it suits them. 'Of course. I don't want to upset him.'

Once Dori was satisfied that Rafferty understood, she allowed her to pass.

'Morning!' he cried as they entered.

'Hello, Giacomo,' Rafferty said. 'My name is Ashley.'

She made her way to the end of the bed and perched in a spot where she could see Giacomo and keep Dori in the periphery of her vision.

'Do I know you?' he asked. His eyes glazed over as if he was struggling to place her. 'Are you one of my girlfriends? If not, would you like to be?'

'No,' Rafferty said with a hint of laughter. 'You don't know me yet. Your friend Dori said I could come and talk to you.'

'Dori? How is she?' he exclaimed. 'I haven't seen her in years.'

Rafferty glanced towards the doorway where Dori was standing. Dori's face fell, and, at Rafferty's sympathetic gaze, she gave a 'What can you do?' shrug. *Ascension, my ass,* Rafferty thought. This was straight-up dementia.

'Dori's just over there,' Rafferty prodded gently. She pointed towards the doorway.

'That old witch? She's not my Dori. Looks like her mother, though!' Giacomo gave a hearty chuckle.

Rafferty didn't know what to say. A second glance towards Dori suggested this was a frequent problem, and Rafferty didn't want to push it. What could she learn from an old man who didn't appear to know what was going on?

'Giacomo, tell me about your son.'

'Son? He's only little. Where's his mother gone? Haven't seen her either. Lots of people going missing around here...'

Could he be talking about an actual disappearance? Rafferty made a note to check for any historical mispers in the area just in case.

'Who, Giacomo? Who has gone missing?'

His eyes glazed over. Dori dashed forward to prop him back up against his pillows, put a Sippy cup full of water into his hands, and then, just as quickly, stepped back.

When he spoke, he seemed to have no idea where he was. 'Who are you?'

'I'm Ashley. We just met.'

'Why are you on my bed? Are you my girlfriend?'

So much for what Rafferty had read online about mornings being the period in which dementia patients were most lucid.

'We were talking about people going missing.' Rafferty tried to steer the conversation back towards fertile ground.

'He's got to go, got to,' Giacomo said.

'Who's got to go?'

'Him. He's got to go. Guy's gotta go. Nothin' but trouble, he is.'

'Guy Rosenberg?' Rafferty clarified.

Giacomo became animated. He seemed full of energy, almost rocking back and forth where he sat upright in his bed.

'Gotta go! Gotta go! I gotta go.'

'Calm down, Giacomo.'

'GOTTA GO!'

'That's enough!' Dori cried. 'Out! Get out, Inspector Rafferty! And don't you come back. Nobody is allowed to interfere with Giacomo's ascension, nobody. I've worked far too hard to have you mess it all up. His spirit *will* make it to that higher plane.'

Dori looked deadly serious. She seemed ready to try to carry Rafferty out herself.

'I'm going, I'm going,' Rafferty said. *But I can't promise I won't be back with a warrant*, she added in her head.

Giacomo was still muttering "he has to go" as she made her way back down the corridor to her shoes. If the Collective was a cult of personality, then it wasn't Giacomo's personality, not anymore.

Chapter 24: Crossing the Ts

D r Larry Chiswick hated working weekends. Somehow, *pretending* to work in the office on a Saturday morning was even worse. There was no good reason that he couldn't have sent his report off yesterday after he had completed the autopsy. Despite his initial suspicions that Maria might not be up to the job, his new diener had performed admirably. Given the classic petechial haemorrhaging, it took little effort to conclude that Guy Rosenberg had been smothered, and then someone had shot his corpse at point-blank range. A strange set of circumstances to be sure, but not the weirdest case he'd ever dealt with.

Complex circumstances and creepy cultists notwithstanding, the forensics were relatively straightforward: Guy had been smothered and then shot.

Except complexity was what Chiswick required. Without something to explain why a perfectly good report happened to be delayed over a weekend in a way that strongly benefitted a friend who was illegally investigating a murder, it would be not only Morton's neck on the chopping block but Chiswick's too.

That was why, at nine o'clock on a Saturday morning, he found himself in his dinky office in the basement morgue at the new New Scotland Yard building. A steaming mug of pour-over coffee sat on the desk just out of reach so he couldn't knock it over. The new Chemex brewer in this office beat the crap out of the old push-for-gruel machine he'd had to share with everyone else in the old Scotland Yard building. What he didn't like was the lack of name change. It was so confusing when people said they'd be at 'Scotland Yard'. He never knew which one they meant.

He typed slowly, knowing that it was possible for the IT department to pull up his keystroke history in the event that Professional Standards opened an investigation. He'd already recorded the report onto his personal Dictaphone so all he had to do was type it up. He'd had Maria write out a working summary for him to pass on to Morton. The poor girl had looked confused when he'd insisted it be done by hand. It wasn't as if he could explain that he didn't want it uploaded to the police database before Monday morning.

He picked up his coffee and sipped it as he scanned what she had written. It didn't quite match what he'd said.

Guy Rosenberg was a thirty-four-year-old man in relatively good health. At six foot one, he weighed ninety-two kilograms, putting him in the slightly overweight category. The pathologist notes significant liver damage indicative of alcohol addiction.

Evidence collected:

Hair

Genital swab (vaginal secretion present)

Blood

Fingerprints

Scrapings from under nails

Trace swabs from clothing

Clothing

There wasn't much for Chiswick to go on. The toxicological samples that Maria had hand-couriered to the lab were yet to be processed, so those sections in his report were currently blank. Not that it mattered. Guy Rosenberg had been smothered, full stop. If he'd been drunk or high as well, that probably wouldn't change cause of death. It did, however, give Chiswick an excuse to wait until Monday before putting his report onto HOLMES. Diligence was never a bad thing.

He grabbed the secure landline phone from the other side of the desk and hit the speed dial button for the forensics department.

'SCD 4.'

'Hi, this is Doctor Larry Chiswick. I'm chasing an ETA on several samples sent to your office yesterday.'

'Which case?'

Chiswick reeled off the case number from his notes.

'Guy Rosenberg? It's not marked as expedited in our system.'

'Well,' Chiswick said, 'get it marked as urgent. I need those results, and I need them now.'

He didn't, of course. It was just a ruse to justify the delay in his report. He slammed down the phone before they could answer and turned his attention back to his coffee. It had cooled just enough for the fruity flavours in the beans to come through. He leant back in his chair and wondered where he could pilfer a digestive biscuit from. Maybe Morton had some in his corner office upstairs.

All in a day's work.

• • • •

MORTON'S SATURDAY MORNING was interrupted by a text message from Kieran O'Connor at the Crown Prosecution Service. It simply read:

Meet me at The Spencer in an hour.

Google said it was near the river, halfway between Terra Farm and Kieran's home.

Curious enough to comply, Morton found the infamous Irishman lazing in a chesterfield at the back of the pub, a little after eleven. The young lawyer was wearing shorts and a T-shirt, a far cry from his usual three-piece suit and Barrister's bands. Morton almost didn't recognise him.

'God, I'm starving,' Kieran moaned. 'Just another hour until the kitchen opens. I did get us some crisps, though.' He shoved a packet towards Morton.

Cheese and onion. 'No thanks.'

'Suit yourself. Look at this menu. It's actually pretty good. Don't you miss the days when pubs just used to be about the booze? No? Me neither.'

It took all of Morton's restraint not to strangle him. *Just tell me why I'm here,* he thought.

'You're awfully chatty this morning.'

'It's easy for me to be chatty and casual. I'm not the one who's about to get fired.'

Morton's blood ran cold. 'Silverman knows?'

'Not yet,' Kieran said through a mouthful of crisps. 'But she will sooner or later. If Ayala's already calling me off the record, there's no guarantee he hasn't told anyone else.'

Of course it was Ayala who'd called the CPS lawyer.

'I don't need him to keep his gob shut for long. Just a couple of days. Chiswick's holding his report 'til Monday. If I can't exculpate Stephen and Abigail before then, I'll recuse myself first thing Monday.'

Kieran leant back. 'You know that won't be enough to solve the case, and there's no benefit to being involved. Quit now while you can. Before this comes back to bite you in the backside.'

'Can't.'

'Why not? Stephen didn't do it. You're his alibi. You can't alibi the prime suspect *and* investigate him at the same time. Just walk away now and you're free of all this mess. It's not too late to let this crap roll downhill.'

'I can't let someone else investigate,' Morton said. 'Because they'll immediately think that Stephen could be the killer.'

Another handful of crisps went into the lawyer's mouth. 'You weren't with him when the gun went off?'

'I was.'

'Then what's the problem?'

'Guy Rosenberg didn't die from a gunshot. Someone smothered him during the night before his corpse was shot.'

The lawyer cottoned on quickly. 'Two attempted murders by two people?'

'Could be... Or perhaps it's just one person covering up the smothering with the siren call of a shotgun? Maybe they thought we'd assume that a man shot in the chest at point-blank range had died because of that gunshot. If someone smothered him and then shot him to muddy the waters, doesn't that strike you as risky? And why do it when I was there? '

'It's ballsy,' Kieran agreed. 'But you weren't there. From what Ayala said, you were the last one on the scene.'

'I was staying at Stephen's bungalow on the other side of the farm.'

Kieran crunched through another mouthful of Walkers. 'Presumably, your killer knew that.'

'Maybe. What I don't get is why someone would commit murder on the one night that a police detective was around. It's almost asking to be caught. Any other night and nobody would ever have known that a murder had taken place. They've even got pigs on-site, for God's sake.'

'Strange indeed. You'll work it out,' Kieran said. 'So, you think that Stephen could have smothered him while you slept? On his wedding night?'

The lawyer's tone was so sceptical that Morton found himself playing devil's advocate. 'It's not impossible.'

'And you didn't recuse yourself from the investigation because...?'

'Because the dead guy used to date my son's new wife.'

Kieran dropped his bag of crisps. 'Shit. Now I see why you're not handing this off.'

'Indeed. Either I uncover the killer, or I let someone else work to put my eldest son in jail.'

'That's a bit of an assumption. I'll say it again, as your friend and as a lawyer, do your family a favour and recuse yourself right now, David. Before this gets messy. Once there's a written record proving that you're acting against procedure, you'll be out of a job, and worse, you'll lose your pension too.'

'Is it? Who'd get it if I recuse myself? It can't be anyone I'm friendly with, so that rules out all of the good investigators. Hell, I trained half of them! If it gets kicked to one of the handful of coppers who hate me, they'll seize on Stephen as the obvious suspect and never let go. Because of me.'

Kieran picked up his crisp packet, now bereft of half its contents, and set it back upon the table. 'True, the few you're not on good terms with are feckless eejits.... but surely Stephen's wife is his alibi? Weren't they... you know, doing what newlyweds do?'

Morton leant forward to steal a crisp, eliciting a cry of protest. A horrible thought came to him: two murder methods, two people. What if it's a husband and wife team, each the alibi for each other? It screamed reasonable doubt.

'Walk me through it one more time,' Kieran said. 'Nothing is making much sense to me. You've got a cult hiding away in their own little bubble, totally cut off from the world. If someone in the cult wanted Guy Rosenberg dead, they could have quietly offed him and fed him to the pigs or tossed his body into the Thames. Nobody would have been able to ID him that way.'

It was the same thought that Morton kept coming back to. 'There's only one good reason I can think: collective responsibility, if you'll excuse the pun. If Guy's murdered while only members of the Collective are on the premises, the cult is culpable as one of its members has to be the killer. If the same murder were to be committed while outsiders are on Terra Farm, it would muddy the water, as they've now got two suspects to point the finger at who don't belong: Sarah and me. Come to think of it, they were awfully keen that we stay the night.'

It hadn't been their intention to stay. They'd have gone straight home after the ceremony if Morton had had his way. As it was, he'd had a few too many beers and had wound up crashing in Stephen and Abigail's spare room. It was terrible luck.

'Not a bad theory. So, what're you going to do?'

'Kill Ayala, for a start,' Morton said with a nervous laugh. 'Then see if I can solve the case before the pathologist's report is uploaded to HOLMES and I have to recuse myself.'

'And Chiswick is going along with this?' Kieran said.

'Until Monday morning at nine o'clock.'

'Then you're fecking buggered. You can't find a killer in... forty-odd hours.'

'Just watch me,' Morton promised. He rose to go.

'Wait a minute! You can't make a big dramatic promise like that and then feck off. Sit.'

Morton hovered.

'*Sit down*, David. I'm not letting you walk out of here. I need to warn ya about Purcell first. From what I hear, he's walking into all the bungalows to investigate.'

'Well, yeah?'

'You don't have a warrant.'

'It's a crime scene!' Morton protested.

'No,' Kieran said. 'It's not. The south-east bungalow is, but a court might consider each bungalow to be an individual property. It's not just one farm. There are eight little homes, with people who live there. Let's get a warrant next time unless you want to add to the trouble you're in.' He looked at Morton seriously. 'You can feck off now.'

Chapter 25: Following the Money

The yoga instructor, Tracey Cox, set up camp in a local park for midday on Saturday. She'd already been out to several other locations to run classes, and this was the last class of the day, intended for old-age pensioners. It was a slower session with easier poses and far less demanding clients who were happy to pay up just for the chance to stretch in the sunshine.

Rafferty had followed Tracey up the hill on the off chance that her sojourn out of the compound had some connection to the case. It wasn't as if she had much to do on-site at Terra Farm: they'd talked to all the witnesses, gathered what scant physical evidence there was, and now everything seemed to be stalling. Morton's "golden forty-eight hours", the window with the greatest chance to quickly solve a murder, and more crucial than usual, was halfway gone and they were no closer to catching the killer than when Rafferty had first arrived on-site.

There was some talk among the team about mutiny. That was Ayala's doing, and while she sympathised with him, there was no way she'd backstab Morton. Nobody wanted to be caught with their pants around their ankles when Silverman realised the investigation was illegal, but that wasn't a good enough reason to grass. She didn't dare say it to the boss's face, but there was still every chance Ayala would seize the opportunity to climb over the corpse of Morton's career if he thought that meant his own shot at promotion.

Tracey was wandering between the mats, fixing the posture of her clients, when she saw Rafferty leaning against a tree.

'You look stressed, Detective. You're welcome to join us. It's ten pounds for the session. I've got a spare mat that you can borrow.' Her voice was saccharine sweet.

'No more than usual,' Rafferty lied. 'I just want justice for your friend Guy.'

'Thank you, dear. I appreciate that,' Tracey said. 'But you won't find it by following me around all weekend.'

'I...' Rafferty started to protest, but then a shadow came over her that made her turn away. A large elderly man shuffled into view. There was a distinct smell of weed in the air.

'Trace,' he said in a hushed, urgent tone, 'I need to—'

'Not now, Frank,' Tracey said. 'Can't you see I'm helping Detective Inspector Rafferty here with her inquiries?'

The man called Frank looked from Rafferty to Tracey and back again.

'Ah. I'll come find you later.'

Tracey smiled sweetly. 'Much later.'

Before Rafferty could even question what had just happened and who the hell Frank was, Tracey had rushed over to one of her students.

'Now, just raise your head so your spine aligns. That's it.'

'Tracey,' Rafferty said, interrupting her. 'Who's Frank?'

Another sickly-sweet smile. 'Don't you mind about Frank. He's been trying to ask me out for years. I never have found a way to say no that he didn't interpret as "not today". Now, how about that lesson?'

· · · ·

FOR LUCY REED, THE Saturday morning sojourn into town was a brief respite from the lunacy of the cult. It had taken months before they had trusted her to come and go, and even more time before they stopped sending someone with her, but finally she was alone even if it was just for a few minutes in a grotty public restroom.

Thanks to Lorenzo's blanket ban on electronic devices – except for his own, of course – Lucy had to write out her draft article longhand, which then had to somehow be passed to her editor back in the States. Thankfully her editor had a friend at their sister publication in London, *The Impartial*, and one of their guys had been pretty good at subtle hand-offs.

That was how she had come to be in possession of her most frantically written bundle of papers yet. She hastily stuffed the draft inside the larger stack of research papers that she had been quietly accumulating for weeks. As well as copies of her notes, the bundle now included a draft of her tell-all exposé on the Collective. Though it was rough and ready, as one might expect for something that Lucy had scrawled during moments of privacy snatched from her hectic cult schedule, she was proud of her work.

She skimmed through it one last time.

What started out as little more than a hippie counterculture movement has descended into depravity, with members subjugated to the absolute will of the Collective's autocratic despot.

It didn't begin that way. In the seventies, Doctor Giacomo di Stregoni was a renowned psychiatrist and a passionate advocate for deprogramming those who had left cults. Some questioned his methods: they asked how it was appropriate for former cultists to be recruited into what was little more than a new cult.

It was di Stregoni's personal charm, his impeccable academic record, and the ongoing success of the program which bought him a lot of leeway, and his recruitment of the poor, the disenfranchised and the mentally ill continued. In time he built up a cult of personality centered around none other than Doctor Giacomo di Stregoni himself.

In the turbulent eighties, authorities turned a blind eye to allegations that Dr di Stregoni enjoyed sexual relations with many of his patients, and his once-controversial benign-ism (a cult in all but name except without overt malice) moved from squat to squat in West London, fitting in wherever the fabric of society was most frayed.

It was in the late nineties that di Stregoni's "Collective" was lost from public view. A former patient turned group member owned a sizeable chunk of land in Putney upon which di Stregoni founded Terra Farm, the group's secretive home. In the twenty years since, those gates have been closed to all outsiders.

For the last six months, Lucy Reed of New York City's The Objective *newspaper has lived among the group following their ways. This week she witnessed a murder investigation being opened into the death of Guy Rosenberg, a young man who had grown up in the Collective and who had never chosen to abide by the group's rules.*

As the senior Mr. di Stregoni himself has fallen prey to Alzheimer's, control has passed to his son Lorenzo. This illness has been explained away within Terra Farm as "ascension", the notion that Giacomo's mind has ascended to a higher plane of existence. This is underpinned by a system known as Priority, a grade assigned to each member of the Collective which denotes their place in the hierarchy. The cultists toil away in the hope that they too can gain higher Priority, which comes with privileges ranging from their own home to a key to the gate, and, one day, "ascend" just like Giacomo di Stregoni.

The younger di Stregoni has proven to be a keen dictator-in-waiting. As well as masterminding this new Priority system, he has implemented a raft of new rules to test his authority, including the vulgar practice known as "seclusion", which demands that any woman on her period be placed in a dark room alone with nothing more than a dog bowl full of water until their time of the month has passed...

Satisfied that it was up to snuff, or at the very least that her editor could whip it into publication-ready shape without further input from her, Lucy stopped reading and folded the notes inside a copy of *The Impartial*. She flushed the toilet just in case anyone was listening and headed back out into the sunshine, where she proceeded to sit on the green bench opposite the post office. She put the newspaper by her side and waited.

A few minutes later, a man in a suit sat down beside her. He too had a copy of *The Impartial,* which he proceeded to read at leisure, and then, without saying a word, he folded his own copy to match hers and put it between them. He then fumbled with his mobile phone for a few minutes before nonchalantly standing up. Only his copy of *The Impartial* remained on the bench, and Lucy's copy, complete with her draft article and all her notes tucked inside, was gone with him. It was so quick, so easy that nobody could have spotted the hand-off. Within the hour the draft would be scanned and emailed to her editor in New York, ready for the morning news cycle.

Chapter 26: Empty Bed

In the thirty years that Bernadette Schofield had been a nurse, she'd seen everything: blood, vomit, urine, and worse. She'd cleaned it all up, and she'd done so with a smile. She'd dealt with undermedicated patients and overmedicated patients. She'd been sworn at, punched, kicked, and abused by drunk, high, and pathologically unstable patients.

Nothing could shock her anymore, so when she started her midday shift with a quick tour of the wards, she wasn't surprised to see Claudia Sozler's bed empty.

Her mind jumped to the most logical conclusion she could think of, all the while a tiny voice expressing doubt. Claudia had probably gone just to the ladies' room.

By the time Bernie finished chatting with the other patients on the ward, ten minutes had passed, and her pulse began to race when she realised that Claudia still hadn't reappeared. It didn't take more than ten minutes to nip to the loo, especially when it was right across the hall.

Her second assumption was equally straightforward: Claudia could have gone to the bathroom and tripped en route. That seemed plausible. Bernie had certainly picked up a collapsed patient or two. In fifteen seconds, Bernie strode the length of the ward and crossed the hallway to the ladies'. It was a single toilet. She knocked loudly. No answer.

'Is anyone in there? This is Nurse Schofield,' she called out. When there was no answer, she spoke again: 'I'm coming in.'

The door was unlocked. It opened easily at her touch.

Empty.

Hadn't Miss Sozler been interviewed by the police? Bernie began to get a sinking feeling in the pit of her stomach. Door number three, then. Could she have nipped out for a cheeky cigarette? Bernie didn't think the young woman was a smoker, but she couldn't rule it out. She ran from the bathroom to the nearest window with a view of the hospital's sole smoking area. Squinting against the sun, she looked up and down. There was no sign of her there either.

'Shit,' she muttered under her breath. An urge to go and have a cigarette came over Bernie, even though she'd quit decades earlier.

Bernie paced up and down. One last try. She returned to the ward and looked to see which of Claudia's wardmates were awake and alert.

'Ladies, did anyone see the young lady in the corner leave?'

'Me.' The voice belonged to a wizened old woman with more wrinkles than hair.

With a loud squeak, Bernie pivoted on her heel to face the patient. 'Did she say where she was going?'

'Nope. I thought she was just off to the bathroom. Poor dear has been up and down all morning. Her visitor went with her.'

'Visitor?' Bernie questioned. It wasn't yet visiting hours, and none of her colleagues had mentioned shooing an early bird away.

'Yes, a much older woman in a drab grey cardigan. She wasn't here for more than a minute or two.'

'When was this?'

'About an hour ago. I tried to tell Nurse Andrews there was an out-of-hours visitor on the ward, but she said that I had to stop being so nosy.'

Panic began to set in. The police had been questioning Claudia, and then an unknown woman had taken her away from the hospital without so much as telling any of the nurses.

Forget Discharge Against Medical Advice. This could be a kidnapping.

Chapter 27: Shadows and Vapours

Morton had barely finished lunch when Mayberry ran into the incident room, breathless and exhausted.

'B-boss, your ph-ph-phone?'

Confused as to just what was happening, Morton looked at his phone. Three missed calls, all from Rafferty, all in the last few minutes.

'What's going on?'

'C-C-Claudia. Kidnapped.'

'And we know this how? Rafferty?' Morton asked.

Mayberry nodded. He was breathing heavily, having run the length of the compound, and by the time he could stammer out the details, Morton's own stress levels had begun to spike. They didn't know much yet. A nurse had reported her missing to hospital security, who in turn had rung the police when they saw Claudia's name was attached to an active investigation in HOLMES. The system was working as it ought to. If Sozler had been kidnapped, it had to be connected. The most obvious suspects were the cultists, except they were right here on Terra Farm.

'Who's left the compound today?'

'M-Marta, T-Tracey, L-L-Lucy, a-and...'

'And?'

'And w-well... A-Abigail isn't h-here.'

'She's in custody,' Morton reminded him. 'And there she'll stay until I work out what to do with her. She can't come back to Terra Farm, not while we're investigating.'

The other members of the Collective ought to have noticed her absence by now. If they had, they were doing a damned good job of pretending they hadn't. Perhaps they had incorrectly assumed that she was with Stephen and Sarah. Sooner or later, he'd have to phone home and see whether his son had calmed down yet.

'W-what now?'

'Go pick up Rafferty. She's somewhere in town. I'll call ahead and let her know you're on the way. Go with her to the hospital and help her however she needs. I'm counting on you two to find Claudia Sozler safe and sound, and every second counts. Whatever you need to do, you have my authority to do it. Stick to the Abduction and Kidnapping procedure where you can. Loss of life is a much bigger concern than finding any kidnapper. Sozler's safety comes first. You got it?'

'Y-yes.'

'Then go.'

Morton watched as Mayberry sprinted out of the bungalow. He hoped he was doing the right thing. There was no way he could investigate an alleged kidnapping and solve the murder at the same time. Rafferty was the one he trusted most to deal with it sensitively. She had extensive experience in dealing with victims of violence and sexual abuse from her time with Sapphire, and with Mayberry's organisational skills and penchant for spotting patterns, they made for a formidable duo. Where Rafferty was quick to action, Mayberry was slower and more deliberate.

And it helped with Mayberry's occasionally problematic stutter. He frequently commented on how much he appreciated having someone by his side to take the pressure off so he wasn't trying to interview suspects alone.

As Morton heard the roar of an engine coming to life in the distance – presumably Mayberry driving away – he turned his attention back to the incident room boards. As was customary, Mayberry had written the notes. He had the neatest handwriting, and he was pleased to take on any task his speech disorder didn't affect.

For this investigation, there were two boards. The first board covered the official investigation concentrating on the suspects who could plausibly have shot Guy Rosenberg.

The full suspect list was there: Giacomo, Lorenzo, Lana, Pauline, Lucy, Doreen, Marta, Tracey, Darren, Stephen, Abigail, Sarah, and Claudia.

The same suspect list was on the second, "unofficial" board.

Morton put a red line through Claudia's name. She had been in seclusion at the time of the gunshot, and unless she had a way of teleporting out of a locked room and then back inside, she couldn't have smothered Guy either.

Likewise, Morton had struck off Sarah as well as Stephen and Abigail. Morton had been with them the whole time, and he knew in his gut that his family was innocent.

That left nine suspects. He took a yellow pen and crossed off Giacomo and his nursemaid Doreen. Both were old, frail, and had given each other an alibi. It was plausible that one of them could be faking ill health, so he was reluctant to use a red pen.

Seven. Seven plausible suspects, Morton mused. Two of them, Darren Heggerty and Pauline Allchin the groundskeeper, lived on the west side of the compound. They struck Morton as the least likely suspects of the bunch if only due to lack of physical proximity. The unmarried women, Lana and Lucy, had been equally far away in the north-east corner. Either of them would have had to run past the widows' bungalow to get to the crime scene.

The most obvious suspects were those in the adjacent properties: Lorenzo immediately to the west, Marta and Tracey to the north. The older women were less likely if only because the recoil on the shotgun would have been substantial, and, perhaps less fairly, because murder by shotgun was a typically masculine murder method.

Lorenzo was the most obvious suspect except for the lack of gunshot residue on his hands. Unless he had fudged the timeline somehow, he had to be ruled out of the official investigation. Nothing ruled him out of having smothered Guy, however.

'Hmm,' Morton mused aloud. What if the timeline had been faked more than once? What if there had been not one but two rounds of gunshots? That would be one heck of a forensic countermeasure. Accurately working out where a sound had come from was a challenge at the best of times. If the killer had shot Guy using a silencer and then fired the gun again later on, or fired a different gun, or even had an accomplice fire a gun, it confused everything. The gunshots that had awakened Morton could have been a deliberate ruse, used to draw him out of bed and keep him focussed on a gunshot that was totally unconnected to the actual murder. His head throbbed. He could play this wheels-within-wheels game all day and get no closer to the truth.

Hear hooves, think horses, not zebras. It couldn't be that complicated. Someone had tried to shoot Guy to death. Someone else beat that person to it.

Except that still didn't put Lorenzo in the frame. Even if he had shot at the floor to wake everyone up, it would have left gunshot residue on his hands, and there would have been damage wherever the bullet struck. Purcell's team had found no indication of such damage.

The only way Lorenzo could have done it would have been for him to shoot Guy earlier using a silencer, giving him time to thoroughly clean his hands before someone else shot the ground with the gun. At that point, Lorenzo, with clean, gunshot residue-free hands, could have then taken the gun and run over to "discover" Guy's body. That would fit the timeline and allow him to be waiting for Morton on Guy's doorstep with a recently fired gun and no gunshot residue on his hands.

Except that required an accomplice. And it was needlessly complicated. Nor did it fit with death by smothering.

Even for one of Morton's cases – and he'd had some peculiar murders to investigate over the years – the idea that three people had been involved in the death of Guy Rosenberg stretched all credibility. Unless Lorenzo and an unnamed accomplice were responsible for both the smothering and the shooting?

Talk about wheels within wheels. The idea of a man being smothered, shot but not shot, and then the sound of a silenced gunshot used to mask the first gunshot, which in turn hid the smothering... It was enough to make Morton's head spin.

Confronted with the prospect of driving himself mad arguing around and around in circles, he called the one person in the world who could talk him out of it: his wife.

'Hey,' he said.

'Hi. Our son isn't too pleased with you.'

'He's still angry, then? She left me with no choice. I had to arrest her. She lawyered up instead of talking to me, and let's face it, we don't really know her from Adam.'

'But you don't have to keep her locked up in a cell. Trust your son's judgement. He hasn't married a murderer. She could come here. You know I'd keep them both safe here.'

He hasn't married anyone, Morton thought. He'd gone through some cockamamie cult ritual and ate a few BBQ chicken wings. As if that counted. He didn't dare say that.

'I'd like nothing more,' he lied. 'Before that can happen, I need her to start talking, and I need to know she won't run straight back to Terra Farm. Our killer is still on the loose, and we've now got another misper.'

'Who?' Sarah asked.

'Claudia.'

'The young lass? Lorenzo's girlfriend?'

'That's news to me. I think you might be talking about Lana? Blonde, waif-thin, talks like she's posh when she's clearly not?'

'Oh,' Sarah said. 'Yep, that was who I was thinking of. She and Lorenzo were as thick as thieves on the night of the wedding.'

'Right. I don't think that has much bearing on the investigation. Nothing so far does. I'm stuck going around and around in circles.'

'How so?'

Morton relayed the whole sorry state of affairs.

'It's like you always say to me: strip out the impossible and whatever remains must be true. This isn't that complicated. It can't be.'

'What's your theory, then?'

Sarah paused for a moment. 'Someone tried to shoot Guy to death. Someone else beat that person to it.'

'I had the same thought. But there's no evidence either way.'

'You'll find it. You always do.'

He wasn't so sure. 'I will,' he said confidently. 'Tell Stephen I'll get Abigail out as soon as it's safe to do so. And ask him what he knows about this ludicrous priority system.'

'Priority?'

'Just ask him. He'll know. Text me his answer, would you?'

He hung up. The time for chit-chat was over. Progress was what he needed. The clock was ticking. If he spent any more time on the ridiculous wheels-within-wheels theory, he'd run out the clock. A two-gunshot theory didn't rule out anyone. Distance wouldn't matter, and the killer would no doubt have been alive to the possibility of gunshot residue evidence.

If he kept thinking of ever-more-elaborate plans, it would be Monday morning before he knew it.

Sarah was right. The simplest explanation was the most likely to be true: two people had tried, one had succeeded. Was he right that killing Guy on Stephen's wedding night was a way to point the finger at the outsiders? So far nobody had so much as suggested that he or Sarah had killed Guy.

Something was amiss. Why hadn't they just killed Guy and fed his body to the pigs? Any other day at all, and this would have been plain sailing for the killer. Perhaps it was just bad timing. Morton shouldn't have been there. If he hadn't been drinking, he and Sarah would have driven home, and the killer could have offed Guy without any police witnesses to open an investigation.

Morton desperately wanted to pin it on Lorenzo. The man was thoroughly repugnant. He was so arrogant that it was hard to believe that anyone would commit murder on Terra Farm without his say-so. Perhaps that was it. Perhaps Lorenzo hadn't ordered Guy's death, so the killer couldn't simply feed him to the pigs in plain sight.

Whatever was going on, Morton wasn't going to solve it sitting around ruminating. He looked at the clock. Forty-five hours left.

It was no time at all to find two would-be killers and conclusively prove Stephen's innocence. If he could solve the actual murder as well as the attempted murder, he could go home happy and his sleight of hand with the coroner's report would never see the light of day.

It was a big ask. Morton pushed down the feelings of helplessness. He could feel sorry for himself on Monday. It was time to crack on and finish sorting out warrants so Purcell wouldn't land him in even more hot water.

Chapter 28: Echoes of the Past

The security team at Charing Cross Hospital proved very helpful. Within minutes of Rafferty's arrival on-site, she and Mayberry were sequestered away in a room full of CCTV monitors, and complete control had been handed over to Mayberry. One of the hospital's security team lingered in the background, allegedly there to help if needed but seemingly content to browse Reddit on his phone while the police worked.

Even the parking, a whopping two pounds and forty pence per hour and prepaid to boot, was barely a fly in the ointment of what seemed like a promising start to the investigation.

It was only a side-shoot of the murder investigation, and yet, with Morton's full blessing to use his authority to commandeer resources, it felt like Rafferty was once again in charge of her own case. Unlike Ayala's sullen and resentful approach to her leadership, Mayberry was happy to take orders, and he carried them out quickly and efficiently.

'Who taught you how to do this?' she asked as she watched him effortlessly navigate the complexities of an enormous CCTV setup with dozens upon dozens of cameras.

Mayberry flashed a proud smile. 'B-B-Brodie.'

That explained it. One of the Met's more recent hires, the Scottish tech wizard had been poached from some Silicon Valley firm. He was a bit rough around the edges, even for a Glaswegian, and yet for reasons unknown, he had taken a shine to Mayberry. The pair of them were frequently spotted in Brodie's office amicably eating in silence. It was always junk food, of course. She could totally understand the allure of an occasional Five Guys burger and a milkshake, but what the boys found pleasant about Wotsits, Rafferty couldn't fathom. The taste wasn't her thing, but what really ruined them was the texture. The way they stuck to her teeth... yuck. But if it made them happy, she was happy to turn a blind eye.

'Th-there!' Mayberry shouted. He excitedly wagged a finger at one of the screens. There, in grainy black and white, was Claudia Sozler.

'Why is publicly funded CCTV always so grainy?' Rafferty complained aloud. She eyed the hospital security guard accusingly. He was still absorbed in whatever he was doing on his mobile phone and so didn't notice.

'B-better p-places to spend the m-money?' Mayberry said.

'I suppose. Where is this camera, anyway?'

'By the car p-park entrance.'

The CCTV didn't show much, as the camera angles were limited and there were far fewer cameras than necessary to provide the sort of blanket coverage Rafferty had hoped for. They were looking for the woman whom Claudia had left with as much as Claudia herself. From what Nurse Schofield had relayed via Mayberry, they were looking for an older woman in a drab grey cardigan. It was a pretty generic description, so Rafferty didn't expect much.

'L-look.'

She followed the line of Mayberry's gaze, and sure enough, there the grey cardigan woman was, trailing a few feet behind Claudia.

'Can we blow up that footage? I need to see her face.'

Mayberry's hands danced over the keyboard, his fingers furiously tapping away with the click-clack sound of a mechanical keyboard assaulting Rafferty's eardrums.

Despite Mayberry's best efforts, the image was too grainy to make much out.

'Is there anything we can do with facial recognition to see where else she pops up on CCTV?'

'M-maybe B-Brodie could?'

'Give him a call, then, and while you're doing that, I'll go visit the ward. Text me if you guys find anything.'

• • • •

THE WARD WAS THREE flights up. From the corridor, Rafferty had a view back east across the city. The hospital's name, Charing Cross Hospital, was a misnomer. It was situated in Hammersmith, nearly five miles west of Charing Cross Road, which made the parking seem even more extortionate.

She spotted a nurse up ahead.

'Excuse me?' Rafferty called out. 'Could you tell me where I can find Bernadette Schofield?'

'She's up at the nurses' station.' The nurse spoke with a Filipino accent, reminding Rafferty just how reliant the NHS was on overseas staff to fill in the gaps. There simply weren't enough people joining the profession, and it was no surprise why. It was thankless, underpaid, and carried a great deal of stress dealing with the burden of life-and-death care every day. It even made the police pay complaints pale by comparison.

'Thanks,' Rafferty said. She mustered a smile and was flashed a very brief one in return as the nurse scurried past her.

The nurses' station was comprised of three desks arranged in a "U" shape. A pleasant-faced, middle-aged woman was sitting behind the forward-facing desk, tapping away at a laptop. Sure enough, her name badge read *Nurse Schofield*. Although she was wearing earphones, Rafferty could hear tinny pop music from five feet away. The break in light from Rafferty's shadow caused her to glance up.

'Detective Inspector Rafferty. May I have a word?' Rafferty spoke loudly to try to make herself heard over the sounds of Ed Sheeran.

It wasn't enough. Bernadette yanked out the earphones. 'What?'

'DI Rafferty,' Rafferty repeated. 'I'm here about Claudia Sozler, your missing patient.'

The nurse leapt to her feet. With one hand she slammed the lid of her laptop down, and with the other, she offered Rafferty a firm handshake and confirmed that, yes, she was Bernadette Schofield.

'Call me Bernie. What's the latest news?' she demanded.

'It appears,' Rafferty said cautiously, 'that Claudia walked out with a woman matching the description you passed on to my colleague. Can you tell me what your impressions of Claudia were? Did she strike you as agitated or anxious at all?'

It took Bernie a moment to consider her answer. 'I think she was. I see a lot of domestic violence cases, and Claudia struck me as pretty typical. She was afraid of someone. That much was obvious. But there was more to it. She kept going on about a man, so we had to give her Olanzapine on arrival.'

Two questions flitted into Rafferty's mind. She went for the easy one first.

'What's Olanzapine?'

'It's an antipsychotic,' Bernie said. She leant heavily against the counter of the nurses' station as if she was too tired to stand unaided, and it was only then that Rafferty noted the bags under her eyes and the weariness in her expression. 'Miss Sozler was in pretty bad shape from her time locked up, and we didn't want her struggling too much. Her heart was already racing, and we had to give her oxygen to keep her O2 saturation up. Whatever he did to her, it wasn't pretty.'

Whatever he did. Even in the chaos of a kidnapping operation, it struck Rafferty as odd that the assumption was always that a man did it.

'Whatever she did,' Rafferty corrected. It had, after all, been Pauline Allchin who had locked her up.

'A woman did this? On her own?' Bernie asked sceptically. 'Or because a man told her to?'

Touché, Rafferty thought.

She abandoned the argument and tried to steer the conversation back towards what mattered. 'What was Claudia saying about a man?'

'She kept sobbing and saying that it wasn't fair, that they didn't deserve this, that they'd make him pay. It was all jumbled nonsense,' Bernie said. 'The poor thing was delusional.'

'But she didn't mention a name?' Rafferty said. 'All she said was that it's unfair? You sure that you didn't miss something? She didn't mention any names? Guy or Lorenzo, perhaps?'

'Dead certain,' Bernie said firmly. 'She just kept saying that it wasn't fair. And no, I'd have remembered if she'd mentioned a name.'

Interesting, Rafferty thought. Who were 'they'? She and the mystery woman? She and Guy? And what was unfair? Guy's death?

If Claudia knew about that, it begged the question of how she knew. Even if she'd heard the gunshots, she'd been locked in a cell until Purcell had found her, so she couldn't possibly know that Guy was the victim, could she? Unless she'd overheard it from the police on the way from seclusion to the hospital?

Whatever, Rafferty thought. It didn't matter. Her immediate focus had to be finding Claudia and making sure she was safe. If anyone from, or working for, the cult was after her, then Rafferty had to get to her before they did. The police were keeping a keen eye on the known cultists, but who knew how many friends or employees they could have off-site? It seemed absurd to assume that *all* of the cultists lived on Terra Farm, or that they couldn't hire in thugs from outside to do their dirty work.

'Can you show me the ward which she disappeared from?'

'Sure, but there's nothing unusual about it.'

Bernie wasn't wrong. The ward was identical to all the others. Claudia's bed was the same as every other, all heavy metal and sterile white cotton sheets. Even her place in the ward, at the far end with a view over the car park, was unremarkable. Rafferty's fishing expedition was drawing blanks. From Claudia's bed, it was a short hop to the bathroom, a little further to the nurses' station, and further still to the lift.

'How did Claudia get past the nurses' station without being seen?' Rafferty asked. She regretted her question the moment the words had left her mouth. Bernie's entire demeanour shifted from weary but welcoming to obviously on edge.

'We can't see everything,' Bernie said defensively. 'Claudia dressed before she went. Anyone who spotted her would have assumed she was a visitor leaving, assuming anyone had even been on the nurses' station at that moment. If there are emergencies, it can be unattended for short periods.'

Claudia certainly could have left when she spotted that the coast was clear if her intention had been to escape unnoticed. Equally, a kidnapper could have used the same tactic of waiting for an emergency to arise somewhere nearby and then slip out unnoticed. It was all too easy to arrange.

'I understand,' Rafferty said quickly, hoping to appease the nurse. 'I didn't mean it as a slight. I just meant, is it possible she could have walked out?'

'Or been walked out,' Bernie finished for her. 'It's been going around in my mind all day. I know I've been busy, but surely I would have noticed a kidnapper waltzing in here out of visiting hours and then spiriting away one of my patients. If Claudia had made any sort of noise, I'd have come running to help. Surely she would have screamed?'

'Alas,' Rafferty said sadly, 'fear can cow us into silence. Are you sure nobody saw anything?'

Bernie hesitated. 'Well... one of the other patients thought she saw a visitor, but didn't give any details.'

'You don't believe the witness?'

'No,' Bernie said firmly. 'The woman in question is dosed up with opiates. She's not reliable. And she only said she saw a woman in the corridor. There's a constant flow of people going to and fro. What will happen now? Do we need to take this to MARAC?' Bernie was referring to the Multi-Agency Risk

Assessment Conference, a group meeting chaired by the police and attended by all the agencies involved in high-risk domestic violence cases.

'No,' Rafferty said, knowing that this situation didn't warrant it. 'I assume someone here did a risk assessment when she arrived, and I know all calls to us get flagged as "I" for Immediate.'

When Bernie continued to look confused, it was Rafferty's turn to explain jargon. She told her how police calls could be flagged as I, S, or E for Immediate, Soon, or Eventually. It was the police equivalent of triage and meant that, for example, calls from the residences of sitting Members of Parliament would always get an immediate response.

'If you're sure....' Bernie sounded dubious.

Rafferty was. By continuing to treat the disappearance as a kidnapping, authority to investigate the alleged crime remained with the police. If they treated Claudia as simply having left against medical advice, and having walked out under her own steam without coercion, then they had no right to pursue her, as Claudia was an adult with every right to make a bad decision. Rafferty's gut said that Claudia knew something important, something that might break the case wide open, and she had long since learned from Morton to always follow her gut.

'Bernie, I'm totally sure about this. We have to follow the Abduction and Kidnapping procedure, and we have to act fast. If Claudia has been intimidated and taken against her will, then time is of the essence. I need to find her and to do so as quickly as possible. Here's my card. If you or any of your colleagues think of anything at all, call me day or night, okay?'

'Okay.'

• • • •

'LADDIE, THAT JUST WON'T do, will it?' Brodie's voice boomed in the Charing Cross Hospital CCTV room, reverberating in the confined space. He'd been ten minutes away down the road, watching football at Stamford Bridge, when Mayberry had called. He hated being interrupted cheering on The Blues, and every little setback was making him more and more resentful that he was missing the big game against Arsenal.

'N-no.'

They stared at the screens showing the car park. It was here that they'd hit a dead end. They knew whoever had taken Claudia Sozler away had come from the garage and left the same way. It should have been simple, except for a gaping hole in the CCTV coverage that meant they couldn't follow the pair beyond the door from the hospital.

'It ain't our fault,' the hospital's security guy snivelled, dabbing at his nose with a filthy Kleenex. 'We don't run the car park, do we?'

While they owned the land, the car park was managed for them, so the CCTV system the hospital had installed began and ended at the car park entrance.

'Are there cameras down there?' Brodie asked.

The security guy looked disinterested. His cheerful demeanour at the initial excitement of a police investigation in his security suite had dissolved into disdain that they were still there and continuing to waste his time.

He huffed into his tissue once more. 'How would I know?'

'Fer feck's sake,' Brodie muttered. He stood and beckoned Mayberry to follow him. 'Come on, laddie.'

'W-where are we g-going?'

'To the car park, laddie!'

Brodie accelerated as he turned out of the door into the corridor, his long strides closing the short distance in no time. Mayberry was forced to intermittently jog to keep up with the giant Scot. They arrived at the car park entrance in no time. Just inside were the Pay-And-Display machines, Brodie's first target.

'W-what are you l-l-l-looking for?'

Brodie sighed unhappily as he inspected the ticket machines. 'I was hoping these machines would be card only, and then we would ha'e got a record of everyone parking in here. Shame they're cash. How nineties.'

'N-now what?'

'We make a map of all the CCTV cameras in here, then go find the management company and ask them nicely if we can see the footage. If that doesn't work, we call Morton and tell him we need a subpoena.'

It was a lot of work, and there were no guarantees that it would yield any usable footage.

'And if that d-d-doesn't help?'

'Then we look at CCTV cameras on the roads around the hospital. Claudia Sozler can't have been driven through this bit of London without appearing on a camera somewhere, and once we get a match, we should be able to get the vehicle registration plate of the kidnapper.'

Chapter 29: The Good Doctor Pontificates

Chiswick spent his afternoon pretending to work while really browsing eBay looking for vintage records to add to his already burgeoning collection of sixties and seventies vinyl. He had been mindlessly clicking away when the phone rang.

'Hello?'

'Dr Chiswick, please.' It was a man's voice, polite, with a hesitancy that suggested the speaker was nervous.

'Speaking,' Chiswick said slowly. His voice dripped with the contempt of a man interrupted during the crucial closing moments of an auction for an original nineteen seventy-three pressing of Pink Floyd's *The Dark Side of the Moon*. 'Who is this?'

'This is Chris Budew from SCD4. I'm calling about the tests you ordered on case M416 Guy Rosenberg.'

If anyone had been in Chiswick's tiny office just off the morgue, they'd have seen a shocked look on his face. Not only had the Forensics Department taken him seriously, but they'd actually managed same-day turnaround on a Saturday, which was unheard of outside a serial murder or terrorism case. Chiswick's excuse for delaying his report was beginning to disappear faster than a pint of Guinness placed in front of Kieran O'Connor on a Friday evening.

'Okay?' Chiswick said. It just had to be the Rosenberg case when they finally pulled their finger out, didn't it? Chiswick took a sip of his tea and watched the time on his eBay auction count down towards zero. Three minutes left. 'What about the results, then?' he asked impatiently.

'Well,' Budew said with more than a trace of admiration in his voice, 'I don't know how you knew it, sir, but you were right. There was something unusual in the bloodwork, and so I expected to find something when testing the trace samples that you swabbed from his lips.'

Get on with it, Chiswick thought. Two minutes.

'And you found something,' Chiswick said. He took care to try to keep surprise from his voice. It was quite nice that poor Budew was impressed by his genius.

'Yes, sir. Guy Rosenberg had over forty cardiac glycosides in his system.'

Chiswick sputtered, the remnants of his tea going everywhere. '*What?* Rosenberg was poisoned?' he practically bellowed.

'Yes, sir... Didn't you... suspect?'

One minute. 'Err, yes. Just tell me what you can about what he was poisoned with.'

'The cardiac glycosides indicate that the victim came into contact with toxins derived from lily of the valley.'

Le muguet, Chiswick thought. The infamous French flower given on the first day of May every year as a symbol of good luck. It had become massively popular for weddings ever since the Duchess of Cambridge had chosen it as her bridal flower.

'You're one hundred per cent sure?'

'Yes, sir,' Budew said. 'The combination of glycosides is unique.'

'I'll be damned,' Chiswick muttered. 'Murder three ways.'

'Excuse me, sir? I didn't quite catch that.'

'Nothing,' Chiswick said quickly. 'Thanks for your call. Can you email me over your report?'

'Absolutely. I'm doing so now. Good day, Doctor.'

The line went dead. It took a few seconds for Chiswick to register that the timer on his eBay auction was now ticking down the final seconds. Five, four, three... Before Chiswick could so much as click to bid, let alone confirm his bid, the timer refreshed.

Auction closed.

No Pink Floyd today.

'Damn it!'

Chapter 30: The Window Closes

Despite the size of the car park at Charing Cross Hospital, there were remarkably few security cameras. Hours of donkey work looking for them, calling the operator of the car park, and then finally reviewing all the CCTV coverage that was digitally transferred, had all come to naught.

Mayberry was sitting with Brodie in the back of his car in the far corner of the car park. Brodie had his laptop open on his lap, the heat emanating from it no doubt uncomfortable against his chunky thighs. His phone was tethered as a personal hotspot. Despite the 4G connection, it was dreadfully slow.

'This'll take a while, laddie. Unlimited data. Yeah, right. Knowing our luck, I'll get done for not adhering to the Network's fair use policy... and then we'll have a fun expenses claim to get yer man Morton to sign off on. Anyway, d'ye nae hae something else to be going on with?' Brodie looked at him expectantly.

'L-like w-what?'

'You could try going door to door, laddie? There are dozens of businesses around here. Most of them have CCTV out front.'

'R-really?' Mayberry sounded doubtful.

It was a long shot. Even if they managed to access CCTV footage that had been recorded during the time period that the kidnapper was known to be in the area, the chances of images of Claudia or her kidnapper being picked up by some random business's cameras were slim to none. And of course, just because the kidnapper had entered via the car park didn't automatically mean that she had a car. Even if she did drive, notwithstanding the possibility of a stolen car, the likelihood of identifying the mystery woman that way relied on her number plate being caught on camera at just the right time and with her in view. No chance.

'Unless you've got any better ideas, laddie?'

Mayberry didn't.

'Then skedaddle. I've got work to do.'

· · · ·

TIME WEIGHED HEAVILY on Rafferty. She found herself pacing the ward that Saturday evening unable to think of anywhere else to go, and unwilling to return to Morton empty-handed just yet.

The boys had found nothing on their CCTV search so far, and the woman matched no known police databases. Trying to track Claudia's past was just as difficult. She was a ghost who had no friends anywhere in the world. She'd grown up in the system, bounced from home to home, and had somehow landed at Terra Farm shortly after her eighteenth birthday. She had no public social media accounts of any kind. No Facebook account, no Pinterest, no Instagram, and no TikTok. What kind of young person hid from the entire internet?

For a while, Rafferty had hoped that the alleged kidnapper was one of the cultists. As she understood it, there weren't many former members whom Claudia could have made contact with. Understandably, the members of the Collective were an insular bunch who practised what they called exclusion, which in reality meant the absolute and uncompromising ostracism of former members. Rafferty and Sarah had chatted about that on Friday evening via WhatsApp. Morton's wife was studying psychology part-time at Birkbeck, and one of her lectures had been on how cults use "in groups" and "out groups" to make members feel special. She'd said it was called "othering", and that by creating a distance between the cult and the real world, it bound the cult closer together.

The theory fit. The Collective, now that it was under Lorenzo's leadership, operated under a series of arbitrary rules that served only to reinforce that Lorenzo's word was law. As the cultists themselves said, they had to obey anyone of higher priority without question or delay. Members weren't allowed to leave Terra Farm unless on Collective business, women were pressured into agreeing to seclusion whenever they were on their period, and marriages were used as an opportunity for members to pledge themselves to the cult rather than to each other. Each of the rules seemed to be borrowed from religions and cults past and present, and then renamed as if Lorenzo had invented it all.

Giacomo would have recognised that if he were still lucid. He was a textbook case of late-stage dementia, and what a fall it had been. Back in the day, he had enjoyed a burgeoning reputation as a Z-list celebrity psychiatrist, often appearing on popular radio. That reputation had rapidly become ancient history as the man succumbed to the vicissitudes of age. It was hard to reconcile the angry, gibbering, drooling wreck in the northern-most bungalow with the idea of a charismatic, handsome young psychiatrist with the raw magnetism to convince others that he ought to be their rightful leader.

What the founder had done might not have risen to the level of illegality – the cultists were, by and large, mentally competent adults who could make their own decisions – but the whole set-up bore marked similarities to the gaslighting techniques

Rafferty had observed in abusive relationships back when she worked for Sapphire, the Met's sexual offences investigation team.

The helpful nurse, Bernie, was now off-shift, and so Rafferty had found herself explaining her presence to yet another shift nurse. All the nurses were sympathetic but couldn't offer much in the way of practical help.

The route from ward to car park passed by the ladies', the nurses' station, one lift, a stairwell, and a long winding corridor that went past a little shop. Rafferty had even stopped in to see if any of the shop workers had seen anything. They hadn't. They'd been much too busy ripping off patients with extortionate price-gouging on everything from toothpaste to sanitary towels.

A quick jacket potato in the hospital cafeteria had been Rafferty's only break. She was shocked to see how many unhealthy options were available to buy inside a hospital. Why on earth was a hospital café serving up chips and slices of pizza that were so laden down with cheese that the grease was visible from the other side of the room?

Her final pass of the day was when she found the mother lode. The ward Claudia had been on specialised in domestic violence cases. It was only when she was washing her hands in the ladies' toilet, the very same one that Claudia had used, that she spotted a poster above the hand dryer.

Big bold text on the poster read:

If you're frightened, you're not alone. Call us.
24/7 Confidential Freephone...

There was a number underneath and a phone affixed to the wall beside it.

Rafferty cursed. How on earth hadn't she thought of it sooner? The woman on the CCTV was neither a cultist nor a kidnapper. She was a volunteer from one of the many domestic violence women's shelters dotted around London. That was why Claudia Sozler had followed her so willingly. Claudia trusted her.

A sudden brainwave hit her. It was more morbid curiosity than investigative instinct, but after a brief knock to ascertain that the coast was clear, she nipped into the gents' bathroom next door to see if the same sort of posters were on display there.

Two things struck her immediately. First, the gents' was much cleaner than the women's bathroom. There was less, not more, urine on the toilet seat, and there were no tampon wrappers on the floor. That was a surprise. She'd always imagined the men to be the messier sex.

The second was the complete absence of domestic violence advice. Where the women's bathroom had loud, clear, unambiguous advice in big, brash lettering, the men's room was devoid of any such posters. It was almost as if those behind the scheme thought men couldn't be victims of domestic violence. Rafferty knew this to be a falsehood. She'd investigated plenty of cases where women had abused men, though admittedly not as many as vice versa. And then there were plenty of male on male abuse cases.

It stuck in her throat. It just seemed totally unfair to exclude half the population from help that they might need. She knew the same problem was replicated across London's many domestic violence shelters. Frequently they were women-only or women-and-children. In one case that Rafferty had worked, a woman had fled to a shelter only for her son to turn thirteen during her stay there. Per their draconian rules, he'd been thrown out on his birthday to return home, she had followed, and the father had beaten them both half to death before Rafferty could get there.

Once she was back in the ladies' bathroom, Rafferty wedged the door shut for privacy, and then lifted the phone off of the hook. She quickly dialled the number from the poster.

'London Domestic Violence Helpline, this is Cynthia. Who am I talking to?'

Rafferty held the phone between her cheek and shoulder so she could scribble notes while on the phone. 'Hi, Cynthia. This is Detective Inspector Ashley Rafferty of the Metropolitan Police. I believe a witness in my murder investigation may have called this number yesterday from Charing Cross Hospital and subsequently been taken to one of your shelters. I need to speak to her urgently as she may have important information.'

'Umm... can you hold, please? I'm just a volunteer, and I'm gonna need to transfer you to my supervisor.'

Cynthia didn't wait for an answer before the hold music began to play. It was Symphony No. 9 by Beethoven, played by a full orchestra. It wasn't half bad, though that didn't stop Rafferty's patience fraying with every passing second.

Eventually, the music stopped, the line crackled, and a different voice spoke.

'Hello, who is this?'

'Inspector Rafferty, Metropolitan Police.'

'Shame on you, Inspector Rafferty! This line is for real victims.'

Rafferty's brow furrowed. 'I'm calling about a victim I need to speak to. Did a Claudia Sozler call you yesterday?'

'You know I can't say. Data protection, safeguarding, can't prove who you are, and all that jazz.'

Rafferty forced herself to breathe. 'I'm happy to verify my identity. You can ring the Scotland Yard switchboard by Googling for the number and then ask them to put you through to my mobile.'

'That won't be necessary,' the woman on the other end of the line said gruffly. 'I still can't tell you anything.'

'Miss...?'

'Riccardo.'

'Miss Riccardo, I have an open kidnap investigation here. I need to know if Claudia has been kidnapped, or if she's safe.'

'Ho, ho, I thought you said she was a witness. You keep changing your story, Inspector Raffly.'

'It's Rafferty,' she corrected coldly. 'And kidnap and murder are not mutually exclusive.'

'Don't you get smart with me. I am simply not going to reveal who is and isn't a client. You're a woman. You ought to respect that our shelters are safe spaces. Good day to you!'

And the line went dead. Rafferty swore. What a bloody jobsworth. It was a murder investigation, for Christ's sake. Couldn't she exercise just a little bit of discretion?

Rafferty knew there were rules that were there to protect women, but they didn't exist to stop the police talking to a key witness in a murder investigation. She briefly considered calling straight back, but stayed her hand. It wouldn't do any good. *Where should I go from here?* she wondered. She could call Kieran and see if the Crown Prosecution Service could compel the helpline to disclose Claudia's whereabouts.

Or maybe, just maybe, she could call an old colleague at Sapphire and see if she could find Sozler that way. There were only so many domestic violence shelters in London, and it was odds on that Sozler had been taken to the nearest one with space. If Rafferty could exclude the oversubscribed shelters, and then visit each in turn starting with the nearest, she might be able to locate Sozler tonight rather than losing precious hours working with the lawyers.

She texted Mayberry: *Give up on the CCTV. I think I've found her. Come join me at Charing Cross Hospital. Bring food, I'm starving.*

• • • •

THE DOOR-TO-DOOR SEARCH wasn't going any better than the trawl through the hospital car park's CCTV footage. Brodie's hunch was that whoever had left the hospital wanted to put some distance between it and them, and the easiest way to do that was to nip up the A219, under the monstrosity that was the Hammersmith Flyover, and then join the Great West Road. That route, less than a mile or so, would open up most of London as the A4 joined up with so many other arteries.

What Brodie had hoped to find were CCTV cameras along the first stretch of that route. Despite the huge number of tiny shops, cafés, estate agents, and fast-food takeaways, there were far fewer cameras than he'd have liked.

The task was complicated by the time. A lot of the shops were closing, and of those that were open, many only had cameras covering their front door without any view of the road.

The bigger problem, however, was Mayberry. Brodie couldn't carry a warrant card, nor could he demand access to CCTV. That had to come from Mayberry. But with the detective's continued stuttering, many of the business owners simply didn't take them seriously.

Brodie and Mayberry had spent what felt like an eternity walking miles on foot, stopping in every open shop on the way.

The most promising lead on Mayberry's list was a jeweller's right before the Hammersmith flyover. He had a hunch they'd have a camera or two in light of a recent spate of "smash and grab" attacks on jewellery shops by thugs on motorcycles. Many jewellers were now even more cautious about security than usual, and jewellers were already notoriously paranoid. This one was no exception. CCTV cameras pointed both north and south, and each had been positioned carefully so that both the shop's frontage and the road were in plain view. It was the perfect set-up to catch ram-raiding bikers, which also meant it ought to have caught all the other cars passing by. It was still a long shot. Even if they could identify every vehicle that passed by, and by extension the registered owner of each, it was still a stretch to turn that into actionable intel about Claudia's whereabouts.

Nevertheless, Mayberry rang the doorbell and hoped for the best. It was the kind of jewellery shop that scrutinised customers through the cameras to decide whether to let them in. He held up his police ID, and the door buzzed. Brodie followed him inside.

The woman behind the counter smiled politely. She was dressed in a fine grey suit with two gold buttons, complemented by a white blouse. Unsurprisingly, she was also adorned with enough of the shop's merchandise to make it look like she was going to a wedding. Gold and diamonds glinted in both ears while an ornate necklace hung around her neck. It was made up of concentric circles of differently coloured gold sprinkled with tiny, bright diamonds.

'Gentlemen, what can I do for you today?'

'W-w-we need to see your CCTV,' Mayberry stammered.

She folded her arms, pulling her suit taut around her. 'Do you, now? And why would that be?'

'A w-w-woman h-has—' Mayberry began.

Brodie leapt in. 'What my colleague, Detective Sergeant Mayberry, is trying to say is that a woman was kidnapped from Charing Cross Hospital earlier today by car. We believe it may have passed by the front of your shop. We would be grateful if we could check your CCTV in case the car was caught on tape by your cameras.'

She looked from Brodie to Mayberry and back again cautiously. 'And what did you say your name was, Detective?'

Brodie shook his head, his great mane of red hair immediately visible in his peripheral vision. 'Not a detective, ma'am. I'm just the tech guy.'

'Then why,' she asked, 'are you doing the talking? Shouldn't the good sergeant be the one asking for permission to compromise my clients' privacy?'

'Ma'am, we don't want to intrude on your clients' privacy at all. We just need to see the road outside. You can play us back the CCTV and cover up the side of the screen with the shop visible using a bit of cardboard if that's your concern.'

She still looked doubtful.

'I'm s-s-sorry,' Mayberry stammered. 'I h-h-have aph-ph-phasia.'

Her expression softened. 'I had an uncle with that. Right, let me see that ID again, up close this time if you don't mind. My eyes aren't what they were. Then I'll sort you out.'

No sooner had the jeweller finally let them see the CCTV than Mayberry's phone buzzed. It was Rafferty. He showed it to Brodie:

Give up on the CCTV. I think I've found her. Come and pick me up at Charing Cross Hospital. Bring food, I'm starving.

'Go on, laddie,' Brodie said. 'I'll stay here just in case there's anything to be found. I'll get an Uber if I need to.'

• • • •

RAFFERTY HADN'T BEEN a part of their world for the better part of a decade, but her colleagues at Sapphire treated her like an old friend who'd never left.

She found them in the back of Tolpuddle Street in Islington. It wasn't a familiar haunt for Rafferty, as, back in the day, she'd been based in Southwark. The seven-mile drive had taken over an hour thanks to horrendous traffic, and it was beginning to feel like a very, very long day.

Mayberry had come with her. She'd intended to bring him inside, but at the last minute, she'd decided to leave him in the car. His aphasia was worse than ever, and she didn't have the time or patience to explain his disability yet again. Besides, he was busy doing the paperwork to record the investigation trail so far, a task she would have hated, and it would be easier to reconnect with her old colleagues on her own. She'd called ahead but had only spoken with the desk sergeant, so she had no idea whom she'd find once she was inside the station. Sapphire was a close-knit group, one that changed on the reg as most of its staff only did a year to a few years before rotating out to a less-intense unit.

The moment she walked into the station, a woman shouted out her name. 'Ashley!'

It took a second for Rafferty to recognise the older woman. Had her hair changed? Or had she lost weight?

'Jan?' Rafferty said tentatively.

'You do remember me!' Jan beamed.

When Rafferty had known her, Jan had been the newest member of Sapphire. She'd joined right before Rafferty had left for her stint with the probation service. Now the fresh face was wrought with wrinkles, she was greying at the temples, and she was carrying several extra pounds.

Jan threw her arms around Rafferty in a big hug. 'How the hell are you? We thought you'd left the service!'

'I'm good,' Rafferty lied. She was tired, stressed, and desperate to have this whole illegal mess of an investigation behind her. 'I did take a break, went to probation for a while, and then Morton poached me back to work for his MIT.'

'*The* Morton?' Jan said in awe. 'That's amazing. What's it like working with him? I've heard he's like Sherlock Holmes on Adderall with a perfect memory, and that he solves cases just by looking at them.'

Rafferty burst out laughing. 'I wish! He's got a good memory, sure, and he's smart, but he's just a man. He'd be the first to tell you it's hard work, a great team, and more than a bit of luck that gets us most of the way there, and today I need to borrow a bit of your hard work.'

'Sure, sure,' Jan said earnestly. 'But come and say hi to the guys first.'

Jan grabbed Rafferty by the wrist and led her through to the back of Islington Police Station. They walked through a door marked Sapphire, and it was there that they found the rest of the unit huddled around a cramped table.

'Guys,' Jan said. 'This is Sergeant Ashley Rafferty.'

Rafferty blushed, debated letting it slide, and then corrected them. 'It's Detective Inspector Rafferty these days.'

'Ooh, get you! Enough chit-chat. Inspector Rafferty needs help with a case.' Jan turned to Rafferty expectantly. 'Go on?'

Rafferty hadn't expected to be so suddenly or so publicly put on the spot. 'Err, right. I'm trying to find a woman who is a material witness in a murder investigation down in Putney. We thought she had been kidnapped initially, but it appears that, during a trip to Charing Cross Hospital, she may have called the DV helpline number in the ladies' toilets and been whisked away to a shelter somewhere in the city. The helpline won't tell me where she is or even if they have her, and I need to find her by tomorrow.'

A sharp intake of breath from one of the men sitting at the back of the room drew Rafferty's attention. He was a rotund man with a ruddy complexion, and he looked decidedly dubious.

'Inspector, you know as well as I do that these shelters must always be safe spaces. They won't just give up the identity of their clients.'

'I know,' Rafferty said reassuringly. 'And I wouldn't have asked if it were anything other than a murder investigation. We believe she may have been romantically involved with the deceased. I need to ask her about that.'

'And if you don't like her answer?' he asked, hinting at the notion that Claudia Sozler could be the killer.

'She's not a suspect,' Rafferty said flatly. 'We have conclusive exculpatory evidence. She's a witness, and only a witness.'

Newly mollified, the fat man nodded in Jan's direction as if to give her permission to reveal something.

'We don't know where she is for sure,' Jan said. Her tone was apologetic. As she spoke, she booted up her laptop, clicked around, and then a printer hidden in the corner that Rafferty hadn't noticed hummed to life.

Jan fetched the printout and laid it on the table. 'Ultimately the choice of whether they co-operate is probably down to whoever is running the desk and what state your witness is in. But this is a list of the nearest shelters that had vacancies earlier today. Like you said, if you go to them one by one, you might find her that way. Sorry we couldn't give you something more specific.'

It was as much as Rafferty could ask for. The rest would be up to dogged determination, legwork, and a bit of luck. If she worked down the list with Mayberry, they could cover the most likely shelters tonight and, if necessary, resume their search first thing in the morning.

'Give me the list.'

Chapter 31: Three?!

It was early evening when Morton got the call from Dr Chiswick. Less than five minutes later, he had shut himself inside a bedroom in the north-west bungalow, shut the curtains, and collapsed onto the bed, desperate for a few minutes of shut-eye before he could stare at the board in the incident room once more. The allure of the Red Lion Inn grew stronger by the minute.

Three killers. Could this investigation get any more ridiculous?

No other case had ever been so stressful. He'd gone undercover. He'd had his life and liberty threatened by the likes of the Bakowskis. He'd even come close to divorce after their shenanigans had caused a serious rift with Sarah a few years back.

But never before had he felt so powerless, so helpless, and so useless. It was nearing the end of Saturday, and so he had just a day and a half until Chiswick's deadline when he'd spill the beans to Silverman and all hell would break loose. It wasn't his pension he was worried about or even his job. He wasn't far off retirement as it was, and they'd paid off the mortgage years ago. What he was worried about was taking others down with him. His team's plausible deniability was wafer-thin, and they didn't deserve to be reprimanded. Worse still, Stephen and Abigail would be firmly in the crosshairs, and so too would he and Sarah be for aiding and abetting them after the fact.

It didn't help that the whole thing was media catnip. One whiff of a "murdered three times" story and the Fourth Estate would be whipped into a frenzy beyond even the legendary

DeLange murder that he had investigated last year. When they then learned that the murder had taken place inside a cult and that a young, vulnerable, not to mention beautiful woman had gone missing... well, that was enough to have television vans parked in front of Terra Farm twenty-four-seven for months.

He heard the front door swing open. It had to be one of the team; only they had the keys. Morton rolled over and pulled himself up into a sitting position, paused so he didn't stand up too fast and get dizzy, and then languidly stretched as he stood up.

Ayala was waiting for him in the living room. His eyes were as wide as saucers.

'Did you see?' he asked earnestly. He was holding an iPad in his hand with the case files displayed on the screen. The toxicology report was now part of the record.

Morton swore. That was the first concrete detail in writing. He'd successfully kept the smothering off the books until now. But now that the poisoning had been officially recorded, there was no possible excuse for him not to recuse himself.

'Come on, boss, you're still in the game,' Ayala said. He was surprisingly upbeat. 'The poison didn't kill him. It was just an attempt. You can still investigate the *actual* death, right?'

Morton sensed a trap. When was Ayala ever this helpful? Was he really going to bat for Morton in his hour of need? Or was this an attempt to give Morton enough rope to hang himself and free up Ayala's dream role? Worse yet, was Ayala playing it both ways? If he pretended to support Morton and Morton somehow solved the murder, he would be the hero of the hour for staying loyal. If Morton didn't solve it, Ayala hadn't personally done anything illegal and could freely gun for Morton's job. Win-win for him.

'*Just* an attempt?' Morton seethed. '*Just* an attempted murder? Have you lost your mind, Bertram? Any one of us could have poisoned him. Stephen, Abigail, even Sarah. Me being on this case is so absurd that... Did you hear something?'

There was a rustling noise outside as if someone were lurking beneath the window.

'Go check,' Morton said, his voice barely above a whisper.

Ayala disappeared. Morton held his breath and strained to hear any noise outside. Ayala was gone for a good few minutes.

'Nothing, boss. Must have been a fox or something.'

'Strange. I'm sure... Never mind,' Morton said.

'You're stressed, boss, that's all,' Ayala said. For a split second, it looked like he might try to hug Morton, and then he thought better of it. 'Let me make you a cup of tea.'

That old standby, Morton thought. The great salve of British men and women everywhere: tea.

Nevertheless, Morton allowed Ayala to put the kettle on. As they waited for it to boil, Ayala carried on nattering away.

'This isn't as big a deal as you think, boss. All eyes were on Stephen and Abigail that night. There's no way the bride or the groom could ever get enough time alone to poison someone, is there?'

'You saw the poison in the report,' Morton said. 'It's lily of the valley, Abigail's bridal flower.'

'Which grows all over Terra Farm, and anyone could have had access to it. You've not been caught with your pants down just yet, boss. Silverman can't reasonably expect you to turn over a case at eight pm on a Saturday night during a misper. The logistics alone mean you've got some time to arrange a hand-off. Who would you hand off to? DCI Chumley's on holiday, DCI Halasz is on maternity leave, and DCI Brissenden won't work Sundays if it means he misses church. I'd say you can still take until Monday morning without it resulting in a professional misconduct case.'

Did Morton have a bit of time? Or was Ayala trying to lull him into a false sense of security? He seemed to swing back and forth as predictably as a pendulum. One moment he was telling Morton it was all fine. The next, the world was crashing down.

Morton hated this case. He couldn't trust his family. He couldn't trust his team. And he certainly couldn't trust any of the members of the Collective.

All he had was his gut, which told him he had to assume he had time whether any remained or not. All he could do was carry on trying to solve the case, and in doing so exonerate his son and "daughter-in-law".

'Then,' Morton said slowly, 'we'd best get cracking. Get everyone in here ASAP, even Kieran. I know he's not part of the team, but he might be able to buy us a bit of time on the paperwork.'

Ayala scurried off to fetch the team while Morton sipped his cup of tea. It was helping.

Chapter 32: No Go

It was after dark when Lucy Reed ventured out of Terra Farm once more.

The day had been an eventful one. There were murmurings of a disappearance, the police were buzzing all over the farm like flies on rotting fruit, and, most importantly, Lucy was only hours away from her article going to press.

All she needed now was to meet her contact in Putney Heath. The plan had been agreed upon months earlier, sitting in her editor's corner office at *The Objective*'s Madison Avenue HQ. Back then, Putney Heath had been nothing more than a series of squiggles on Google Maps.

Now it was a sweltering, midge-infested maze of dog poo and gas canisters. The dogs couldn't be helped. Nature was nature, and even the best dog owner missed it every now and again. But the gas canisters were heinous. They were strewn wherever the local junkies got high. Unluckily for Lucy, the meeting points were the worst of all for it.

Step one was the "following" check. At precisely six o'clock local time, she made her way across a tiny stone bridge no more than five feet long. It crossed one of the two streams that fed King's Mere, the local pond-cum-swamp. The second stream, twenty feet further south, had an identical bridge. Her contact walked over it until they passed in the middle. As usual, he was carrying a yellow umbrella.

'Good evening,' she said to him.

'Good evening,' he said back.

And just like that, she confirmed that neither of them had been followed. It was simple, easy, and it worked. There was a slight risk that someone else might greet her, but the combination of an unusual umbrella, the time of day, and the general disinclination of Londoners to greet a stranger were strangely reassuring.

She looped around to the west of the Mere until she found herself once again walking towards her contact. This time, he had a note balled up into his fist. As they passed, he pressed it into her hand and carried on walking. She suppressed a smile. The whole shebang felt like something out of a twenties spy movie. Nevertheless, she followed protocol and waited until she was halfway back to Terra Farm before curiosity got the better of her and she unfurled the note.

Instead of a copy of the finished article, or even a congratulatory "well done", there was a thumbs down drawn in pencil along with the words:

Not enough.

She swore, tore the paper into confetti and tossed it into a hedge.

By the time she was back at the farm, her anger had subsided and her resolve was firm. If *The Objective* needed a bigger story, she'd get them one.

Come hell or high water.

Chapter 33: The Shelter

The third women's shelter on the list was in Acton. It looked to Rafferty's untrained eye like three downmarket family homes knocked together. There was a B&B sign out front with the No Vacancies sign lit in neon. Rafferty wasn't convinced by the imposter signage; there wasn't even a phone number on it. In a road full of two-up, two-down terraced homes, it stood out like a sore thumb. Several cars, most of them older and none of them clean, were parked outside.

They were now just over six miles away from Terra Farm. It didn't sound like much, but in London that meant a solid half hour's drive or the better part of an hour on public transport. To Rafferty's mind, it was close enough to be accessible and yet far enough away to feel safe.

'Are we in the r-right p-place?' Mayberry said. He was looking at the B&B sign as if he was confused.

'I think so,' Rafferty replied. 'I've got a good feeling about this one. Let's go find out.'

As they approached the front door, Rafferty noticed movement in the front window as if someone had spotted them and was on the way to intercept them. A small but unsubtle CCTV camera was affixed to the wall above the door and appeared to be motion-activated as it swung in their direction when they reached the end of the path.

Before she could knock, the door swung open. A woman a little older than Rafferty blocked the doorway. She looked from Rafferty to Mayberry and frowned.

'Didn't you see the sign? No vacancies,' the woman said firmly. She stepped back almost immediately, her right hand moving to slam the door.

Rafferty's lightning-fast reflexes came to her rescue as she managed to jam her foot in the door before it closed.

'Detective Inspector Rafferty,' she said. 'I'm here to see Claudia Sozler.'

There was a momentary flash of recognition on the woman's face before she frowned and held up her hands as if she'd never heard the name in her life. Finally, they were in the right place.

'I don't know what you're on about,' the woman said.

'Yes, you do,' Rafferty said, her voice now barely more than a whisper. 'I know this is a women's shelter, and I know Claudia is here. She's a material witness in a murder investigation, and I need to speak with her urgently.'

'If this place is what you think it is, then how dare you bring *him* with you.'

Rafferty glanced left in the direction the woman was glowering, and only when she paused did she realise that the *him* to whom the woman was referring was poor, sweet Mayberry.

Rafferty swelled with indignation. 'He's a police officer, and he has spent a lifetime protecting women.'

The woman's glare turned to Rafferty. 'Be that as it may, if this were a women's shelter, and I ain't saying it is, mind you, then no man would ever be welcome, would they? Now, you mind removing your foot from my door, please?'

'Please,' Rafferty said. 'I just need to know if she's all right even if I can't see her. Is Claudia here?'

The woman's expression softened, but not for long. 'I can't and won't tell you who's here. Adults get to go where they want and do what they want, short of you having a warrant that says otherwise, and they expect their privacy, ya know? You never heard of the Data Protection Act? Get lost before I have to call in a complaint to your supervisor. Who would that be, by the way?'

'We're going.'

Rafferty led Mayberry back to where they had parked. As they left, the door shut with a bang behind them, and Rafferty could feel eyes on the back of her head as if the woman were watching.

Sure enough, when Rafferty glanced back as she opened the car door, a pair of beady eyes was watching them from the front room.

Chapter 34: Recap

Despite the lateness of the hour, Rafferty and Mayberry were incommunicado, which only added to Morton's rising stress levels. Three murders, or rather, two attempted murders and one actual murder. How on earth was Morton supposed to figure it out with half his team off chasing a ghost, and just one day – a Sunday, no less – left on his ticking clock?

'They're not coming, boss,' Ayala nudged gently. 'Can we get started?'

Morton looked up bleary-eyed from his seat on the sofa in the living room of his son's bungalow. Present were Ayala, Stuart Purcell, and, just so they didn't mess up and unknowingly trample on the cultists' legal rights once again, Kieran O'Connor, all of whom were waiting for him to explain exactly what they were all doing sitting in the living room of a bungalow on the grounds of a cult at this ungodly hour on a Saturday evening.

'Thanks for coming, gents,' Morton said. His voice was beginning to crack from hours of talking. 'What's the state of play? Purcell?'

'The forensics are limited,' the chubby crime scene tech said with a sour expression on his face. 'Everyone in the Collective has been pretty much everywhere. DNA and fingerprints are nigh on useless. As you know, nobody had gunshot residue on their hands or clothes, which means the killer must have washed thoroughly before we tested them.'

'At the risk of asking a stupid question, is there any way to avoid being covered in gunshot residue?' Ayala asked.

'That all depends on what you mean when you say GSR,' Purcell said. 'The weapon, in this case, is a shotgun, so the cartridge it was loaded with contained the projectile, or bullet, the gunpowder as propellant, and a primer inside the case. We found the cases by the bed, and we were presented with the gun itself by Lorenzo di Stregoni, who we definitively proved did not fire the gun.'

'I assume you swabbed the dead man himself,' Kieran interrupted to suggest the possibility that Guy had, in fact, committed suicide.

'No gunshot residue there, and the wound profile isn't consistent with a self-inflicted injury. It would have taken some sort of jury-rigged mechanism to hold the gun a couple of feet from his chest at the angle he was shot at, and we found no such mechanism. Can I get back to my point, please? I was under the impression that time is of the essence.' Purcell's tone was terse.

Morton smiled at him weakly in an attempt at diplomacy. 'Please, Stuart. Nobody here is questioning your integrity or thoroughness. It's been a stressful weekend, and I'm sure Kieran just wanted to double-check that we'd covered all the bases in the light of the timeframe we have to work in, and the likelihood that this is going to receive major press coverage if the details leak.'

'Thank you,' Purcell said. 'When we look for trace evidence of GSR, what we're really looking for is a near-unique fusion of lead, barium, and antimony.'

'Near-unique?' Kieran said dubiously. Morton could practically see cogs turning as the lawyer thought of the "beyond reasonable doubt" standard.

Purcell frowned. 'We used to think this combination in the quantities found in gunshots was unique, but it's not, as PbBaSb is also found in the lining of car brakes. While it isn't therefore conclusive, it is strong circumstantial evidence. We're not dealing with a murder in a garage where PbBaSb might reasonably be in the environment anyway.'

Kieran leant forward in his seat. 'What about the risk of contamination, then?'

'I'm not a GSR expert,' Purcell said, his pitch and voice getting louder as he became defensive. There was no love lost between the scene of crime officer and the CPS lawyer, especially since the latter had already taken them all to task for conducting illegal searches.

'Nobody said you were,' Morton said softly. 'If you don't know, we can come back to it later. It's not exactly probative when we didn't find any trace of gunshot residue anywhere.'

'Oh,' Purcell said as if he was realising the question was merely academic. 'There are concerns that contaminants in cars and police stations could affect the evidence. Right now, we report one to three particles of PbBaSb as inconclusive, and the Forensic Science Service is always refining the definition.'

Kieran nodded along thoughtfully. 'But still probative?'

'I suppose,' Purcell said. He turned to appeal to Morton. 'Can we move on? I still have a lot of evidence to review.'

'One more question, then,' Kieran said, much to Purcell's chagrin. 'If the presence of GSR is probative, then how valuable is its absence in this case? Surely any defendant is going to point to the lack of GSR and simply say, "reasonable doubt"?'

'You're the lawyer,' Purcell said. 'That's one for you. As a matter of forensics, a thorough scrub with oxidising bleach would get rid of it. The same can be said for blood, tissue, fingerprint, and many other types of evidence. It's amazing what bleach can do to a crime scene.'

The lawyer sat back, defeated. 'Fair enough. Sorry, you go on.'

'As I was saying, we didn't find much. None of the cultists tested positive for GSR, and none of their clothes tested positive either. We swabbed several dozen of the Collective's white robes from all over the compound. Nada.'

'Then what on earth *have* you found?' Kieran asked.

Purcell frowned, pretended that the lawyer didn't exist, and spoke directly to Morton.

'My team found a large quantity of top-quality marijuana just outside the compound. The packaging bore evidence of rough handling, which in my experience would be consistent with being thrown over a fence.'

'So, someone lobbed it over the hedge,' Morton said. 'Good work. I assume it's too much for personal use?' When Purcell nodded, Morton said, 'Any trace of drugs inside the compound?'

'I could smell it in the widows' bungalow,' Purcell said. 'Nothing back from the lab just yet.'

Marijuana testing would be miles down the priority list. If the police raided every location where marijuana could be smelled, they'd have to raid half of London.

'Where would they have got it from?' Kieran asked.

Purcell's face was turning more and more ashen as if he were under a spotlight. He was terrified of the lawyer and it showed. 'The same place as anyone else, I guess? Possibly even on the darknet?'

'An anti-technology cult buying weed on the internet?' Kieran mocked. 'Come on. Can we go back to the "significant quantity"? That's got to be dealing.'

'That was my suspicion too,' Purcell said. 'The cult seems to have odd finances. As far as I can tell, most of their money is coming in from selling yoga classes to the local community. It's enough to pay the bills and to scrape by. Marijuana would top that income off nicely.'

Morton's mind whirred. The combination of yoga and weed... It was quintessentially hippie. It didn't sit well with the authoritarian streak that Lorenzo had demonstrated. Perhaps it was a hangover from the halcyon days of Giacomo's leadership.

'So, how are they transporting the weed?' Kieran asked. 'I haven't seen a garage or driveway.'

Kieran had a point. The entrance to Terra Farm down the long path between the hedges was barely wide enough to walk two abreast, let alone drive down.

'They've got a jeep,' Ayala said. 'I heard Lorenzo saying that Guy always left it messy.'

'Where?' Purcell demanded sharply. 'I haven't seen one.'

Ayala waved a hand in the vague direction of the main road. 'Maybe it's parked out in the lane.'

'I haven't checked that!' Purcell jumped to his feet as if he was going to go and start looking for trace evidence at nearly ten o'clock at night.

'Hold your horses, doughnut,' Kieran said. Purcell immediately scrunched up his face in a mix of anger and shame. The lawyer certainly knew how to push Purcell's buttons, and his love of Krispy Kreme doughnuts was legendary in the force.

'What now?!'

'You'll need a warrant,' Kieran said. 'The jeep is on a public road.'

'And how do you propose we get that?'

Kieran's expression was smug. 'Guy Rosenberg didn't have any official documentation, according to the background checks that Mayberry did. If he was driving that jeep, he was doing so without a driving licence. That ought to be enough to take a look. Don't go poking around until after I've sorted the paperwork, all right?'

Morton cleared his throat. 'Gents, this is fascinating, but weed is the least of my concerns. For all I care, the whole lot of them can burn a bushel of the stuff and get as stoned as they want. We have a murderer – or three – to catch.'

'More if there are co-conspirators,' Kieran chipped in helpfully.

'Thanks, Kieran,' Morton said, his sarcasm biting. 'Really helpful. Let's go from the top here. At some point during the night of the wedding, Guy Rosenberg was poisoned with lily of the valley. Enough of the stuff was found in his bloodstream to kill him, except someone else smothered him before the poison could get him.'

'Did he look like he'd been poisoned? Any slurred speech? Exaggerated movements? Confusion?' Ayala asked. 'We know someone poisoned him, but do we have any idea how? Was the poison injected, ingested, contact-based?'

Morton paused. He had seen Guy Rosenberg a few times that night. 'I thought he was just drunk.'

The symptoms weren't dissimilar: vomiting, loss of control, thirst. Rosenberg was a known drunkard – Abigail had said as much at the wedding – and so, with all of the festivities and his own tipsiness, Morton hadn't paid much attention to the victim's final hours.

'Was he?' Ayala asked.

'I think so,' Morton said. 'He was definitely knocking back the booze. Chiswick reckons that our victim ingested poison, as there was trace evidence on his lips and he couldn't see any injection sites. Apparently steeping lily of the valley in water releases the toxins. If he drank a glassful of water laced with the stuff, it would explain his symptoms and easily be masked by his insobriety.'

'Clever,' Kieran said. 'And very popular across the channel, where they call it *le muguet*. It's cheap, it's readily available, and a drunk guy wouldn't necessarily notice if his water tasted a bit off. Whoever was behind it managed to poison a man right under the nose of a detective chief inspector. But there was one flaw, wasn't there? It didn't kill him. Would it have done without the *novus actus*?'

Morton nodded. 'He was hours away from dying of the poison, and there's no way he'd have got any treatment while he was passed out alone in his bungalow.'

'Except someone smothered him before the poison took effect,' Kieran said. 'And then someone shot his corpse. Murder three ways. It's unheard of. Three killers, or one very creative murderer looking to cover their tracks?'

That was the question Morton had been pondering ever since his call with Chiswick. He still didn't have a good answer. It was certainly *possible* that one person had committed all three attempts, but what would have been the point?

'I don't see it,' Morton said flatly. 'The poison meant he was done for, end of story. Why risk smothering someone if you've already set the wheels in motion?'

'Maybe,' Kieran said cautiously, 'they thought the poison had failed, that they'd not administered enough for a fatal dose, and the smothering was a fallback. Or they got impatient.'

'But then why not smother him in the first place? He was a known drunk. It wouldn't have been hard. And then why the gunshots, for that matter? Whoever shot him had to think they were killing him. Nobody goes to that much effort to simply defile a corpse.'

'Unless, again, it was about covering up the real cause of death. If Chiswick hadn't been taking his time over the report – yes, I know you begged him to hold it 'til Monday morning – then he'd never have bothered with the detailed tox screens, and we'd probably have been none the wiser about the poisoning. That would-be killer nearly got away with it.'

It would never have come to light if Chiswick hadn't gone above and beyond in his quest to delay the formal autopsy report. If the killer had been trying to trick the police into looking for a shooter – a violent form of murder favoured by young men – then the police could have overlooked the poisoning, a method much more likely to be used by women. It left Morton stuck with the same wheels-within-wheels logic he'd been grappling with throughout the case. Was one attempt designed to cover up another? Or was each independent of the other?

'Purcell, what're the stats on the gender divide in poisoning?' Morton asked.

'Err,' Purcell demurred. 'Offhand? I'd guess the split is about eighty-twenty women to men. But don't take my word for that.'

Four in five. Those were good odds that the poisoner was a woman. Ignoring Abigail and Sarah, Morton had six female suspects: Tracey, Marta, Doreen, Pauline, Lucy, and Lana. He reeled the names off to the group.

The lawyer burst out laughing. 'That,' he said, 'has to be the most geriatric-sounding list of suspects I've ever heard of.'

Despite the absurdity of it all, the tension seemed to evaporate from the room. Kieran was right. Why on earth would one pensioner, let alone three, decide to take up a life of murder in their dotage?

It was down to Ayala to try to steer them back on topic. 'All right, boss, how about we list 'em off. Murder attempt one, the poisoning. Right now, anyone could have done it, but our six women are the prime suspects. The smothering was done overnight, so physical proximity isn't important, and that implicates anyone strong enough to smother a drunk. I could see any of them having done it except for Giacomo because he isn't *compos mentis* enough. And our shooter, murder attempt three, required access to a gun which we know is owned by Pauline, and so it's more likely to be someone living nearby, right?'

'Unless all the cultists already know who the killer is and are covering for each other,' Kieran said, suggesting the Orient Express scenario: all of them were in on it. 'They're not exactly the most honest bunch.'

Morton felt his eyes began to close. It was getting on for eleven, and they were still no closer to catching the killer than they had been at the start of the meeting. Everyone was still a suspect except for Claudia Sozler, who had been locked up throughout the entire night.

'Gents, unless someone here has had a eureka moment and can break this thing, let's call it a night. Thank you all for coming in. We've got one day left to solve a murder. Let's get some sleep and hit it afresh tomorrow.'

No one had any further ideas, and so they dutifully filed out of the bungalow. Morton debated staying on-site and then, with a heavy heart, he began to lock up. The Inn was only a few minutes away, and he'd soon collapse into a warm, safe bed, well away from the lunatics of Terra Farm.

One more day and this whole ordeal would be over... one way or the other.

Chapter 35: Empty Nest No More

Having another adult in the flat was a novel experience for Sarah Morton. Long gone were the days of having two boisterous boys knocking about the house they used to live in, scuffing up furniture and emptying the fridge as if they were constantly ravenous. They'd downsized after the boys had moved out, partly because they didn't want to rattle around a big, empty house, but mostly because they wanted to be closer to the centre of London. The new place was a stone's throw from the Thames, the theatres of the West End, and too many world-class restaurants to count. In return for giving up a garden and square footage, they'd gained a view to die for and a gated community.

It didn't hurt that Sarah no longer had to spend most of her time scrubbing an enormous family home. These days, a Roomba did the bulk of the housework. What it couldn't manage, a weekly visit from their housekeeper saw to. The Roomba buzzed about, to-ing and fro-ing around her feet. It reminded her of Stephen. He was furtive, sneaking around the flat as if she might bite, or worse, engage him in conversation. She had yet to corner him to ask about this priority malarkey. He spent most of his time hiding away in the guest bedroom, where she could hear that he was on the phone, whispering to God-knows-who.

When she heard the tap running in the kitchen, Sarah jumped at her chance to check in on her son.

Stephen looked up guiltily and then turned towards her. 'Hi, Ma. Did I disturb you?'

'Not at all,' she said. 'Have you managed to talk to Abigail? How's she coping?'

He set down his glass and perched his bum on one of the stools by the breakfast bar. Sarah leant on the other end of it, waiting for him to answer. 'Honestly, I don't know. I'm not allowed to talk to her,' he said after a pause. 'Everything is so surreal right now. I only got to talk to her once, her one phone call and all that. I've been trying to find her a more competent solicitor. She doesn't deserve to be locked up, Ma.'

'Your father's doing what he thinks he needs to do to keep her safe.'

'Well, sod Dad and his "I know best" attitude. She could come here, couldn't she? There's room enough, and don't tell me you haven't spotted the police cars driving past the front of the building every half an hour to check up on us.'

'Maybe your father knows something we don't. That Claudia girl ran away, after all.'

'Well, she's nuts. She swans around like she owns the place, all airs and graces, talking about what she's going to do to this building or how she'd tear down the pigsties. It's just not helpful. That isn't what the Collective is about.'

'Then what is it about?'

'Sharing. We share everything. We've got communal land, communal dining, even communal washing facilities. Everyone has a part to play, and everyone is expected to pull their weight.'

She watched her son intently as she asked her next question. 'And what about this priority stuff?'

'What about it?'

'How do you feel about it?'

He didn't say anything for a moment. 'Well, it makes me a bit uncomfortable, to be honest.'

'Why?'

'Because it's at odds with how I understand the Collective. The whole point is that we're all equals, comrades in arms, part of something bigger than ourselves.'

'And priority goes against that.'

He nodded. 'It's insane to say we're all equal but that some are more equal than others. Just look at Guy's house. Priority seven, even worse than Abigail and me, and he gets a shack of a home while Lorenzo and Giacomo have every mod con and luxury. I don't mind paying my dues, but...'

'But it's not fair.'

'Then again, life isn't. And I can't afford London, Ma. You know that. I've bounced from job to job, achieving diddly squat. With the Collective, I've got somewhere to live, a real bricks and mortar house, and I've got a purpose. I have no responsibilities other than tending the land, doing a bit of DIY here and there, and mucking in with the cooking.'

'Sounds idyllic.'

'It is, Ma.'

'Except someone killed a man, Stephen.'

'Can we change the subject?'

'Okay,' she said, shrugging as if she didn't care. She did, but she knew if she pressed him on it, he'd clam up and go hide in the bedroom again. She picked what she thought was the safest, least-contentious topic she could think of. 'What're you planning on doing while on your honeymoon? Spot of scuba diving? You used to love that.'

They were due to fly out on Tuesday morning and wouldn't be back until the end of the month.

'Err, Ma... about the honeymoon... we can't take it.'

'*What?*' Sarah's own temper rose. They'd only just paid the final instalment on the trip, a once-in-a-lifetime all-inclusive trip to the Maldives complete with seaplane transfer, private villa, and scuba excursions. 'Why on earth not?'

'Abigail won't go.'

'Because?'

'Because, Ma, honeymoons are an unearned luxury, a shiny bauble to distract us from our spiritual needs.'

That was news to her. When she'd told him about the trip, he'd been grateful for such a generous wedding gift. Sarah stood up. Her son was a foot taller than she, but while he remained perched on the stool, she could look him right in the eye. 'Unearned? Your father and I earned every penny of that money and we booked the trip months ago, but you're only telling us *now*? You know it's cost us a fortune. With your blessing. What's changed?'

'Lorenzo says–'

Of course it was one of Stephen's new friends who had put this idea in his head. She wanted to yell at him, to scream and swear. Instead, she bit her tongue, swallowed deeply, and counted to ten.

Her son had always been like this. He lurched from one thing to another, never staying long enough to put down roots. He wouldn't – or perhaps couldn't – stay in one job for more than six months. No doubt that was her own fault for spoiling the boy, wrapping him up in cotton wool whenever life got hard in the way only a mother could.

'Honeymoons are important. It's a chance for the two of you to spend some time alone together, to make memories that'll keep you smiling when times get tough. And they will get tough, sooner or later. You need to know that what you've got is worth fighting for.'

'I do know that, Ma. I don't need a fly 'n' flop to tell me that.'

She wasn't convinced. The Maldives had been his dream destination since he was a teenager. If they'd still been in the old house in Hammersmith, she'd have frogmarched him upstairs to his childhood bedroom, where an A3 poster of Maldivian beaches used to hang on the wall beside one of Jet from The Gladiators.

'But what's the harm in going? It's all paid for. Wouldn't want to waste that?'

'Then you and Dad go,' Stephen said. 'I'm not sullying my soul for this. It's not worth it.'

Her knuckles turned white as she leant against the breakfast bar. There was no arguing with him. Not today. Logic was gone and hippie Stephen was back.

'Maybe we will,' Sarah said tersely. 'But what are you going to do instead? There's a job going over at–'

This time, he cut her off. 'I don't need a job. I've got one.'

More news. 'Doing what, exactly?'

'I'm going to train as Mr Heggerty's apprentice.'

An image of a looming hulk of a man, silent and sullen, came into Sarah's mind. She'd met him at the ceremony. 'The Terra Farm handyman? You've spent a decade travelling the world, studying at multiple universities, and you want to be a *handyman*?'

'Someone's got to do it,' Stephen said. 'So why not me? The Collective needs someone to keep the place shipshape, and Mr Heggerty won't be young enough to do it forever. Besides, we're hoping to build a couple more bungalows, expand the place a bit. That needs all hands on deck. Especially now Guy's gone.'

For a moment, the murder had slipped her mind. Not only was he going back there, but he was going back into the lion's den. 'Someone murdered him.'

'And Dad will get justice,' Stephen said smoothly. 'Don't let one bad apple ruin a good bunch, Ma. The Collective are good people. They're kindly, simple folk who eschew technology. It'd do you good to get away from your screens and your stress too.'

He stood. 'And I think it's time for me to get back to finding Abigail a solicitor. Nice chat, Ma.'

Chapter 36: A Dirty Deal?

Morton had just finished locking the front door to Stephen's bungalow when he heard a sound in the darkness. It was the same rustling noise that he'd heard earlier in the day.

He shuffled towards the bushes. Was he imagining something? Perhaps it was one of the boys coming back? A lost mobile? A sudden thought?

As he turned back to the front door, a flash of movement caused his muscles to tense with anticipation.

There, on the doorstep, was Lucy Reed, bold as brass.

'Detective Morton, I need to talk to you urgently. Inside. Keep the lights off. I don't want to be seen.'

Morton froze. Was this a trick? Or was the case about to break all on its own? Sod it. He unlocked the door once more, left the lights off, then allowed Lucy to pass before slowly shutting the door. The lock clicked shut.

'Further in,' she whispered, 'in case someone sees us through the window.'

Her paranoia was extreme, and if she was about to betray the cult, that was understandable. When they had made it into the middle of the hallway with all the doors closed so nobody could see them, Morton heard her breathe a sigh of relief.

'I have not been completely honest with you, Mr Morton,' Lucy said in a low tone that was barely audible. 'I'm sure you already know that.'

'You're the killer?' Morton asked.

'Heavens, no!' Lucy cried.

'Then what?' Morton demanded. 'We know you never entered the country under the name "Lucy Reed", and you're obviously an American. You don't even try to hide the accent.'

'It's true,' she said. 'Lucy Reed isn't my real name. But my real name is of no concern. I'm a journalist with *The Objective*. I trust you've heard of us. I've been undercover with the Collective now for nearly six months, and I know everything you need to know to break this case. I suspect you can't do it without me.'

Morton arched a disbelieving eyebrow. He had heard of *The Objective*. It was a sensationalist rag with links to London's *The Impartial*, the latter of which had once been run by a man convicted of orchestrating the most complicated murder Morton had ever investigated.

'Or more precisely, should I say you can't do it in the timeframe that you need without my help. We both know you shouldn't be on this case.'

'So why are you talking to me now? You could have revealed who you were on Friday morning if you wanted to assist with our investigation. What's changed?'

'Sozler's disappearance and Rosenberg's death,' Lucy said. 'The combination is a powder keg waiting to explode all over the papers, the TV news, and the internet. You're lucky we're so off-the-grid here or you'd already have been swarmed by paparazzi. But you mark my words, sooner or later, the news cycle is going to spin up and they'll be all over you, all over this case, and all over the Collective. You're not the most discreet of men. You didn't even notice when I lurked under the window to listen in on your discussions.'

Aha! He *had* heard someone at the window. For a moment, his biggest problem in the world was making a mental note to say 'I told you so' to Ayala, then reality bit back.

'And your involvement in this is...?'

'I deserve this story,' she said fiercely. 'I've worked this story for months and months. I've *lived* this story. I've gone along with the most absurd rules, put up with being thrown in a shed while I'm on my period, abstained from alcohol, and built relationships with those who live here. I've done the donkey work, and I will not let some British hack waltz in at the last moment and steal my limelight. I want an exclusive, and I want you to serve it up on a plate for me.'

She stared at him, unblinking. He could see the determination on her face. This was her big break, her first massive story, and, for a moment, Morton wondered if she'd kill to keep it.

'Think about it, Mr Morton,' she continued. 'Together, we can shape the narrative. We can keep your family out of it. We can protect your career. And we can catch a killer.'

A killer? Morton thought. Lucy Reed didn't know everything.

'And what do you want?'

'I want everything. I want access to your reports. I want quotes. I want to make my piece a Pulitzer-worthy smash hit that explodes this pathetic little cult, and I'm going to do it with or without you. The only question is, do you still want to be a police officer on Monday morning or not?'

Blackmail. That was all it was. As if this dreadful weekend couldn't get any worse.

'No,' Morton said flatly. 'Never ever try to blackmail me again, or I'll arrest you for blackmail and throw in a charge of perverting the course of justice for good measure. Don't forget, you've only ever given me a false identity. That's a slam dunk prosecution in anyone's book.'

It was mutually assured destruction. She could destroy his professional life. He could put her in prison for a very long time. It was a standoff that was in neither of their interests to break. Nevertheless, Lucy seemed unsurprised by his answer.

'Take a night to think it over, David,' she said coolly.' I wouldn't want to see you break your family apart over this.'

Before Morton's rage could drive him to do something he would regret, she walked out, leaving Morton standing alone in the bungalow's hallway.

He bolted the door and then headed for the incident room. He'd never get more than a fitful night's sleep of tossing and turning anyway, so he might as well spend his final hours as a policeman staring at the evidence.

Two wannabe killers plus one successful murderer, and he was no closer to catching any of them.

Chapter 37: Le Muguet

That Sunday morning, bright sunlight streamed into the incident room. Morton turned over, forgetting where he was, and promptly rolled off the sofa and onto the floor with a crash.

He was still dressed, still exhausted, and still no closer to catching the killer. He missed Sarah dreadfully after just two nights apart. He debated sending her a text and then he saw the time. Best to let her sleep.

As he stretched out, his cramped neck and shoulder muscles complained. The medicine cabinet above the hob beckoned. Two Neurofen and a sip of water later, he turned his attention to food.

His stomach was too queasy to even attempt a proper breakfast, so he grabbed a slice of toast before chugging down the rest of his glass of water. Despite his showering every day, the thirty-degree heat meant that Morton smelt about as bad as a homeless person, and if he could smell it, so could everyone else. But there was no time to remedy that when there was work to be done. He fell back on the old teenage standby: a liberal application of deodorant.

When Morton began to look for lily of the valley, or *le muguet* as Kieran had called it, he found it everywhere: in borders, hanging baskets, and even around the edges of the vegetable garden.

It was so prevalent, so obvious, that the poison used to murder Guy Rosenberg had been right under Morton's nose the whole time. He'd have noticed the flower sooner had there been the slightest hint that this was a poisoning case. The gunshots and the smothering had been the perfect distraction, keeping Morton off the ball for two of his three days.

So as to avoid any paper trail, the team had taken to using self-deleting messages to discuss *le muguet*. That made it even harder to follow the three tracks of the investigation.

And poison changed *everything*. The conundrum was obvious: if everyone had access to the flowers, then nobody stood out. All of the cultists, from Giacomo to Claudia Sozler, could have picked a few. It didn't take a genius to throw them in a bucket of water and wait. Even Claudia Sozler's alibi began to fall apart. Her being in seclusion at the time of Guy's death didn't pre-empt her planning his death and ensuring that he came into contact with the poison whilst she was locked away.

If anything, Morton's suspect pool was getting larger rather than smaller. Nearly everyone was back in the frame, and he could feel the pressure of the clock ticking. It reminded him of a time when, in a sweltering exam room, he'd fallen asleep during a test only to awake when the examiner called out into the silence: *Ten minutes remaining!*

This was exactly the same feeling. Time was slipping away, and the task at hand seemed more difficult than ever before.

If the murderer's potential ease of access to poison and/or the victim couldn't give him a suspect, he'd have to narrow things down another way. Whoever had poisoned Guy Rosenberg knew enough about plants or poisons to pick an obscure way to commit murder. Lily of the valley was almost unheard of as a poison in Morton's experience. Although there had been a famous spate of poisonings using it in France in the late nineties, with *le muguet* hitting the front page of *Le Monde* over and over, it hadn't ever made the headlines here. Alas, Morton thought, there was not so much as a hint of a French connection in the cult.

The offer Lucy Reed had made last night surfaced in Morton's mind. She could be bluffing, and yet, Morton reflected, there had been something in her tone, a certainty that made it seem almost a foregone conclusion that she, Lucy, could help him break the case. The question then became, could he bear to pay such a price? He had already compromised his professional principles once this weekend. He shouldn't be on the case at all. It had taken the loyalty only a father can feel for Morton to break the rules after three decades of impeccable service.

He pushed away the thought of taking her offer. Maybe he'd reconsider later when he was truly desperate, but not yet. The day was still young, and Morton hoped they could break the case without his resorting to taking Lucy's sordid offer. But without any insider information, how was he to whittle down the suspects until only one person remained, one person who was beyond all doubt the poisoner?

The bride and groom seemed unlikely. All eyes had been on them that night, and that sort of reasonable doubt was wide enough to drive a truck through. But he couldn't exclude them as much as he wanted to. Slipping poison into a water glass took but a moment.

He kept coming back to the statistics. Poisoning was almost uniquely a woman's way to kill, and to choose a bridal flower seemed somehow even more feminine.

There was something old-fashioned about it too. Once upon a time, murders using foxglove had been popular on British television for largely the same reasons a killer might choose *le muguet*: it was readily available, not suspicious to own or possess, and it worked. This murder was simply a more efficient twist on the classic plant-based poisoning.

Morton's mind felt cloudy. He hadn't slept properly, and the atmosphere on Terra Farm was beyond claustrophobic. Despite the ticking clock, Morton knew that taking a short break was the smart choice. Sometimes, standing still was the best way to move forward.

He signed himself out at the gate, where two constables from the East Putney station were still standing guard just off the cult's land, and wandered in the general direction of the river. He was parched, so he swung into a local corner shop to pick up a chilled bottle of water. By the time he reached the Thames, Morton had drunk the entire bottle. Thirst quenched, he found a bench facing inland at the edge of Wandsworth Park and sat down. He glanced around to make sure he was alone and then called Sarah. She answered almost immediately.

'Hey,' he said, mustering as much casual cheer as he could. 'Stephen in earshot?'

He could hear Sarah's voice like a knife cutting through butter on a hot day. 'He's in the other room. How's it going?'

'Badly,' Morton said. 'I'm no closer to solving this crime than when you left. Three people tried to kill Guy Rosenberg, and everyone is lying about what they were doing, when they were doing it, and even who they are.'

'Nothing new there, then,' Sarah said. Morton could hear the faint smile in her voice.

He chuckled weakly. 'Except for the blackmail.'

'*What?*'

'One of our cultists is apparently an undercover journalist,' Morton said. 'She knows I shouldn't be on this case.'

'Oh, God. How much does—'

'Not money,' Morton whispered. He felt suddenly tawdry as he furtively checked that nobody had come into earshot. 'She wants inside access, stuff she can print.'

'But... you don't have anything.'

As if that were the only problem, Morton thought. 'And I'd get fired for professional misconduct.'

There was a silence that hung in the air. Morton could just imagine his wife biting her lip as she debated whether or not to say what was on her mind.

'Say something, would you?'

'Well... and don't shoot me for saying this... but you're going to be fired anyway if you don't break this case by tomorrow morning when Silverman gets into the office. If it's not something totally illegal, maybe we should do the deal? This is Stephen's life we're talking about.'

'I won't. I can't. No way. No how. Never.'

But he would.

Chapter 38: Rafferty Returns

Take two, Rafferty thought as she drove back to the quiet suburban street where she believed Claudia Sozler was hiding in the women's shelter. This time she had come alone and had parked her car well out of sight.

She was banking on the staff working in shifts. If the same woman appeared in the doorway once more, Rafferty's plan would quickly fall apart.

After she got out of her car, she looked into the wing mirror, dabbed a finger in her bottle of water, and artfully smudged her mascara. Guilt slowly built as she assumed the persona of a domestic violence victim. She had to remind herself several times that she was doing the wrong thing for the right reasons. Rafferty was convinced that Claudia held the key to breaking the case, and she was the only one with a chance of getting to her. The only other approach would be to try for a search warrant, but without any hint that Claudia had done anything illegal, it would be hard to come by.

Nobody seemed to notice as Rafferty shuffled towards the door, her posture hunched and her head low. She knocked and waited. It took a moment for the door to open, and then a woman appeared. Rafferty held her breath, half-expecting her plan to backfire. Thankfully, an older woman had answered the door. She was dressed in a knitted cardigan that looked homemade and had the stern, but not unkind, expression of a school headmistress.

'You looking for a room?' the woman said, pointing at the B&B sign.

'N-no,' Rafferty said, aping Mayberry's stutter to disguise her own voice. 'I c-called a number at the h-hospital, and they said to c-come here.'

The woman stood aside, let Rafferty shuffle past into a narrow hallway, and then clicked the door softly shut.

'Sorry, love, we weren't expecting anyone else tonight,' the kindly woman said. 'Go on, first door on the right. You sit tight, and I'll bring you a cup of tea.'

Rafferty did so. She was in. But she still had to find Claudia. She looked around. The front room was like an old-fashioned tea shop with fussy floral decorations. On the floor underneath the window was a big box of toys. With a jolt, she realised that women brought their children here too.

The woman reappeared before Rafferty had a chance to look around any further. Now that she was no longer hunching over, Rafferty could see that the woman wasn't nearly as old as she had first thought. She was probably somewhere in her late forties or early fifties, with shoulder-length blonde hair elegantly cut to frame a heart-shaped face, and had a warm, comforting smile. If Rafferty had been in trouble, she knew she would have trusted this woman immediately.

'I'm Elaine. What's your name?'

'A... Abigail,' Rafferty said. She had almost given up her real name without thinking. Instead, she stole the name of Morton's new daughter-in-law.

'Okay, Abigail. What brings you here?'

She had cut to the chase much faster than Rafferty had expected. She had three options: tell the truth and risk getting thrown out, tell a half-truth and say that she knew Claudia from Terra Farm, or perhaps just borrow a story from an old case. She'd already told one lie. In for a penny, in for a pound.

'I was at Terra Farm with Claudia,' Rafferty said, opting for the half-truth. She really had met Claudia there. This was the acid test: if Claudia wasn't here, the confusion would be obvious.

'Oh, honey, I'm so sorry. Did they lock you up too?'

Rafferty gulped. She hated lying. Thankfully, she didn't have to; the kindly woman took her silence and downcast eyes as affirmation.

'It's okay if you're not ready to talk. Let's get you set up in one of the bedrooms, and then, if you like, I'll bring you breakfast if you haven't had anything.'

It took all of Rafferty's effort not to 'fess up and admit she was a police officer. Instead of coming clean, she meekly allowed herself to be led upstairs.

She paused on the landing. 'Can... can I see Claudia?'

'Hmm, let me ask her,' the woman said. She disappeared down the long hallway, and Rafferty heard a knock followed by voices that were too quiet for Rafferty to make out what was being said.

When the woman returned, she gave a half-smile. 'Fourth door on the left. When you're done, take room fifteen.'

She handed Rafferty a key and headed off down the stairs.

It was with trepidation that Rafferty slowly approached the door to Claudia's room. She knocked and then opened the door without waiting for a reply. Claudia was inside, sitting bolt upright on a single bed staring blankly at a wall. She looked much better than when she'd been stretchered out of the compound, but there were still dark circles around her eyes as if she hadn't slept in days.

It took Claudia a moment to realise that there was someone in her doorway. For a few seconds, everything was calm. It was only when she realised that Rafferty wasn't Abigail that she panicked.

Claudia scrabbled backwards on the bed, her back flat against the wall, until she was in the very corner. Her skin seemed to pale even more until she was ghost-like. Rafferty had mere seconds until Claudia screamed the house down.

'Don't come any closer!' She spoke in a raspy, quiet voice that Rafferty could only just hear.

Rafferty stopped just inside the door and held up her hands to show they were empty. 'I won't hurt you, Claudia. My name is Ashley Rafferty. I'm a detective with the Metropolitan Police. You're not in trouble, I promise. I'm only here to talk to you. Please.'

Claudia's eyes darted between Rafferty and the hallway as if she wanted to bolt. 'You... you lied. They said you were Abigail.'

'I did,' Rafferty said. 'And I'm sorry about that. I had to come and talk to you, to make sure you're all right.'

Claudia continued to press herself against the wall, cornered. Rafferty could see her trembling. 'You don't care about me. Nobody does. Not anymore.'

'Yes, yes, I do. I wouldn't be here if I didn't. If you want me to go, I'll go.'

Rafferty waited, the seconds passing by painfully as she hoped that Claudia wouldn't take her up on that offer.

'Why would you care?' Claudia said at last.

'Because what they did to you – seclusion – wasn't right.'

'I don't care about that.'

'Then, what do you care about? What made you run? Did they do something worse?'

A terse nod. Rafferty chanced a half-step closer.

'*Him*,' Claudia said, her voice laced with venom. She pulled even further away, tucking her legs up against her chin and wrapping her arms around them.

Could she be talking about Guy? Or was the culprit the man everyone seemed to hate? 'Do you mean Lorenzo?' Rafferty asked.

A nod.

'Why? What did he do?'

Claudia began to slowly rock back and forth. 'It's not fair. We didn't deserve it. We didn't.'

Another step forward. Claudia froze in place, her sobbing abating for a moment. 'What was it that you didn't deserve?' Rafferty said.

'We didn't deserve it. We didn't. He should have left us alone. Alone. We didn't deserve it.'

'We?'

The rocking grew faster, more violent. 'We didn't! We didn't! We didn't deserve to die.'

She knew that Guy was dead? How? She'd been locked up.

'How did you know?' Rafferty asked. 'Weren't you in seclusion?'

Faster and faster, Claudia rocked. Her chants grew louder and louder. 'We didn't! We didn't!"

Footsteps echoed outside the room, and then the door was flung open. The kindly older woman was back, her expression sterner than ever. 'That's enough, dears. Come away now, Abigail.'

For a moment, Rafferty debated identifying herself as a policewoman. Then she thought better of it. Claudia wasn't going to give her anything more meaningful to go on, and she now knew where Claudia was and that she was safe.

Rafferty allowed herself to be marched from the room.

'She'll be okay, dear,' the woman said. 'I'll talk to her.'

'Thank you,' Rafferty said, forcing herself to flash a grateful smile.

'Now, room fifteen. Just along there.'

Rafferty thanked her again. 'Is it okay to smoke?'

'Not inside.'

'I'll nip out for a quick one, then.'

Rafferty bounded down the stairs, out the front door, and then, as soon as it had shut behind her, slunk off into the night. She needed to have words with Pauline post-haste.

If Claudia knew that Guy was dead, that meant she couldn't have been in seclusion the whole night.

At the start of the interview, Claudia had been the only suspect with a rock-solid alibi.

Now, she was a potential murderess.

Chapter 39: Sunday Funday

Sunday morning provided a new challenge for Ayala. He needed a search warrant to search inside the cult's jeep, but the Magistrates' Courts were all closed on Sundays. It was his first time making an out of hours application, and he felt wrong-footed by the informality of the process. He was used to filling in long forms, then queuing in the courthouse corridors before finally being allowed to ask a magistrate for what he wanted. Instead, he got to go directly to a magistrate's house. After a brief consultation with Kieran O'Connor to double-check the procedure, Ayala was on his way to the home of Joseph Elkins, the nearest magistrate to the Collective. Elkins lived in one of the big Victorian homes on the outskirts of Putney. Ayala found the place easily enough, though parking proved a little more of a challenge.

On the doorstep he found himself explaining to a bathrobe-clad magistrate why he needed a search warrant.

'It's a murder case, then?' Elkins said. He was holding a pen and an official-looking form from the Ministry of Justice website which had clearly been printed just before Ayala arrived. The ink was still wet, the tell-tale sign that he'd used a cheap inkjet printer.

'Yep,' Ayala said.

Elkins ticked the "indictable offence" box on the form.

'Thanks for the courtesy call to warn me you were on the way,' he said amicably. He glanced at the form and paraphrased it monotonously. 'Do you have reasonable grounds to believe the jeep contains evidence or material of beneficial importance to a trial?'

'I do.'

'Right,' Elkins said. He ticked the box, wrote out the location of the jeep and the number plate, and then time-stamped the form. He copied the lot onto a second form and handed Ayala a copy. It didn't look very official.

'That looks like the sort of note my mum used to scribble to get me out of physical education.'

Elkins smirked. 'That, Detective, is a pukka search warrant. But yeah, she ain't much to look at. Same could be said of you.'

He stepped back, shutting the door. In a sulk, Ayala stomped back to his car, where he looked at himself in his wing mirror. Sure, there were bags underneath his eyes and creases coming in at his temples, but it was still a handsome face.

'I look a damned sight better most men my age,' he muttered to no one.

Chapter 40: Sisters in Arms

Once she'd briefed the boss on the latest developments, Rafferty went in search of Pauline Allchin. The groundskeeper was sitting under a tree near the pigsties, her eyes closed.

'Pauline?'

Her eyes flicked open. 'What do you want?'

There was a spot of shade a few feet to Pauline's right. Rafferty sat down cross-legged. 'I spoke to Claudia last night.'

'You found her, then? Where is she?'

'Can't tell you that, I'm afraid,' Rafferty said.

'Is she okay?'

'She's safe. For now.'

'What does that mean?'

'It means that she thinks someone wanted to kill her. When I spoke to her, she just kept repeating herself over and over again. All she could say is "it's not fair".'

The top of Pauline's lip twitched. 'And what's that got to do with me?'

'Everything,' Rafferty said. 'You know what goes on in the cult. Morton saw you outside Guy's bungalow after the gun was fired. Claudia wasn't there. She was in seclusion, right?'

A terse nod.

'And you've soundproofed the room you lock women up in.'

For a moment, it looked like she'd deny it. Then she said: 'I have.'

'Then, how did Claudia know that Guy had been murdered?'

Pauline lurched forward and hauled herself to her feet. 'I don't have to talk to you, do I?'

'No,' Rafferty conceded. 'But if you want to help your friend, then you should. Who wanted to kill Guy and Claudia? If you don't tell me what you know, we can't arrest them. And we can't protect Claudia.'

Pauline didn't say anything. But she didn't walk away, either. Rafferty stood, touched her arm gently, and looked her in the eye. 'Claudia thinks of you as a mother, doesn't she? Like she's the daughter you never had?'

For the second time in two days, a pang of guilt struck Rafferty. She didn't like having to be manipulative, and she hated how good she was at it.

A tiny tear rolled down Pauline's cheek. 'I can't,' she said.

'Yes, you can. You've got Claudia's best interests at heart. So do I. Help me to help her.'

'You know the rules around here. I have to do everything I'm told.'

'Without question or delay.'

'Right,' Pauline said. 'Then you know what you're asking me to do.'

'To have a little chat? Just us girls? Provided that no crimes have been committed, I'll keep everything you say off the record. You have my word. Now, will you sit back down?'

They resumed their seats, neither quite sure of the other. Pauline took the gamble, swallowed, and then, like a flood, the words came tumbling out.

'I don't like the rules. Lorenzo isn't like his father. Giacomo, for all his faults, only ever had the greater good in mind. What Lorenzo did was cruel. Those who refused his will were...

removed from the cult. When he took over, he came down hard on anything he didn't agree with. First, it was talking to outsiders. That was no longer allowed. Then it was the priority system.'

'Which you went along with.'

'Like hell I did.' Pauline rolled up her sleeves to show a series of burn scars crisscrossing her arms. 'He purged the naysayers with fire. I fell in line. You would have too.'

'Until Claudia came along.'

'She was so sweet, so innocent. She just wanted what we used to have, a simple happy life. I wanted that back too. When she found *it* out, I knew I had to help.'

Spit it out, woman, Rafferty thought. 'What did she find out?'

'She thinks Guy is the rightful owner of Terra Farm.'

'Could she prove that?'

'It's complicated,' Pauline admitted. 'You know it was Clementine Rosenberg's land, right? Her late partner left it to her.'

'Right. And she left it to the cult?'

Pauline shook her head. 'We all thought that. There used to be a file full of legal documents in Giacomo's office, including Clementine's will.'

'And?'

'It disappeared. One day it was there, and then it wasn't.'

Rafferty wasn't yet convinced. 'Someone shredded old paperwork?'

'The day after Claudia stuck her nose in,' Pauline said. 'Bit of a coincidence. She wasn't even a dweller back then.'

'A what?'

'A dweller. Someone high enough priority to get to live on Terra Farm.'

Several thoughts came rushing to Rafferty as she parsed the importance of what Pauline had just said. 'There are *more* of you? Not living on the farm? How many?'

'A few. Not as many as there used to be. Anyway, Claudia knew all about wills. She had an A-Level in law. And she wanted to know why Guy was disinherited. It was his mother's farm, after all, so he should have inherited it.'

'What did she do?'

Pauline folded her arms. 'She did what brash young people are prone to do. She went straight up to Lorenzo and demanded to see the paperwork.'

'What did he say?'

'That it was long gone. Except it wasn't. I'd seen it there when I went to talk to Dori. He got rid of it after she started asking questions, not before. Then he started love-bombing Claudia.'

'Love-bombing?'

'Massive displays of affection. We all took part. We had to. For the next couple of weeks, she was everyone's best friend. She moved onto the farm where he kept her so busy, she didn't have time for Guy. It's one of the things he does to keep us in line. Lorenzo knows who is where, when, how much they're eating. He's petty enough to take away your food if you cross him. One day, he's your best friend. The next, you're eating vegetable slop while everyone else feasts on steak.'

Classic cult conditioning. Sarah had warned Rafferty about it. 'And then?'

'Then, just as quick, he told everyone to shun her. We stopped paying her attention, threw her in seclusion, and punished Guy for fraternising with a higher priority member without permission.'

'She was *higher* priority than Guy?'

'Yep,' Pauline said. 'Lorenzo did that to piss Guy off. He's a seven, she's a six. Mad, isn't it? Guy had been here his whole life, the poor man.'

It was all so arbitrary.

'Then,' Pauline continued, 'I got to know her. Seclusion is barbaric, so I did what any woman would. I let her out. As much as I could, anyway. If I saw someone coming on the cameras, back in the cell she went. We got to talk, a lot, and I think she was onto something.'

'Hold up a minute,' Rafferty said. 'I'm really confused here.'

'About what?'

'The Rosenberg surname. If Clementine was a Rosenberg by marriage–'

'By birth,' Pauline said. 'Around here, the women don't take the men's surnames. Or they didn't under Giacomo's rules. I have no idea if Abigail will become a Morton.'

'Right. So Clementine and Marta were both Rosenbergs at birth... but Marta is a Timpson now?'

'She got married before she joined the cult. She was already a Timpson when she came to us, so she just kept that name. Giacomo wasn't bothered.'

Rafferty was starting to understand. Marta's name change was essentially grandfathered in. 'And then Guy is also a Rosenberg. How come he took his mother's name instead of his father's?'

'She said she didn't want him to know his father, that it was better for him to simply be a Rosenberg all his life.'

It all clicked. Two sisters, one married and kept her maiden name, the other didn't. Guy had kept his mother's maiden name. 'Now I think I get it,' Rafferty said slowly. 'So, what was she going to do with this information?'

'You mean what has she done with that information. She dragged poor Guy into town to speak to a lawyer.'

The revelation stunned Rafferty. While she knew the cultists had lawyered up whenever they were interrogated, the thought that the young, naïve couple had actually consulted a solicitor hadn't crossed her mind. She recovered quickly. 'Do you know who they hired?'

'Mr McPhail of McPhail and Harbottle down in the village.'

'When was this?'

'The day before Guy was murdered.'

Chapter 41: Tick Tock

The clock was ticking towards midday and Morton had made some progress, though not as much as he'd have liked. The hunt for Claudia was officially over now that Rafferty had found her safe and sound at the domestic violence shelter. On the off chance that someone in the cult would find her, or, more likely, she would move on under her own volition, Morton had assigned Mayberry to keep a watch over the shelter.

He'd phoned to verify that Lucy Reed really was an undercover journalist. The newspaper had confirmed it almost immediately despite the time of his call, and so he stood outside her bungalow with a moral dilemma: could he really choose the lesser of two evils?

He could. Morton knocked on the door. When Lucy answered, she ushered him inside.

'It's just me,' she said as he looked around for Lana, the other woman who shared the unmarried women's bungalow. 'We can talk, but keep your voice low. The walls have ears around here.'

She should know, Morton thought. After all, it was Lucy who had eavesdropped on his own team meetings.

'What exactly do you want from me?' Morton asked. 'I can't give you anything illegal.'

'You know what I want,' Lucy said, smiling sweetly. 'I need an exclusive. Give me access to your staff, your reports, and all the evidence. Let me write the narrative that makes you the big shot who solved the case and caught the Collective killer.'

'And in return?'

'I'll give you a murderer. I'll even go first as a sign of trust.'

239

Morton stared down at her. She was standing so close, he could smell her breath.

'No,' he said flatly.

She looked crestfallen. 'No? Are you sure about that, Mr Morton?'

'How about I don't arrest you for obstructing my investigation?' It was Morton's turn to proffer a too-sweet smile.

She shrugged. 'You could. I'm willing to risk it. But if I go down, I'm taking you and your whole family with me.'

Morton felt his jaw clench. From the gleam in her eye, it was obvious she knew she had him.

'Tell you what,' she said. 'For now, give me a mobile phone and a laptop, and when I need to get out of here, you let me leave quietly. No obstruction charges, no blackmail charges, just a journalist and a cop helping each other out. Oh, and I'll need somewhere to work away from prying eyes.'

'And where would that be, exactly?'

'Anywhere I can write my article,' Lucy said. 'I can't do it without tech. Let me use one of the rooms in Stephen and Abigail's bungalow. I know you've blacked out the windows for privacy, so pretend you're interrogating me while I get the article done, and while I'm doing that, you can arrest a killer.'

She held out a hand. Morton looked it for a long time as if it were a viper that might bite. Reluctantly, he shook it.

'Now, spill the beans.'

She grinned. 'You're going to like this. I assume you've background checked everyone here.'

'Naturally.'

'Then you know Darren Heggerty doesn't exist, at least not one who was born July 4th, 1965 in Swindon. Mr Heggerty isn't who he says he is.'

Morton motioned for her to keep talking.

'If I'm right, he's your murderer.'

Over the next half an hour, Lucy told Morton what she knew. By the time she was through with her story, Morton knew that Darren Heggerty was the name of a child who had drowned aged eleven in 1974 and that the man now using that moniker had assumed his identity.

'And how can you prove he's a killer?'

'I didn't promise to *prove* it,' Lucy said. 'I just said I'd tell you who they are. If you want more, I want more. Now, can I have that laptop, or shall I go and out you to the chief of police?'

As if he had any choice. Bloody journalists.

Chapter 42: Flattery Gets You Everywhere

The offices of Harbottle and MacPhail were, as Rafferty had expected, closed to the public for the weekend, and yet, as Rafferty approached, there was clearly a car parked out the back. When she called Brodie to have the licence plate checked, he read back the name Jonathan MacPhail, the junior named partner. By the looks of the state of his car, MacPhail wasn't the most successful lawyer in town.

It seemed her luck was beginning to turn. Even though it was a Sunday, MacPhail was in his office. Rafferty knocked loudly on the door. When nobody answered she knocked again, and again, and again. Finally, she knocked on the window at the side of the building where the lights were on.

'Mr MacPhail!' Rafferty yelled. 'This is the police. We need to talk to you.'

She continued to yell, attracting curious looks from passers-by. She was willing to scream until she was too hoarse to continue if she had to.

Eventually, a click signalled the opening of the front door, and a disgruntled MacPhail appeared. He was a beady-eyed little man with too little neck and much too large a belly for the crumpled shirt he hastily pulled down to try to cover it.

'I'm trying to work here,' MacPhail said. 'Clear off or I'll call the police.'

Rafferty flashed her ID. 'Mr Jonathan MacPhail, I presume?'

He huffed. 'Guilty as charged, Inspector. Come in before you scare half of Putney away, will you?'

Inside was a clean, empty reception room painted the corporate blue and grey of Harbottle and MacPhail. There was even a fish tank, which Rafferty found mesmerising. She wrenched her attention away from the school of neon tetras looping around a plastic shipwreck and stared down at the vertically-challenged lawyer.

'Well?' MacPhail demanded. 'What do you want?'

'I'm investigating the murder of Guy Rosenberg.'

'Never heard of him, and we don't do murder cases. Or any kind of criminal matters at all.'

Rafferty eyed him coldly. 'I'm not here to instruct you. You had a meeting with a couple, Claudia Sozler and Guy Rosenberg, last week about a property dispute.'

'Can't say if I have. Client confidentiality.'

Rafferty had anticipated the line. 'That wasn't a question, it was a statement. I can get her here in ten minutes,' she bluffed. 'Or we can have a quick chat off the record. Our little secret. That'll be the quickest way for you to get back to work. Five minutes and I'm out of your hair. It'll save me going to get a warrant, and it'll save you hours too.'

He seemed to consider if it were worth his time making her come back. 'Off the record? Hmm. Definitely no Rosenberg. I'd have remembered a name like that. What did you say the other one was? Sozler? That rings a bell. Sozler, Sozler, let's see...'

'It was about a property called Terra Farm.'

'Oh, you mean the lunatic,' MacPhail said. 'She came in for a free initial consult. Bloody freeloaders. But she wasn't with anyone else.'

'You're sure? There wasn't a man with her?'

'100%.' MacPhail walked over to a water fountain in the corner and poured himself a cup. 'Want one?' He pointed.

'No, thank you. So, you met with Claudia. What did you think of her case?'

MacPhail snorted. 'Her case? She was off her rocker, talking about some cult that she thought her boyfriend owned.'

'What if she's not insane?'

His eyes went sideways. 'You mean she really was in a cult? Here? In sleepy old Putney? My, my, that is a turn-up for the books.'

'The cult is real,' Rafferty confirmed. 'The property known as Terra Farm was allegedly willed to the leader of the cult, but I can't find any record of probate.'

'What kind of land is it? Are there any buildings on it?'

'Eight bungalows and a barn.'

That piqued his interest. MacPhail whistled. 'That's an easy five mil right there, so it's well over the threshold for probate. You got a minute?'

'Sure.'

He walked towards a door at the back of the reception, unlocked it, and beckoned Rafferty to follow him. Their destination was the room with the lights, the window of which Rafferty had tapped on. He took a seat behind his desk and flipped up the lid on his laptop.

'Where is this place?'

Rafferty gave the address and then followed up with all the other details while the lawyer made notes. By now, MacPhail was too curious to remember that he'd only promised her five minutes. He scrawled enthusiastically on a yellow notepad, umm-ing and ahh-ing as she spoke.

'Hmm, you're right,' MacPhail mused. 'No sign of probate at all.'

'So, what does that mean?'

'It means that Clementine Rosenberg's estate never lawfully passed to anyone,' MacPhail said. 'And no inheritance tax has been paid to the government.'

'Giacomo di Stregoni doesn't own Terra Farm? At all?'

'Nope,' MacPhail said. 'Let me check something...'

While Rafferty watched, the lawyer beavered away at his laptop. The silence was punctuated by more umms and ahhs, as well as the occasional 'that's interesting'. By the time MacPhail was done researching, he was bouncing on the balls of his feet as if he were Marco Polo arriving in Beijing for the first time.

'Unregistered land! Of course!' he cried. 'That explains it.'

Rafferty looked at him blankly. 'Excuse me?'

'Have you ever bought a house, Inspector?' MacPhail asked. When Rafferty nodded, he continued: 'Then you'll have gone through the process and dealt with the mountain of paperwork that a property transaction entails. It used to be that *everything* was done on paper. The chain of conveyances documents we call a deed proved ownership over time, all recorded in one neat little bundle of paperwork. Then we moved towards a centralised system run by the Land Registry. It was a revolution. By having a public record of who owned what, we did away with all the disputes arising from poor and fraudulent paperwork, and the government began to guarantee who owns what land.'

'So?' Rafferty asked. She had no idea why she was being given a lecture.

'So, Inspector, the property you call Terra Farm wasn't registered at the time that Clementine Rosenberg inherited it. She didn't need to register it, because back then the database didn't yet exist. Now it does, and so the land was registered by Giacomo di Stregoni. See here.' He spun his laptop around to show Rafferty the current record.

'Then he does own Terra Farm,' Rafferty concluded.

'Not necessarily.' MacPhail now had a twinkle in his eye. 'When Giacomo became the alleged owner, he registered the land for the very first time. To do that, he had to fill in a form called an AS1. Though I suppose one might wonder if he could make an adverse possession claim... No.... Of course not... The real owner wasn't excluded... and it's not been probated anyway...'

'Stop waffling, man, and spit it out,' Rafferty said tersely. The clock was ticking, and MacPhail was making no sense whatsoever. Thank God she wasn't paying him by the hour. Or paying him at all.

'Short version, then,' he said. 'If there was no probate, the property didn't legally change hands, and Giacomo di Stregoni must have used fraudulent declarations to take control of the land.'

'Why didn't anyone do something when she died?' Rafferty asked.

'Because,' MacPhail said, his grin now wider than the Cheshire cat's, 'as far as the probate record is concerned, Clementine Rosenberg never died.'

Chapter 43: It's Always the Quiet One

The man who called himself Darren Heggerty was officially a complete mystery. He was the quietest of the suspects, and so Morton knew little about him except that Darren had joined the cult early on.

As Lucy had told him, there had indeed been a boy called Darren Heggerty who matched the name and date of birth supplied by the imposter. The real Darren Heggerty had died in a car accident on the way to school, aged eleven. Presumably, the imposter had adopted the dead boy's name deliberately, as it seemed too unlikely that the combination of the name and date of birth were mere coincidence.

Morton took Mayberry with him to confront Darren. He was alone in his bungalow when they arrived. The front door was wide open. Inside, Darren was splayed out on an old sofa, his nose buried in a battered John le Carré paperback that had seen better days.

'Darren Heggerty?'

Darren held up a hand. 'Just a minute. I've got three pages left.'

For a moment, Morton debated yanking the copy of *The Constant Gardener* from his hand, but that was too savage. Even he would be desperate for the ending. He gave the man ninety seconds to finish.

'Thanks for that,' Darren said. 'What can I do for you, gents?'

'You can come down to the station,' Morton said.

Darren paled. 'Why?'

'Because we know you're not Darren Heggerty. The real Darren Heggerty died in 1974.'

The man calling himself Darren Heggerty glanced around furtively as if he was looking for an escape route. Morton stood between him and the door. He wasn't concerned. Even if Darren managed to get past both him and Mayberry, he would still have to contend with the matter of a perimeter fence, the only way out of which was through a heavily locked gate that was currently manned by uniformed police officers.

Morton had seen so many criminals get hit by a fight-or-flight response, and it often made his job that much easier. Innocent men rarely ran.

Darren, however, was not most criminals. Morton watched as he wrestled to control himself. He slumped over, the veins on his forehead throbbing, evidence of a high pulse rate.

'Am I under arrest, then?' he asked.

Morton was taken aback. He had not expected a cultist to be so matter-of-fact. The only way that Morton could compel Darren's attendance at the station was to arrest him.

He thought quickly, opting to bring Darren in on a lesser charge of giving a false name to the police. 'Yes, you're under arrest for obstructing a police officer in the execution of his duty pursuant to section eighty-nine subsection two of the Police Act nineteen ninety-six.'

Obstruction wasn't necessarily the best charge to stick the man with, but with only a false name to work with, it was enough for now. It only carried a one-month prison sentence or a level three fine. That didn't matter. Morton just needed to take him in, process him, and run his fingerprints and DNA against the police databases. Who was the man calling himself Darren Heggerty? And why had he been hiding out in a cult for decades?

As Morton recited the formal caution, Mayberry pulled Darren to his feet, spun him around, and fastened a pair of stainless-steel cuffs around his wrists.

Just as Darren was about to be dragged out, he made the smartest move available to him, and, just as the others had threatened to do, he lawyered up.

'I want a solicitor, please,' he kept repeating as Morton and Mayberry frogmarched him out of his house and towards Morton's car in full view of the whole Collective.

Chapter 44: That Unforgettable Smell

The jeep was filthy. Clearly, it hadn't been driven in a while. There was a thick layer of dust covering the outside of the car, and, on the bonnet, someone had cheekily scrawled "Clean Me". Ayala watched as Purcell crowbarred the passenger door open. Back and forth he tugged until the door sprang open, spewing dust from the inside in a thick cloud that descended upon them both.

'Thanks for that, Stu,' Ayala muttered before spitting into a nearby bush to get the worst of it off of his lips and teeth.

Purcell grinned. With so much dust in their hair, they looked like pensioners. He burst out laughing.

'Calm down, dear,' Ayala said. 'Pull yourself together. We've got work to do.'

'Right, right. What're we looking for? Just weed?' Purcell asked.

'I can smell it already.' Ayala pinched his nose. The dank smell of marijuana was unforgettable. It reminded him of wandering around Amsterdam Nieuwmarkt, which reeked of the stuff. 'That and anything else the cultists might be hiding off the premises.'

'Looks pretty empty to me,' Purcell said. 'There's no doubt in my mind there was marijuana in here at some point. You think they were dealing?'

'It fits with the hippie vibe,' Ayala said. 'And it would explain how they can afford to live. One yoga instructor can't front living costs for thirteen adults, after all.'

'So, where do you want me to start?' Purcell swept an arm across the car theatrically. 'There are going to be samples everywhere. I could spend months processing it.'

'The boss won't pay for that, and we're in a rush. Let's start with the steering wheel, see who's been driving this old banger.'

Purcell set to work straight away. He opened up an enormous kit bag, donned his facemask, and then pulled out a black powder.

'It's a rough-textured steering wheel, so I'm using this rather than silver aluminium,' he explained as he applied the powder. Before long, whorls of fingerprints began to appear. Purcell got so close that his nose was almost touching the car. He was breathing deeply as he studied each in turn.

'What're you doing?' Ayala asked.

He was paying particular attention to the ten and two positions, where the driver would most likely have gripped the wheel. 'I'm looking for the most complete print. These are all partials.'

'Then what? You get comparator prints from the cultists?'

Purcell backed out of the car, set the prints down, and said: 'Already did. Most of them agreed easily enough. To get the rest, I printed their houses and assumed the most common print belonged to the occupant. Obviously, I'll double-check that if we need to.'

'Nice,' Ayala said. 'As long as it's legal.'

Purcell demurred. 'Kieran's been on my arse about that.'

'Can't believe you let him get away with calling you Doughnut.'

'What am I supposed to do?' Purcell turned his back on Ayala to carry on working.

Ayala looked at him. 'Stand up for yourself, maybe? He's like Morton: totally full of himself. I don't know if he's just obnoxiously unaware or if he's deliberately bullying you. Either way, you've got to tell him.'

'I will,' Purcell promised.

Yeah, right, Ayala thought.

'Nearly done lifting the wheel. Three possible latent prints. I should send the samples back to the lab straight away. I'll do that, but I'll also see if I can do the comparison right now if you'd be so kind as to pass me that camera. Even if it's not legally admissible, it might get the investigation moving again.'

Once the prints had been digitised, Purcell transferred the files to his laptop by Bluetooth and opened up the analysis programme that would compare them to the cultists' fingerprints. The laptop's fans whirred louder and louder as the laptop strained to process the data. Finally, it beeped to indicate a result.

'Bingo, match found.'

'Who?'

'You won't like it.' Purcell turned the screen to Ayala.

The fingerprints belonged to Guy Rosenberg. The dead guy was their mystery driver.

Another dead end.

Literally.

Chapter 45: Class of 1974

While Morton was off waiting for Darren Heggerty's solicitor to arrive, Mayberry had been tasked with finding out more about the dead boy the suspect was impersonating. Naturally, he went straight to Brodie to ask for help. He met the Scot in his spacious office, where Mayberry handed over bacon sandwiches he had brought with him as an apology for ruining Brodie's weekend for a second time.

'No need tae do this, laddie,' Brodie said. He happily squirted oodles of tomato ketchup on his sandwich anyway.

'I w-wanted to.'

'Well, thank ye. Now, what're we looking tae find out?'

'Who o-our s-suspect is, t-the one p-p-pretending to be Darren Heggerty.'

'The dead laddie we looked up?' Brodie said. 'Let's see what we know about 'im.'

The death had occurred so long ago that Brodie could only find a handful of newspaper clippings in the archives. Darren Heggerty had died in a car accident just outside a now-defunct school called Dulwich Prep.

'Small s-school?' Mayberry asked.

'Aye,' Brodie said after a pause to look it up. 'Six boys of his own age in that year. Very posh place for a buncha southern twats, by the looks of it.'

Mayberry wondered how well the imposter had known Darren Heggerty. He knew the dead boy's date of birth, which spoke of familiarity. Had he stumbled across that in a newspaper and then remembered it years later? Or had he simply looked up old death notices in the hope of finding a plausible identity to assume? It seemed an odd bit of trivia for someone unconnected to the real Darren Heggerty.

'C-could our imp-p-poster be one of h-his schoolmates?'

Brodie smiled. 'I like the way ye think, laddie. Let's have a butcher's.'

While Mayberry peered over his shoulder, Brodie looked up each in turn. It was the fourth of the five boys who proved most interesting.

'See here, laddie.' Brodie pointed at the screen where Mayberry could read the name Dominic Winslow. 'This Dominic hasn't been up to much lately. No tax return, no death certificate, no driving licence. Looks like he disappeared off the face of the earth.'

'Any n-news articles?'

After a few more searches, Brodie whistled. He brought up an archive of *The Impartial* newspaper dated for the twenty-second of January, 1988.

Dulwich. A woman's call to her husband cost her dearly when it resulted in her death as well as that of her eleven-year-old son this morning. Angela Heggerty was driving her son to school when her Ford Fiesta careened off the road and into a tree. Angela died on impact.

'She was gone when I found her,' said Corbyn Tewk, the Head of Maths for Dulwich Prep, 'and poor Darren Heggerty didn't last long enough to make it to hospital. It was such a shame. He was a bright young man with an exciting future ahead of him.'

Now the school staff are campaigning against car phones while driving. Prefect Dom Winslow had this to say: 'These phones just aren't safe. They took my best friend away, and you could be next. Don't risk it. Use a landline or talk in person. There isn't anything you need to say that's so urgent it's worth dying for.'

Brodie was pleased with himself. He was beaming when Mayberry tore himself away from the story.

'Dominic Winslow, who are ye? And where the hell have ye gone?' Brodie asked aloud.

Chapter 46: The Big House

It was all hands on deck. While Morton and Mayberry were taking the man calling himself Darren Heggerty to New Scotland Yard to be interviewed, and Ayala was out front searching the jeep with Purcell, Rafferty was left flying solo. She headed off to talk to Kieran O'Connor. They had arranged to meet at his home in Cheyne Walk, a twenty-minute drive across the Battersea Bridge. She had clocked the SW3 postcode as soon as he'd texted her to confirm his address, and yet, when she parked outside, the evidence was incontrovertible. She'd never realised just how wealthy the lawyer was. Surely the Crown Prosecution Service didn't pay this well?

The house was laid out over five floors, including the basement and loft conversion. It was separated from the River Thames by a tiny strip of public garden and the road itself.

A woman answered the door. She was impeccably dressed, with her make-up done up as if she were about to head out to a wedding.

'You must be Ashley,' she said. 'I'm Tara. Kieran's in his office.'

'Where's that?'

'Oh,' Tara said. 'Up the stairs all the way to the top. His door's always open. Do you want me to show you?'

'No, no, I'll find it.'

Rafferty grew more impressed as she ascended. The house was beautiful. There were gilt-framed paintings on the walls, luxurious curtains draped in every window, and tasteful curios and knick-knacks scattered atop antique furniture. How the other half lived!

His door was indeed open. The man himself was sitting at his desk, Mont Blanc pen in hand, scribbling away furiously.

She knocked on the open door. 'Am I interrupting?'

'Come in, come in,' Kieran said as he spun around in his office chair.

The glistening river visible through the window drew Rafferty's eye. She could see right across the Thames. Cadogan Pier lay on the left, and beyond it on the other side of the river, Rafferty had a beautiful view of Battersea Park.

'Grand, isn't it?' Kieran said as she admired the view.

'Very much so. Are you sure you work for the government? Not a hedge fund?'

He laughed. 'Pretty sure. I pretend to work, anyway.'

'So,' she said, pausing before asking the totally irrelevant question she was dying to ask. 'Who's Tara?'

Kieran blushed. He looked happier than Rafferty had ever seen him before.

'My fiancée,' he said.

'*What?*' Rafferty exclaimed. 'When did this happen? I thought you lawyers worked all hours God sends. How did that leave you enough time to date? And, more importantly, how have you kept her a secret? She's gorgeous!'

'Four months ago,' Kieran said. 'It's insane, I know, but this woman is amazing. She's smart, she's kind, she's funny—'

'She's loaded,' Rafferty said.

'Hah, that too. But this is actually my house.'

'Come again?'

'This is my place,' Kieran repeated. 'I inherited it from my grandfather a few months back. He was a politician.'

'Wow! Just... wow!' Rafferty was not-so-quietly impressed.

Kieran had kept his wealth very low-key. She had assumed the dapper suits and silk ties were simply a lawyer thing. She stood there slack-jawed with surprise.

'You know that gormless look doesn't suit you.'

'Oi!' Rafferty raised a hand as if to smack the cheeky lawyer and then thought better of it. 'If I'd known you were this loaded, I'd have said yes when you asked me out last year.'

He laughed awkwardly along with her and then hastily changed the subject. 'What query was so urgent that it was worth interrupting my morning of shopping in Sloane Square for?' He didn't sound sorry at all to be missing the chance to explore the Peter Jones department store for the umpteenth time.

'Our vic, Guy Rosenberg, may have been seeking to reclaim an inheritance. The land that Terra Farm is built on belonged to his late mother. Last week, his girlfriend Claudia visited a local lawyer about that. They thought that because there was no probate of the will, the estate had not been administered, and so Giacomo's registration of the previously unregistered land was invalid. Does that tally with what you know?'

Kieran looked impressed. 'Did you practice that speech? I like it. If you ever fancy joining the dark side and cross-training as a lawyer, let me know. To answer your question: I'm not a land lawyer.'

'But you do know the answer,' Rafferty pressed. 'If it makes any difference, only the cultists knew she'd died, and Guy was a child when it all happened.'

'Hmm,' Kieran said.

'Hmm?'

'Look, I really don't know much about this area of law. It's finicky and technical, and there are all sorts of time limits I might not be cognisant of. But if I had to guess, then I'd say that Giacomo's registration is invalid. He can't inherit without going through probate, and from a cursory search of the relevant databases, that hasn't happened. In the absence of a will, the next of kin, i.e. Guy, ought to have inherited.'

'And what happens now? Who benefits from Guy's death?'

It was a good question. 'Cui bono indeed?' Kieran said.

'This land dispute has to be important,' Rafferty said. 'Conservatively, we're talking about at least five million quid's worth of prime real estate in Putney. That's worth killing for.'

'Before I give you my theory, I'll caveat again that I've done no research, and this isn't my specialism. I think the estate of the mum...'

'Clementine Rosenberg,' Rafferty supplied.

'Right, her estate,' Kieran said. 'It would need to go through probate. Tax would have to be paid given the value of land in Putney, and only then would Guy have inherited. That leaves two possible beneficiaries: firstly, anyone Guy has included in his own will.'

'We haven't seen any sign of a will.'

'Okay, then the second is his next of kin,' Kieran said.

'He had nobody,' Rafferty said. 'What about a partner? Would Claudia inherit?'

Kieran's brain seemed to tick away as he thought. 'No,' he said firmly. 'From what I suspect, she doesn't meet the definition of a dependant, and they weren't married, were they?'

Rafferty didn't think so, but it was entirely plausible they could have undertaken the cult's "binding" ceremony.

'Does a weird ceremony between nutters count?' Rafferty asked.

The answer surprised her. 'It might if they think they were married. That could be enough to create a dependency in law.'

'Now, that is a weird outcome. What about the second possibility?'

'The second possibility is someone who wanted control of the land to stay where it is,' Kieran said. 'Giacomo has the strongest interest there. His own beneficiaries would then benefit in the future. Who would he leave his own estate to?'

'He's got a son, Lorenzo.'

'Then Lorenzo is a natural suspect,' Kieran said. 'And so is anyone who fervently believes in the cult. If they lost the land, it's hard to imagine life continuing as it is on Terra Farm. The Collective would be history.'

Rafferty sighed. 'Then all of them *except* Claudia and Pauline are suspects.'

'I'm afraid so. But there may be one silver lining here.'

'What's that?' Rafferty asked.

'Only the cultists who knew about Guy's visit to a lawyer would have a motive. Find out who knew, and use that to narrow down your suspect pool.'

Chapter 47: Another One Bites the Dust

Darren Heggerty took an age to confer with his lawyer. It was getting on for three o'clock by the time Morton finally got to start interviewing him. If Darren wasn't his man, Morton knew that his ticking clock was almost up, and with it his career.

Morton shuffled his notes nonchalantly as he took a seat opposite the suspect and his lawyer, which infuriated both of them. 'Thank you for coming in, Mr Heggerty. Or is it Mr Winslow?'

The silence was as deafening as it was damning. Until that moment, Morton had wondered if they were clutching at straws. Now he knew that Brodie and Mayberry's research had been right. One boy died, another disappeared, and then, miraculously, the dead boy reappeared. It was the miracle he'd been praying for all weekend.

'Don't look so surprised. We know everything.'

Normally, when confronted with their past, suspects would either deny everything or clam up and refuse to speak at all. The number of times that Morton had seen a suspect repeat 'no comment' for hours on end was unreal. But Winslow didn't do that.

Instead, he *smiled*.

'What's so amusing, Mr Winslow?'

'It's over,' Winslow said. 'It's really over.'

'It is indeed,' Morton said. His stomach turned queasy. It was never this easy. 'You tell me how you killed Guy Rosenberg, and I'll personally talk to the prosecutor about a sentencing recommendation in light of an early guilty plea,' he promised.

The smile vanished.

'I didn't kill Guy,' Winslow said. He looked in bewilderment at his lawyer.

And there it is, Morton thought. *The blanket denial.*

'Oh, really?'

'Really.'

Morton's gut turned over again. It wasn't the butter-wouldn't-melt expression on Winslow's face that irritated him. It was the fact that Morton believed him.

'Then why is it "all over"?'

His lawyer leapt in. 'I think I need to consult with my client.'

Again? Morton thought. He glanced at his watch. He couldn't afford to lose much more time if Darren wasn't the killer.

'If you didn't kill Guy Rosenberg, we'd be willing to consider a plea deal.'

Winslow waved off the offer. 'I don't deserve one.'

'Mr Winslow,' the solicitor said, 'I would advise that you listen to the police offer and–'

'I said I don't deserve one,' Winslow repeated. 'Not after what I did.'

'What did you do?' Morton asked.

Again, the lawyer tried to drag Winslow out, but Winslow went on. 'No, I've been under Lorenzo's thumb for long enough. This is better than I deserve. Here's the deal that I want: I tell you everything I know, everything I did, and you throw the book at both of us. I'm going down, and I want to take that bastard with me.'

It was an easy offer to agree to. Lucy Reed's assertion that the man in front of him was a killer rang in Morton's mind, but if Winslow hadn't killed Guy, whom had he murdered? 'Okay, start talking. Who did you kill?'

'Joanna Winslow,' he said. 'My wife.'

'How did you kill her?'

'She slipped,' Winslow said. 'We were arguing in the hallway. She was scratching at me, screaming insults. I raised my arms to fend her off, not trying to hurt her at all, and we wrestled. I must have pushed her away, because the next thing I knew, she was stumbling. I saw it in slow motion. She toppled backwards, all the way down the stairs. Her body made a horrible cracking sound as she bounced to the bottom, and when I managed to pull myself together enough to run down after her, she was dead.'

There were tears in Winslow's eyes. Morton's gut said he was telling the truth. It sounded like an accident.

'Why were you arguing?'

Winslow looked away. When he turned back, he asked: 'Do I... have to tell you?'

'Nope,' Morton said gently. 'But if there's a good reason, it might help your case and your conscience. Do you want to take some more time to talk to your lawyer again?'

'No, no, I've told you this much,' Winslow said. 'It feels good to get this all off my chest, if truth be told. I've been carrying this with me for so long.'

His voice was turning hoarse, so Morton poured him a glass of water.

'Take your time, Mr Winslow.' *Just not too much,* Morton thought. He still had to catch Guy Rosenberg's killer.

'She got depressed. We were trying for a child, and it didn't happen.'

'Infertility?' Morton asked.

Winslow shook his head. 'Miscarriages. Her family had a history of them. She was frustrated, angry, justifiably so.'

'She took it out on you?'

'At first, it was verbal. She'd berate me, belittle me, and insinuate I wasn't enough of a man for her.'

'Did it escalate?'

Winslow nodded. 'She started to make the comments in front of other people. She told her friends I was firing blanks, that I couldn't get it up, even that I'd had a vasectomy. I hadn't. It was different stories every week.'

It sounded like emotional abuse to Morton.

'She told me to "man up" whenever I protested. Before long she was slapping, scratching, and eventually biting me. Whatever I did was wrong, and she punished me for it. Over and over, she'd hit me while telling me that I wasn't good enough, that I was unworthy of her, that I couldn't give her the baby she so desperately craved. I felt like a failure. I hated it.'

Emotional *and* physical abuse. 'What did you do?'

'Nothing at first. I let the resentment build. I had no one to talk to. She had long since cut off all my friends, and I have no family left, so she was my entire existence. On some days she was the most wonderful woman I had ever met. On others it was hell. The continued push-pull broke me. I wasn't strong enough to handle it. When she flipped out on the day she died and started clawing at me, I pushed her away. I didn't mean to kill her. I just wanted her to stop yelling, to stop hurting me.'

It still sounded like an accident. Morton would never be able to make a murder case out on these facts, and he wasn't sure he wanted to. Even manslaughter seemed like a stretch.

'What did you do after she died? How did you end up at the cult?'

Winslow dabbed at his eyes again. 'I told the policeman who came to take my story. He said he didn't believe me, that no man would ever be so pathetic. He insinuated that I had killed her deliberately, that nobody could fall backwards like that by accident.'

'So you ran,' Morton concluded.

'To my shame, I did.'

'Where did you go?'

'I got all my money out of the bank. It wasn't much, and then I took everything valuable that I could carry, and I fled for central London. I had heard about the squats in the West End from the news. Lots of landlords were moaning that their second homes were being broken into by groups of organised squatters. I asked around the homeless folks, and I found them easily enough. I moved from squat to squat, begging for money to get by. Eventually, I fell in with Giacomo's lot. They seemed better than the drug-addled fools I'd met on the streets. They were kind and they fed me. They made me feel like I belonged. When they asked who I was, I panicked and said the first name that came into my mind, Darren Heggerty. And that was it. I was stuck living a lie.'

Morton remembered what he'd learned about the cult's beginnings. The group had started as hippie counterculture. It wasn't hard to see a man on the run, a man with nothing to live for, falling in with such a group.

'And you stayed because Giacomo found you out.'

'Not at first. I stayed because I liked it. Giacomo was a good man once. Eventually, I confided in him. He told me to tell nobody, that they wouldn't look at me the same way ever again. No smoke without fire, he said. I'd have left when Lorenzo took over...'

'But he blackmailed you?'

Winslow hung his head. 'Yes.'

'So you stayed, you did his bidding, and you kept quiet.'

'And every day, it's torn me up inside.'

Morton reached over to the tape recorder and hit pause. 'I don't blame you. Mr Winslow, you were the victim of abuse. You're not a murderer.'

A glimmer of hope shone in Winslow's eyes. 'I'm not a good person, Mr Morton,' he said. 'I've done bad things for the Collective.'

'Then now's the time to redeem yourself. I'm going to turn the tape back on and you're going to tell me everything, okay?'

He did so.

'Mr Winslow, what did Lorenzo di Stregoni ask you to do?'

'He had me become his eyes and ears in the cult as well as his enforcer. Whatever I saw or heard, I reported back to him. Then there was the dodgy stuff.'

'Okay. Like what?'

'He had us selling marijuana.'

'How did that work?'

'We asked the non-dwellers to prove their loyalty to the Collective. It was easy. They were so desperate to get in that they'd do anything. God knows where Lorenzo found 'em, but he did.'

'You grew it?'

'For a while. Marijuana was always part of the Collective. We were hippies, after all. Lorenzo escalated it all to an industrial scale. Eventually, he decided it was too risky to grow it ourselves, so he found a supplier elsewhere and we became middlemen. Guy drove the parcels out, the non-dwellers sold it and passed us back the money.'

Dealing by proxy. It was clever; Morton had to give Lorenzo that. He found patsies willing to sell weed for him and took all of the profits. Promising them promotion in the cult was cheaper than paying them.

'What was it you did in all this?'

'I... I was the hired muscle. I went out and collected the money.'

'Did anyone ever try to stiff you?'

Winslow glanced at his lawyer, an obvious tell. 'Occasionally.'

'And you collected.'

'I did.'

Morton left it there. If Winslow was acting under duress, the Crown Prosecution Service wouldn't prosecute, and it was clear that Dominic Winslow would be a key witness for the prosecution when the time came to take down the Collective.

'Anything else?'

Winslow exhaled deeply, clearly relieved that Morton hadn't pressed him further. 'Nothing that bad.'

'But there is something.'

'I didn't have anything to do with it.'

'Then you won't mind telling me.'

'Lorenzo used the women to recruit men. He called it flirty-fishing. Send a gorgeous woman out to seduce a lonely man, and then manipulate them both to do his bidding. Lorenzo still uses the technique. It's how Abigail entrapped Stephen.'

Morton stared. Without skipping a beat, he paused the tape recorder. '*You what?*'

'I said that's how Stephen joined the cult. Lorenzo sent Abigail out to find more men, and Stephen was the lucky man. Apparently, she found him giving a speech at Speaker's Corner in Hyde Park about environmental issues, and she knew he was an easy mark. She listened, complimented him and agreed with his ideas, and seduced him. When Lorenzo learned that his father was, well, you, he was apoplectic at first. He soon came around to the idea that having a policeman's son in the fold could be... useful.'

Morton's hands began to tremble with rage. He restarted the tape.

'Interview terminated at... 15:38.'

Without another word, Morton stormed out. As he shut the door behind him, he could hear Winslow's lawyer yelling questions in his wake, demanding his client be charged or freed. Morton didn't care about that right now.

What he wanted to know was what the hell that bastard Lorenzo had done to his son.

Chapter 48: The Joiner

It took all of Sarah Morton's persuasive skills to get her husband off the phone and back to work. Of course she knew what flirty fishing was. He'd agreed to let her handle Stephen, though knowing David, he wouldn't sit idly by on his hands while she took the time to figure out exactly how deep in their son was.

She called Stephen into the living room.

'What is it, Ma?' he asked. 'Is Dad finally letting Abigail go?'

'Sit down, please.'

'Uh-oh,' he said as took the armchair. 'That's your "you boys have misbehaved" voice. I haven't heard that in years. What did I do?'

'You told me yesterday that the Collective are good people.'

'They are.'

She paused. This was like convincing someone that they'd been scammed. The trouble was, nobody ever thought they were stupid enough to fall for it, so they often doubled down.

'Do you think that... Well, is it possible that they're not who you think they are?'

'I know them, Ma. Better than I know you.'

Sarah felt her temper rise. She pushed the anger back down. She arched a quizzical eyebrow at him.

'Sorry, Ma. I didn't mean it like that. I trust them as much as I trust you. Better?'

It was too late. The Freudian slip was out of the bag.

'You ungrateful git,' Sarah said, glaring daggers at him. 'Can't you see what you've dropped your father in the middle of? That he's risking everything to keep you out of jail?'

'If he thinks I deserve to be in jail, he should arrest me,' Stephen said evenly. 'And if he doesn't, he shouldn't have any trouble handing the investigation off to someone else. I didn't ask for any favours, and I don't want any.'

He was so naïve. No wonder Abigail had been able to lure him into the Collective so easily. 'The police don't always get it right. You think those cultists wouldn't stitch you up in a heartbeat? You'd be such an easy fall guy.'

'They're not cultists, and they'd never do that to me. They're my family.'

'*We're* your family. Even when you forget it. Even when you don't invite your brother to your wedding.'

'I did invite Nick,' Stephen said. 'And he said what you said, except he'd have "nothing to do with those lunatics". See why I don't come to you? None of you trust me. You think I'm an idiot who would fall for anything. Well, I'm not, and, for the first time in my life, I'm happy. Can't you just be happy for me?'

'You know Abigail tricked you, don't you?' Sarah said.

His smirk faltered. 'She wouldn't.'

'She did.' Sarah slid across the coffee table one of her psychology textbooks. 'Open it to the bookmark and read.'

The chapter that she'd marked was on flirty fishing. It described how cults used young, attractive women to lure in men. As Stephen read, his face fell. By the end of the chapter, he was crestfallen. He was on the verge of crying when he looked up. Now he knew. Her anger dissipated, and she found herself standing up. She swooped in, wrapping him tightly in a proper bear hug, the kind he'd loved as a boy.

'Fuck!' He jerked backwards, roughly shoving her away as if he were in immense pain.

'What on earth is going on?'

'Nothing.'

'Like hell is that reaction nothing. Stand up and turn around. I felt something on your back.'

'But Mum, I...'

'Now, Stephen.'

He slowly turned, and then, button by button, he began to take off his shirt. Stephen looked at her imploringly one more time as if to beg her to leave it well alone. She wasn't buying it.

'Off.'

The moment the shirt slipped off his shoulders, Sarah swore too. Where normally Stephen's skin was covered in a light downing of fuzzy hair just like his father's, instead there were ugly, red welts that covered his entire back.

'Stephen,' she whispered softly. 'How on earth did this happen? Who did this?'

'It's not what it looks like, Ma.'

Chapter 49: The Grave

The search for the details of Clementine Rosenberg's life and death had yielded sod-all. As far as governmental records went, she may as well never have existed. What little they did know was that Clementine had never legally married and that, before she owned it, the land in Putney had once belonged to her partner Cecil, who, unlike her, had left behind a valid last will and testament. Back then it was just farmland with one bungalow, presumably the larger ornate one now occupied by Giacomo, and the barn.

It confirmed Kieran's theory. Her death had never been officially processed, and so Guy ought to have inherited Terra Farm upon her death. What they didn't know was exactly when she died, where she died, and whether there had ever been a will and testament.

Rafferty figured the place to start was with the older women, those who'd been in the Collective the longest. That meant revisiting Tracey and Marta. As seemed to be their custom, they were sitting on opposite sofas in the living room reading, totally ignoring each other, each pretending they were lost in their respective books. Rafferty was buying none of it. She'd seen the two women bickering through the bay window.

Marta looked up as she entered. 'Miss Rafferty,' she drawled. 'How lovely to see you again. Do come in and grab a seat.'

'We heard you found that traitor, Claudia,' Tracey said.

News travelled fast. Rafferty's expression must have given away her anger that such sensitive information had leaked.

'Pauline told you?' Rafferty asked.

'Nah, we heard that dumpy ginger bloke telling one of his team. Don't think he realises how far voices carry around here.'

Purcell. Rafferty resolved to take it up with him the moment the investigation was over.

'I've got no comment about any of that,' Rafferty said.

'Naturally,' Tracey said. 'So, what can we do for you?'

Rafferty looked across the room to meet Marta's eye. 'Guy was suing to get control of Terra Farm. Did you know?'

Marta twitched uncomfortably. 'No,' she said unconvincingly.

'Hmm,' Rafferty said. 'Do you and Guy have any other family?'

'No, it was just us,' Marta said. 'He was my whole world.'

'Right. So, you're his next of kin. Doesn't that mean that, if Guy was right, Terra Farm ought to be yours now?'

Another twitch. 'Nonsense. It belongs to Giacomo. My sister saw to that.'

'Your dead sister. Why isn't there a record of her death?'

This time Marta shared a glance with Tracey. 'What's it got to do with records? She's definitely dead.'

'Can you prove that?' Rafferty asked, thinking there might be a death certificate lying around Terra Farm after all.

'Absolutely,' Marta said with iron-clad certainty in her voice. 'You're standing almost on top of her.'

Rafferty recoiled. 'You mean...?'

'She's buried in front of this very house – right under the rosebush out front.'

Chapter 50: Flirty Fishing

The cells were deathly quiet when Morton arrived. The women's wing was rarely busy, and tonight was no exception. He navigated on autopilot, his brain still trying to catch up with exactly what had happened this weekend. Three days felt like a lifetime ago, when things were simple and his career and his son's liberty didn't hang in the balance. The worries of letting a new person into the family, virtually unknown to them still, now seemed minor in comparison to the stress of the weekend. Even the idea of reconciling with his son seemed easy. Stephen might be an oddball, even angry at times, but he was still a Morton.

And now, like it or not, so too would Abigail be if the pair of them ever made it to a registry office.

He found her in the cell at the end of the corridor, just as the custody sergeant had said he would. He opened the door and let himself in.

'Before you ask for a lawyer again, I need you to hear me out,' Morton said, closing the door. 'Just listen. Then, if you want a lawyer, I'll call Perkins back and we can have a repeat performance.'

His plea was met with a slow nod.

'The truth is, I don't know whether I should hate you or pity you,' he said, all the thoughts he'd had on the drive over bubbling to the surface. 'Probably both. I know you're a victim in all this too. Nobody deserves to be treated the way Lorenzo has treated you. But I'm God-damned *livid* with you. You dragged my eldest son into the Collective. He's foolish enough to believe that you love him.'

'I do love Stephen,' she croaked. Crocodile tears were forming in the corners of her eyes.

'Yeah, right. I know that Lorenzo ordered you to go and find a man – any man stupid enough or naïve enough to fall for your lies– to ensnare and entrap. What did he promise you? Higher priority? Money? It worked like a charm, didn't it? Stephen's always felt that he didn't quite belong anywhere, and you preyed on that. You offered him validation, a home with what he thought were like-minded souls. And then you betrayed him.'

'I didn't!'

'Liar,' Morton spat. He opened up the photo that Sarah had just sent him. It showed Stephen's back raw, bloody, and blistered. The "C" of the Collective was visible among the carnage.

'He *chose* to do that,' Abigail said. 'I told him not to.'

It wasn't the answer Morton had expected. He thought she'd deny it. 'He wanted this?'

'It's like you said. He wanted to belong. So did I.'

'And you thought you'd get there by deceiving him? By becoming whatever you thought he wanted? By luring him to join the Collective? You just did whatever Lorenzo wanted, whenever he wanted it. Stephen deserves better than that. He deserves better than *you*. You know I have to tell him.'

The crocodile tears rapidly became a flood, reducing Abigail to a sobbing mess. Between cries, she said: 'Please don't tell him. I'm so, so sorry. It might have started out as a trick, but I really do love him. If you tell him, you'll destroy him.'

There was no doubt that Abigail was a master manipulator. In one sentence she had appealed to his emotions, his love for his son, and in the same breath implied that it would be his responsibility if Stephen's heart was broken. She had somehow spun the whole thing on its head so that Morton would be responsible for her actions.

'Nonsense,' Morton said firmly. 'If any harm has been done, it was done by you a long time ago. You started your relationship with my son on a foundation of mistrust and deceit. Do you honestly think you can make my son happy after that?'

He watched as the cogs turned. She seemed to be trying to rationalise what she had done.

'I did trick him,' Abigail said finally. 'Because I had no choice. I just did what I was told. Without question. Without delay. But I do love him. I didn't think I would. I thought...'

'You thought what?'

'I thought nobody could ever love me. If I hadn't found Stephen, Lorenzo would have made me enter into a binding with Guy Rosenberg.'

The phraseology tripped Morton for a moment, and then he realised that the threat of having to marry Guy might have spurred her actions. It also explained why she'd want to kill him.

'It was an arranged relationship?' Morton asked. He pulled his trusty notepad from his pocket and began to scribble notes as they talked.

She bit her lip and then nodded. 'Yes. Lorenzo told me that I had a choice: marry the only single man in the cult vaguely my age or find someone else. I chose the latter.'

'Why?' Morton asked. 'What was so bad about Guy?'

'I didn't love him. And he loved Claudia. Lorenzo only wanted me to marry Guy to make him miserable. He loved to play puppet master, to keep us all wrong-footed all the time. The idea that we could be happy without his say-so undermined his authority.'

'You were happy?'

'Yes,' Abigail said. 'Stephen makes me happy. He's different. He's *kind*. He actually cares about *me*, not just the Collective. Okay, I didn't love him when I met him, but I knew I could grow to love him, if that makes sense, and I did. I do love Stephen. I'm sorry for what I've done, Mr Morton, but I'm not sorry that I fell in love with your son.'

Morton shifted uncomfortably. There was a ring of truth to her protestations. 'Then why did you lawyer up?'

'It's what Lorenzo told us all to do when we were in the barn. Say nothing, ask for a solicitor.'

'But you're talking to me now,' Morton said.

'My secret's out, Mr Morton. I have nothing left to hide.'

'Then tell me straight. Who do you think killed Guy Rosenberg?'

'Lorenzo. Nobody takes a shit without his say-so.'

'Okay. Why?'

'Control. He fears losing it. Lana and I overheard Claudia and Guy talking. The two of them had found a lawyer. They wanted to take back the family farm. They said that they could prove it was rightfully Guy's. Don't ask me how, though.'

Morton felt his jaw drop. She knew about Guy's claim to the farm too?

'Lana would have run straight to Lorenzo,' she continued. 'He wouldn't have let it stand.'

It all came around full circle. If Lorenzo knew that the Collective was about to lose the land, he had every reason to kill Guy as well as every opportunity. He could have used any of his faithful to do it. He could be responsible for the smothering, the poisoning, the shooting, or any combination of them. Or he could be a thoroughly dislikeable waste of space human being who happened to be innocent this time.

It changed nothing. Morton could prove no more than he could at the start of his conversation with Abigail. The thing that kept niggling at him was the timing. Why would Lorenzo have killed Guy on that night in particular? If he'd waited just one more day, Guy's disappearance would have been unnoticed by the outside world. Was Abigail still playing him? Was this all a con? Was she pointing the finger to distract from a murder she had in fact committed herself?

She looked at him earnestly. 'Will you let me out now?'

'No,' Morton said simply, resisting the urge to justify his decision. He could have said that the holding cell was the safest place for her. That was true. He could have said he still didn't trust her. That was true too. More pragmatically, release paperwork took time, and he had little of that left to waste.

What he needed was solid, concrete proof.

And he might have to deal with the devil again to get it.

Chapter 51: The Ask

The drive back to Putney flew by despite the heavy traffic. Morton's mind kept wandering. If the land was due to go to Guy, who would benefit most from his death? The obvious answer was Giacomo, who would otherwise appear to be the lawful owner, but his Alzheimer's precluded him from being a serious suspect. The man couldn't plan breakfast, let alone murder served three ways.

As Abigail had suggested, Lorenzo was the next obvious suspect. If Lana really had overheard Guy and Claudia talking, then surely she'd told him everything. While Morton had already cleared him of the shooting, it was still very possible that Lorenzo was behind the poisoning or the smothering of Guy.

Perhaps the most frustrating thing of all was that Morton had already caught a killer this weekend. It just wasn't the killer he was looking for, and not one, Morton thought, who ought to be jailed for his actions.

It was late afternoon by the time that Morton returned to the incident room in Stephen and Abigail's bungalow. For now, he was keeping his silence about Abigail's transgressions. It wasn't wholly altruistic; his relationship with his son was on tenterhooks at best, and if Abigail denied the facts then it could split the family in two. Sometimes it was best to let sleeping dogs lie.

No sooner had he shut the door behind him, slung his jacket on the coat hook in the hallway, and put the kettle on, than there was a near-silent knock at the front door. Lucy Reed was waiting there, just as he'd requested.

He ushered her in.

'I trust my information proved accurate,' Lucy said. She had a duplicitous smile that showed off far too many teeth.

'Worthless, you mean,' Morton said bitterly.

'Not at all,' Lucy said in an infuriatingly matter-of-fact tone. 'I promised you I'd hand-deliver you *a* killer. I didn't say anything about them necessarily being Guy Rosenberg's killer.' She smiled at him sweetly. 'And before you ask, no, I won't share my source. Journalist's prerogative.'

'You're not here to taunt me. You're here because you still want something and I still need something. What is it?'

She smiled. 'Straight to business, Mr Morton? I can give you information pertinent to Guy Rosenberg's murder.'

Morton regarded her warily. 'And what will it cost me this time?'

'Everything,' Lucy said. 'I want all the crime scene photos, I want the pathology report, quotes from your team – exclusive, naturally – and I want to be kept abreast of every development so when you're ready to arrest the killer, I can get the money-shot picture for the front page.'

A belly laugh erupted from Morton. It was a preposterous request.

'Or,' Lucy said, 'I can end your career here and now with one quick phone call to your boss. At best, you get fired on the spot, and at worst, you get arrested.'

Yet again, Morton felt his temper boil. He was tempted to simply arrest her for attempted blackmail, see out the final few hours of this botched investigation, and fall on his sword when the truth came out. As long as he cleared his family name, he didn't care about his career.

Before that, he still had the obvious counter-threat to repeat. 'Or I can arrest you for assisting the murderer after the fact, obstructing my investigation by giving me a fake name, and then ensure you get deported as soon as you've served your time. In the more immediate future, I can also throw you in jail long enough to ensure that someone else scoops your investigation, and you lose your one big shot at a Pulitzer.'

It was the last threat that did it.

'Meet me in the middle,' Lucy said. 'Exclusive quotes, all the documents that are about to become public knowledge two hours before anyone else, and a heads-up before the arrest so I can make sure I have a camera. Nothing illegal, just a good deal all around. Naturally, you'll bring no criminal charges against me either. In return, I'll shape the public narrative however you want so that your boss never learns of your duplicity. You have my word on that, and you know you can always arrest me if I renege on the deal. It's mutually assured destruction. Go down in flames with me, or we can both walk away with what we want most in the world: justice for you and a juicy by-line for me.'

Morton paused. If it wasn't illegal, and it might get him out of this.

'Deal,' he said. 'So long as you can prove what you tell me.'

She smiled like the cat that had got the cream. 'I can, but it's going to take a little legwork on your part.'

'Keep talking.'

There was a pause, as if she were about to reveal a huge secret. 'This farm belonged to Guy's mom.'

'We know that,' Morton said matter-of-factly. Lucy didn't need to know just how recently he had come by this information.

Lucy looked crestfallen, and then suddenly perked up. 'But did you know Guy was going to try to take back the farm?'

'We did,' Morton said again.

A vein in Lucy's temple began to throb. She looked as if she were fishing in the deepest recesses of her mind for any titbit that she could sell. 'Do you know about the will?'

'What will?'

She had him, and she knew it. 'The last will and testament of Clementine Rosenberg.'

'Do you have it?'

'No, but I know where it is,' Lucy said. 'If I tell you where you can find it, will that suffice for our deal, Mr Morton?'

She definitely had him. Without the will, Morton would find it hard to break the case. If it was a forgery, then handwriting analysis on the signature could break the case. Whoever had forged the will in the first place surely had the strongest motive to prevent the forgery from coming to light. A small voice at the back of Morton's mind warned him that the forger could well be Giacomo himself, in which case the evidential value of the will would be minimal as it was clear that Giacomo was physically and mentally incapable of any of the three murder attempts.

He nodded at Lucy. The deal was on.

'It's in a false bottom inside the lowest drawer by Giacomo's bed.'

How had Purcell missed that? Even with a whole farm to search, it was a massive mistake.

'Who knows about this?' Morton asked. He hoped against hope that Lucy had somehow found out from Claudia or Lana.

'Dori and Marta, at least,' Lucy said. 'I eavesdropped on them on the night of the binding, when they had drunk too much and were arguing about it on the veranda.'

The journalist certainly had a talent for sneaking around to listen in when she wasn't welcome. 'What specifically were they arguing about?'

'Whether to destroy the will,' Lucy said. 'They were worried about Guy's drunken ramblings that the farm was his. Claudia put the idea in his head. Before she was on the scene, he had no such notions.'

And if it wasn't forged, Morton wondered, why would the elderly women in the cult be so keen to see it destroyed shortly after Guy's death? Could they be acting "without question or delay" on the orders of someone above them in the pecking order? Once again, it came around full circle, right back to the big man himself. Of course they would have done whatever Lorenzo ordered.

Then again, there was no proof that he even knew about the dispute. Could they have taken matters into their own hands? Probably. Would they have? Morton doubted it.

No matter which way Morton spun it, he couldn't get away from the fact that Guy's big secret had become common knowledge. The younger women knew. The older women knew. Was there anyone in the Collective who *didn't* know about Guy's claim?

Chapter 52: Unfinished Business

There wasn't a ground-penetrating radar available when Rafferty called to request one. It was a specialist bit of kit, and there was scant call for one most of the time. She tried a few university archaeology departments, but, surprise, surprise, nobody was around to take her call as it was a Sunday. Eventually, she had the idea to look through the news to see if any neighbouring forces had used one lately. Three phone calls, much cajoling, and the promise of a free dinner later, the kit was on its way from Kent Police.

'Sh-sh-should we be doing this?' Mayberry asked.

'If Morton can flout the rules and regs, then I sure as hell don't care about a few dead roses. Dig 'em up! We can't run the radar over it until you do, and the techs are waiting.'

'On y-y-your h-head be it.'

While she waited with an impatient scowl, Mayberry began to hack away at Marta's roses. Rafferty wasn't convinced that it was entirely legal without some sort of warrant, but it was always easier to ask for forgiveness than permission.

Less than two hours after the fateful proclamation that Clementine had never left, the bushes were all gone, and two bored-looking, yet in Rafferty's mind kind of cute, techs appeared at the gate with their ground-penetrating radar. Thankfully, it was just about small enough to make it down the winding gravel path without having to take out the gate. Once it had been put where the rose bush once was, it took them mere minutes to confirm that there was a cavity in the earth about six feet down, just about big enough to hide a petite body. It looked like Marta was telling the truth: they had buried Clementine there.

Digging a hole to confirm that would take a few more hours, and a DNA test to confirm a familial match a few days after that, but it wasn't a priority for the case. Despite Rafferty's protestations that Clementine was just as important as her son, there was not yet any hint of foul play, and the clock was ticking faster and faster as Morton attempted to solve Guy Rosenberg's murder before his career became the killer's next victim.

While it wasn't Morton's top priority, Clementine Rosenberg deserved a proper burial in a proper grave once this was all over. What was pertinent was that Clementine's death had clearly never gone through proper channels. Thus, her assets had never been lawfully distributed, and the true ownership of Terra Farm, therefore, remained with her estate.

Proving Clementine was dead would be the first step to establishing who now owned Terra Farm. Without a body or a death certificate, she was essentially stuck like Lord Lucan: missing, presumed dead. It took seven years for a missing person to be considered legally dead, and Giacomo had tried to register the land before that time had elapsed.

Without a valid will, Guy ought to have inherited as her next of kin, so whoever had doctored and disposed of the will was their prime suspect.

More technicalities. Rafferty debated texting Kieran O'Connor yet again and then thought better of it. For now, her immediate task was to prove or disprove Marta's claim that her sister was buried under the roses. That meant exhuming the corpse. Time to get digging.

· · · ·

AYALA WAS KEEPING A low profile. With Morton off talking to the journalist and Rafferty borrowing Mayberry, he was alone and at a loose end. He had no direct orders, and so he found himself ambling around Terra Farm to people-watch. Truthfully, Ayala didn't want to be on the case at all. It was one thing for Morton to risk his own career, but the boss's recklessness had put all their careers on the line.

Every now and again, he thumbed through his contact list until he found S for Silverman. One phone call dobbing the boss in, and Ayala would be seen as the honest team member rather than Morton's accomplice.

He looked around. By now he was out of sight of the Collective and, he hoped, well out of earshot too. A twinge of guilt hit him as he hit the call button. Silverman's number went to voicemail.

'Good evening, ma'am. This is Detective Inspector Bertram Ayala. I'm terribly sorry to disturb you at this late hour. Could you return my call at your earliest convenience, please?'

Even if she never called him back, Ayala now had plausible deniability. With a bit of finesse, he could play both sides right up until the nine o'clock Monday morning deadline. If Morton succeeded, he'd think of a lie to explain his call attempt. If Morton failed, then Ayala would be right there waiting to take his place. Rafferty had had her chance at leadership, and Morton was long overdue for retirement. No matter how this ended, Ayala needed to make sure this was his time to step into the spotlight.

Chapter 53: Where There's a Will, There's a Way

Morton knew he really had to cover his backside, so he heeded Kieran's advice and procured a search warrant before heading over to Giacomo's bungalow. The remaining time to solve the murder was melting faster than a Mr Whippy ice cream on a hot summer day. The moment he had the green light, Morton dashed into the largest bungalow in search of the will.

Giacomo was snoring loudly when Morton opened the door to the master bedroom. In the armchair on the other side of the bed, Doreen the nursemaid was sleeping soundly too, at least until the creak of a wooden floorboard startled her. She bolted upright, her hands flailing around manically as if she were searching for something.

'Mr Morton!' she cried. 'Don't you knock?'

As she stood, Morton quickly closed the distance between them and then regarded her coolly. Without saying a word, he thrust a copy of the search warrant into her hands.

She squinted at it and then waved her hands in the air. 'It's no use without my reading glasses! What is this rubbish?'

'This is a search warrant authorising me to search Terra Farm for a copy of the last will and testament of Clementine Rosenberg. I have reason to believe it's here in this room.'

Dori nodded. 'Of course, it's right over there. Giacomo keeps all his documents in that bedside unit there.'

With one gnarled finger, she pointed to the bedside unit. 'Try the bottom drawer,' she continued. 'Giacomo made it himself.'

Gobsmacked at how easy it was, Morton opened the drawer. Aside from a few worthless knick-knacks, and a couple of dead batteries, it was empty.

'Just throw that junk on the floor,' Dori said. 'I'll pick it up later. You'll want to pull the whole drawer out and flip it upside down to take the bottom out. He likes to keep things flat, you see.'

'Not hidden, then?' Morton asked drily.

She flitted around him. If she weren't being so helpful, Morton would have ordered her to leave the room. 'Oh, no, we don't have any secrets here in the Collective. He put the false bottom in to keep the documents away from the children, but they're all grown up now.'

The will wasn't a secret at all? Morton quickly tossed aside the knick-knacks and did as Dori had instructed. He flipped the drawer upside down and tapped lightly to loosen the false bottom. It fell out easily and hit the carpeted floor with a soft thud. Morton set the drawer back down facing up and looked inside expectantly. There were dozens of pieces of paper inside. He flipped through a few. Bills. Nope. A birth certificate for Lorenzo. Interesting. Giacomo's academic credentials as a psychiatrist. Also of interest.

But no will.

'Where's the will?' Morton demanded.

She gave half a shrug. 'If it's not in there, then I don't know. Nobody *ever* goes in there. You can see that from the dust.'

Morton wiped a finger across the bottom of the drawer. While there was a light smattering of dust, it wasn't months or years of build-up. Someone had been in there very recently, and presumably, they had taken the will. Why? And if they'd taken it long enough ago that dust had begun to build up again, that spoke to planning and premeditation. And yet, despite that, they'd killed Guy on the one day that a policeman was on-site.

'Who can come in here, Dori?'

Another shrug. 'Anyone, I guess. It's not like we lock the doors. I'm in here most of the time with Giacomo. When I'm out and about, and he's in his wheelchair, anyone could wander in. We don't have any secrets in the Collective.'

Morton rolled his eyes. The cultists had more secrets than they had sane members.

'If I search your bedroom, will I find it there?' Morton asked, testing the old woman.

'Heavens, no, Detective Chief Inspector!' she said. 'I've no business touching Gia's stuff. He might have ascended beyond the need for physical belongings, but I'm not going to touch anything unless I'm ordered to.'

Morton eyed Giacomo carefully. 'From what I hear, the boss wanted rid of Guy.' It was one of the titbits he'd extracted from Lucy, that the old man kept muttering, 'He has to go, he has to go.'

She paled. 'Whatever he says, it's not relevant to this plane of existence. I always think he means that someone is going to ascend. Lorenzo said that priority zeros become part of the collective consciousness. Maybe he's even talking about his own ascension in the third person.' She moved to position herself between Morton and Giacomo as if she were scared that Morton might try to arrest the demented man at any moment.

'Why did he say it, then?'

'I don't know, sir. He says lots of things.... Wait, how did you know about that?'

Morton gave her a thin-lipped smile as if to affirm that he would ask the questions.

'Please, sir, don't take him away from me. He's all I've got.' Her tone was pitiful. The woman standing before Morton was clearly besotted with Giacomo. She had spent her life following him and had become his nurse when he needed one. It was obvious she would do anything for him, though Morton doubted she could be the killer if only because an arrest would stop her from ever seeing him again.

There was scant little to be gained from torturing the woman further. Morton's gut said she was as innocent as anyone insane enough to join a cult could be. He spun on his heel and headed for the front door. It was time to direct his ire at the woman who continued to pull his strings like a duplicitous puppet master: Lucy Reed.

Chapter 54: Another Arrest?

By the time Morton had stomped the hundred yards east to reach the unmarried women's bungalow, he was fuming. Lucy had the place to herself again. With Abigail at New Scotland Yard and Lana practically living with Lorenzo, the journalist had all the time she needed to plot her shenanigans and machinations in peace. When she answered the door, Morton pushed his way in. He could feel that his temper was beginning to fray in the face of an impossible deadline, and yet he couldn't control himself.

'You lied to me,' Morton growled. 'Again.'

Her surprise seemed genuine. 'About what?'

'The will isn't there.'

She smiled, confident that she held all the cards. Morton felt like a fish out of water.

'You've got it,' he accused her.

'Nope.' She smiled too sweetly.

'A copy of it, then.'

Her smile broadened. 'I can certainly get you a copy.'

The veins in his temple were throbbing. He had had enough of her games. 'Hand it over or I'll arrest you, and then you won't be able to finish your article in time for it to be newsworthy.'

'Can't,' she said. The laughter in her voice was beginning to grate.

'Lucy Reed, you're under arr—'

'Tut, tut, Mr Morton. My, what a temper you've got. I said I *could* get it for you. I don't think I can do so from the inside of a jail cell, however. Do you think I could keep any of my paperwork safe in a place like this for very long? Copies are with my editor in New York, and we both know you don't have the time to try to get it any other way. I don't need to add that you'll never be able to compel a US newspaper to give you a copy, either, so don't even think of lawyering up.'

He ground his teeth together. 'What do you want now?'

'Arrest me.'

'What?' Morton wasn't sure he had heard her correctly.

'I need uninterrupted peace and quiet to finish my article tonight,' Lucy said. Both she and Morton were working against a ticking clock: he had to solve a murder, and she needed to scoop the rest of the media to the story. With one killer already under arrest, albeit for a historical crime that Morton didn't truly believe needed prosecution, Lucy's clock was ticking down almost as fast as Morton's.

'You want me to arrest you so that you can write in your cell.'

'No,' Lucy said. 'I want you to *pretend* you've arrested me. I want out of this hellhole, and I want my story. Pretend to arrest me, drop me at the nearest five-star hotel to write in peace, and I'll get you a copy of the will.'

It wasn't a bad idea. Morton didn't seriously consider Lucy a suspect, and taking one more person out of the mix would simplify his job as well as shaking up the rest of the cultists. He thought for a few moments.

'No,' he said finally. 'I'm going to need more.'

She looked almost pleased that Morton was beginning to play her game. 'Name your price, Mr Morton.'

He ticked things off on one hand as he dictated his terms take-it-or-leave-it style. 'Firstly, I want copies not only of the will but of any other pertinent documents you or your editor may have, and I want them post-haste. Two, I want my reputation, and my family's, left well alone. No hit pieces. Three, I want to have editorial approval.'

'Not a chance, Mr Morton. I know my best interests lie with keeping you sweet. You'll have to rely on that to keep me honest.'

There was a steely glint to her eye that said she was serious.

'Okay,' Morton conceded. 'I want a copy before it goes to press as early as humanly possible. Four, I want you to leave the country as soon as possible so I don't get pressure from above to actually prosecute you. Five, we have to make this look good. No cosy hotel room with room service for you. You can write in a ten by eight cell for a night. If you fail to abide by any of my conditions, I'll have the Crown Prosecution Service throw the book at you.'

'The hotel is non-negotiable. If you let me have my hotel, I'll give you my whole article before even my editor sees it.'

She held out a hand. Morton shook it. They had a deal.

'Turn around and place your hands behind your back. Lucy Reed, you are under arrest on suspicion of murder. You do not have to say anything. But it may harm your defence if you do not mention when questioned something which you later rely on in court. Anything you do say may be given in evidence.'

She might think it was mere acting, but by his including the caution, she couldn't argue she wasn't really and lawfully under arrest. The charge would never stick, but so long as she sent over the finished article before it went to press, Morton still had the option of backtracking on his promise and threatening once more to arrest her, which gave him de facto editorial approval whether she liked it or not. He was dealing with a snake, but with his family and career on the line, he was reluctantly willing to sink to her level.

Less than thirty minutes later, with Mayberry driving Lucy Reed across the capital to spend a night not at Her Majesty's Pleasure but at The Royal Albert hotel in Bloomsbury, Morton's phone buzzed to indicate an email. True to Lucy's word, her editor had emailed over copies of Lucy's notes, including a low-resolution scan of the last will and testament of Clementine Rosenberg.

Morton hurried back to the makeshift incident room in his son's bungalow, where he found Purcell twiddling his thumbs. There was an empty box of doughnuts beside him, which Purcell hastily tried to hide. Morton ignored the gluttony, instead pretending he hadn't spotted the Krispy Kreme box. He tapped his pin into his phone to unlock it and then shoved it into Purcell's sugary mitts.

'Make yourself useful. Put the images on that phone onto your portable projector.'

With his eyelids hanging so heavily that he thought he might doze off at any moment, Morton made a beeline for the kitchen to boil the kettle. He rummaged through the cupboards in search of coffee.

'Bugger,' he said. Decaf! How was he meant to work on that?

A shadow appeared behind him. With his nerves jittery from caffeine withdrawal, he tensed up as he turned. Thankfully, it was only Purcell. 'The projector is ready for you, boss. You making coffee?'

'Trying to,' Morton said. 'But it appears we're down to decaf.'

'Yep. I finished the last of the good stuff earlier.'

It took all of Morton's effort not to throttle Purcell.

'But I've got Pro Plus, and there are still a few doughnuts left.'

A few? Morton thought. No wonder the chief scene of crime officer was on the dumpy side. He had a sweet tooth that was the delight of dentists everywhere, and a Pepsi habit to match.

It was a good job Sarah wasn't on-site anymore, as she'd have heartily disapproved. 'Gimme.'

The first bite of his Krispy Kreme was heaven. Between the sugar rush and the caffeine hit from a Pro Plus, Morton found himself wired in no time. The drowsiness of a very long weekend was, temporarily at least, at bay.

'Did your team search Dori and Giacomo's residence, Stuart?'

'I did that one myself,' Purcell said.

'Then, how'd you miss a stash of documents?'

'I didn't,' Purcell protested. 'You talking about the bottom of the drawers? There wasn't anything there worth your attention. It's all logged on HOLMES...'

Morton shot him daggers. 'You mean to say, I've been given the run-around over a document we already knew wasn't in there?'

'I guess so. But you've got a photo now, eh, boss? Where's it from? The quality is abysmal.'

The pair surveyed the photographs of the will. Lucy had used a tiny camera concealed within a pen to collect her evidence, and it showed in the quality of the photos. Morton had to squint to be able to read the loopy handwriting of the will. They read in silence the purported last wishes of Clementine Rosenberg:

I, Clementine Rosenberg, do this day, June 20th nineteen-ninety, set my hand to paper to record my best intentions. I hereby bequeath all my worldly goods to Giacomo di Stregoni for the benefit of the Collective so that he may continue his good deeds and works in assisting those souls who are lost or fallen. It is my wish that Terra Farm be home to the movement, now and always.

'Do you think it's good enough for handwriting comparison?' Morton asked.

'Dunno,' Purcell said. 'I'll find out for you.'

The will was dated for three months before Clementine's death and purported to be a holographic will, the kind where the testator, in this case Clementine Rosenberg, wrote out her wishes by hand and then signed it. There was no witness signature. Morton made a mental note to ask Kieran O'Connor if such wills were ever valid, and if so in what circumstances.

'Why'd it get changed right before she died?' Purcell asked. He was munching through yet another doughnut, and there was a smear of milk chocolate coating around one side of his mouth. Did he ever stop eating?

'Ahem,' Morton said politely and pointed at the corner of his mouth. Purcell got the hint and pulled up his T-shirt to dab the corner of his mouth. Disgusting.

'Wrong side,' Morton chided.

Once the sugary mess had been dealt with, Morton pondered Purcell's question. It was highly improbable for any individual to change their will right before their death.

'Perhaps she knew she was dying?' Morton said. 'If I knew I had months left, I might revisit my will.'

'Or write your first one,' Purcell said. 'This one doesn't have that guff about superseding prior wills and codicils.'

They didn't know yet what had killed Clementine, and they might never know. Something slow, like cancer, would explain the last-minute change of will. Once Rafferty was done exhuming the body, the pathologist could take a look. But that wasn't likely to happen before Monday morning.

'She was in her sixties,' Purcell said. 'Seems a bit young to die?'

Had she been murdered too? If so, why hadn't her body been fed to the pigs instead of buried?

Morton squinted again at the will.

The handwriting was problematic but not much of a surprise. The Collective had begun as a back-to-the-earth movement. While not as extreme as the Amish, the Collective did eschew technology as far as practically possible. They didn't have televisions or radios, and they certainly didn't have broadband. Only the higher-ups were allowed any tech at all. Pauline had her CCTV, and Lorenzo freely used his mobile while keeping everyone else's devices under lock and key. In the world of the Collective, priority meant everything.

Priority. The will didn't mention it. Was that a good thing for the Collective? Morton knew that the whole system of priority was a recent invention, so if it had been mentioned in the will, it would have been a dead giveaway that the will was counterfeit.

'The most troubling thing isn't the handwriting or even the date,' Morton mused. 'What I want to know is why she excluded Guy.'

'Uh... she didn't want to leave him the farm?'

Purcell didn't understand. He was unmarried and child-free.

Morton tried to explain anyway. 'When you have kids, everything changes. One moment, your biggest problem is what you're going to do for date night on the coming weekend or which nifty sports car you'd like to buy. But then this potato-faced little munchkin pops out, and, against all logic, he's the most perfect thing in the world. The moment Stephen was born, I knew why I existed. We don't always get along, but he's still my son, my firstborn, and I'd do anything for him. Going against that sort of primal drive is nigh on impossible. I couldn't cut my kids out of my will if I wanted to, not that I'll have much to leave behind when I go. Clementine doesn't even *mention* Guy. It's not even as if she specifically chose to leave him no bequest. That happens sometimes. I know my Dad cut out a cousin by specifically leaving him a single penny. It's as if she didn't even *think* about him. Or her sister. That's not right.'

'Maybe she didn't think of it like that,' Purcell said. 'If she thought of the cult as her family, maybe by giving them control, rather than directly giving it to a child, she could protect Guy's future. If she swallowed the Kool-Aid as much as the rest of these weirdos, that sort of logic begins to make sense, doesn't it?'

Doughnut had a point. In cloud cuckoo land, the Collective was family too.

'It's possible, I suppose,' Morton conceded. 'But I still think my first instinct is right. This,' he said, waving his hand towards the image on the wall, 'has to be a forgery, plain and simple.'

'You told me once, you always follow the evidence. What evidence are you following now, boss?'

'Five million quid's worth of it,' Morton said. 'That's the evidence I need. Imagine if Guy had wrested Terra Farm back. He'd have sold it out from underneath the lot of them. He'd have been rich, and they'd have been turfed out onto the streets. That's my evidence. In my mind, the mere fact that someone has taken the will since says it's as bent as an eleven-bob note.'

'Who, though? Don't they all have the same motivation? The same opportunity?'

That was the burning question. All of the cultists had the same interest in continuing to live on Terra Farm rent-free.

'Giacomo has the most obvious motivation,' Purcell said, as if he were reading Morton's mind. 'Without the land, he's not got a Collective, has he?'

'He led the Collective before they had the land,' Morton countered. 'Back then, they moved squat to squat. They managed just fine.'

'Squatting isn't as easy as it used to be.'

Touché, Morton thought. 'Okay, but he's doolally. The man can't feed himself unaided.'

'How's that clear him of forging a will years ago?'

In truth, it didn't, unless Morton's gut instincts were right and the forger was also Guy's killer. Just because the date written on the will was nineteen ninety, it wasn't necessarily written then.

'If I can get you the original paper, could you carbon date it?'

'Theoretically, yes,' Purcell said. 'I could check whether the paper the will is written on is old enough to line up with the date she allegedly signed it. Can't do that with just the scan, though.'

Even if Morton could get the paperwork, that would take time he didn't have, and it'd take valuable attention away from elsewhere in the investigation. He had to assume the paperwork might be fraudulent. 'So, let's do what we can do for now. We've got a few handwriting samples from the members of the Collective, don't we? Lucy's coded notes? Dominic Winslow's witness statement and the like? Can we compare those digitally?'

'Compare them, yes. It won't hold up in court, though, without the originals,' Purcell said. 'I'll put them on-screen if you'll give me your phone again.'

Morton proffered it. Purcell gestured for him to unlock it, and then, when he had access, he began to whizz through authentication screens using Morton's fingerprint to gain access to the police computer system.

As he worked, Morton thought about who had been in the Collective back in nineteen-ninety and was still here. Assuming the document really did date to back then, age ruled out Lana, Lorenzo and Guy himself, as they had been mere children back then. Claudia and Abigail were babies, and Lucy hadn't started her undercover work. That left only the old-timers: Giacomo, Doreen, Tracey, Marta, Pauline, and Dominic.

Heggerty *could* have done it. He was certainly capable, and he had every motive to stay in the cult far away from the past he had fled from. As one of the Collective's two enforcers, surely he would have known if Lorenzo had given orders to destroy the will?

Unfortunately, one look at Darren's witness statement immediately discounted him. Morton was no handwriting expert, but the two styles were night and day. The will was written in an elegant looping cursive; Darren's handwriting looked like a drunken spider had been coated in ink and let loose on the page.

'And the same for Lucy's notes?'

A few moments later, they flashed up on-screen. He and Purcell squinted at them. Again, no obvious match.

'What I need is a handwriting sample for all the other cult members who were here back then,' Morton said.

'Right... but they'd be crazy to volunteer that. If they're smart enough to steal the will and either hide it or destroy it, they won't hand over a writing sample.'

Morton sighed. Purcell was right again. It had to be the tiredness getting to him. Purcell was never this sharp. He could try to trick one or two members into writing something down, but it wouldn't work with all of them, and even if he could, Morton didn't have time to get an expert in to examine them all.

'Anyway,' Purcell said, 'isn't it possible that the cult has a designated scribe? With the way they split out responsibilities among members, the handwriting on the will itself might not belong to Clementine.'

This time Purcell had tried to be too clever. Morton flashed him a smug smile. 'Nice try. The handwriting and the signature are obviously the same pen, and they look like the same handwriting.'

'You're willing to make that call from one low-resolution photo? With enough confidence that you're going to stake not only your career on it but mine, Rafferty's, Ayala's, and Mayberry's as well?'

Purcell's question hung in the air. Perhaps Morton was being rash.

But with time running out, he needed to be.

Chapter 55: Family Connections

Too stressed to work, Morton ventured outside to clear his head. He paused on the veranda to admire the setting sun, which cast a pinky-orange glow over the whole of Terra Farm. The mugginess of the weekend had given way to a cool wind that, when combined with the short-term hit from the combination of sugar and caffeine, brought Morton back to full alert.

As Morton paced the grounds, he ruminated over the events of the weekend, turning over each of the suspects in his mind for the nth time. There had to be a missing puzzle piece. The will was involved. He had no doubt about that, even though money was such a tawdry, boring reason to commit murder.

Control, on the other hand, was less common. The hierarchy of the Collective was bound up in their twisted idea of loyalty, the fundamental notion that every order given by someone of senior priority had to be honoured without question or delay. It was so extreme, so fanatical and yet so simple. And it worked. Nobody had grassed Lorenzo up and yet they all maintained that his word was law.

Poison, smother, shoot. Three very different methods and only one of them successful.

The three attempted murders had to be connected somehow. They had all happened on the same night. Something or someone had precipitated three law-abiding if insane cultists into would-be killers.

The issue was the same brick wall he'd been banging his head against all weekend. Nothing was certain. Lana could have done it to keep her man in control. Lorenzo could have ordered any of them to do it for him. The elderly women could have killed him to stay in their homes. They were in their dotage and had little to lose to protect their way of life.

But they weren't long for this world. What was going to happen after they died? Or even just needed to go into a care home? Would Lorenzo simply carry on? Would he stand to inherit Terra Farm from Giacomo? The forged will had used the phrase "for the benefit of the Collective", and yet nobody seemed to think about what would happen if the Collective ceased to exist.

The older suspects had to be Morton's focus. Someone who had been with the cult at the time had had a hand in the forgery. It wasn't Dominic Winslow, as his handwriting didn't match. Giacomo might have forged the will, yet he was incapable of hiding it now, and his lack of physical prowess made it even less likely that he had killed Guy. The two incidents, the murder and the forgery, were, in Morton's mind, inextricably linked, and finding how the two intersected would be key to catching the killer.

All of which brought Morton back to the three women he'd be fixated on all day: Pauline, Marta, and Tracey, the last original cultists still standing. The first seemed too authoritarian, too enamoured of rules and order, to have become a murderess. There was no physical evidence to exclude her, and she was the owner of the gun, but decades of policing experience screamed that she wasn't the killer.

All of that left Morton with just two doddery old ladies as his remaining suspects. Marta jumped out as the most likely. She knew who owned the land, as it belonged to her family. She had been in the Collective at the time her sister passed away, and, perhaps most interestingly, she was Guy's next of kin. Did she now inherit his claim to the land?

Morton rubbed his eyes. His last caffeine hit was beginning to wear off, and the siren song of his double bed at the Red Lion Inn was calling his name once more, but there were a few tasks he had left before he could allow himself to sleep. He had to talk to Marta. She was the last Rosenberg standing.

He meandered slowly in the direction of the older women's bungalow. It was near to Guy's, a fact he kept coming back to. Distance mattered. Terra Farm was much larger than he had realised at first. The mere fact he'd been last to get to the murder scene showed how big it was.

His tired brain kept churning the same old thoughts around. Could Marta have wanted to steal the land for herself? Perhaps. Why, then, would she forge a will leaving it to Giacomo? And then wait twenty years to bump Guy off? Another dead end. Either Marta was playing 3D chess and Morton's mind couldn't keep up, or Marta hadn't killed Guy for personal gain at all. Perhaps she, like the rest of the cultists, simply wanted the cult to continue.

A vision of Lana flitted into his mind. The blonde couldn't be excluded. She had the same interests as Lorenzo, and she seemed determined to one day become Mrs Lorenzo di Stregoni. Could she have acted to steal the will? With its destruction, and no heir able to try to take the land back from Giacomo, her lover would remain in control. By proxy, that gave Lana the same interests that Lorenzo had.

'Damnit,' Morton swore to himself as he walked past the barn. It looked large and mysterious now that it was empty. He found himself drawing closer and closer to the eastern side of Terra Farm, where the widows' bungalow stood. Rafferty was standing where the rosebushes had been earlier in the day, guarding a white forensics tent that now covered the excavation site. She nodded to Morton as he passed.

Perhaps, Morton thought, he could shake something loose by accusing Marta. The lights in the front room were still on. Through the drawn curtains, Morton could make out the silhouette of a woman in the rocking chair by the fireplace. He knocked on the front door, and the silhouette dragged itself to its feet.

The door swung open to reveal Marta. She was alone and seemed entirely unsurprised to find Morton on her doorstep.

'It's about time, Detective. I've been expecting you.'

Chapter 56: Closest Relative

Marta hobbled back inside, Morton following in her wake. Once more, he found himself holding court in a living room.

'Where's Tracey?'

'Out for her evening perambulation, I should think. Much like yourself, no? She'll be back soon if you want to talk to her.'

'It's you that I'm here for, so I'll be quick and to the point. Tell me about your sister's death.'

'Terrible thing, terrible thing,' Marta said. 'I still haven't got over it.'

As Morton stood there, Marta unconvincingly dabbed at her eyes to wipe away non-existent tears. Marta Timpson was no actress. She slumped down into the rocking chair as if she could no longer bear the weight of the world.

'What was it that she died of?'

'It was her time,' Marta said. This time it sounded like she genuinely believed her own trite answer.

'What physically killed her?'

Marta tilted her head and looked at him as if he were a small child asking a stupid question. 'What do I look like, a doctor?'

'Presumably, she saw a doctor,' Morton said.

'Doreen saw to her in the end.'

Saw her off, more like, Morton thought as he suppressed a grimace.

'What was it that Doreen diagnosed her with?' He didn't hold out much hope for a proper answer.

'She was unwell.'

Grr. 'In what way?'

'Well, she died, didn't she?'

He wanted to bang his head against the wall. 'Was it something sudden and unexpected, like a heart attack? Or was she tired and pale for a while?'

'She had grown pallid, grey, tired. She struggled with everything. Pain wracked her body. Her punishment, I think, for her sins. It was her time when it came to be her time.'

'How did you find out?'

She stared at the floor, avoiding Morton's gaze. 'Giacomo told me. He ministered to her during her final moments. All he said was that it was her time. One day I went out. When I came home, she was still.'

'And then what? You just buried her?'

'Of course not,' Marta said. 'We have our rites. We put a sheet over her and left her to rest in the centre of the barn. She lay in repose for five days and five nights, and then, per our custom, her nearest relative dug the grave.'

He imaged a younger Marta breaking a sweat with a spade as she tried to shovel out the clay-rich soil with no help. 'You had to dig that grave all by yourself?'

'Her closest relative,' Marta repeated. 'Guy.'

Bloody hell, Morton thought. *They made a* child *dig his mother's grave?*

'And you *let him?*' Morton growled. 'You didn't help at all?'

'Couldn't if I wanted to,' Marta said. 'Old wrist injuries. My hands aren't good for much.'

It was clear she hadn't wanted to. Here she was, talking about having forced a child to dig his mother's grave, and she had the gall to complain about her arthritic wrists?

'How old was he?' Morton demanded.

It must have taken the boy hours. Morton's mind flashed back to when he had helped his own father dig a koi pond in the back garden. That had been hard enough, and there had been two of them digging through loamy sand.

She folded her arms across her chest defensively. 'Nine. He was nine, okay?'

Nine years old and burying a body. Morton's face contorted into a sneer. 'And now what?'

'And now I'm going to wash my hands of it, Detective Morton. My conscience is clean.'

Chapter 57: Dusk

The sun had set on Morton. Now that daylight had faded and all of his suspects had retired to their bungalows for the night, an unsettling peace descended upon the farm. The hum of the ground-penetrating radar had long faded as the techs moved on to excavating the body of Clementine Rosenberg. He watched as shadows crept across the farm, his team slowly assembling in the incident room for the end-of-day briefing.

'Quiet, isn't it, boss?' Rafferty asked.

'It was,' Morton said, forcing himself to smile. 'How's digging up the body?'

'On pause 'til daylight, I'm afraid,' she said apologetically. 'There's definitely a body down there, but the techs won't dig it out overnight.'

'Damn.' That meant no DNA confirmation before Morton had to solve the case. He'd have to assume that the body was, in fact, Clementine's and proceed accordingly.

'I've got Mayberry babysitting the scene to avoid contamination,' Rafferty continued. 'That all right with you?'

Poor Mayberry couldn't have been back for more than five minutes before he'd been assigned another task. He'd only just driven the "arrested" Lucy Reed out of Terra Farm. It meant that he wouldn't be able to join them for the final team meeting of the weekend. Not that it mattered too much. Mayberry rarely ever contributed to group discussions. His aphasia made that too hard for him.

'Of course,' Morton said.

'Shall we go in, then?'

Morton half-smiled and gestured for Rafferty to go on in ahead of him. He paused for a moment to survey the darkness once more, and then, with the heavy heart of a man who knew he was headed for the gallows in the morning, he dragged himself into the bungalow and clicked the front door shut behind him. He double-checked the lock and then headed into the living room.

At his arrival, a hush fell across the room.

Ayala refused to meet Morton's gaze. Only Purcell, who strictly speaking wasn't even on Morton's team, would look him in the eye. Despite the pudginess of his rosy red cheeks, which Morton normally found endearing, the sallow, waxy look to Purcell's skin and the bags under his eyes reflected the mood of the team. Everyone was exhausted, hope seemed to have dwindled, and it was all Morton's fault. He should never have tried to investigate Guy Rosenberg's murder, and now that he had, the entire team had been dragged down into the mire with him.

Morton fired up the projector.

'As you know, this has been a complex investigation against a tight timeframe. Before I begin, I want to say a personal thank you to you all for trusting me. It's not easy to blindly follow, and yet you've all been willing to put yourselves in the firing line for me and my family.'

'Without question or delay,' Ayala muttered, drawing a smirk from Rafferty.

'Well, then, with my newfound dictatorial authority, we're going to do this meeting in three parts. First, the three methodologies. Second, I want to review what little forensic evidence we have. Third, we'll go around all the suspects in light of each of the three methodologies. Any objections to this approach?'

Again, there were none. Morton felt like he was talking to himself, which, broadly speaking, he was.

There was tension in the air. This was the kind of "get on the same page" meeting that Morton favoured in the middle of an investigation, and his team knew it. With a hard deadline in twelve hours working against them, they needed a miracle. Recapping old evidence seldom broke a case. In this case, the team was already so familiar with the evidence that it was virtually pointless to review it. They'd done the best job that they could given the time constraints imposed on the investigation. Nevertheless, Morton had to try.

'Before we do all that, let's think again about our victim. Guy Rosenberg had been part of the Collective all of his life. Despite one sojourn on his own, he returned to the only family he had ever known, where he fell in love with a younger woman. His mother once owned Terra Farm. If Claudia is to be believed, he was convinced it ought to be his. We also know that he had a drinking problem, and that his six months of sobriety came to an abrupt end on the night of–'

'We know all this, boss,' Ayala said impatiently. He tapped his wristwatch. Morton resisted the urge to throttle him.

'Indeed we do,' Morton said. 'What we don't know is who killed him or why. Somewhere between one and three people chose to try to kill Guy on the same night. Why that night? Did they see the presence of outsiders as a distraction?'

'I think,' Ayala said, 'it's too much of a coincidence to be random chance. Timing has to be key here. Either someone thought you were a good distraction, or they wanted to blame you.'

'Rafferty? What do you think?'

She gave a languid shrug. 'Perhaps it's a setup. Someone might want to sow confusion. We've been chasing our tails all weekend trying to second-guess these lunatics. Murder three ways: insanity, forensic countermeasure, three separate attempts. How're we supposed to unpick that? And there you are, right in the middle of it, hamstrung by being connected to two of the suspects.'

'You think this is all the work of a criminal mastermind? That someone knew I'd be caught between Scylla and Charybdis, and used that to mess up the investigation? Doesn't that sound infinitely more complicated than just killing Guy and feeding his body to the pigs?'

'Then perhaps,' Rafferty said slowly, 'the killer or killers *wanted* to be caught.'

'Okay, why?'

'Guilt? A way out like Heggerty? Or they wanted to expose the land dispute?'

The land. It kept coming back to the land.

'What exactly is the sitch with the land?' Ayala asked.

Morton put the last will and testament of Clementine Rosenberg on the projector. 'Terra Farm belonged originally to Clementine's partner Clive and his family. It was, as the name suggests, a working farm. When she inherited the land, it was before the Land Registry database, so everything was done on paper using deeds rather than having a simple database entry stored with the Land Reg and backed by the government. This is the heart of the problem. This will, which I believe is forged, leaves the land to Giacomo for the purposes of housing the Collective. It doesn't leave anything, not a penny, to either her sister Marta or her son Guy.'

'Who gets it now?'

It was Morton's turn to shrug. 'No idea. It'll almost certainly be contested. Giacomo's too far gone–'

'Ascended, you mean,' Ayala said with another smirk.

'Too far gone to even remember if he forged it. I doubt any of 'em want to be homeless.'

'And they'd all obey Lorenzo at the drop of a hat, anyway,' Rafferty said. 'All that "without question or delay" malarkey. It's good motivation, but I don't see how it gets us closer to catching a killer.'

'What it gets us closer to,' Ayala said, his smirk turning into a snarl, 'is fired. Unless you pull a rabbit out of the hat, we're all goners tomorrow morning.'

Morton paced the room. 'I'm going to say this once and only once. If you don't believe in me, there's the door. Not once have I ever let you down, and during this investigation, I have gone to great lengths to make sure the paperwork reflects only the first attempt we knew of, the gunshot, so that you can pin it all on me if the shit hits the fan. But for tonight I need you all to bring your A-game. I need one last push to give Guy Rosenberg, and possibly his mother too, the justice they deserve. Are you with me or not?'

Purcell and Rafferty were the first to nod. They seemed, if not enthused, at least alert enough to continue.

'Ayala?' Morton prompted.

Ayala looked around dubiously. 'I'm with you,' he said with a hint of reservation.

'Good. If we don't solve this murder in time, I want the three of you, and Mayberry, to throw me under the bus. Get your stories straight, tell them I was a train wreck, that I kept everything except the shooting from you, and that you all voiced concern about me continuing to investigate but that I ignored you... which I did. Got it?'

Three nods, two of them hesitant.

'Then onwards. The first would-be murder. Someone attempted to poison Guy on the night of Stephen and Abigail's *binding ceremony*,' Morton said with a shiver running down his spine. It wasn't truly a wedding just yet, as they had never made it to the Registrar's Office. 'And then someone smothered him before the poison could finish the job. Finally, first thing in the morning, someone shot his corpse at point-blank range, and the noise of the shotgun caused bedlam. Three very different murder methodologies.'

'What are we missing, boss?' Ayala asked. 'Three attempts. Doesn't that mean three murderers? Why would someone try twice, let alone three times?'

'As Rafferty suggested, it could be a forensic countermeasure. Right from the start, we've pretended to be concentrating on the shotgun. Those responsible may think we haven't even noticed the poison and smothering.'

'More simply,' Rafferty said, 'three killers.'

'Right. The poison is a wild goose chase for us. Any of the cultists could have administered *le muguet* to him. He was drinking like a fish, he'd never have noticed it, and the darned thing is all over Terra Farm. So let's look at the other two attempts. The smotherer had to get in, smother him, and get out.'

'Also dead easy if he was blackout drunk,' Rafferty said.

Purcell raised a tentative hand. Morton gestured for him to speak. 'None of them lock their doors.'

'There we go, then,' Rafferty said. 'Walk through an unlocked door in the dead of night, shove a pillow over the face of an unconscious drunk, wait five minutes, walk out. Easy. And again, it isn't going to get us anywhere when anyone on Terra Farm, including Stephen or Abigail, could have done just that.'

Morton's nostrils flared. 'Stephen's not a suspect.'

Rafferty met his stare with a steely-eyed determination of her own. 'Perhaps he should be. He's the newbie. Everyone in the Collective who's joined under Lorenzo had to do something to get in. Why's Stephen been leapfrogged to priority six? Why's he got a cushty bungalow? And isn't it a bit of a coincidence that his new wife used to bang the dead guy?'

Rage bubbled up within Morton. He'd expected it to be Ayala who picked at that scab, not Rafferty. But before he could start yelling, Purcell chirped up.

'What about the gun? Who could have done that? The shooter had to have been capable of firing a shotgun and then scarpering before you could get there.'

Timing. Again.

'Ayala, did you run the distance from here to there and time it, as I asked?'

Ayala looked bewildered. Clearly, he'd totally forgotten that little task. 'Err...'

'Go, do it now. Come straight back, and we'll halve your time.' Morton pulled out his phone, readied the timer, and shouted: 'Go!'

Ayala leapt to his feet, bolted for the door, and ran. Morton didn't want him to have time to prep because Morton hadn't had that luxury on the morning of the shooting.

Two minutes and thirty-seven seconds later, Ayala was back panting and sweating. Morton did the calculation in his head. Ayala's average was one minute, eighteen and a half seconds. The farm was nine acres. With the severe gradient, Ayala's time was pretty impressive. Not that Morton would ever tell him that.

'You're getting a little slow in your old age, Bertram.'

In return, Ayala gesticulated rudely.

'Now, now, Bertram,' Morton said. 'That said, you're faster than all of us, and we're undoubtedly faster than the members of the Collective. We can safely assume nobody else could go that quickly. What I need you to do next, once you've caught your breath, is go back to Guy's bungalow and repeat this exercise for each of the other bungalows.'

'*All* of them?' Ayala exclaimed.

'Just like I asked you to do this morning,' Morton said. He smiled sweetly.

'Fine.'

Once Ayala was gone, Morton exhaled.

'Right. While he's out of the room, I know he's going to dob me in to Silverman before either of you. He might even have done it already.'

'Then we'd better solve the murder, hadn't we?' Rafferty asked.

Morton turned his attention to the whiteboard on which Mayberry had drawn a layout diagram.

'Top left: Stephen, Abigail, and Sarah and I. Top middle: Giacomo and Doreen. Top right: Lucy, Lana.'

He skipped Claudia. She would usually have been in her room in the north-eastern bungalow but that night had been locked up in seclusion inside the groundskeeper's spare room.

'Next row. Middle left: Pauline and Claudia. Then the barn. Then Marta and Tracey.'

He traced a finger along the diagram. It was roughly to scale. Now that Morton knew that Guy's bungalow was over a minute's sprint from Stephen and Abigail's, it made much more sense that the rest of the Collective had managed to beat him to the crime scene.

'Bottom row. On the left is where Darren Heggerty lives. The middle one belongs to Lorenzo. The right one is the victim's bungalow. Is that everybody?'

Purcell stood and jabbed a finger at Lorenzo's bungalow. 'Was Lana with Lorenzo that night? I found women's underwear in his bedroom, so unless he's not telling us something, he has overnight guests.'

Morton shrugged. 'Possibly.'

Mayberry added her name to Lorenzo's bungalow and then put a big question mark in red next to both occurrences of her name.

A breathless Ayala reappeared. His times were written in Notes on his phone. Morton scanned them:

Fifty-five seconds to Giacomo's, fifty-four to Pauline's, forty-one seconds to Lucy and Lana's, thirty-six to Darren Heggerty's, and nineteen seconds apiece to the remaining two bungalows which belonged to Lorenzo and the widows.

'Nice work.'

Ayala was too out of breath to reply, so he settled for a quick thumbs-up. His white shirt, which had been pristine and immaculately ironed first thing this morning, was now stained with sweat.

Morton scanned the times slowly. 'I think we can deduce that our shooter probably isn't Giacomo, Doreen, or Pauline. I'd have seen them coming back this way. The rest are all plausible.'

'Unless they outmanoeuvred you there too, boss,' Ayala said. 'What if they just joined the crowd outside Guy's?'

'Then they'd have been covered in gunshot residue.'

'Would they, though?'

Morton pondered. As he did so, Lorenzo's voice echoed in his mind. He'd said something on the porch. Morton couldn't remember exactly what he'd said, but it had been something like:

No doubt you'll want to test my hands for gunshot residue ... It's not as if I've had time to go and clean my hands...

He swore. Without question or delay. Lorenzo's protestation hadn't been him yelling about his innocence. It had been an *order.* 'You're right. Someone could have washed up, come back, and all I'd have seen is the crowd.'

'When?' Rafferty asked. 'When would they have had a chance to go wash their hands?'

It was a good thought. 'Ayala, I'm going to need you to go running once more.'

'Again?'

'Down to the barn. I think there's a tap there. Can you check if I'm right, please? And if so, where it is exactly?'

Ayala dutifully rose. The front door slammed behind him none too gently as he left.

'Speaking of timing,' Rafferty said, 'our killer needed to wipe down the gun, get outside, wash their hands, and then come back to rejoin the crowd? That takes some serious confidence to do quickly.'

'Or recklessness.' Whether by skill or luck, the gun had been well-cleaned and was devoid of usable prints except those which belonged to Lorenzo, and they were on the barrel, where he'd picked it up.

'And,' Rafferty said, 'they had to get the gun in the first place, though I suppose they could have done it at any time. Do we know when Pauline last used it?'

'She said she'd last used it over a week ago. Something about rats in the barn,' Morton said. 'It could have disappeared from her bungalow at any point since then.'

Ayala reappeared. 'Two taps. One on the northern wall, one on the southern wall. There's soap next to both. Before you ask, it's twenty-four seconds at a sprint from Guy's.'

Twenty-four seconds. Anyone could run that, clean their hands, walk back down, and be lost in the crowds. All while Morton was inside securing the crime scene. He kicked himself. Why hadn't he realised sooner just what Lorenzo was up to?

Morton sank in his seat, dejected. After all that, they'd proved that nobody could be definitively ruled out of anything except for Lorenzo, who was the only person who couldn't have washed his hands clean of gunshot residue.

He heard a loud yawn. He looked up to see Rafferty stifling another one.

'Go get some sleep if you need to,' he said. 'You look dreadful.'

Not exactly tactful, but it was true. There were large, dark circles under her eyes.

'I'll sleep when we're done,' she said. 'And you're not looking too fresh either.'

Ayala cleared his throat. 'When you two are done comparing your beauty regime, I've got a thought to share.'

'Go on,' Morton said.

'If we've excluded the people who live alone – which is just Pauline and Darren, right? – then we *must* have a witness to the shooter returning home.'

'Lorenzo lives alone too,' Morton added, 'unless Lana was with him. It doesn't work. You've just proved it yourself. The killer could have cleaned their hands in the barn. Or the would-be witnesses could have taken a shortcut through the barn and missed the killer entirely. That's how I got to Guy's.'

'But they'd still have had to sneak out of their own home unseen, presumably while carrying a shotgun.'

'Unless, yet again, they planned ahead. The gun could have been stashed anywhere on the site for all we know. I'd have personally stuck it inside a bale of hay where I could easily retrieve it. Hell, they could even have taken it straight from Pauline's that night.'

'Then we're screwed,' Ayala said.

'Not necessarily. We've got time to solve this. One last Hail Mary. I want you to–'

'Run back and forth like a lunatic?'

'No, go to the Royal Albert Hotel. It's just off Southampton Row.'

His expression brightened. 'I know it. I love their cocktails bar.'

'Meet Brodie there.'

He screwed up his face in confusion. 'Thanks, but he's not my type.'

'Funny, Ayala, very funny,' Morton said. 'Lucy Reed is there. She's typing up her article ready for publication.'

'You're *helping* that witch?'

'No, I'm catching a killer, and if I have to make a deal with a hack journo to do it, so be it.'

Ayala looked as puzzled as ever.

'She wants to break this story before we arrest the killer. That means making the UK morning print run. Realistically, that means she's got to have a print-ready article by about two o'clock tomorrow morning. Any later than that, she'll miss the last chance for a stop press.'

'Won't she just break the story online?'

'Fat chance,' Morton said. 'She's been writing a Collective story for months and months. She's not going to settle for having that online if she can at all avoid it. She wants the front page by-line, the glory of a serialised article, and all the accolades that go with it.'

'And Brodie's going to get me this... how?'

'Digital eavesdropping. She has to use the hotel's Wi-Fi. When she sends off her draft article, I want you to be there to get a copy.'

'Ah,' Ayala said. 'You want us to perform a man-in-the-middle attack.'

'What you do in your spare time is none of my business. Just get me that article.'

Ayala gesticulated at Morton once again and then stomped out.

'Call me when you've got something!'

The door slammed again, this time so hard that Morton was surprised it didn't fall off its hinges.

'What about us?' Rafferty asked, waving an arm at Purcell.

'Bed. We really do need a miracle, and that means being sharp enough to figure out how to break this in the next ten hours.'

Chapter 58: A Restless Night

Sleep did not come easily for Morton that Sunday night. What rest he did get was fitful, punctuated by recurring thoughts of failing those he loved. It was a stress Morton was unaccustomed to dealing with, and thus was almost wholly unprepared for. He had made several grave errors over the weekend, and the only way to redeem himself was to solve a nigh-on impossible case.

Murder three ways. The case was as unusual as the Collective. And it was driving him mad.

For Guy not only be a target but to be so unpopular that three separate attempts had been made on his life in one night, his death had to have been precipitated by a solitary contemporary event.

That brought Morton's wandering mind back to the land. To some, Terra Farm was simply home, the place where aimless wanderers had settled to build their life together. To others, it was the physical manifestation of the Collective. Then, finally, it was wealth. But whose wealth? Was it Lorenzo's inheritance from Giacomo? Guy's inheritance from his mother? Or did it truly belong to them all, a property in trust for the Collective?

Or was it about family and honour? Was Guy's decision, with Claudia's support, threatening to unearth old wrongs and tear apart the group?

As Morton tossed and turned, images floated through his mind. The flower, *le muguet*, used to poison Guy. The groundskeeper's gun, left out for anyone to use, and the pillow with which Guy had been smothered. All were within reach of anyone on Terra Farm.

Morton flipped his own pillow over and placed his face back down on the cooler side, and then he pulled one leg out from under the duvet and folded it across the bed so he was lying on his side. The mattress wasn't very comfy, and the night had become too muggy for his liking. How he wished he were back home with the balcony doors open and Sarah by his side.

Morton sniffed. There was a bad smell in the air. It took him a moment to realise that the smell was emanating from him. He hadn't had the opportunity to change clothes for several days. He kicked off the covers, hauled himself to his feet and shuffled into the tiny bathroom to bathe.

The shower helped bring him out of his drowsy state. The thought of a nice clean shirt cheered him greatly.

Clothing!

Why hadn't he thought of it before? The killer had to have washed their clothes, because Purcell had found no trace of gunshot residue on any of the clothing that the cultists had been wearing or on the clothes that he'd retrieved from each of their homes.

Lorenzo's voice rang loud and clear in the back of his mind once more. This time, Morton was in no doubt as to exactly what had been said.

It's not as if I've had time to go and clean my hands and bleach my clothes.

Bleaching clothes. Not even just washing them. *That* had been Lorenzo's order, words that served as a reminder to the killer lurking outside the house that their sleeves would have been smothered in gunshot residue.

It would have taken *ages* to hand-wash the robes, and nobody had had enough time to do that when Morton had assembled them all in the barn straight away and held them while they were initially interviewed.

But they could have dashed off and thrown the robes into a washing machine while Morton was securing the crime scene. Even if he'd heard it, Purcell wouldn't have given a second thought to the whirr of a washing machine.

But where had Morton seen a washing machine? By now he knew Stephen's bungalow like the proverbial back of his hand, and there was no washing machine there. The other bungalows were likewise lacking. Except one. He'd seen two in his time on Terra Farm and they were both in the widows' bungalow.

The killer had to have gone there.

If, as Morton suspected, Tracey and Marta were responsible for washing everybody's clothes, then it made sense that the killer had to go to their home. Whoever had killed Guy must have put their clothes straight in the wash and then found something else to wear instead. Would Tracey and Marta have noticed someone going into their home? Or had they been too preoccupied by the drama outside Guy's bungalow that morning?

Perhaps each had assumed the other had run the machine.

And if they did everyone's washing, the killer could have borrowed clean skivvies right there and then.

Unless the shooter was one of them, after all? They were the closest to the crime scene. It would have been easy to throw a robe in the wash, scrub their hands, and then head back down to Guy's in time for the circus.

Without skipping a beat, he hopped out of the shower, wrapped a manky threadbare towel around himself, and grabbed his iPad. Excitement ran through him. He was within a hair's breadth of cracking this case.

Time to work backwards to go forwards.

Assumptions were all he had to go on, so he decided to try a few thought experiments. In Morton's experience, most poisoners were women. Whoever had poisoned Guy had probably done it by spiking his drinks at the binding. Naturally, the easiest way to do that would be if you were running the bar. That night, Marta had been pouring the drinks. His second-best guess was Doreen. He'd seen her carrying glasses to and fro that night.

If he assumed Marta was behind *le muguet*, who then was the shooter? She wouldn't need to shoot him, but she lived in the nearest bungalow and had access to the washing machines. Could Marta have poisoned Guy and Tracey shot him?

On the other hand, following the same logic, perhaps Marta had shot him, making Dori the most likely suspect in the poisoning. Unless it was Tracey and Dori?

None of them seemed to have much motive.

And Marta had been outside the bungalow when Morton arrived on Friday morning. If she was the killer, it took serious balls for her to go and help Morton by fetching a telephone while she was covered in gunshot residue. Unless that too was a ruse and Lorenzo had been sending her off to dispose of the evidence on the way. Could they all be in on it?

Morton stood. The same old problem kept coming back to haunt him. He could argue himself round in circles for hours, each theory sounding just as good as the next.

And he still had a third method that could literally have been perpetrated by anyone.

If Marta really had just hobbled off to fetch a mobile, and he was right about the need to access the widows' bungalow, then perhaps Tracey was in on it? She too had access. But she had no real dog in the land-ownership race unless she was acting at Lorenzo's behest.

If one of his hunches was right – that the shooting and poisoning attempts were some combination of the older women, Dori, Marta and Tracey – then, assuming each attempt was by a different person, the smotherer had to be one of his remaining suspects.

Stephen and Abigail were out. He refused to even consider it. Pauline struck him as unlikely, though that was only gut instinct. Heggerty had confessed to one murder. Surely he wouldn't confess to one while hiding another?

Lorenzo had been too drunk to function. Claudia had been in seclusion.

That really only left Lana in the third prime suspect slot. She knew about the land issue and could have killed to protect her and Lorenzo's future. And, as Lorenzo's live-out mistress, Lana had the best experience slipping in and out of the bungalows undetected thanks to her frequent moonlight sojourns to his bungalow.

It also explained why Lorenzo had been so quick to shout about gunshot residue. He hadn't had time to go and clean his hands, but his words could have served as a warning that someone else needed to. Someone he genuinely cared about.

If he had identified Lana as a possible killer, he might have thought Lana had shot Guy, never realising she had killed him but by another means. She had been right there when he made the remark about washing hands.

Had Morton cracked it?

His elation flooded out of him like a popped balloon. Even if all of this rampant speculation were true, he couldn't prove any of it.

There was one thing for it: a big gamble. He had to call a meeting in the barn and see how much he could wheedle out of the group. There had to be one thing, one tiny sliver of evidence, to tell him which suspect had done what, when, and why. He wasn't entirely convinced the Crown Prosecution Service would be able to do much with it – even the miracle worker that was Kieran couldn't prosecute without any evidence – but it was his best bet at saving his team, saving his career, saving his family, and keeping his promise to Claudia.

One thirty-odd-year career gambled on the spin of one meeting. One chance to save himself. One last shot at catching three killers.

He looked out of the bay windows at the darkness of the farm.

Bring it on.

Chapter 59: The Fourth Estate

S leep had still not come for Morton when his phone rang shortly after midnight.

'Morton,' he said, his tone groggy.

'B-boss, ch-ch-ch-check your email.'

His brain went into overdrive. *Mayberry!*

'Ayala got the draft article?'

'Y-y-yes, sir,' Mayberry said. Even with the crackle of a dodgy phone line, Morton could detect a hint of pride in his voice. As Morton darted for his laptop, he grinned. His deal had paid off.

'Attaboy, Mayberry. Now bring her back here for eight o'clock. Wait outside until I text you.'

He rang off without waiting for confirmation. Time was short, and he had a draft newspaper article to read.

Within a few clicks, he had it on his screen. While Lucy had written it for *The Objective*, it was also going to be syndicated in the UK by *The Impartial*.

The headline was bold but understated:

The Collective: A Family of Killers.

It lacked a certain panache, Morton thought. He would have thought Lucy and her editor could come up with something snappier. Perhaps there was a reason Lucy Reed had never had a smash hit article before.

Thankfully, the article itself was dynamite. The front page showed a photo of Giacomo in his heyday posing with Clementine Rosenberg. She was holding a baby in her arms. The caption read: *Cult leader and his first "bound" partner pictured with their son, Guy.*

Morton blinked. Guy?

He squinted. The boy in the picture. It wasn't Lorenzo. It really was Guy!

That changed everything, didn't it?

If Guy had been Giacomo's son, then surely Giacomo was his next of kin. The land wouldn't go anywhere, regardless of whether or not the will was a forgery. If it wasn't, Giacomo had inherited lawfully. If it was, Guy ought to have inherited so it would pass into his estate, and then Giacomo would take ownership from there. Did the other cultists know? This inverted the motivations. Now it wasn't killing to stop Giacomo losing the land, it could also be killing to see him inherit it after all. If they knew. And if they understood the law as Morton did. And if he was right.

Morton suddenly felt even more out of his depth. He skimmed the article quickly, looking for new information, anything that could hint at what knowledge each cultist was working off of. Soundbites jumped off the page.

Di Stregoni Junior has proven himself a keen dictator-in-waiting, and upon taking control he almost immediately implemented a raft of new rules to test his authority, including "Seclusion", a practice in which women on their period are placed in a dark room on their own with nothing more than a dog bowl full of water until their time of the month has passed.

It was dynamite, and Morton knew it would sell papers. It also had the benefit of being true, a quality Morton did not generally ascribe to the press. Perhaps his views had been coloured by once arresting the then editor-in-chief of *The Impartial*, the sister to Lucy's newspaper, *The Objective*. It was hard to let bygones be bygones.

Misogyny in the cult ran rampant. Women were treated as second-class citizens who were expected to defer to their menfolk, do their domestic chores, and, until he fell ill with dementia, service Giacomo di Stregoni's sexual needs. At one stage, Giacomo even attempted to instigate separate languages for men and women, only for the whole thing to fail as neither gender could remember the terms Giacomo had suggested, and thus everyone quickly reverted to English.

No wonder then that the only men permitted in the cult by di Stregoni were those that he did not consider rivals.

And yet, rivalry among the women was fierce. With almost all of them sleeping with Giacomo, jilted feelings were typical. No individual demonstrates this more than Marta Timpson (née Rosenberg). The sister of the late Clementine Rosenberg, the original owner of Terra Farm, Marta was given guardianship over her nephew Guy (pictured above). The Objective's undercover reporter once heard her say in confidence that "The boy is a constant reminder that I am barren. My failure to give Giacomo a child was what drove him into the arms of my sister."

Morton's jaw dropped. *Of course!* Marta didn't want the land. She hated the man, not for being a drunk or a wreck, but for being a living, breathing reminder of the sister she had hated and the man who had spurned her.

Whenever a cult member became problematic, the cult would, according to the writing of Giacomo, "put the old dog out of its misery should its mewling bark threaten the common peace". It was not a rule they applied to the leader himself despite his advanced dementia, which was explained away as "ascendance", a state the group aspired to in order to "transcend the banality of human existence".

But for the other practices instigated by their erstwhile leader, the cult would have died out. The practice of "flirty fishing", in other words using the most attractive women to lure in young men under the pretence of a relationship, has swelled the ranks of the cult in recent years. Even the son of DCI Morton, lead of London's foremost Murder Investigation Team, has been taken in by this ruse.

'Bitch!' Morton spat. He snatched up his phone. Mayberry didn't answer, so he left a voicemail. 'Mayberry, make sure our journalist friend makes it back to the farm. I need her.'

An idea had popped into his head. He would give all the cultists a copy of the article at once, with Lucy Reed present, and see what it shook loose.

Against his better judgement, he carried on reading in case of more titbits. There was mention of Darren, naturally, though Lucy had nothing new to share and had made up a quote or two to support her narrative.

It was the final section that gave Morton pause once more.

The cult founder's son, Lorenzo di Stregoni, shared his father's passion for control, but not for the cult. The Objective can exclusively reveal that Lorenzo planned to sell Terra Farm after his father's death. Clearly, he did not know that the land was subject to a dispute, as Clementine's estate had never been properly probated. Di Stregoni Junior was overheard saying that it was only a matter of time before Giacomo's physical body failed now that he had ascended, and that all Lorenzo and his partner Lana had to do was wait.

That was enlightening. *Hmm*, Morton mused. Did Lorenzo now have a claim anyway as Guy's half-brother? Did it matter? With Guy dead, Lorenzo was his father's next of kin and had effective control over his affairs. It seemed Lorenzo was as smart as Morton had initially thought, if he was willing to bide his time and wait for what he thought was his.

Morton had everything he was going to get. It was time to start preparing. In a few hours, all the cultists would be gathered in the barn and he could reveal his cards and make his best guess. With the final ace in the hole – Lucy's article – Morton was now as equipped as he ever would be. It was time to shake the tree and see what rotten fruit fell out.

Chapter 60: The Calm Before The Storm

That Monday morning, Morton rose at daybreak. As soon as he turned on his mobile, the barrage began. Chiswick had texted to confirm that his report would be uploaded at ten o'clock. Abigail had been released without charge after Stephen had procured her a more competent defence solicitor. And Lucy Reed's story was going to press as expected. The morning copies of *The Impartial* were already en route to newsagents all over the capital, promising all the lurid details would be revealed in part one of her "explosive exposé of the sordid tale of the Collective cult".

So far, she had kept her word and avoided tarnishing the Morton name. Abigail and Stephen were conspicuously absent from part one, though with five more parts yet to be printed, Lucy still had Morton over a barrel.

He forced himself to choke down a small breakfast at the Red Lion Inn, a stale croissant paired with yet more coffee. As he chewed it over, he shut his eyes, visualising the night of the binding once again. Images of Lana and Lorenzo floated into his mind. They had looked every bit the smitten young couple in the first flushes of love, an image totally at odds with everything he'd learned about Lorenzo over the weekend. While the de facto leader had come across as creepy during the ceremony, he had been totally at ease during the reception. Had that been an act too?

Then there'd been the older women. They'd been the only ones to talk to him. Poor Dori was totally besotted with Giacomo and totally enthralled by the lies Lorenzo had peddled. She had to know that Giacomo hadn't "ascended" and yet she wanted to believe so much that she bought into it all completely.

Guy himself had been misanthropic, drinking at breakneck speeds. If he had really been about to wrest control of the land from Lorenzo, why wasn't he on cloud nine? He hadn't acted like a man about to come into a vast sum of money.

Everything about this investigation wrong-footed Morton. This was a closed-shop community, a place where life and death went unnoticed by the outside world. Guy's murder could have taken place one day earlier – or later – and the killer would have got off scot-free.

So why on earth had they killed Guy on the one night that an outsider, a police detective to boot, was on-site? The timing *had* to be key to solving the riddle. The killer, or killers, needed a rock-solid outside witness to the murder. Unfortunately, Morton didn't yet know why. He returned to Terra Farm a little after seven a.m. with not much more to work with than he'd had three days earlier. His first task of the day was to finalise the logistics. As well as his own team, he needed a large, visible police presence in case things turned nasty. So far, the Collective had been compliant, perhaps because of the ongoing police presence. That could turn in a heartbeat when Morton began arresting them en masse.

There were a lot of minor crimes to deal with. Some of them were easy, slam-dunk affairs. Nailing Pauline Allchin for improper storage of a firearm, or even making an arrest under the Births and Deaths Registration Act ought to be easy. Someone should have reported Clementine's death after all, though he'd have to ask Kieran O'Connor exactly whom that responsibility fell upon.

He put the thought of those crimes from his mind. There were bigger fish to fry. If everything went perfectly this morning, he'd have arrests for murder, two attempted murders, and, if he could swing it, fraud. One notable absence in his mind was that the law didn't criminalise running a cult per se. The fact that the Collective existed didn't affect Morton's ability to arrest them at all. He had to treat them like any other citizens and arrest them only for the crimes they had committed.

Morton was busy marking out the whiteboard with a map to show where he wanted each of them to stand when he assembled the suspects in the barn. Next to the map, he had a list of each of the cultists' names as well as the offences he intended to arrest them for. Several were still marked with huge red question marks.

The team arrived shortly after he did, joining him in the incident room. They looked sombre as they traipsed in, eyes downcast, faces tired.

'Mayberry, what on earth are you doing here? I said eight, didn't I? And where's Lucy Reed?'

The younger officer hung his head. 'She's g-gone,' he mumbled. 'Her h-h-hotel room was empty this m-m-morning.'

'Gone?' Morton roared. 'Gone where?' A shrug met Morton's furious glare. 'Get on the phone to border security. If she tries to get on a plane, train, or cross the Channel Tunnel, I want to know.'

When he was gone, Rafferty sidled up to him. 'That was a bit harsh. You know you'll solve this.' She gestured at the whiteboard. 'You've always got a plan.'

Ayala's voice came from over the breakfast table. 'Only if you count "winging it" as a plan.'

'I'll pretend I didn't hear that,' Morton said.

'Good, and we'll pretend we haven't broken the law every which way this weekend.'

Keep focussed, David, Morton thought to himself. 'I assume you've all read Lucy Reed's article?'

They both nodded.

'Then you know Guy Rosenberg is Giacomo's son.'

'Does that change anything?' Rafferty asked. 'Legally, I mean.'

Morton demurred for a moment. He hadn't had a proper reply from Kieran about how Guy's relationship changed the land ownership dispute. All the prosecutor had said was: 'Do I look like a sodding land lawyer to you?'

'Nope,' Morton said. 'Probably not. We could get into wheels-within-wheels logic again arguing that Guy's next of kin now is one of the di Stregoni men.'

'Because that logic has got us so far this weekend,' Ayala said.

'Quite. Do I detect a note of sarcasm, Bertram? Can we stop with the jibes and have an honest conversation, please?'

His sergeant gave a forced smile. 'If you do, it's because you've mishandled this from start to finish and Silverman is going to have your guts for garters if you don't pull a rabbit out of the hat, boss.'

'Outside. Now.'

The pair walked out in silence, only the tap of Ayala's brogues on the wood flooring echoing down the corridor.

Morton shut the front door behind him, glanced around for eavesdroppers, and then, when he was sure they were alone, said: 'I know you're not happy. I'm not either. If you want to leave, leave.'

Ayala did. Without saying another word, he marched off towards the gate.

'Well, that backfired,' Morton muttered to himself. He returned to the incident room to find Rafferty examining Lucy Reed's article.

'Ayala's not feeling himself. It'll be just the two of us today, so let's adjust the plan accordingly,' Morton said. He nodded at the printout. 'Still poring over that? Did I miss something important?'

'No,' Rafferty said. 'But I keep coming back to one thing: Lorenzo and Lana wanted the land.'

'That's obvious,' Morton said. The article literally said so.

'But didn't he already have it?' Rafferty said. 'He's in charge of everything going on here, after all. Or maybe he was ready to flog it, and a murder on the premises is a damned fine reason to disband the Collective for good.'

It was plausible. The same £4.5million payday that Guy and Claudia were after would no doubt be equally appealing to Lorenzo and Lana. Maybe Lorenzo too had noticed that the cult was rapidly ageing. Morton said as much.

'Except,' Rafferty said, 'he brought in Stephen by using Abigail. Why refresh the cult's membership if he was planning on winding it down? Wouldn't he have been better off just waiting and letting it die off naturally?'

'Perhaps. But he needed money in the interim. The cult provided him with the means to live comfortably. His father isn't dead yet, and some of the others could live for another thirty years. I don't think he's got the patience to wait it out.'

'Then maybe that's why Guy had to die on Friday.'

Morton waited for her to finish her thoughts. When she didn't, he prompted her. 'Because...?'

'Because this crystallises the land dispute. It's out in the open. Either it's Giacomo's, therefore it's Lorenzo's, or it was Guy's, and, if Lorenzo's his brother, as Lucy suggests in her article, Lorenzo still wins as his next of kin. Like you said, with Guy dead, the Collective is brought into disrepute and he has the perfect excuse to bring it all to a head, toss the last few cultists out, and sail off into the sunset with Lana as a multi-millionaire.'

It was as good a theory as any of those that Morton had dreamt up. Unfortunately, it suffered from the same fatal flaw: a complete lack of evidence either way.

'Okay. Let's pretend you're right. Which of the three murder methods did he use?'

'All of them,' Rafferty said. 'He tries to poison him. It doesn't kick in quickly enough. He smothers him. That does work. But you might leave before Guy's body gets found. Then, to make sure you investigate, he has Guy shot and then stands on the veranda, literally holding the murder weapon, and waits for you.'

'I suppose in your theory, he's not covered in gunshot residue because someone else fired the gun.'

'Not only that,' Rafferty said, 'but he used you to help him get away with it. You saw him, you saw the gun. You followed your nose and didn't let him out of your sight.'

'Justifiably!'

'Didn't say it wasn't. But while you were keeping a close eye on him, the killer had time to bugger off, wash their hands, ditch their dirty clothes, and then come back again before you've even got your shoes on.'

'Don't you start on me too.'

Rafferty stepped closer to him. 'I'm not starting on you. I'm giving you my take. Don't question my bloody loyalty. I'm not the one who's just stomped off with his knickers in a twist. Mayberry and I are right here with you, balls deep in this mess. We'd appreciate it if you stopped trying to pretend you've got all of this under control for five minutes. We can figure this out, but only if all of us work together.'

Morton's shoulders sagged. He exhaled deeply. 'I'm sorry.'

'Accepted. Now, we know Lorenzo didn't use the gun. We also know he implemented the whole priority system. Does their need to obey him "without question or delay" extend to murder?'

'Perhaps,' Morton said. 'Perhaps not. Some of the cultists are more loyal to Lorenzo than others. I think there's a schism on the farm. He's got his "true believers" who have fallen for all of his bullshit hook, line, and sinker.'

'Who are they?'

'I'd say Tracey, Dori, maybe even Abigail and Claudia.'

'All women,' Rafferty mused. 'Just like his father's followers. You didn't mention Lana. Isn't she a true follower?'

'I'm not convinced. She's too wick to believe all his crap. She's also, according to Pauline, the only young woman exempted from the practice of seclusion. I think she's his partner in crime, not his obedient lackey.'

That was Morton's assessment too. From the moment he'd met Lana at the gate on the morning of the wedding, she'd struck him as odd. 'Damn it. She was the one who took our phones at the gate.'

'And you just handed them over?' Rafferty asked, incredulous.

'She said it was so nothing would disturb the ceremony,' Morton mumbled.

'Not heard of Airplane mode?'

He kicked himself. He hadn't been happy about it at the time. And they'd been so rushed.

'Don't beat yourself up too much, boss. These con merchants can be awfully convincing.'

'We'll see who's convincing when I round them up, put the fear of God into 'em, and see if we can divide and conquer these lunatics.'

His bravado won a smile from Rafferty. It disappeared a split second later.

'What?'

She pointed at the clock. 'It's show time.'

Chapter 61: Hell Hath No Fury

One by one, the cultists were escorted to the barn.

To avoid any doubt in their minds about what was about to happen, Terra Farm was full of uniformed officers. Two escorted each cultist into the barn while more surrounded the perimeter.

Morton had even had Stephen and Abigail brought back to the farm, though they were cowering in the corner of the barn, guarded by Sarah, and avoided eye contact.

Only three cultists were missing: Claudia, who was still at the women's domestic violence shelter with uniformed officers who were making sure that she stayed there, safe and sound; Darren Heggerty, who had yet to be released from the Met's custody; and finally, Lucy, who was, at this moment, stuck in a detention room at Heathrow, having tried to fly out of the country without telling Morton. He'd deal with her later.

The remaining cultists were waiting in the barn. None had attempted to run or asked for a lawyer, not even Lorenzo. Morton hadn't given them the chance. Before they could say anything, he'd given each of them the same spiel: ask for a lawyer and come down to the station to be formally interviewed, or simply come to the barn to listen to him talk to all of them. For added curiosity value, he'd given each of them a copy of Lucy's article.

Many of them had been reading it when the last member of the Collective, Lorenzo, was brought into the barn. At that point, they'd hastily folded their copies or stuffed them into their pockets, a hush falling almost instantly.

Between cultists and constables, the barn was so busy that Morton could barely see. He walked slowly from the northern entrance in a giant circle, counting to make sure he hadn't missed anyone. Everyone was there who needed to be: Giacomo and Dori, Tracey and Marta, Lana and Lorenzo, Stephen and Abigail, and Pauline. Their expressions were a mix of shock, curiosity, and fear. Only Lorenzo's was unreadable. He looked as cocky and laid-back as ever, at least until Morton handed him the last copy of Lucy Reed's article.

'Bit of light reading for you, Mr di Stregoni,' Morton said with a grin. He watched as Lorenzo's eyes parsed the headline: *The Collective Killer: Life, Death and Betrayal in a Cult.*

It wasn't the snappiest of titles, but it was a real improvement from Lucy's original headline.

Underneath it was the tagline: *An exclusive six-part exposé from our undercover correspondent.*

The cat was among the pigeons now. The cultists knew their secrets were tumbling out, and with five more parts yet to come, they had no idea what else was about to be revealed. That nervousness could give Morton the edge he needed.

His confidence was short-lived. To address the group, he climbed on top of one of the largest bales of hay to survey the barn.

And saw Silverman lurking by the south door. Next to her was a sheepish-looking Ayala. He hadn't left the farm after all. Instead, he'd ratted Morton out. Morton swallowed, cleared his throat, and ignored his unwanted guest as he called for silence.

'First of all, I'd like to say thank you for co-operating this morning. If at any point you wish to talk to a lawyer, please say so. I am recording this for the record.'

He looked around for any objections. None were forthcoming. Legalities dealt with, Morton pressed on.

'This weekend has been... challenging for everyone involved, not least because none of you have been forthcoming with the truth.'

Hardly surprising, that. Murder suspects not playing ball with the police. *Come on, David. Think.* He paused for a moment just as Silverman's glare caught his eye. He'd totally forgotten that he was still pretending to only investigate the shooting. Time to deal with that.

'For the last three days, I've been working on the assumption that one of you shot Guy Rosenberg,' Morton said slowly. 'And for three days I've been wrong.'

Confusion spread among the cultists. Morton watched their reactions to this pronouncement, trying to discern who might already have known that Guy had already been murdered. Nobody jumped out at him. Either they didn't know or they had world-class poker faces.

'This morning,' he continued, 'I received an advance copy of the pathologist's report. It's almost as interesting as the article you've all been reading.'

Pauline raised a hand. 'Are you saying Guy wasn't shot with my gun after all?'

'He was shot,' Morton said. 'But he'd been dead for several hours by then. Someone shot his corpse.'

This time, they did look surprised. To Morton's right, Dori leant heavily against Giacomo's wheelchair as if she could no longer stand unaided. Lorenzo, meanwhile, looked almost pensive.

'So, how did he die?' Lorenzo asked. 'The drink finally got him?'

'Drink wasn't the only thing in his system,' Morton said. 'Someone poisoned him. But you already knew that, didn't you, Mr di Stregoni?'

Lorenzo shook his head slowly. 'You think I poisoned him?'

'Don't you control everything that goes on here? From what I've been told, nobody takes a leak without your approval. What was the phrase, "Without question or delay"? That sounds pretty controlling to me.'

'I simply expect people to respect their superiors.'

'That's you, is it, Mr di Stregoni?'

Lorenzo puffed out his chest. 'Around here? Damn right it is. This is my Collective, and I'm proud to lead it.'

'Bit hard to do that from behind bars, isn't it?'

'Not if I didn't kill anyone.'

'Then surely you're not in charge?' Morton said. 'You can't have it both ways, Lorenzo. Either you're the big kahuna and Guy was murdered at your say-so or you're not quite as important as you think if your subordinates can kill one of your members without you knowing.'

Lorenzo looked as if he was about to lose control there and then. His eyes narrowed to slits. His hands balled into fists. Morton was left in no doubt that if there hadn't been a barn full of constables between them, Lorenzo di Stregoni would have decked him.

'Temper, temper, Lorenzo. You might have inherited Daddy's name, but you don't have his talent for controlling people, do you? He ruled this farm with an iron fist for decades. You couldn't manage it for two years, could you?'

Lorenzo worked his jaw, his nostrils flaring. He said nothing.

'One more thing you won't be inheriting is this farm,' Morton said. 'Isn't that right, Lorenzo? You knew this place wasn't really his.'

'No comment.'

'Is this another secret your members have kept from you? From what I've been told, it was common knowledge around here that Guy and Claudia were going to sue for control of Terra Farm. They'd even found a lawyer.'

Another glare. Lorenzo looked over to Lana just for a second, barely long enough for Morton to notice. 'It's news to me,' he said.

'Is it, now?' Morton said. He turned to Lana. 'Is it news to you too?'

This time it was Lana's turn to glare. 'Fine,' she said. 'I knew. So what? It was complete nonsense. Everyone around here knows that Clementine was Giacomo's greatest fan. There's no way she wouldn't have wanted him to have it.'

Giacomo's greatest fan. That was one way to put it. 'She was sleeping with him,' Morton said. It wasn't a question. He knew as much from Lucy Reed's article.

'He slept with everyone. That was his thing.'

Lorenzo looked awkwardly at the ground.

'Got something to say, Mr di Stregoni?'

'Yeah,' he said. 'Are you going to get to the point, or are we all going to stand around and chat about my dad all day?'

'My point,' Morton said, 'is that I think you killed Guy to stop him from taking over the farm.'

Lorenzo laughed. 'Well, I didn't. So you won't be able to prove it.'

'You didn't tell the killer how to get away with it?' Morton said. 'As I recall, you said, "It's not as if I've had time to go and clean my hands and bleach my clothes." That wasn't an offhand remark, was it? You wanted the killer to go and clean up so there would be no evidence. That's what we call aiding and abetting.'

'Call it what you like. I can't remember saying that, and even if I did, it doesn't mean that I wanted anyone to do anything. Sounds like an innocent enough remark to me. Is that all you've got? I know you don't have any real evidence. You know I didn't fire that gun.'

That, Morton couldn't deny. Lorenzo's hands and clothes had been swabbed before anyone else's. There really wasn't any physical evidence to go on.

'Didn't you want your brother dead?' Morton asked.

'No,' Lorenzo said. 'I didn't even know he was my brother until a few minutes ago when I read the article you handed me. It doesn't surprise me, though. Dad loved the ladies.'

Several of the women glared. Dori looked especially offended. So too did Marta. Had the older di Stregoni been stringing them all along?

Then it hit Morton. Lorenzo had said those words. There was no doubt about it. But it hadn't been Morton who'd remembered them. Morton rounded on Marta.

'You,' he said, jabbing a finger in her direction. 'You're the one who reminded me. You wanted me to think it was Lorenzo.'

And now I'm going to wash my hands of it, Detective Morton. My conscience is clean.

She hadn't been decrying her innocence. She'd been reminding Morton what Lorenzo had said. She wanted him to remember Lorenzo's words. The cultists had hammered home the point that they had to obey the orders of those above them in priority.

It changed everything.

He'd been wrong from the off. It wasn't someone killing Guy to *hide* the cult's wrongs. It was an attempt to *expose* them.

Morton smiled as relief flooded through him.

'You're very clever, aren't you, Marta?' he said. 'Always quietly pulling the strings in the background. Never the leader, just the one behind the throne, puppeteering away. You told me about Lorenzo, and there's only one reason you'd do that. You wanted me here. You know, it's been driving me mad all weekend. Why kill a man on the only night that a police detective is on-site? Except it didn't work, did it?'

He looked around to mass confusion.

'Someone poisoned Guy. They slipped him a concoction derived from *le muguet,* or lily of the valley. It's a bridal flower, and you've got it everywhere here. Like the more commonly known foxglove, it can kill a man. But it's not quick. That was the first attempt on Guy's life. And you, Marta Timpson, wanted me to witness it. You wanted this investigation, and you wanted all the press attention. No doubt there are reporters at the gate.'

Marta said nothing. She folded her arms and looked at him, poker face still firmly in place.

'When it didn't kill Guy straight away, you needed to keep me on-site. No wonder you kept topping up my drinks.'

'I was on bar duty, Mr Morton. That's what barmaids do.'

'You got Sarah and me to drink enough that we couldn't drive home. Stephen, who was it that suggested we stay on your sofa?'

His son shrank away from the collective gaze of the barn as if slinking back behind his mother would save him from answering. Finally, he said: 'Marta.'

'And then you realised that even if I stayed overnight, it might not be enough. If we'd left in the morning first thing, which by the way we would have, we'd never have even known Guy was dead. We'd have left, Lorenzo would have seen to his corpse, and the whole plan would have failed. So you shot him. You shot your nephew point-blank in the chest, didn't you, Marta? And then you walked back to your bungalow, swapped your gunshot-residue-covered tunic for a fresh one and ran the washing machine.'

'Unless Tracey did it,' Marta said. 'She lives in the same bungalow.'

At that, Tracey ran towards Marta. The policemen standing by had just enough time to intervene. She flailed wildly. 'You *traitor*!' she screamed. 'You *descended* a long time ago, and we all know it. Just because Gia chose Clementine over you.'

'Like hell he did.'

'You know it's true!' Tracey screamed. 'You couldn't give him a child, could you? You useless, barren witch. So he knocked up your sister, and you killed her for it. And now you've gone and killed your nephew. All because you couldn't handle being alone.'

Marta looked at the exits. There was no way out. 'Do you know what it's like? Living day to day with a useless brat who reminds you that your man cheated on you with your sister? Every time I looked at Guy, I saw *her* smiling back at me, mocking me. The boy ought to have been more, much more. I could have given him back himself. He is the true son of Giacomo di Stregoni. Not that he ever dared claim that mantle. I'm not sorry that he's dead.'

With a strength Morton would never have imagined that she possessed, Marta leapt towards Tracey, her bony fingers going straight for Tracey's throat. Constables leapt in from all sides to pry them apart.

Then, as soon as the drama had started, it was all over. Handcuffs clicked around Marta's wrists. They had her. She gave a languid shrug as if she knew she'd been beaten and was now resigned to spending the rest of her life behind bars.

Lorenzo watched, a smile spreading slowly over his debonair features. Not only did he think he was he was off the hook, he clearly thought he'd got rid of a troublemaker. 'Time to get going now, then, Chief Inspector. You've got your woman.'

It was Morton's turn to smile. 'I'm not done yet,' he said.

'Why not? You've got your killer.'

'The poison didn't kill him either,' Morton said.

A collective gasp echoed around the room.

'You're joking, right?' Lorenzo folded his arms. 'You're saying someone drugged him, someone shot him, and *someone else* killed him? You're having a laugh, Mr Morton.'

Morton turned to face Lana. 'Got something to come clean about, Miss Hayworth?'

She looked at him blankly, defiant. 'No.'

'So you didn't sleep with Guy Rosenberg last Thursday and then smother him while he slept?'

It was the perfect opportunity. She'd known all about Guy and Claudia's plan to claim the farm, and the wedding night was the first time in months he'd been drunk.

She pulled a face. 'I didn't sleep with that freak!'

'But you did kill him.' Morton said 'And all to protect Lorenzo. Not that you'll ever be thanked for what you did. He doesn't love you.'

She turned to her beau just as he began to protest that it wasn't true, that he did love her.

'You bastard! I killed for you. I dealt with the will for you.'

'And now you'll go to prison for him too,' Morton said. He gestured for her to be handcuffed.

As Lana was being dragged away, Lorenzo stared after her. His was the stare of a man who had just realised that he didn't know the love of his life after all.

'You said you dealt with the will,' Morton said to Lana. 'What did you do with it?'

'No comment,' Lana said.

'No matter. The fact you had to destroy it speaks volumes. Guy was the real owner of Terra Farm. That threatened you, didn't it? If Guy took it over and chucked you all out, you'd have to get a real job. No more freeloading off the Collective. No more easy drug money, no lording it over the rest of the Collective. That goes for you too, Lorenzo.' Morton motioned for Lorenzo to be handcuffed too.

The brash leader stared at him.

'Lorenzo di Stregoni, you're under arrest for grievous bodily harm contrary to section eighteen of the Offences Against the Person Act eighteen sixty-one. You do not have to say anything.

But it may harm your defence if you do not mention when questioned something which you later rely on in court. Anything you do or say may be given in evidence.'

'What?' Lorenzo yelled. 'I haven't hurt anyone. You've just proved Marta and Lana did it without me.'

'You haven't hurt anyone? You sure about that? ' Morton looked over to his son. 'Stephen, would you kindly show Lorenzo your back.'

Slowly, reluctantly, Stephen did as he was asked. The same horror that Sarah had seen in her kitchen days earlier was now visible for the whole Collective to see: a gruesome letter C burned into his back, blistered and oozing pus.

'He wanted that,' Lorenzo said derisively.

'Nevertheless,' Morton said. 'Nobody can consent to that level of harm.'

Evidently, Lorenzo wasn't *au fait* with the case of *R v Brown*. Consent was no defence in law.

It wasn't a murder charge, but it still had a potential sentence of life imprisonment, and if Morton knew Kieran O'Connor at all, the prosecutor would demand the maximum.

As Morton watched the arrestees be hauled away, Silverman fought her way across the barn to him.

'I suppose you think you're clever, David.'

'Always.'

'Two weeks suspension. Without pay. Starting right now.'

'Fine,' Morton said. He handed over his handcuffs. 'In that case, I think I'll go spend some time with my wife, my son and my new daughter-in-law. I'll leave you and Ayala to sort the paperwork.'

Chapter 62: The Heir and the Spare

C laudia retched.

For the umpteenth time today, she found herself slumped over, worshipping the porcelain throne.

And as it was now late afternoon, she couldn't even call it *morning* sickness.

She retched again, feeling her throat burn, the taste of vomit rising to her lips. Her antenatal care team had said it would get better by week twelve. That moment couldn't come soon enough.

In the distance, she could hear children running, screaming, giggling. Even in the shelter, life went on. So long as you didn't want to bring a teenage boy with you, anyway.

Soon, it would be time for her to leave.

They weren't throwing her out. They rarely ever did that. Only last week, they'd upgraded her from the tiny emergency room she'd been allocated on arrival. Her new digs had an en suite, her own cooking facilities, and, when she said she didn't have anything of her own, they'd given her clothes, toiletries, even a basic smartphone.

Nice people were so easy to take advantage of.

And Claudia knew she was an expert at taking advantage. The baby in her belly was proof of that.

He was her insurance, her backstop, and she intended to protect him with her life. She pulled herself up off the floor, stooped over the sink to swill out her mouth, and made a beeline for the fridge. She hoped a glass of milk would take away the taste. It didn't.

She slumped down on the bed, alone with her thoughts. When she'd joined the Collective, she'd had no one to protect her. She'd been sleep-deprived, forced to do menial labour, and it felt like every man on the farm had tried to have his way with her.

Two had succeeded.

Neither of them were lovers. They were a means to an end, and a lucrative one at that. Guy's claim to Terra Farm had been obvious right from the start. It had been his mum's home, so why shouldn't it be his?

Except the fool didn't want it. He said he knew. He'd always known. Marta had told him when he was old enough to understand.

But Guy was weak. Too weak to fight for himself. Or for her.

He'd let them throw her in that filthy cell. The only glimmer of hope had arisen from befriending the groundskeeper, earning her trust by not straying too far when she let her out of the cell. It wouldn't have done for Lorenzo to learn his rules were being flouted.

And when she'd found Guy a solicitor, he'd still refused. She'd had to do all that on her own too.

She turned towards the desk where her handbag was. She unzipped it and fished inside for the prize she'd kept safe all along: the last will and testament of Clementine Rosenberg.

Not the fake. She had no idea where that had gone. Presumably, Lorenzo had burned it long ago, thinking that proof of his father's fraud was gone with it.

No, this was the original, the real will, kept safe by Marta Timpson all these years and given to Guy on his eighteen birthday. She scanned down it again, her eyes searching for the most pertinent line:

I, Clementine Rosenberg of Terra Farm, Putney, being of sound mind, declare this to be my Last Will and Testament, revoking all prior Wills and codicils.

.... hereby bequeath Terra Farm and all its contents to my son, Guy Rosenberg of Terra Farm, and his issue to be kept in the family, forever and always.

She smiled, a smug satisfaction rising through her.

Even if the courts didn't believe her when she told them that she and Guy were bound, there was no denying the life growing inside her belly. One little paternity test and Terra Farm would be hers.

So long as the baby wasn't Lorenzo's.

Chapter 63: Into the Sunset

Paradise. That's what it was. Absolute bliss. White sands, tropical seas, complimentary champagne, and the bridal suite to boot. The Maldives were everything that the travel agent had promised and more.

'I can't believe the kids turned this down,' Morton said as he supped his third cocktail of the afternoon.

'All the better for us,' Sarah said. 'And only a couple of hundred quid to swap the names over. I thought the whole holiday was going to be a write-off.'

After all that had happened, Stephen and Abigail had decided not to get legally married after all. Not yet, at least. The pair of them were currently house-sitting back in London, getting to know each other outside of the confines of Terra Farm. Who knew whether they would make it in the real world?

The cult was now gone, so they'd have to make it or not on their own. So would the other members of the Collective.

They'd all got their comeuppance in the end. Except, perhaps, two of them. Morton hadn't seen or heard from Claudia since the arrests. As she was no longer a person of interest, he no longer cared.

The American got away too. No blackmail charges, nothing. She'd fled the country, and the Crown Prosecution Service couldn't be bothered to extradite on such flimsy evidence. But somehow, karma had still caught up with her, as a rival newspaper had managed to get the final scoop before she did. Morton smirked. *Wonder how that happened.*

He set down his drink. 'Shame we've got to go home tomorrow, isn't it? If I retired, we could spend the next forty years travelling the world, seeing sunsets.'

'Just like BK times.'

'BK?'

She grinned. 'Before Kids. We could do it, you know. You should've retired years ago.'

He laughed. 'Hey, we're not that old.' He quickly changed the subject. 'I suppose I'd better turn my phone on and see what we've missed while we've been away.'

'If you have to.'

The phone slowly booted, messages flooding in. Most were boring. The kids were fine, Kieran wanted to know if Morton was going to be coming to the Arsenal match the previous weekend, and an unknown number wanted to talk to him about a personal injury claim for a car accident he hadn't been in.

He lazily flicked the screen, pulling up his email inbox.

One email from Silverman caught his eye. The subject line read:

Notice of Termination

Morton let out a guttural growl.

'Ayala! I'm going to kill you!'

Made in the USA
Middletown, DE
03 August 2021

45276262R00215